The Defender:

In Evils Grasp

Reggi Broach

Front cover art by Emma Dillon
Back cover art by Kay Broach

First Printing: 2018
ISBN-13: 978-0-9989620-3-0
Library of Congress Control Number: 2018939442
R.B. Enterprises, Harrison, TN
Reggi Broach, Harrison, TN
Copyright 2018 by Reggi Broach

Acknowledgments

In all our lives there are times when we wonder if God is still there, if he still cares, if he's listening. This is often referred to as the "dark night of the soul." No matter how dark things get, He is still with us.

I struggled with writing this particular book because of the darkness I could see in it. My husband, Ron, encouraged me to push forward with it "as is." Thank you, Shannon for the read-through looking at the same things and the words of wisdom.

We've gone through some of our own "dark nights." God has not forsaken us. My acknowledgment is to praise God for his faithfulness through adversity and aloneness.

My husband, Ron, has worked so very hard with getting my books published, formatted, marketed, and working on making them available as audio books. I could not have done all of this without him.

As with all the books I've written, I am grateful to those who encouraged me to write them, and to those who read them. My family, my co-workers, and my Keith Street family and friends have all been so supportive. Thank you all so much.

Thanks to Emma and Kayleigh for designing my book covers.

I am also very grateful to my editor who does more than edit. Thank you, Janelle Musick, for your editing, educating, encouragement, advice, and friendship.

CIF SHIP: *SS Evangeline*

Explorer Class Ship with atmospheric maneuvering capabilities

Drive Capabilities:
- Tachyon
- Matter/Antimatter

Weapons Capabilities:
- Minimal laser
- EMP and tachyon defensive weaponry
- Electromagnetic shields
- Electromagnetic deflectors

Personnel Accommodations:
- 14

Mission:

To establish a Commonwealth presence on all technologically undeveloped worlds, or worlds that have not chosen to ally with the Commonwealth, despite non-spatial developments. To report any world where the invasive forces of the Liontari have a foothold.

Crew Manifest

The crew is to consist of two teams. The primary team is the ship's crew, the secondary team is the diplomatic mission team. Each team is to act as support personnel for the opposing team as needed.

- **Captain David Alexander**
    * Ship's Crew, aka Prisoner #7138
- **Commander Brynna Alexander**
    * Diplomatic team leader, aka Prisoner #7139
- **Lt. Commander Braxton Flint**
    * Architectural Engineer – Diplomatic team, aka Prisoner #7140
- **Lt. Commander Lazaro Dominick**
    * Chief Engineer – Ship's Crew, aka Prisoner #7141
- **Lt. Commander Jason Adams**
    * Physician – Diplomatic team, aka Prisoner #7142
- **Lt. Thane Ryder**
    * Pilot – Ship's Crew, aka Prisoner #7143
- **Lt. Alexia Flint**
    * Psychologist – Diplomatic team, aka Prisoner #7144
- **Lt. JG Marissa Holden**
    * Navigation – Ship's Crew, aka Prisoner #7145
- **Lt. JG Laura Adams**
    * Nurse, Botanist – Diplomatic team, aka Prisoner #7146
- **Ensign Aulani Ryder**
    * Comm & Computer Tech – Ship's Crew, aka Prisoner #7147
- **Ensign Cheyenne Dominick**
    * Linguistics – Diplomatic team, aka Prisoner #7148
- **Chief Petty Officer Jake Holden**
    * Security – Ship's Crew, aka Prisoner #7149

Contents

Acknowledgments 3

CIF SHIP: *SS Evangeline* 4

Crew Manifest 5

PROLOGUE 7

CHAPTER ONE – THE TRAP 11

CHAPTER TWO – DAY ONE 59

CHAPTER THREE - JAKE 71

CHAPTER FOUR – DAY TWO 105

CHAPTER FIVE – DAY THREE 139

CHAPTER SIX – DAY FOUR 171

CHAPTER SEVEN – DAY FIVE 207

CHAPTER EIGHT - LIONTARI 239

CHAPTER NINE – DAY SIX 271

CHAPTER TEN – THWARTING EVIL 311

EPILOGUE 377

PROLOGUE

Captain Alexander found himself once again standing on the surface of Galat III. The villagers around him were celebrating their new alliance with the Commonwealth. Everyone was having a great time eating and dancing. The Captain felt as though he were an invisible observer in the midst of the commotion. Wait, this was familiar. It was the dream again. His conscious mind tried hard to wake him. He thought he was done with this dream. It wasn't supposed to happen again. He tried to turn away and shut his eyes. He didn't want to see what he knew was coming, but his head wouldn't turn, and his eyes wouldn't close. The pack of wild dogs attacked as expected and destroyed the people of Galat III, leaving only the Captain and his crew standing. The Captain looked down expecting to once again see the blood of all Galat on his hands. His hands were clean. His uniform was clean. Wait, that wasn't supposed to happen. The dream had changed. The wild dogs howled then turned their attention to the Captain and his crew, who were still spread out around the area staring at the decimation in horror. Knowing it was useless, the Captain still searched his uniform for a weapon. The alpha male of the wild dogs lowered his head and snarled at David. It moved slowly towards him. David looked up to see where the rest of the crew were. The crew were no longer scattered around the area, but now they were standing behind him surrounded by the vicious animals. He looked back at the dog threatening him.

Another new element of the dream had materialized. The dog had a collar and a leash. David's eyes followed the leash to the hand holding it. The man holding the leash was none other than Supreme Executor Luciano Hale, ruler of the Commonwealth. David and his crew recognized him as a renegade superior being, formerly in the service of Pateras El Liontari. The dog leapt at David, but the leash kept him just out of reach. David's consciousness continued to try to wake him. Something or someone wasn't done with him yet. The dog continued to leap at him. He was so close, he could feel the animal's hot breath on his face. The Captain wanted to back away so badly, but his arms and legs wouldn't move. The dog stopped jumping and straining at his leash. He howled six times. A bright light appeared in the shape of a man. The light was so bright David had to look away. His conscious mind became frustrated. He was able to move to protect himself from the light, but not the attacking dog. David shielded his eyes. The bright figure stepped between David and the dog. The dog and his master faded away along with the dogs encircling the crew. David started to thank the figure in front of him until a noise caught his attention. It was the sound of an ax hitting a tree. He looked around to find the source. No one was there. His conscious mind was finally allowed control.

Awareness slowly began to creep up on Captain Alexander. What was that pounding sound? He moaned in disappointment. It was his own head. He guessed it would be awhile until the pounding stopped. He took a deep breath evoking an uncontrollable onslaught of coughing accompanied by shooting pain in his sides. He moaned again. He wasn't sure the deep breath had been worth it. This pain was familiar, his ribs were likely broken or at least fractured. There was a metallic taste in his mouth. Another thing he was familiar with, the taste of blood. It seemed a lot of people liked punching him in the mouth. David began to move around, slowly taking inventory of all his body parts. Everything seemed to be working, he thought. That was good, although the aches and pains evoked by his movements were none too pleasant.

Now that he knew the condition of his own body, David began to test out his surroundings. He was lying face down on a padded surface which smelled quite rank. In the course of flexing his limbs, he had found the boundaries of the padding. It was apparently an old mattress, very old, judging from the stench. David opened his eyes slowly and pushed himself onto his side. His left eye wasn't working very well, but neither was his right for that matter. What little he could see was dark, blurry, and there were two of everything. He rolled a little further and found the wall near the edge of his mattress. He pushed and pulled himself into a sitting position. He looked around the room. Yes, there were two toilets, two sinks, two doors, and two dim lights. He held up one of his hands. Yup, ten fingers on that hand and probably ten on the other as well. The Captain quickly got bored with his own sense of humor. He took another slow deep breath. He coughed again, but less violently this time. David reached up and touched his face. His left eye was swollen nearly to the point of being unable to open. He touched his nose. It was bruised and bloody, but surprisingly not broken this time. The last time he had taken a beating like this was on Drea. He hadn't been so lucky that time. He nearly died from that beating. This didn't feel lucky. It felt painful.

The fog began to clear from his mind. Where was he? Now he remembered. He was in a Commonwealth jail cell. Where was the rest of the crew? Maybe they were in nearby cells. How did he get here? His uncle, Admiral Robert Deacons, had set a trap for them. His mind began to replay the events leading up to his current predicament.

Prologue

CHAPTER ONE – THE TRAP

Three months ago, the crew of the *Evangeline* were loyal to the Commonwealth who had commissioned them on their current journey. Their mission to seek out the strongholds of a powerful enemy known as Pateras El Liontari wasn't what it appeared to be. Startling truths had broken the bond with the Commonwealth who cared for and groomed them for this mission early on. Those truths resulted in a carefully concealed treason.

The ship's captain, David Alexander, led his crew down the treasonous path. His uncle, Admiral Robert Deacons, surprised the crew on Tudoren by bringing them some new technology to enhance their missions. He discovered the crew's disloyalty and attempted to put an end to their traitorous behavior. His actions caused the death of his own nephew. Arni Sotaeras Liontari, son of the Commonwealth's primary enemy Pateras El Liontari, confronted Admiral Deacons on Tudoren and reminded him of his history with Pateras. Robert, when faced with the overwhelming truths of his own past and the Commonwealth's treachery, rejoined Pateras.

Pateras healed Captain Alexander's mortal wounds and restored his life just prior to the Admiral's departure. With his own treasonous act, David's uncle reported his nephew's death to the Commonwealth supposedly ending his treasonous leadership. The crew of the *Evangeline* now followed the resurrected Captain Alexander in the service of the Commonwealth's proclaimed enemy, except for one.

The only man aboard the *Evangeline* who had not renounced his loyalty to the Commonwealth was the security officer, Chief Petty Officer Jacob Holden. He had offered his voluntary cooperation to his traitorous Captain for several reasons, namely to protect his own wife and unborn baby.

When their mission began, it was deemed of such immense importance, the Commonwealth took some rather stiff measures to see that no one dropped off the mission. An unexpected pregnancy, being a primary reason for leaving a mission, was dealt with prophylactically. The measures included temporary sterilization of female crew members prior to the mission and involuntary termination of any such events during the mission. Captain Alexander had intervened in the doctor's performance of his Commonwealth mandate to end the pregnancy and saved the life of the child, his security officer hadn't known at the time, existed. Knowing his wife's pregnancy was against the regulations was the only thing keeping the Security Chief from turning his entire crew over to the Commonwealth for prosecution and re-education.

Captain David Alexander, now presumed dead by the Commonwealth, took the *Evangeline* to Romajin, a technologically advanced society, about two days from Tudoren. The Security Chief's wife was now in desperate need of clothing that fit her expanding shape and items for the baby after she delivered. The ship was not equipped for these circumstances.

The *Evangeline* had been out of contact with the Commonwealth due to some highly unusual solar activity. As they were now leaving the Tudoren system, contact was about to be reestablished. Their stalwartly loyal Commonwealth security chief was again a source of concern.

Captain David Alexander and his wife, Commander Brynna Alexander called Jake into the Captain's office to talk. "Security Chief Jake Holden reporting as ordered, sir."

David and Brynna were already seated at the table in David's office. "At ease, Chief. Take a seat."

Jake sat down across from the couple. "Is there a problem, sir?"

"Not yet, Chief. I just want to prevent one before it happens. I expect my uncle will be contacting you when he receives Brynna's reports on Tudoren. What do you plan on telling him?"

Jake didn't hesitate before answering. "What do you want me to tell him, sir?"

David and Brynna cast a sideways glance at each other. David shifted in his seat. "Do you plan on telling him I'm alive?"

"No sir, I don't. It doesn't matter in this respect, who I'm loyal to. I won't put Marissa and the baby in danger, and I won't put your uncle in the position of dealing with you. If he thinks you're dead, he won't come after this ship or its crew. If you have a reason for me to tell him, then I will, but I'd really rather not. Just tell me what I can and can't say."

"You wouldn't lie to me, would you, Jake?" David studied Jake's face.

Jake wasn't about to mince words. "Yes sir, I would. I won't lie to you if it endangers the safety of my family. I also didn't lie to you when I said I didn't want to put your uncle in that position. I won't do that to you, or to him."

"So, what would you lie about, Mr. Holden?" David knew it was pointless to ask such a question, but he had to try.

"Whatever is necessary to protect my family."

"I suppose the question now is: how many times have you lied to me? Which is conversely followed by: how many lies do I know about? I'm sure you wouldn't want to clear any of that up, would you?"

Jake gave the Captain no indication of his innocence or guilt. "That's an exercise in futility, sir. If I have lied to you, I'd just do it again to keep perpetuating the same story. If I haven't lied to you, you still wouldn't know whether to believe me or not."

The two stared at each other. Brynna felt the room filling with testosterone and animosity. "Gentlemen, let's move on to the problem at hand. The Admiral will contact you, Chief. What do you plan on telling him?"

"I told you, I'll tell him whatever you want. Commander, I'll confirm your report, that despite your best efforts, the Baldesar Province remains loyal to Pateras. I'll also confirm, Pateras was not found or introduced to the other two Provinces."

"Is this where the lies to protect your family come into play?" David jumped in.

Jake's expression never changed. "Absolutely. You're lying to the Admiral's board to protect the crew."

David looked sorrowful. "I suppose I am. I don't like lying, but I need to buy some time. I'm doing whatever I can to defend these helpless populations and this crew. If it were for personal gain or might cause the detriment of others, I guess I would find another way."

Brynna tried to encourage David. "We aren't perpetuating a falsehood, Captain. We're just keeping certain facts to ourselves."

The Captain shook his head. "We're lying to the Commonwealth. I am anticipating a day when we will be openly opposing them instead of hiding in the shadows."

Jake continued to stare at the Captain devoid of emotion. "If it helps, I'll give you a full report of everything I tell him. What do I tell him about our next destination? He's going to want to know why we're stopping on Romajin."

"We've been out for nearly eight months. We're stopping to restock and with our communications problems on Tudoren, I want to run the ship through an intensive diagnostic. I'm also going to want to send some of David's personal items back to his family."

David gave Brynna a startled and concerned look. "You're getting rid of my stuff? What are you trying to get rid of?"

Brynna gave him an impish grin. "You're dead. You don't need your stuff anymore. I thought your poor mother would like some mementos. It's what everyone would expect me to do."

The fretful look on David's face was priceless, even Jake couldn't help grinning. "I'm not dead! I need my stuff." His voice was nearing a whimper. "I don't even have a lot of stuff."

"Relax dear, I'm going to send a few token items. If you were actually dead, I would put your clothing into the ship's stores. Your pictures are all computer files. I can copy those onto a data crystal and send the copy to your mother. I do think I should send your medals to her, though."

Jake and Brynna could see David going through a mental inventory. Except for his civilian attire, he really didn't have much more than that. All his personal possessions were placed into storage before they started the mission. He kept a few decorative items to put in his office which included his medals. His thoughts went back to when he had earned them. At the time, they meant something to him. He had worked hard to earn those achievements. The sweet taste of victory in his mouth when he earned them was now leaving a bitter aftertaste. The Commonwealth had cost him a great deal. The medals were a painful reminder of that cost. Perhaps Brynna was right; his mother might appreciate them more than he did.

Brynna could tell by the changing look on David's face, his thoughts had gone south. "Captain, you earned those medals. They represent your hard work, not the Commonwealth's intentions. Perhaps you should decide what to send to your mother, sister, and brother."

David shook off his negativity. "Alright Commander, I'll

take care of it. Chief, is that a sufficient answer for you to give the Admiral if he asks?"

"Yes sir. I don't suppose we can anticipate every question he may ask. I'll do my best to keep him at bay."

"Chief, he knows Marissa was brought back to life. If he asks you if I'm still dead, can you convince him I am?"

Jake looked surprisingly worried. "I sincerely hope so."

David felt like they had covered the subject as thoroughly as possible. "Okay, Chief, I would appreciate a report after the Admiral contacts you. You're dismissed."

Jake stood up to go. "I know you still don't trust me, but I appreciate the effort you're putting forth."

David stood up. "You've made your position pretty clear. I keep hoping you'll see things the way we do. Our lives are in your hands on a daily basis. Remember this one thing, your life has also been in my hands on a daily basis. I could've left you behind or spaced you if I had chosen to."

Somehow the thought hadn't really crossed his mind. Jake's naturally pale complexion became even lighter for a moment. He swallowed hard. "Yes, Captain." Jake saluted his Captain and disappeared into the corridor.

David stared at the closed door for a second before sitting back down. "What do you think?"

Brynna shook her head. "I don't trust him. He's been surprisingly forthcoming about his intentions, although I feel like he's hiding some key facts."

"Oh, he's definitely hiding something. He's biding his time to turn us in. I just wish I knew whether our time on Romajin was the time, or not."

Brynna frowned. "There's no way he would risk Marissa and the baby. I bet it will be after the baby is born. We need to make plans for what to do as soon as the baby delivers."

David nodded. "We've got a few months before we need a

plan in place. You never know, Jake may join us by then."

• •

Brynna got her "official" reports off to Admiral Deacons as quickly as possible. The things she didn't put into her reports were things the crew did after the initial negotiations were complete. The missions on the second and third continents started as a standard Commonwealth first contact mission. As soon as their goodwill gestures were underway, Brynna presented Pateras to each population. Cheyenne always programmed the data modules with a copy of the Ancient Texts and a historical account of Arni's death on Drea. Jake never seemed to react when Brynna changed her mission parameters. She still didn't feel like he was accepting her goals. He also stopped uttering snide comments under his breath and making disapproving faces.

It didn't take long for Admiral Deacons to respond to the reports. He made a perfunctory call the next day to Brynna to see how she was handling her husband's recent death. Assuming their communication might be monitored, she gave him the expected cold, disengaged responses, but assured him the crew was supportive and functioning as expected.

"Commander, are you comfortable continuing to head this team up as is?" Admiral Deacons bluntly questioned her.

"What do you mean, sir?"

"You've been through some traumatic circumstances. It would be hard for anyone to continue this mission. This also puts you short staffed. I could pull you off the mission and replace you with another couple to bring the crew back up to full staffing. I could also send another Diplomatic Mission Team leader out there and give you a field promotion to Captain."

Brynna was caught off guard by the Admiral's offer. The Admiral knew perfectly well David was alive. She quickly discerned he was trying to cover himself appropriately. She hadn't considered these possibilities though. Her hesitation was certainly plausible. "Admiral, I would rather not make any changes just yet. Lt. Flint filed reports on my mental capacities. I am functioning within acceptable parameters right now. I'm not inclined to make such major changes until I'm further from Tudoren. Since that's where David… died, I think things will get easier away from there. Please give me a little more time."

The Admiral appeared to study her carefully. "Very well, I will give you some time. I am going to put you in for that promotion though. If you are in command of the ship *and* the mission, you need the rank to go with it."

"Yes sir. Thank you, sir. May I ask a personal question."

"Of course, what is it?"

"How did David's family take the news? Are they alright?" Brynna bit down on her lower lip. She knew he couldn't answer her adequately, but it would look suspicious if she didn't ask.

"They didn't take the news well at all. I – I'd rather not go into detail, if you don't mind."

"I'm sorry, Admiral. I know this hasn't been easy for you either. Please convey my condolences to his mother, sister, and brother… if you think it's appropriate. I know the circumstances were not what anyone would have wished. Were you able to contact his father?"

"No, I haven't located him yet. My mother, Jessica and Abigail did want me to extend their sympathies to you, Brynna."

"Please thank them for me. I will try to contact them later when the pain of it has worn off a little."

Admiral Deacons face grew dark, "I doubt this sort of pain will ever wear off. Brynna, they really fell in love with you. They were pleased with David's choice, but I'm afraid you will be a constant reminder to them of what they lost."

"I understand, sir. I'm sorry if that's a problem for you too, Admiral."

"I'm a soldier, Brynna. I know how to set aside my feelings… most of the time." The Admiral was ready to be done with this part of the conversation. He was afraid if they talked too long, one of them might slip up. He abruptly changed the subject. "I need to talk to your security chief. Could you hail him for me?"

"Of course, Admiral." Brynna's hand moved to touch the appropriate controls.

The Admiral interrupted her movements with one more quick question. "Commander, I'm not going to receive any nasty surprises when I talk to him am I?"

"None that I am aware of, Admiral. For the record, I have not coerced the Chief in any way. He will tell you whatever is on his mind."

"I do have one more question, Commander."

"Yes, Admiral?"

"Has the Tudoren sun's solar activity settled down?"

"Not really, sir. It got worse just before we were ready to leave the planet and knocked out *all* our communications for three days. The day before we launched, the activity dropped way down and gave us a window to leave the system. The window closed right after we left."

"That sounds just a little too convenient, Commander."

"You can send a ship to check it out if you don't trust me, sir. I strongly suspect, Pateras is responsible though. I have reason to believe he's protecting this world from the Commonwealth. We can get back in. It'll just take a long time without tachyon drives. I know you want to neutralize the threat, Admiral, but they aren't getting out of there any faster than we can get in."

"Very well, send me to your security chief."

Brynna pressed the buttons and hailed the chief. She told him the Admiral was awaiting his report and connected the two. For the next twenty minutes, David and Brynna dangled in suspense. Jake forwarded a recording of the entire conversation back to the anxious couple. The conversation seemed to be exactly what they expected. Jake made no attempt to inform the Admiral of David's presence. He *did* send a file in a hidden carrier wave out to Admiral Garcia. He put the file on such a low-level frequency to disguise it underneath his transmission to Admiral Deacons.

● ●

As the crew prepared for their visit to Romajin, they took extra precautions to hide files they didn't want discovered. Once everything seemed secure, David and Brynna began to relax.

Late the next morning, the *Evangeline* reached orbit around their latest destination. Brynna contacted the CIF base on Romajin to get landing clearance for the *Evangeline*. David, Jake, and Marissa boarded the shuttle. The shuttle headed for a remote area on the opposite coast from the CIF base. Commodore Gary Vardin met Brynna and the rest of her crew as soon as the ship was settled.

"Commander Alexander, I'm Commodore Vardin. It's a pleasure to meet you."

Brynna smiled as cordially as she could, considering the number of things she was now trying to keep hidden. She saluted the man then smiled. "Thank you, sir. I hope you don't mind the unexpected visit. Our ship needs a little TLC. Our food stores are getting low, our communications array needs a full diagnostic, and we need to replenish our data modules. My crew would also appreciate some food that doesn't come from a package."

"Oh, absolutely!" The Commodore seemed eager to please her.

Brynna turned to present the crew to the Commodore. "This is my second in command, Lt. Commander Braxton Flint and his wife, Lt. Lexi Flint, our ship's psychologist. This is Lt. Commander Lazaro Dominick, my chief engineer and his wife

Ensign Cheyenne Dominick. Ensign Dominick is our linguistics officer. This is Dr. Jason Adams and his wife, Laura. Laura is a medical officer and botanist. This is Lt. Thane Ryder, our pilot, and his wife Ensign Aulani Ryder, our communications officer. My navigator and security chief are visiting friends on the west coast."

"You know, I have heard about these new Explorer Class ships, but hadn't seen them until now. Would you mind giving me a tour?"

Brynna smiled. "Of course, Commodore, this way." Brynna led him on a tour of the ship including a visit to the guest quarters. When they reached the shuttle bay, Brynna explained, "I'm sorry the shuttle isn't here for you to see. Since some of the crew wanted to visit their friends on the west coast, I let them take the shuttle."

The Commodore continued to smile as he responded to her. "Oh, yes. I wondered about that. I'm glad they're getting some down time. Being an explorer class vessel must mean your missions are quite stressful. I'm not trying to pry into classified information. It's purely supposition on my part. If your supply officer can send me a list of everything you need, we'll get you restocked and on your way as fast as we can. Forgive me for asking though. Where's your Captain?"

Brynna's face sobered. "Captain Alexander died in the line of duty two months ago. Admiral Deacons has put me in for a field promotion to Captain."

Commodore Vardin's smile faded briefly. "Oh, Commander… Commander Alexander? I'm sorry, was he your…?"

Brynna grimaced purposefully. "He was my husband, yes. This crew is comprised completely of married couples. I know it's highly unusual, but so is our mission."

The Commodore remained straight faced. "My condolences on your loss, Commander. Forgive me for prying into such a painful matter. Hopefully your stay here will help you relax a little. I have guest housing available here on the base if you like. They are nice apartments with a splendid view. The recreational facilities are excellent. They are at the disposal of you and your entire crew. If there is anything you need, don't hesitate to ask. Those really are beautiful ships. I envy you Commander. I envy you a lot. My aide will show you around the base, and he can also direct you to some local attractions off-base." The Commodore was smiling again. It was slightly unnerving how cheerful he was. His overarching cheer was starting to bother Brynna. After thinking about it for a while, she decided she was being paranoid and let the matter drop.

The crew got settled in their temporary quarters, and then promptly headed into town to do some sightseeing and try the local delicacies. Brynna gave the crew a discreet warning not to buy lots of "baby" items. They had already been ordered not to visit with Jake and Marissa for the length of their stay. The Captain and Commander didn't want anyone connecting the crew with Jake and Marissa.

● ●

David, Jake, and Marissa rented a cottage directly on the western shore. The cottage sat on a cliff overlooking the ocean with a path down to a sandy beach. They also arranged for a private vehicle, complete with driver, to escort them in and out of town. Jake and Marissa were anxious to go shopping.

David had no desire to shop but didn't want to remain alone at the cottage. The young Captain took the time to visit a museum in the historic district. The museum was an old five story home owned by one of the founding fathers of the area. The building had been updated to include elevators and modern restroom facilities, thankfully. A young woman greeted David at the door and handed him an antiquated piece of technology as a souvenir. She informed him the thin folded paper was known as a brochure. The young woman giggled. "It's what people used before data pads, bracelet interfaces, and ear buds. It has a map to guide you through the museum." The woman appeared to enjoy the befuddled looks of her clients. David fumbled with the paper trying to figure out how to work it. The woman tried not to giggle again and showed him how to unfold it and turn it around to see the information on both sides of the page. She demonstrated folding it in opposing directions, so he could see only small relevant sections at a time. David thanked her for her help and began to follow the map on the first page to the first room.

David walked through the halls perusing the displays. He eventually wandered into a room dedicated to the cultural development of the planetary population. He saw a wide variety of religious beliefs listed. Pressing a button on one of the displays, a holographic projection began to show various religious movements. The voice denounced the movements as dangerous and primitive. It interlaced its censure by extolling the virtues of the Commonwealth. David was growing annoyed with the indoctrination until the mysterious voice moved onto a familiar topic. The narrator mentioned one religion as being particularly insidious. An image of Ancient paper writings similar to images David had seen on Drea appeared. The voice droned on about an ancient writing of a timeless being known as the Father and Creator of all life. This selfish being demanded that all serve him and no other, eliminating all choice. The voice defamed the ancient worship of this imaginary god as a method of controlling the masses. The narration began to close its soliloquy with a final verbal lauding of those who put away such primitive beliefs. The last phrase got David's attention. "Actual hard copies of several ancient religious books can be found in the upstairs library archives."

David tried hard not to run as he made his way to the

elevator. He got up to the level with the library archives and stepped out cautiously. The area was empty except for one library attendant. He moved around the room casually. The attendant seemed to be paying him an inordinate amount of attention. The woman didn't appear to be the "library" type. Her stance was almost military in nature. She was working on a task in front of her but was clearly paying attention to David despite her task. David gave her a polite nod as he continued to wander casually around the room. It struck him as odd when she simply nodded back to him without straying from her task. The other attendants in the rest of the museum were quite warm and friendly. David began glancing at more than the displays. There seemed to be a superfluous number of security cameras in this area. There had been several in the other areas of the museum. This room had two or three times as many cameras.

David decided to press the attendant for information. "Do you get a lot of theft or vandalism in this part the museum?"

The woman looked annoyed that he had spoken to her. "I'm sorry, sir. I'm not at liberty to discuss the museum's security with you."

David smiled disarmingly. "I'm sorry. I didn't mean to pry into things that weren't my concern. I just noticed a larger number of security cameras up here than on the other floors. I work a security detail myself frequently. Forgive me, I know better than to ask such questions."

The woman managed a weak smile. David spotted the display he was looking for and moved closer to it. He casually pulled his scanner out of his pocket. Despite being in civilian attire, David preferred to keep certain gear with him at all times. He glanced over his shoulder in time to see the woman press a silent alarm button. David got his scan as quickly as possible while setting his scanner to monitor approaching human heat signatures. Seconds later his scanner flashed a warning indicating two vehicles with somewhere near twenty people were pulling up outside the building. "Uh-oh, time to go," David thought to himself. After one last glance at the building layout on his scanner, David slid it into his pocket and carefully removed his weapon from its concealed holster. The attendant was concentrating on her computer screen and didn't see David slip up behind her. The Captain saw her reaching surreptitiously for a weapon under her desk. Grabbing her left arm, he hastily twisted it behind her back, and pulled her out of reach of the weapon. Shoving his own weapon into her ribs, he ordered, "Turn off the audio-visual feeds to the entire building and delete all records for the last two hours."

The woman hesitated and stammered, "I – I'm just a librarian. I don't have access to security protocols."

David twisted her arm more tightly causing the woman to let out a small yelp. "That's not true. You and I both know you aren't a librarian. You are a trained security officer, although your training seems slightly inept. Do it now."

The woman reached down and placed her hand on the computer screen. "Computer, shut down all primary audio-visual feeds."

David pushed the weapon into her ribs a little harder. "And secondary…"

The woman glowered at him. "Computer, shut down all primary and secondary audio-visual feeds and delete all primary and auxiliary recordings for the past two hours."

David slipped a data crystal into the computer interface. "Run the program." Once the program was activated, he removed the crystal and slipped it back into his pocket.

The woman ran the program as ordered. David sat the woman down in a comfortable chair near the elevator. He pushed the button for the elevator. As soon as it arrived, David sighed. Looking at the angry woman, he apologized, "I'm sorry about this." He raised his weapon and fired. The woman convulsed violently several times then collapsed. David caught her and leaned her back into the chair, so she wouldn't fall in the floor. He had used a heavy stun setting so it would take her awhile to give the approaching security force any kind of description of him. The Captain stepped onto the elevator and pressed the button for the second floor. The car stopped as requested, but David remained on it. He pulled out his brochure. Opening it to its fullest size, he pressed the button for the first floor then began to flip the map back and forth awkwardly. The doors opened. He stepped out in the face of ten armed troops. His eyes grew wide. He pulled his arms and brochure back up against his body and stepped to the side. The troops gave him a brief glance and moved hastily into the elevator. A second group headed up the stairs. As soon as the coast was clear David hastily folded his brochure and exited the building. He walked casually to the end of the block. He picked up his pace the instant he turned the corner. He spotted a mass transit stop ahead. He pulled the hood of his jacket up in time to hop aboard. He wasn't sure where he was headed, but he needed to put some distance between himself and the museum. David kept his head down, trying to look dejected or tired. Several stops later he got off and hailed Jake.

Jake's voice answered promptly. "Yes Captain, what do you need?"

"I need to be picked up as soon as possible. Where's the vehicle?"

There was a pause as he heard Jake move around for a moment. "Marissa's in a dressing room trying on clothes right now. Do you want me to just send the driver to get you?"

"That's fine, Jake. Make it quick though."

"What's wrong, Captain?"

"I'll explain it later. Suffice it to say, I got some unwanted attention."

"Yes sir, stand by." Jake pulled his own scanner out. He viewed a layout of the city. The Captain was located northeast of them. "Captain head three blocks east then turn north. That will put you on the most direct route back to the cottage. I'll have the driver pick you up along that route. Captain, is there something I need to be concerned about?"

"I hope not. When you're ready to approach the cottage, hail me. If I don't answer or if there's a problem, don't come back." The Captain began walking the direction Jake indicated.

"Captain, you've got me worried."

"If it turns out to be a problem, just head for the shuttle and move it to another city. I think I covered my tracks fairly well. If I didn't, I'll make sure I protect both of you. Get that vehicle on its way, please." David cut off his connection and moved more quickly.

Jake contacted his driver and gave him the Captain's location. The driver picked David up a few minutes later and drove him back to the cottage. David sat down in a chair and began to kick himself for making such rookie mistakes. He set his scanner up to warn him of approaching vehicles then packed a survival kit. If he had to run, he wanted to be prepared. The cottage had little to offer in the way of survival gear. It did come equipped with a small boat and some scuba gear. David located the boat's tracking device. He wanted to be prepared to disable it quickly. Several hours passed without occurrence. The Captain turned on a news monitoring station on the computer. The news mentioned an assault on a librarian at a local museum. It claimed the attacker was mentally unstable and extremely dangerous. The report gave a vague description along with an artist's computer-generated rendering of the attacker. The picture displayed on the screen. It was a definite likeness of the Captain. David frowned and kicked himself again.

The sun began to go down. It was going to be a beautiful sunset. Jake hailed the Captain as he and Marissa approached. Marissa sensed something was wrong but didn't ask any prodding questions. When she heard the Captain say everything was all clear, she had to ask, "Jake, what's going on?"

Jake laughed sarcastically. "I don't have a clue. The Captain said he got some unwanted attention today."

Marissa hastily opened a news channel in the vehicle as they drove down the private drive to the cottage. The first picture that popped up was the artist's rendition of an unknown attacker in the Museum Library. She recognized the picture at once and gasped, "He attacked a librarian?!?" There had to be more to this than the information provided by the media. The second the vehicle came to a stop, Marissa was out of it and in the cottage.

Jake took the time to ask the driver to bring their packages inside, then asked him to stay close by for a little while. Jake hurried in to find David and Marissa in the kitchen. Marissa was sitting on a bar stool just outside the window between the kitchen and living area. She had already asked the Captain what happened. He was simply waiting for Jake before he responded. David was leaning against the kitchen counter sipping on a glass of water looking annoyed. Jake settled in next to Marissa. He didn't bother asking any questions. The Captain seemed ready to unload without further invitation.

David told the two what he found and how highly guarded it was. When the two heard the entire story they sat there incredulously for a moment before speaking.

Jake gave another sarcastic laugh, "and you called me, trigger happy? You've shot more people on this mission than I have. I couldn't even shoot the person I should have."

David shook his head. "I should have left the *instant* I knew something was up. I was so consumed with curiosity and my desire to learn more about the history of Pateras, I couldn't just walk away. It interfered with my better judgment. I made a rookie mistake." David paced back and forth. He wanted to kick something badly.

Jake glanced at their driver as he put down a load of packages and headed back to the car. "Captain, with the precautions you took, I doubt they could trace you back here very quickly. On the other hand, our driver could recognize you from the pictures on the news."

David sighed. His options were limited. They could leave and move the shuttle to a new location. The shuttle could be traced to other landing sites so that wasn't a great option. They could attempt to bribe or blackmail their driver. They could take him prisoner. He could take off in the boat and leave his crew members behind. He would only have to stay hidden for a couple days, just long enough for the ship to be refit.

As if reading his mind Jake offered, "I could rig a jamming device to cut the news feed and outside communications."

David nodded. "That works for now, but what about tomorrow when you go back into town?"

"There's a smaller town northeast of here. We could go there instead. I doubt there would be as much publicity. I can also just try to keep him too busy to link in to any news channels. I do need to know what you want me to do if he figures it out."

David walked over to the nearest computer. He pulled a data crystal from the storage compartment. He slid it into the slot. A minute later he pulled it out and handed it to Jake. "There's two hundred untraceable credits on here. Tell him if he waits until we're gone to report me, we'll leave another two hundred for him. He's an innocent civilian. I don't want him hurt."

Jake took the crystal and slid it into his pocket. "And if this doesn't work?"

David shook his head again. He had a disgusted look on his face. He leaned forward and placed his palms on the kitchen counter. "I don't know. I guess we just sequester him for a couple days, then take the boat out to sea, and let the ship pick us up out there. Brynna can send someone out here to pick up the shuttle. How could I be so stupid?"

Jake smiled as he pulled out his own scanner and configured it to interfere with all communications channels.

David found Jake's grin annoying and out of place. "Jake, what are you smiling about?"

Jake grinned even more. "I'm just glad to know you're human. I've never seen you make a mistake or get rattled. It's comforting… in a way."

"Thanks… I think." David grimaced and walked outside.

• •

The next morning David stayed behind and monitored the news to see if things had calmed down. He noticed he was no longer the top story. He was still in the top ten mentions though.

Jake dropped Marissa at a store while he drove on down the road. He stopped at a small restaurant on the edge of town. Computer stations were common in restaurants and cafes. He asked the driver to come inside and wait at the bar for him. He told the driver to watch for his signal then join him at the table. Jake chose a private table in a corner.

While the driver waited, Jake hailed Admiral Garcia. It took a moment to get past the Admiral's Administrator. It felt like longer than a couple minutes, but the Admiral's face finally appeared. "Security Chief Holden, what can I do for you?"

Jake glanced around to be sure no one could overhear him. "I want to know if he's agreed to my proposal."

"He has, although there's a slight addendum. You and your wife will be arrested with the others. You will be detained and questioned. Once it has been determined that neither of you is a threat to the Commonwealth, you may collect your belongings and leave. You will receive amnesty from any prosecution and an honorable discharge from the CIF. The Executor himself said he would provide you with a ship. Do we have an agreement?"

Jake thought for a moment. "I want it in writing with the Executor's seal on it."

Admiral Garcia smiled. "So be it. I'll have it to you within the hour. Can I contact you back here?"

"Yes, Admiral."

Jake disconnected the call and ordered a stiff drink. He waved the driver over. "Feel free to order whatever you like, my treat. We're going to be here for an hour."

The driver walked back to the bar and ordered a light lunch. Jake sat back down with his drink and waited. He downed the first drink in one swift gulp and ordered a second. The second one he sipped slowly. He looked down at his hands. They were shaking. It had to be from excitement although he didn't feel excited. He felt nervous. What was there to be nervous about? He was bringing criminals to justice and getting to settle down with his family. Yes, he was betraying his shipmates, but they betrayed their commission first. He truly hoped Marissa would understand and forgive him.

Less than thirty minutes later, Jake's terminal beeped at him. He moved his drink out of view then answered the call. Jake was startled to see the face of Admiral Deacons appear in front of him. "Chief Holden, you lied to me. It seems I am the last to know my nephew is still alive. Why is that? Do you care to explain your actions?"

Jake looked at the drink sitting on the far side of the table and wished it was now closer. He swallowed, but his mouth was too dry. "Admiral Deacons, I apologize. I meant no disrespect, sir. I – I didn't... I didn't want to put you in the position of bringing your own nephew to justice. I know it must have been hard for you to tell the Captain's family he was dead. I didn't want to put you back in the position of bringing him to justice and telling them all over again. I had one other reason for not telling you, sir. They were watching me. They didn't trust me, and they knew you would be keeping in touch with me. I lied to you to earn their trust. Forgive me." Jake stopped speaking and nervously waited for the Admiral's reply. He tried to moisten his lips, but his mouth was still far too dry.

Admiral Garcia moved into the picture behind Admiral Deacons. "Chief Holden, I have the documentation you requested. I'm sending it now. Admiral Deacons will be handling the arrest of your crew. You've done a good thing, Chief. Let me know if you decide to re-enlist. I could use a man like you."

"Thank you, Admiral. I was just doing my job, sir."

Admiral Garcia disappeared leaving him in the uncomfortable eye of Admiral Deacons. Jake hesitated while the Admiral glared at him. "How did you want to do this, sir?"

The words were hard to form. It made the Admiral sick to his stomach. "What is the status of your crew?"

Jake swallowed hard again. "I suppose you already know we're on Romajin. The Captain, Lt. Holden, and I are on the west coast of the Northern Continent. The rest of the crew landed at the CIF base on the East Coast. I don't know if they were staying on base or not. We weren't supposed to contact each other until it's time to leave. There is a situation here that we could use to our advantage, though. The Captain had a… uh… an altercation of sorts with a librarian in a local museum. There's a warrant out for his arrest and a citywide manhunt."

The Admiral's face changed. He seemed to be having trouble swallowing the story. "Excuse me?"

Jake gained some confidence back and spoke with more conviction. "The Captain discovered a display in a local museum that contained some of the Ancient Texts. He got a little overzealous. When he went to check it out, the so-called librarian was undeniably a CIF agent there to locate followers of Pateras. She had the Captain pegged right away as something other than a tourist. She sounded the alarm. He knew if he were detained even briefly, it would set off alarms all over the place. He stunned her with his Tri-EMP and took off."

Admiral Deacons rubbed his face and jaw as though he could wipe away the thoughts and implications. "Chief, I need to get the crew arrested while they are on the ground, and it would be best if they were altogether. If I try to get them separately some may escape. Suggestions?"

"I could let the Commander know we have a problem and try to lure her and the crew out here." Jake thought for a minute. "I could possibly talk my wife into leaving the mission and settling here. I could ask the crew to come out here for a farewell party."

"I have a better idea. I'll tell the Commander, we know the Captain's alive. I'll offer to help the crew escape. The crew can meet at the shuttle port. I'll meet them at the shuttle to give them travel credentials with new identities."

"Meet the crew? Here? Where are you, sir?"

"I'm about one day away from you. I'll be there before sunrise on the West Coast. How can I reach the Captain?"

Jake shook his head. "I'm not sure you can. Because of the incident in town, we've been blocking the comm channels to prevent our driver from finding out what happened. You might be able to get through to him right now because the driver is with me. I doubt he's currently jamming those channels. I can give you the access code to the cottage, but he's going to wonder how you got it. I suggest you contact the Commander and let her reach out to us."

The Admiral pondered the security chief's words for a moment. "You're right. I'll contact the Commander. I would like you to send me that code anyway, just in case. Is your driver going to be a problem?"

Jake glanced at the driver who was finished eating and casually watching his employer for new instructions. "I don't know, sir."

"I assume you're watching him right now?"

"Yes sir."

"Let me speak to him."

Jake waved the man over. The driver promptly joined him at the table. As soon as the curious man was seated, Admiral Deacons introduced himself. "Sir, my name is Admiral Deacons of the Commonwealth Interstellar Force. What is your name?"

The man was taken aback by such a high-ranking official addressing him. He was accustomed to dealing with people of wealth, fame, and power but rarely someone of this stature. "M – My name is Adam Franklin, Admiral. What can I do for you?"

"It seems one of my men got himself into some trouble there the other day. I would really like to deal with this internally and keep it as quiet as possible. It seems his face has been showing up on the news. He's wanted by the local authorities. As I understand it, he got drunk and acted inappropriately. He's currently on leave and staying with Mr. Holden and his wife. He knows he made a mistake and he's keeping a low profile. As soon as he returns to his duty station, I plan on court-martialling him."

Mr. Franklin shifted anxiously in his seat. "Uh… Okay, what do you want from me, sir?"

"I need you to do whatever Mr. Holden requests of you. The first thing is, don't report him to the local authorities. It would put the CIF in a bad light. The CIF doesn't need any negative publicity. You understand, of course?"

"Of course, sir. Will there be anything else, sir?"

Jake volunteered another piece of information. "I believe

there is a small reward for your cooperation. I have a two hundred credit retainer and an additional two hundred credits will be available later. The credits are non-taxable." Jake slid a data crystal towards the man.

The Admiral knew either the Captain or Jake had put some thought into the situation. He diligently seconded Jake's offer. "Can I count on your cooperation, Mr. Franklin?"

The man looked down at the data crystal then back up at the Admiral's face. "Yes sir, I'm glad to do whatever I can for the CIF." He slipped the crystal into his pocket.

The Admiral turned his attention back to Jake. "Chief, I'll be in touch. Keep the comm lines open."

"Yes, Admiral." Jake closed the conversation and downloaded a copy of his amnesty agreement onto a data crystal. As a precaution, he sent a copy to his private files aboard the ship. He turned back to his driver. The man had a troubled look on his face. "What's bothering you, Mr. Franklin?"

"Your friend, hasn't been even remotely drunk in the entire time I've seen him. That story was a smoke screen."

Jake smiled. Mr. Franklin was an astute individual. "Yes, it was. It would have been better for him if he *had* been drunk. The Admiral's fury over this incident knows no bounds. I really wouldn't want to be in his shoes when the Admiral gets ahold of him. You want to know the worst of it?" The man nodded for Jake to continue. Jake grinned even bigger. "Our friend is the Admiral's nephew. He has embarrassed his uncle several times over. The Admiral's tired of it. He's going to make his nephew pay dearly for this one."

Adam smiled and shook his head. "I wish I could listen in on that conversation."

"Me too, more than you'll ever know." Jake was anxious to see the Captain face justice for his treason, not the incident in town. A minor assault couldn't compare to treason.

Jake settled his bill for the food and drinks. He hastily gulped down the rest of his own drink and left the restaurant. Mr. Franklin pulled the vehicle up out front. The two rejoined Marissa to shop.

• •

That evening when they returned to the cottage, the Captain was already asleep. It was unusual for him to go to bed so early. Jake took advantage of the time and sent most of their purchases back to the shuttle. Marissa felt like she had bought enough clothing for herself and supplies for the baby. She was glad to take a break from the arduous task of shopping. She was thankful Jake took the initiative to load her newest acquisitions. Once Adam was on his way to the shuttle port with his load, Jake prepared a simple, but tasty meal for him and Marissa. He served their meal out on the patio overlooking the beach. Jake was surprisingly relaxed. He turned on some soft music and invited Marissa to dance with him under the starry night. Marissa was puzzled by the unusually relaxed nature of her normally tense and uptight husband. She wasn't sure why he was in such a mood, but she did enjoy it. Without bothering to clean up the dishes, Jake and Marissa slipped off to their room and shut the door.

Jake had prepared enough food, so the Captain could eat if he woke up. He left the Captain's food in the kitchen while he spent time with Marissa. A couple hours later, David woke up and went to the kitchen in search of food. He found what Jake left for him, warmed the plate up, and sat down to eat it. Jake finally wandered out of his room to clean up the dishes. He gathered the dishes from the patio and brought them back into the kitchen. "Captain, are you okay?"

David looked up from his plate of food. "I think so. Why?"

Jake glanced at a clock. "You went to bed really early. I thought perhaps you were sick or something."

"Yeah, I was a little confused by that too. I was fine then had this driving urge to eat a huge lunch and get a nap. I'm not sure why I slept so long. I woke up feeling like I hadn't eaten in a week. I almost feel like I'm storing up for a rainy day."

"Maybe you're finally relaxing enough to eat like you should, and the food isn't ship's rations."

David smiled weakly, "It's possible on both counts but something… feels… off."

"Maybe you're *about* to get sick?" Jake offered.

"I hope not." David took another hearty bite of his food. "By the way, you're a decent cook, Chief."

"Thanks, Captain."

David finished his plate and helped Jake clean up. Jake started to return to his room when he remembered he hadn't told the Captain about their driver. "Captain, I forgot to tell you…"

Jake was interrupted by the computer screens flashing a hail from Commander Alexander. When David and Jake saw who the hail was from they cast worried glances at each other. Jake's worry was contrived, but David's was genuine.

David let Jake answer the hail while he stood just out of sight. Brynna's face appeared and the first words out of her mouth were, "Jake, I need to see the Captain. It's urgent."

David stepped into view. "I'm here. What's wrong?"

Brynna bit down on her lower lip like she frequently did when she was worried. "David, I got a call from your uncle. He knows you're alive. There's a warrant being issued right now for the crew's arrest. Your uncle said he would meet us at the shuttle port where you are tomorrow. He's prepared credentials with new identities for the entire crew. I've got the crew split up and traveling separately to the west coast. We're going to rendezvous at the shuttle port out there, then take the shuttle to the nearest Interstellar Port. We can book passage out of the system there."

"Why would the Admiral agree to do that? It could get him arrested." David leaned over placing tightly clinched fists down on the desk in front of him. His face reflected the gravity of the situation.

"I think… I think he feels like he has a second chance to save your life. Your death must have rattled him worse than he let on." Brynna's words sounded hollow even to her.

"Can you reroute the crew to the Stellar Port?"

Brynna squinted at him. "You think it's a trap?"

"It's a strong possibility. If someone wanted to capture us, they would want us all together so we couldn't sound the alarm. If even one of us escaped capture, the message of Pateras could go anywhere. Can you redirect the crew?"

"No, David, I can't. I ordered them to shut off all comms. I didn't want anyone to be able to track them."

"I guess I'll just get there early and try to warn them off. Brynna, don't come here. Head for the Stellar Port."

"David, I should be there to help."

"If you come here, you'll just get caught too. Stay away Commander; that's an order. Somebody has to get this message out."

A flash of pain crossed Brynna's face, then dissolved as she acknowledged her orders. "The crew is supposed to rendezvous with you at 0800 hours. The Stellar Port is only an hour from you. I'll wait for you for three hours then I'll board the next ship out."

David's face revealed no emotion. "Acknowledged, Commander. Remember, Pateras will always be with you. His power surpasses the Commonwealth."

"Yes sir. David, I love you. I hope you're wrong about this being a trap."

David reached up and touched Brynna's face on the screen. "Me too. I love you, too." He reluctantly disconnected the call.

David looked up at Jake. He knew somehow Jake must have had something to do with this, but for once, he *seemed* innocent.

A heavy silence fell on the two men. Jake finally broke the silence, "What are your orders, sir?"

"Get some sleep, Chief. We're going to need to head to the shuttle port early in the morning. We'll look for the crew and send them via regular transport to the Stellar Port. If the coast is clear, I'll bring our shuttle to the Stellar Port myself."

"Captain, you can't be seen wandering around this public Shuttle Port. You're a wanted man. Why don't we drop you at the shuttle? You can meet with the Admiral while Marissa and I collect the crew and arrange to meet you at a secondary shuttle dock. If the coast is clear, move the shuttle to the secondary slip and pick us up. I can let you know which slip we're in as soon as I see you in the air. If you get captured, you won't be able to tell them where the crew is because you won't know."

The Captain opened his mouth to object. Before he could speak Marissa interrupted from behind him. "Captain, Jake's right. This is the best way to handle it."

David had been so wrapped up in his own thoughts he hadn't heard her come in. He turned to see her standing in the doorway.

Marissa was wearing a silk robe wrapped tightly around her. The robe managed to accentuate the growing bulge in her belly. Her dark hair flowed gently down her shoulders in sharp contrast to the lightly colored robe. The Captain wasn't used to seeing the crew dressed so casually. Despite the laxness in military protocol, the Captain had been adamant about keeping the crew's privacy protected and maintaining a definitive amount of decorum. Her clothing wasn't revealing in the slightest, but the nature of the garment made her seem… vulnerable.

"It's weak, Jake. I would rather the crew just headed for the Stellar Port on their own."

Jake shook his head, "It's too risky and time consuming. We need to put as much space between us and this planet as fast as we can. If the crew's faces start showing up on mass transit audio/visual monitors, it puts all of us at risk. Their faces are less likely to show up on a private docking slip. This is the best way, sir."

The Captain felt like he was being sucked into a place he couldn't escape. He sat down sullenly in the chair at the desk. "You win, Chief. We'll do it your way. You two better get some sleep. I'll take the watch since I've already had a nap. We'll head out by 0600 hours local time."

Jake and Marissa acknowledged their orders, packed up as much as they could, then laid down and tried to get some sleep. Their tension levels were high enough, the two had to resort to self-hypnotism to get sleep.

David went to his room and programmed his scanner to alert him to approaching traffic of any sort. He took a shower, shaved, and put on his uniform. If he was going to get caught, he wanted the public to know he was a Commonwealth officer. Seeing a Commonwealth Officer get arrested was headline news. The public would want to know why. It also might serve as a distraction, so the crew could escape.

As the troubled young Captain put the rest of his belongings into his travel bag, he picked up the data module he had brought with him. Surely, he was missing something. There must be some way out of this. The data module had several uses. He didn't want to disturb his sleeping crewmen, so David carried the data module out to the patio. The moon was full. The air was crisp and clean. The ambient light was minimal, clearing the way for thousands of stars to pierce the darkness. David turned on the data module. A message from his Uncle Rob was waiting for him. David played the message.

"David, your family is safe. They're under my protection. I

have to keep this short. I told you I would only do a hard send if I'd been compromised. I don't know if I have been or not. I have the distinct impression they're testing me. I think I would prefer to fail this test. David, this is a trap. They're coming for you and your crew tomorrow morning. If they don't get you, they'll know I tipped you off, and I'll probably be arrested. I'd rather have that happen than see you and your crew caught. If you show up tomorrow, I'll have to arrest you. Please… Run!"

The image faded. David stared at the empty space above the holographic imager. He looked up at the stars. "Pateras, what do you want me to do? I can't run and let my crew be taken. What should I do?"

David felt a presence behind him then a hand on his shoulder. "Arni?"

"Yes?"

"What am I supposed to do?"

Arni stepped around and sat down in another chair facing the ocean. "What do you think you should do?"

David frowned. "I don't like this game."

"It's not a game, David. What you do is up to you. My father has a plan to deal with whichever you choose."

David sat there still considering his options. "I don't really have a choice. It's my job to protect my crew. I suppose I could just run and leave my crew to take their chances. I can't do that. I'll do whatever it takes to defend this crew from the Commonwealth. It's my fault they're in danger."

Arni shook his head. "You're taking far too much responsibility on yourself. Exactly what do you consider my responsibilities to be?"

"I'm following your lead. I depend on you to give me my orders and protect me when I get into trouble. I follow your lead like the crew follows my lead."

Arni shook his head again slowly. "This isn't a military

chain of command. David, your crew gave themselves to me. They are my responsibility, not yours. Let go of them. Put their well-being in my hands."

David rocketed out of his seat and began to pace back and forth on the patio. The cool breeze blew through his short hair. He looked back at Arni. His first inclination was to say, "No." He trusted Arni with his own life. Entrusting him with the lives of the crew was a different story.

"What exactly do you think is going to happen to your crew if you put their welfare in my hands?"

"I… I don't know. I'm a Captain. It's what I was trained to do. How do you expect me to do anything else?"

Arni spoke slowly to give his words time to sink in. "We've had this discussion before. I know this is hard for you. You are a man, one man, a finite human. I'm not. Who's better equipped to take care of them?"

David stood there in the moonlight feeling a buildup of energy that could only be attributed to the presence of Pateras. It was hard to describe. A chill ran through his body causing his skin to erupt with goose bumps while filling him with a warmth and comfort beyond understanding.

David turned placing Arni directly in front of him. Arni asked him one simple question. "Who am I?"

The power of Pateras reached a crescendo within David's innermost being. He felt Pateras' presence well up within him and surround him. In the face of his own insignificance and Pateras' power, David knelt on one knee. "Y – You are the son of Pateras, the most powerful being in the universe. You gave your life to save me and my crew."

"I am more than just the son of Pateras. You've been in my father's presence. Wherever I am, my father is. Have I not proven myself to you? Your crew gave themselves to *me*; they are no longer following you. *You* wanted this, almost as much as I did.

If it is my father's desire to allow your crew to die at the hands of the Commonwealth, then why struggle against it? Did you dislike being in my father's presence?"

The guilt of withholding his crew from Arni pressed on David's heart. He lowered his head. He could no longer bear to look Arni in the eye. Arni had restored Marissa to life before any of them had chosen to follow him. He saved David's own life several times over and brought *him* back from the dead. Arni had died, and Pateras brought him back to life. Pateras had the power of life and death. David wondered why he was having trouble letting go of the crew. He finally forced himself to look back into the eyes of his benefactor. "I'm sorry. You've proven yourself, time and again. Forgive me. I trust you to do whatever you think is best. The crew is yours."

The heaviness lifted from David's spirit. Arni offered David his hand to stand again. David accepted it and stood to face his – his, what was their relationship? Was he truly a god? The idea still seemed hard to swallow. The years of indoctrination had taken their toll. He just couldn't wrap his brain around the idea just yet.

Knowing his thoughts, Arni answered his unspoken questions. "Pateras is the ONLY GOD. If it's easier for you, he is your Father and your friend. He is a constant companion to all who desire his presence."

A faraway look crossed David's face. "Does that make you my father, or my brother,… or my friend?"

Arni smiled at the simplicity of David's question. "I am all of those and more."

David's confusion didn't clear up, but he decided to just accept it. "What's going to happen tomorrow?"

"My father is reaching out to the last member of your crew. It's going to cost you and your crew a great deal. Do what you need to, but don't fight this. No one will be lost. Put the days ahead in my hands. I'll get you through them. The only way out of this is to go through it."

David nodded. He wasn't enthused about it. "This is for Jake's benefit?"

Arni nodded. "He's the only one who hasn't joined me, despite his appearance. His eyes will be open very soon, if you're willing to walk through this with me. Are you willing to do this for Jake?"

David remembered a talk he had with Jake and Thane after an altercation occurred between the two. David asked the two if they would be able to trust each other with their lives. Arni was asking the same thing of him only the threat was not hypothetical. "If you think this is worth it, then I'll do it."

Arni smiled. "Jake's worth it."

"What's it going to cost us?"

"Let me worry about that. You can't stop tomorrow from happening. You can still run, but it will cost you more than you know, if you do. I know this is going to be difficult. Brynna had to trust me when she thought you died in the temple fire. Now I'm asking you to trust me. You and your crew will be arrested. If you run, you will be the only one who escapes. If you take Jake and Marissa, Jake will get you caught later and you'll lose his respect."

"I'll lose his *respect*? He's about to betray me. I don't think he has much respect for me."

Arni smiled again. "He respected you enough to arrange to have you arrested and not executed. One of his conditions for turning you in was the crew would be retrained. He respects you more than even he knows."

David was having trouble accepting yet another concept. He began to wonder why he bothered talking with Arni. It always seemed to leave him more curious than when he started. He asked one more question. "So tomorrow, follow Jake's plan and get myself and my crew arrested. What about Marissa and the baby? Are they going to be alright? Is there anything else I should know or do? Any words of wisdom?"

"All you need to know is that no matter how bad it gets, I will be there with you. I asked Brynna to put your life in my hands and her trust in me. I'm asking the same of you. Whether Marissa and the baby survive or not, I need you to trust me. Stay strong and don't fold. I have limited Luciano. He can only do what I allow."

David burned Arni's words into his brain. He didn't want to forget one word. He knew he would need those words soon enough.

Arni turned to walk away. "Lay down and get some more sleep. Nothing will happen tonight. I have the watch."

David blinked and Arni was gone. The Captain replayed his last words in his mind. His commander had given him an order. He needed to follow it. David walked inside and laid down on the sofa. He positioned the pillows to make himself comfortable then went to sleep, as ordered.

His dream of Galat played through his troubled mind again as he slept. Something was different this time though. The wild dogs tried to attack him again. This time a leash held them back, just out of reach. The dogs howled several times then laid down at the crew's feet.

• •

David awoke early that morning to Jake shaking his arm. David gave Jake a blank stare for a moment until things began to clear up for him. In a flash, his conversation with Arni the night before came back to him. David sat up quickly.

Jake's look of consternation and befuddlement finally came to a head. "Captain, I thought you were standing watch last night. What happened? Are you sure you aren't getting sick or something?"

David stood up before answering Jake. The longer he looked at Jake's face, the angrier he became. "I'm fine," David snapped. He abruptly left the room to splash some water on his face.

Jake glanced curiously at Marissa. "What was that all about?" Marissa just shrugged her shoulders and finished getting ready to go.

David came back in a moment and headed for the kitchen. He found Adam Franklin had prepared breakfast. "Mr. Franklin, I forgot to tell you we were leaving early this morning. Did Jake or Marissa tell you?"

Adam was somewhere around fifty years old with salt and pepper colored hair. He seemed to enjoy his job of caring for cottage guests. In addition to driving for the crew, he had performed numerous tasks around the property which now included a delicious smelling breakfast. Adam smiled at the Captain. "No, they didn't tell me. We have another friend in common." Adam handed David a plate of food and a data crystal. "Leave this data crystal in the shuttle. You'll need it later."

David looked curiously at the data crystal wondering what was on it. Seeing the question on David's face, Adam volunteered, "It's the bribe, your Chief offered me to keep my mouth shut. Arni said to take it, then return it to you this morning."

David took the crystal and slid it into his pocket. "Are you… human or…"

Adam shook his head. "No, I'm a messenger of Pateras. Arni did have one request. He asked that you not be angry at Jake. Jake will be worth it."

Before David could say anything more, Jake and Marissa walked in. The three ate quietly with little discussion. The task ahead of them weighed down all conversation. After they finished eating, they loaded themselves and their remaining luggage into the vehicle. Adam drove the group directly to their landing slip. He helped load their baggage onto the shuttle.

Before climbing into the shuttle, David stuck his head into the vehicle to talk to Marissa for a moment. "Marissa, I'm sorry. I'm not going to be able to keep my promise… at least not the way I thought I could. You're in the hands of Pateras now. Trust him, no matter what. It's the best I can do."

Marissa sat there staring at him. His words just weren't making sense. What did he mean? David backed out of the vehicle. He started to close the door, but Marissa jumped out before he could. She grabbed him in a tight hug. David froze for a second then returned the hug. Marissa whispered a tearful, "Thank you!" She released him and climbed back into the vehicle. He heard her mutter something about "stupid hormones," as she wiped away tears.

David reached the shuttle as Jake finished stowing the rest of their gear. Jake bounded down the few steps from the shuttle. He was far too excited for a man about to be arrested. David placed one hand on Jake's chest and shoved him against the hull of the shuttle. "Jake…" David heard a dog or coyote howl just beyond the perimeter of the shuttle port. He looked to see the animal staring at him. It howled five more times then jumped away into the brush. The dog in his dream had howled six times as well. Jake's eyes followed the Captain's, but the significance was not evident to Jake. David turned his attention back to his traitorous security chief. "Jake… when this is over, you're going to owe this crew more than you can ever hope to repay. I only hope they can forgive you."

Jake's guilt was now plain to see. "What are you talking about, sir?" He tried to look innocent. The Captain wasn't buying it.

"I had a talk with Arni last night. He didn't tell me everything, but he did tell me enough. He said you're worth everything we're about to go through. You better make sure he's right or my back won't be the one needing to be watched."

Jake shoved the Captain away from him. "You're a traitor. You all are. I covered my back." Jake started to walk away then turned back. "If you knew this was a trap, why didn't you walk away?"

"I told you. I'm doing this for you, Mr. Holden."

Jake shivered. The Captain's words struck too close to home. He walked over to the vehicle and got in beside Marissa. Marissa was turned the other direction and hadn't seen the exchange. Jake was glad she had no untimely questions for him.

• •

The driver chauffeured the couple to the main terminal. As the vehicle came to a stop, Marissa looked at Jake. "He's going to let himself be captured to protect the crew, isn't he?"

Jake gave a gruff. "I don't know… maybe. You start looking for the others while I reserve the secondary hangar. I'll hail you when I have the slip number."

Jake and Marissa walked into the small but busy terminal. They looked around warily. Marissa quickly found Jason and Laura. The couple looked weary from a long night of travel. They gave Marissa a brief description of their trip as they changed from shuttle to shuttle during the night and even rode a "scenic" train for part of their journey. Marissa told the couple to spread out and find the others then meet back in this same spot in fifteen minutes.

• •

After Jake and Marissa left the Captain alone at the shuttle, David started his preflight check offs. He opened the hangar bay doors and kept a watchful eye on the perimeter. Ten minutes before the eight o'clock hour, a car rolled up. Admiral Deacons stepped out and walked hastily to the shuttle. The Admiral appeared annoyed. David set up his scanner to jam all communications within a thirty-yard radius.

Seeing it was now safe to talk, Robert spoke first. "David, didn't you get my message? This is a trap. If you stay here, you'll be arrested and so will your crew."

"I'm sorry, Uncle Rob. I didn't get your message until the crew was already out of touch. I couldn't just run away and let them get caught. If we go down, we'll do it together."

"That's truly a noble sentiment, David, but you have to get the word out about Pateras. If you get arrested, I can't get you out of this."

"Uncle Rob, if I escape, it could have some ugly repercussions for all of us. If I'm caught, by you, they won't have reason to doubt you."

"David, please don't do this. I don't know if I can handle seeing the things I know they'll do to you."

"I can't handle walking away, knowing my crew will face those things without me. Uncle Rob, please don't worry. Arni has things under control. You just need to be the angry Admiral. You're allowed to recuse yourself. Under the circumstances, no one would blame you. Leave us behind. Keep the family safe and please don't tell my mom what they're going to do to me. I don't want her to be sick from worry."

Robert shook his head. "I don't think I understand, but I'll accept your decision. Here's two data crystals. Put this one in your pocket… and this one leave hidden here in the shuttle. The first one is a set of phony new identities. These identities have been tagged. If you use those anywhere, it will send up red flags all over the place. The second set, haven't been tagged and are usable. They don't need to find that set on you. If you can escape and get back to the shuttle, you can use these to leave the planet."

David took the second crystal and tucked it into the slot containing blank data crystals under the control panel of the shuttle. He slipped the first one into his pocket as instructed then stood up to escort the Admiral out of the shuttle. The Admiral stood to leave but stopped David before he could go any further. "If you're determined to go through with this, then there's something you should know."

David studied the Admiral's face trying to decipher his message before it was vocalized. "I'm going to do this. I doubt there's anything you could say to stop me."

"Brynna's already been arrested. They picked her up an hour ago. She's being transported here in case you don't come along peacefully. When I come for you, I'm going to behave cruelly. I'm going to rub her capture in your face. It needs to be new information to you. Do you understand?"

David looked down at the floor. "Why didn't you tell me this earlier?"

The Admiral was almost embarrassed by his answer. David was still not looking him in the eye, nevertheless, Robert had to look away. "I – I thought if I could convince you to run, I could let you know later she had been taken. I knew you wouldn't leave if I told you we had her. Since I can't convince you to leave, then you should know all the facts going into this."

David's demeanor had been that of a man on his way to his own execution. That now changed. He stood up straighter. His eyes met the Admiral's eyes. Robert saw fire in them. He hoped he hadn't made a mistake telling David about Brynna. "David, what are you going to do?"

"I'm going to do the same thing as before, only better. My crew needs to see me confident, not defeated. This is part of Pateras' plan. I'm going to embrace it instead of being dragged into it kicking and screaming like a child at bath time." David gave his uncle a small but sincere smile. "I know for a fact Arni has everything under control. He told me not to fold. You do the same thing. Don't let them find you out."

David held out his hand to the Admiral. The Admiral looked down at it. Something finally clicked. Robert reached out and took David's hand and pulled him in for a familial hug. He held his sister's oldest son for a fleeting moment. The moment held a lifetime of flashes. Robert saw David as a newborn, a feisty toddler, an adventurous boy, a proud cadet at the academy, and a strong officer of the Commonwealth. The Admiral quickly released the young man he was quite proud to call his nephew. He moved hastily towards the door to hide the emotion he felt building within him. He covertly wiped away one small tear as he stepped onto the top step of the shuttle. He called back to David. "Don't mess this up. I couldn't live with myself… or your mother." He cast David a weak grin then was gone.

David smiled to himself. It was time to go. He closed the hatch, got into the pilot's seat and requested permission to launch. In a moment, the clearance came through. He launched the shuttle and put it into the appropriate holding pattern around the port. He opened a comm line to Jake. "Okay, Chief, where's the party?"

After an awkward pause Jake answered. "We'll meet you in hangar twenty-five."

David acknowledged him then hailed flight control requesting permission to put down in hangar twenty-five. Flight control gave him a slight ribbing for being fickle before clearing him to descend again. David manipulated several controls then finished his circle and followed the path to his new berth. He gently brought the shuttle into the enclosure. Jake was waiting for him to power down to close the hangar doors. As soon as the engine shut down, Jake pressed the control. The closing doors signaled the troops waiting in the nearby hangars to move in. David put the shuttle into a low energy mode to keep the engines warm, just in case. He stepped confidently out of the shuttle and down the steps. The crew loaded their bags into the shuttle storage compartments. David and Jake visually scanned the perimeter. They were both looking for the same things, but not for the same reasons. The two heard multiple doors open on all sides of them. The hangar door opened widely allowing dozens of troops to swarm in. In a manner of seconds, the crew and shuttle were surrounded. Shouting came from all directions. The crew reacted by immediately pulling their own weapons and forming a defensive circle. A voice from behind the troops called out, "HOLD YOUR FIRE! NOBODY FIRE!" Admiral Deacons stepped into view. "Captain Alexander, I suggest you order your crew to stand down before anyone gets hurt."

David was standing in a defensive position alongside the crew. He and Jake were both standing in front of Marissa. David slowly stepped forward holding his weapon pointed upward and his hands in a position of conditional surrender. "Admiral, we'll stand down, but there's something you need to know. We have a pregnant crew member. As a courtesy, please see to her safety."

The Admiral stood, feet planted firmly in full view of David, but surrounded by his troops. "You're in no position to make demands, Captain."

Before he could respond Thane jumped in. "Captain, I'd rather go down fighting than face what they plan to do to us."

David glanced sideways at Thane, "Take it easy, Lieutenant Ryder. All they have to do is stun us and it's game over either way." David turned his attention back to the Admiral. "Admiral, I wasn't making a demand. I was asking as a courtesy to protect my crew as any good commander would do. Please, promise me she won't be harmed."

The Admiral paused for a moment. "If she and your crew surrender peacefully, no one will be harmed. Send her out, and I'll transport her with me."

David holstered his weapon slowly then turned to face

Marissa. A myriad of emotions displayed on her face. She was afraid, angry, and determined. She held her weapon defiantly. She knew what the Captain was about to ask of her. She began to shake her head at him. Tears slowly began to roll down her face. "Captain… no… please don't make me do this."

David spoke gently to her. "Marissa, give me the Tri-EMP." The Captain placed himself directly in front of her weapon. Being religiously responsible with a firearm, she could not point it at her Captain. His close proximity forced her to lower the weapon. David slowly pried it from her hands. He pulled her in and hugged her as she began to sob openly. He whispered something only she could hear, "The Admiral will protect you." He followed up by saying things he wanted the others to hear. "I spoke to Arni last night. This is a part of Pateras' plan. This will be over in six days. Can you be strong for six days?" Marissa nodded. David released her into Jake's free arm.

Jake kept his eyes on the men pointing their weapons at the crew. Despite his loyalty to the Commonwealth and the part he played in setting this up, he wanted to be certain things went according to plan. Jake kissed his wife gently and caressed her face for a moment. He offered her platitudes of his own. "It's going to be okay. I promise. I'll get us out of this. You'll be okay."

The Admiral folded his arms impatiently across his chest. "I'm waiting, Lt. Holden. Keep your hands in the air, and walk over here slowly."

Marissa stepped out of the circle with her hands in the air. She took a few steps then looked back at her shipmates. Everyone cast anguished glances at her. Her eyes landed back on Jake and the Captain. Jake continued to reassure her. Somehow the Captain's reassuring nods offered more comfort than Jake's did. Marissa walked on over to the troops who promptly spun her around, placed binders on her wrists, and escorted her towards the perimeter. The Admiral instructed one of the officers to place Marissa in his personal shuttle. They heard him give another instruction although no one could make it out.

David kept Marissa's weapon pointed down at the ground. As soon as she was out of sight, the crew quickly began to weigh in on David's obvious plan to surrender without a fight. Some questioned him while others refused to accept it as the only option.

Seeing the fight still in the crew, the Admiral did what he could to drain it out of them. Despite his appearance, he didn't want anyone getting hurt. "Captain Alexander, the rest of your crew needs to put their weapons down and surrender now."

"Admiral, please give us a moment and we will all surrender."

"Let me give you something to think about while you consider your options." The Admiral waved at someone, just out of sight to come forward. The guards escorted another prisoner forward. It was David's wife, Commander Brynna Alexander.

David stared hard at Brynna. She seemed in good condition, just tired and frustrated. The guards forced Brynna to her knees in front of them. Five of the crew knew the Admiral's loyalty lay with Pateras. David and Brynna were two of the five. David had warned the Admiral to protect himself by playing the staunch soldier. Robert didn't like this part of it, but he played his part rather convincingly. "Captain, the penalty for treason of this nature is death. Should I start with your wife?" Brynna's guards moved slightly behind her on each side. They drew their weapons. A heavy silence filled the room as the weapons were heard powering up.

Despite knowing the Admiral was bluffing, David started to launch himself, weapon in hand, at the men taking aim at his wife. "ADMIRAL! DON'T DO THIS!" Jake and Thane caught the Captain and held him back.

The Admiral stood there firmly. His arms again folded resolutely across his chest. "Tell your crew to drop their weapons and surrender peacefully." Braxton cast a sideways glance at the Captain. He was one of the five who knew the Admiral served Pateras although his behavior was an unnerving contrast to that position.

The Captain promptly ordered the crew to lower their weapons and surrender. The crew slowly obeyed. One by one they laid their weapons on the ground and kicked them away. The Admiral ordered the crew to place their hands on their heads, face the inside of the circle, and get on their knees. When the last crew member hit the floor, the troops moved in and hastily secured their prisoners. The crew was cuffed and pulled to their feet one by one. David was handled differently. He was pushed face down onto the concrete floor. His arms were twisted roughly behind him. The troops placed binders on his wrists and ankles. A special binder was placed around his neck. This binder could provide an electrical charge via a remote operated from bracelets like the crew used.

With the crew now secured, the Admiral escorted Brynna over to join the others. Admiral Deacons' stomach churned with disgust. His face reflected his sentiments. Admiral Garcia stood in the background watching him closely. Robert's disgust was not aimed at the Commonwealth crew's treason, but Admiral Garcia interpreted it as such. Admiral Deacons placed himself in the center of the crew. Turning to make eye contact with each one, he addressed the group. "Listen up! You are under arrest and charged with high treason. Under these circumstances, the Supreme Executor has authorized immediate execution. He does, however, believe your miserable lives might still be worth saving. So long as you behave, no one will be harmed. If you resist at all, your Captain will be punished."

The Admiral waved to David's guards to pull him forward. With David in the center of the circle, Robert motioned to the guards to step back. The Admiral walked in a casual circle around David carefully making eye contact with each crew member. "You will notice the device around your Captain's neck. This collar can generate varying amounts of electrical current through the Captain's body. It can be small enough to be painful. It can be debilitating, or it can be deadly, whichever I choose." Robert walked over directly in front of David. He couldn't give the verbal warning he wanted. He stared directly into David's eyes and visibly set his jaw and clinched his teeth. Seeing what was about to happen, David followed the Admiral's example. He swallowed, and quickly braced himself as the Admiral turned away and continued his address. "Just so we're clear, if you resist, this happens." The Admiral touched a button on his bracelet. A fiery charge raced through the Captain's body. Every muscle in his body locked up. Pronounced veins in his head and neck accented the redness of his skin. A groan forced its way through his clenched teeth as he twitched and swayed with the ongoing pulsations. The Admiral released the button and David collapsed to the ground. "Are we clear?" The crew appeared to be in shock. No one answered. Admiral Deacons repeated his question, "Are we clear?"

Being the senior officer, Brynna answered for the crew. "Yes-s-s Admiral," she hissed at him. "The crew will comply with all instructions."

David shook his head to clear it. The jolt had been rough. He supposed the setting had been low. His eyes finally began to focus. His gaze landed on Cheyenne who was ready to cry. David forced his jaw to relax and his facial muscles to comply with his demands. He locked his gaze on Cheyenne, "Chey – enne, n – no satisfaction."

The Captain had given her those instructions once before on Drea. Cheyenne knew the Captain was ordering her to be strong. The cloud of sorrow dissipated, and she took on the demeanor of a Commonwealth soldier, stopping the tears before they came. She set her jaw firmly and responded, "Yes sir! No satisfaction."

The Admiral split the crew up into small groups and transported them back to the military base on the East Coast. Once on base they were each placed in separate cells. Admiral Deacons placed Marissa separately in barracks housing under guard and made sure she had adequate food and water.

CHAPTER TWO – DAY ONE

Except for Jake and Marissa, the crew's first day of captivity was mostly what they expected, or feared. The men and women were quickly separated from each other and escorted to different sections of the Romajin brig. This prison was an older facility and unrenovated. It was old, damp, and smelly. They fully expected to have their clothes taken from them and be dressed in drab prison attire. Each one was scanned for contraband, processed into the prison, and placed in individual cells still wearing their civilian attire. A tracking device was implanted into their shoulders along with a stimulant to keep them awake.

Most of the crew had taken only brief naps the previous night as they attempted to travel to the west coast and escape the planet. David, Jake, and Marissa were the only ones who received a decent amount of sleep prior to being arrested. Because of her pregnancy, Marissa wasn't given the stimulant. She was implanted with the tracker and placed under guard away from the rest of the crew. The other crewmen saw Jake placed in a cell near them. They didn't see that he was later removed and placed in base housing.

Admiral Deacons gave strict orders to Commodore Vardin to see to it the crew were handled carefully. "Supreme Executor Hale is coming to oversee the crew's re-education personally. If any of them don't survive, this will be on your head."

"Of course, Admiral Deacons. I assume you do want to begin the process of breaking them. Where do you want to begin?"

Admiral Garcia interrupted before Admiral Deacons could answer. "Let's get the security chief and his wife interviewed and see if we can clear them to be released. I suspect the Chief will be easy to clear. I'm not so sure about his wife though. She may need to be re-educated."

Commodore Vardin got a concerned look on his face. "I'm not sure if I can do that. She's the one who's pregnant, right? Re-education could cause her to lose her baby."

Robert jumped in before Edgardo Garcia could answer this time. "Conduct the interview. If she can't be cleared, then we'll wait for the Supreme Executor to make that call. He has an agreement with Chief Holden. He may put off her re-education until after the baby is born. See to it she's properly cared for until the Executor gives us further instructions."

It wasn't the call Admiral Garcia would have made, but he wasn't about to start such a petty argument in front of a subordinate officer. Waiting another day or two for the Supreme Executor would make little difference for this one crew member.

Commodore Vardin wasn't quite sure which Admiral to address with his next question. He made eye contact with both then asked, "What about the rest of the crew?"

Admiral Deacons took a strong lead despite feeling nauseated. "Put them on bread and water rations, initiate identity removal protocols, interview each one at length using the normal re-education methods, and keep them away from each other. Don't even let them pass each other in the halls."

The Commodore and Admiral Garcia glanced at each other curiously. Admiral Garcia was technically the superior officer, be that as it may; he wanted to evaluate Admiral Deacons' resolve in this situation, so he tried to say very little. The Commodore had only honest questions.

"Admiral, did you want them stripped down to their undergarments?"

"No, not yet. I want to start out easy until the Executor has completed his own evaluation. You can rotate the thermostats on their cells back and forth to extremes. I don't want them on the edge of delirium when the Executor tries to interview them. The second he's done with them, we can go full force."

"What about their Captain?"

Admiral Deacons walked around the room. He stopped to stare out the window. After a moment of silence, he looked back over at the two. "Edgar, you know this isn't easy for me."

Admiral Garcia studied Robert's face carefully. "Do I need to give the order?"

Robert shook his head. "No, I can do it. I just wanted you to know. I'm not a heartless monster." His voice got lower. "Commodore, work the Captain over. Make sure no accidents happen. He, above all, needs to be alive when the Supreme Executor arrives. Captain Alexander is the only reason the Executor is coming. Are we clear?"

"I understand, Admiral. I will oversee the process myself."

"One more question, sir."

Admiral Deacons was well past being ready to leave this conversation behind. "What is it, Commodore?

"The women… part of the identity protocols… they call for…"

"Hold off. Keep them protected from that until we're ready to push the process one hundred percent. Some of them may choose to return to the Commonwealth. If we push them too hard too fast, it might strengthen their resolve."

"Yes sir." Commodore Vardin excused himself and set to work.

Admiral Garcia walked over to Admiral Deacons. "Robert, I'm sorry about this. If you need to walk away from this, just let me know. I know this is hard on you. You've done a surprisingly good job, under the circumstances."

"Thanks, Edgar. I'll let you know when I reach my limit. I will say this; my limit is getting close. I want to stay in this as long as I can. I don't want to disappoint the Supreme Executor or give him cause to doubt me."

"I think you've already put his doubts to rest. Why don't you take a walk? You look like you need some fresh air."

• •

Captain Alexander was taken to a high security section of the prison. The tracker was implanted in his shoulder along with the same irritating medication to keep him from resting. The medication made him feel like his skin was crawling, and his heart pounded loudly in his ears. He forced himself to start a vigorous exercise regimen to push his body to metabolize the medication faster. His workout was interrupted a few minutes later by Commodore Vardin and two guards whose demeanor reminded him of the thugs he encountered on Drea. The guards were not dissimilar to their Drean counterparts.

Commodore Vardin was far too cheerful when he entered the small cell. He seemed to take a lot of pride and joy in his work. He proudly informed the Captain that Admiral Deacons had sent him to begin his retraining.

David had been exercising on the smelly old mattress on the floor of the cell. He rolled to his feet and took a defensive stance. Arni hadn't told him to submit and take his beating. In the absence of instruction, he chose to defend himself like any soldier would. Being outnumbered and drugged, his reactions did little to improve his situation. A couple hours later David regained consciousness and found himself face down on the smelly mattress, alone in his cell with numerous painful swollen injuries.

He pulled himself into a sitting position and took inventory of his injuries. His eyes were bruised and swollen. They weren't focusing, and he was seeing double. His ribs were either severely bruised or possibly fractured. After his third painful fit of coughing, David slowly pushed and pulled himself to his feet and headed towards a position between the two sinks his eyes insisted were in the room. He fumbled with the cup sitting on the edge of the sink. He filled it with water and raised it to his lips. His hand shook as he lifted the cup, spilling a small amount of water down his hand and arm. He tried to drink the water quickly to keep from spilling any more. His haste evoked another fit of coughing. The pain in his ribs forced him to drop the cup in the sink and double over to protect the pain in his sides. He stumbled back to the mattress and collapsed.

A wave of nausea swept over him, explaining why the mattress probably smelled so bad. As soon as the coughing and heaving subsided, David rolled over onto his side to escape the smell of the mattress. His breathing slowed to normal. Looking around the room, he realized he had seen this place before. This was the room he had seen in a dream. This was the abysmal time and place Arni warned him about. The place where he would be tempted to give up. David took a quick inventory of his own mental condition. Yes, he was in pain and filled with uncertainty, but he wasn't hopeless. David frowned, as much as his swollen lip would allow. This could only mean one thing; his situation was going to get worse before it got better.

"Arni, you said you would be here for me when this day came. Are you here?" David waited quietly listening and searching the room for some sign Arni was there and listening to him.

Finally, a very soft voice whispered in his mind. "I'm here. You won't see me, but I will never leave you alone. Sometimes you just need to trust that I'm here."

"You were in my dream. The dream was different. Why did it change?" David normally wouldn't have continued a verbal one-sided conversation, but since he was alone in his cell, he didn't see the harm and it felt more reassuring.

The voice in his head spoke softly in his mind again. "It's because this time you had me with you."

David was having trouble remaining conscious. He suspected he had a concussion. He desperately wanted one more question answered. "What about the blood? There was supposed to be blood on my hands. What happened to the blood?"

Arni's voice came back again before he lost consciousness. "I wiped your guilt and crimes away with my own blood. My death paid your debts and forgave all your crimes. My father loves you and no longer holds you guilty of any of the crimes in your past."

David passed out again, reassured he wasn't alone. He took comfort in knowing he was forgiven and favored by the most powerful being in the universe.

• •

Two hours later, the Commodore reported back to Admiral Garcia and Admiral Deacons. "Captain Alexander's first *interview* is complete. I participated in the interview myself. He's one tough character. His injuries are minor, although he will feel them for days, maybe weeks. I may need to see the doctor for my fist. I think I broke a bone in my hand. It's swollen pretty badly. It's been a long time since I got to get personally involved like this. I forgot how invigorating it could be." The Commodore was oblivious to the disgust on Admiral Deacons' face.

Admiral Garcia stood up in defense of his friend. "Commodore Vardin, must you be so callous? Captain Alexander is Admiral Deacons' nephew. This is very difficult for him. Just keep your reports as succinct as possible. He doesn't need a play by play commentary."

Commodore Vardin knew this case was personal. He hadn't realized just how or why it was so personal until now. "I'm sorry, Admiral. I didn't know. I'll keep you posted. I'll make the surveillance channels available to you, so you can look in on him whenever you like."

Admiral Deacons couldn't look the man in the eye. He seemed to spend a lot of time looking out the window. He was feeling a lot like a caged animal. "Thank you, Commodore. Apology accepted. You may return to your duties. Admiral Garcia, do we have an ETA on the Supreme Executor?"

"Not yet. Perhaps we should interview the security chief while we wait." Admiral Garcia suggested. He understood his friend's difficulty and decided it might be best to give him some time. He left his friend alone in the office.

Robert pulled up the surveillance video of David's cell. He saw his nephew lying face down on a mattress on the floor. He was apparently unconscious but breathing. Robert slammed his fist on the desk. Looking around the room, he knew better than to call Arni's name out loud. He asked one question aloud, "WHY?"

No answer came. Despite his frustrations, Robert accepted Arni's silence this time.

• •

The rest of the crew, except for Jake and Marissa, were alone in individual cells. Each one, after receiving the irritating stimulant, was pulled one at a time into interrogation rooms. They were questioned and bullied to determine the extent of their resolve to follow Pateras. None were beaten like Captain Alexander, but they weren't handled gently.

The interviews went late into the evening. As each member of the crew entered their interview they were given prisoner numbers. They were told they no longer had names, only numbers. Their interrogators berated and shamed them for embarrassing their friends and families. They offered bribes, blackmail and outright threats.

Each crew member reacted similarly. Each one was totally uninterested in the bribes. Not one person hesitated to turn down the offers of promotions or rewards to change their loyalties. The threats and blackmail were received gravely. Some said nothing while others bravely postured a lack of fear, daring their captors to do their worst. Brynna was one of those who stood up to her captors.

Admiral Garcia was the one interviewing Brynna. "Prisoner 7139, what's going to happen to your poor parents when they find out their daughter is guilty of treason? What about your younger brother? He's just getting established in his career. When word gets out about this, he could lose his job. I could make sure that happens. You know that don't you?"

Brynna glared at the Admiral. "I'm sure you could, Admiral, but I haven't been tried and found guilty. If this comes out and there's been no trial, this will blow back on you and Executor Hale. My brother is young, he'll bounce back."

Admiral Garcia got down in Brynna's face. "You really think I can't touch you? Try me. I can have your entire family arrested on charges of suspected treason. I may even find some evidence that you've been sending messages including classified information to your family for months."

Brynna didn't waver. "You can't find what isn't there."

"No, but I can manufacture it! What's going to happen to your poor little niece and nephew? They'll have to be placed into protective custody. They probably won't get the same care as they would from their own loving parents." Admiral Garcia stepped back to let her consider his words.

Brynna's face was displayed on the screens located throughout the room her face was larger than life on the walls surrounding her. It was intimidating for her to see every flicker of emotion displayed so obviously.

Admiral Garcia turned so his face was not clearly visible to her, but he watched her face on the screen in front of him. "Prisoner 7139, I've been studying your husband's history. Did he tell you what happened to his aunt in the prison on Mara?"

Brynna tried to stop her face from reacting. She was unsuccessful. Her body was reaching a point of exhaustion. Her emotions were being pushed to extremes and the stimulant in her system caused her to react faster than her mind could stop it.

Admiral Garcia continued to push her buttons. "You know I would hate to have something like that happen to your family… especially not one of those precious little children."

Edgar kept his face turned away from her. He didn't want there to be any chance she could find weakness in his threat.

Brynna wanted very badly to lash out at the man with a litany of threats of her own making and scream out at him. She knew that was the reaction he wanted so she clenched her jaw tightly and refused to respond. Through her clenched teeth she finally responded. "Be careful. You may not know exactly what you are dealing with. Pateras is in control, not you and not Executor Hale. You may find tragedy occurring in your own household."

Admiral Garcia, angered by her threat, turned around swiftly and got back in her face again. "If he's so powerful why do I have the upper hand? I've got you and your entire crew under my control."

Brynna smiled. "If I'm under your control, why are you working so hard to make me comply?"

Admiral Garcia turned beet red. He backed away from her slightly. He smiled evilly at her in return. "We'll soon see who's in charge." He pulled back enough to backhand her. Brynna braced herself as the painful blow landed.

Brynna turned her face back to stare into his eyes. "Are you familiar with the Ancient Texts, Admiral? Someone on one of the twelve Explorer Teams will take out Supreme Executor Hale. I don't suggest you stand too close to him when that happens. You wouldn't want to get caught in the fallout."

Admiral Garcia had all he could take of her impudence. He jerked her up from her seat and shoved her at the two guards waiting outside the interrogation room. "Put her back in her cell, and bring me the next one."

Their first two hours in their cells, the heat was cranked until the temperature reached one hundred degrees. The crew stripped their clothing down as far as they dared then started pouring water on themselves from the sink. Each cell, including the Captain's, had a rough shower. The water wasn't heated so if it happened to be winter, the water could be rather brisk. Captain Alexander's compromised condition kept him from observing the facility immediately. As the crew reached the point of dousing themselves with the moderately warm water, the guards reversed the thermostats in their cells and took the temperature down to half what it had been previously. The temperatures rotated every two to three hours throughout the night from one unbearable extreme to the other, preventing the crew from getting more than a few minutes of sleep at a time.

The crew's first day and night of captivity was the longest of their lives. The thing that concerned them the most was not knowing what was happening to their shipmates and how long their captivity would last. Most didn't have the information Arni had given David. Only a few had heard David's message that their incarceration would last only six days. After the grueling course of their first day, six days might seem like an eternity.

Chapter Two – Day One

"Chief Petty Officer Jacob Holden."

Jake was sitting in an interrogation room when he heard Admiral Garcia walk in calling his name. Jake's hands were still bound behind his back preventing him from saluting the Admiral. He at least attempted to stand at attention. "Admiral Garcia, Chief Petty Officer Holden reporting as ordered."

"Take your seat, Mr. Holden."

"Yes sir." Jake sat back down.

Admiral Garcia activated the computer in the room. Computers were integrated into most tables and desks. They were also accessible through control panels in the walls of most rooms either by voice activation or by keyboards. Voice activation was not always practical. He pulled up the Chief's duty record, his personal history files, and his recent reports. He studied the files carefully. As he looked over the information in front of him. Periodically the Admiral would glance up at Jake. Jake sat there quietly waiting.

It felt like an eternity before the Admiral finally addressed him. "Chief, despite being the lowest ranking man aboard the *Evangeline*, you have an impressive record. You managed to make it up through the ranks to chief petty officer in record time. It takes most men twenty years to make it that far. You did it in a quarter of the time."

Jake was uncertain how to respond. He decided to just acknowledge the information. "Yes sir. Thank you, sir."

The Admiral stared at the young man for a minute. Jake was still uncomfortable from waiting for the Admiral to review his file. His comfort level didn't improve under the Admiral's stare. When his discomfort reached a peak Jake finally asked, "Admiral, have I done something wrong? I tried to do everything asked of me. I know I failed on a couple things…"

Admiral Garcia interrupted before Jake could finish. "Chief, I do have a few questions for you. First question, who are you loyal to? Pateras or the Commonwealth?"

Jake scowled. "I have always been loyal to the Commonwealth. That hasn't changed. I'm not sure how I can prove it to you. I handed the entire crew of the *Evangeline* over to you. If that doesn't prove who I'm loyal to, I don't know what else to do."

"Why did you draw your weapon when we came to arrest you and the rest of the crew?"

"I was told I would be arrested along with the crew. I assumed it was to protect me from the others. I had no intention of firing against the troops who came to arrest us. I knew the Captain wouldn't allow us to get into a non-winnable firefight. I kept the appearance of being one of them until we were arrested, just in case."

The Admiral folded his arms across his chest. "Just in case of what, Mr. Holden?"

"In case you needed to use me against the crew after our arrest. The Captain doesn't trust me. He knows I betrayed him. If the others don't know I betrayed them, I might be of some use to break and retrain them. I still think they're worth saving. The crew is a cohesive force when they work together."

The Admiral stared again for a moment. "You would be willing to help us with the re-education process?"

"Yes, Admiral, although I do have my limits, sir."

"And just what are your limits, Chief?"

"I respect this crew. I've spent the last few months protecting them and putting my life in their hands. I'll lie to them. I'll spy on them. Don't ask me to physically harm them in any way. I can't do that."

The Admiral seemed skeptical. "You can lie to a crew you respect?"

Jake smiled ominously. "I've been lying to them for the last two months. If you prefer to tell them I was the one who betrayed them, then so be it. It no longer makes a difference to me. I just want my pardon, my wife, and to go my way. If you don't need my help to break the crew, that's fine with me. I'm just anxious to put this Pateras business behind me."

"Tell me, Chief. What is your opinion of Pateras?"

"He's a powerful being. I don't know if the Commonwealth can defeat him. I seriously think you should establish some sort of peace treaty. If you want me to stay and fight him until the end then that's what I'll do, but I'm not confident the Commonwealth can stand against him."

"What makes you think we can't defeat him?"

"He can bring the dead… the obviously dead, back to life. I saw him heal one of the crew without even touching him. What happens if he wants to take the living and just… wish them dead? He appears and disappears at will. How do we fight that? If you gave me orders to kill Arni the next time I saw him, I would follow that order to the best of my ability. Pateras already brought Arni back from the dead. Who's going to be able to see that he stays dead?"

"Arni died?"

Jake paled when he realized he had given the Admiral new information. He had given his word not to discuss what happened on Drea.

"Yes sir. The Captain's agreement with the Dreans for our release was contingent on one of us being executed. The Captain was scheduled for execution and the rest of the crew were to be released after his death. Arni somehow took his place. We've seen him alive since then." Jake skipped as many details as possible. He knew the Admiral wouldn't be satisfied if he hadn't elaborated.

"You hesitated, Chief. Why?"

Jake lowered his head. "I – I gave my word."

Admiral Garcia frowned. "Why would you give your word, fully intending to keep it, about such an important matter?"

Jake's pallor was a faint shade of green. "Things didn't happen on Drea like the Captain reported. We weren't convicted for the crimes committed by the Commonwealth fifty years ago. We were charged and convicted for our participation in the genocide of the Galatan population. The Dreans took it upon themselves to speak for the Galatans. They have a legal precedent allowing one person to take the punishment of all others involved in a crime. They choose punishments that fit the crime. When one person takes the punishment for others, the punishment is pro-rated based on the number of participants. The Captain was supposed to be hit with twelve separate jolts. Each jolt was less than lethal. The last one was designed to be lethal. Arni somehow managed to change places with the Captain right under everyone's noses and no one saw anything. The Captain's reports referred to a religious leader known as the *Intercessor*. *Arni* was the Intercessor. We saw the Captain secured between two pillars and Arni walking around freely minutes before the execution. I saw them put a hood over the Captain's head. Arni walked away. He was nowhere near him. After it was all over, the Commander demanded to see the body. She *knew* it wasn't the Captain. It wasn't. Part of the agreement to release us was that we keep the presence of Pateras on Drea quiet. The Captain also knew our orders included preventing the death of Arni. He tried to follow that order. I swear he did. He just wasn't the same after that.

"I intended to keep my word because of the agreement with the Dreans. They didn't have to spare any of us. I felt like I owed them at least my silence.

"Admiral, I don't serve Pateras and I don't trust Arni."

"Why, Chief? Everything you've mentioned seems straight-forward. Other than the fact that he's our enemy, why don't you trust him?"

Jake's face contorted nearly into a snarl. His face flushed. "Arni had the power to *stop* the tornado that killed my WIFE. He had the power to control the very forces of nature. Did he use his power? No! He let her DIE! Every *bone* in her body was *broken*. Yes, he brought her back, but what sort of cruel, sick monster would do that? He did it just to make a point!" Jake struggled for words. The ones running through his mind were not the kind you used in front of a superior officer. His struggle was exacerbated by his anger. Jake was no longer simply angry, he was seething. His heart was pounding inside his chest. Every muscle in his body flexed. His face was bright red, and his nausea over saying more than he should was now gone. Jake took another moment to calm down. He forced his muscles to relax and slowed his breathing. It took his heart a little longer to get the memo.

Jake started speaking again, this time more slowly and calmly. "I intended to keep my word because I owed the Captain my life. I also felt like I owed Arni. He gave Marissa back to me. He didn't have to bring her back, but he did. I was grateful for that, yet still angry he let her suffer and die. My silence seemed to be small compensation for that. I know Arni was executed for us. This gets back to why I don't trust him. A being who has power over life and death allows himself to be killed; just how much of a sacrifice is that really? Another reason I planned on keeping quiet was that no one wants to see another entire civilization wiped out. Galat's destruction rattled all of us. The last reason is, my word means something to me. If I give it, I keep it."

The Admiral stared at Jake as he tried to process Jake's outburst. "Alright, Chief, your reasons make sense. Why break your word now? Is it because your future is at stake?"

"Yes… No… Maybe…" Jake's feelings of shame and nausea began to recur. His word was important to him. He hadn't meant to break it. "Part of it was a slip of the tongue. It – It's been a fact of life for us, not something we couldn't talk about aboard ship. Maybe part of me is just ready to get everything out in the open. I've been playing the part of a spy for two months. Spying isn't my thing. I'm a security officer. I'm supposed to be visible, upfront, and obvious. I like things to be straightforward and simple. I'm ready to be done with the spy business."

Admiral Garcia leaned back in his chair and laced his fingers behind his head. "We're almost done here, Chief. I just have a few more questions. How did you get from Drea to Galat?"

Jake raised his head slowly. A voice inside him warned him to answer carefully. A gnawing sensation began to grow inside his belly. Jake knew the Commonwealth would go after the Drean technology if they found out about it. They wouldn't hesitate to kill whoever stood in the way. Jake rolled his head back and forth. He didn't want to answer the question, not the way he should. The Admiral was seconds away from demanding an answer when Jake decided how to answer the question. "Arni took us back there from Drea. The guy can apparently go anyplace he wants and he doesn't need a ship to do it." His story was mostly true. Arni had appeared and disappeared at will numerous times. The thing Jake didn't want to mention was that in this case, Arni had escorted several crew members back to Galat using some advanced tachyon-based technology. Jake was no engineer and couldn't even begin to explain it. He preferred not to go down this road. If he mentioned it, Admiral Garcia would use Cheyenne to force Lazaro's cooperation in explaining as much as he could about the technology. Jake didn't want to see anything happen to Cheyenne.

"What was your hesitation this time, Chief?"

"I was just reliving my frustration. The Captain insisted on going despite my objections. He seemed *obsessed* with Galat." Jake shook his head slowly again as though he could shake the memory from his head.

The Admiral leaned forward and propped his arms on the table in front of him. His eyes would dart periodically to the computer screen behind Jake. It finally dawned on Jake, the Admiral was scanning him. He had programmed the computer to monitor Jake's vital signs. He wanted to be sure Jake was being honest with him. Jake swallowed hard. He hoped he was passing this test.

"Is there anything else I need to know, Chief?"

Jake chose the safest answer. "Probably. There were numerous false reports filed. Is there something specific on your mind? We could go over the reports, if you like." Jake knew his answer would be honest yet unrevealing.

"Maybe later." The Admiral waved the guard forward. "I'm satisfied for now. I do need to wait for the Supreme Executor to arrive before I can completely cut you loose. I'm going to release your restraints. You will be confined to the barracks under guard until I talk to Executor Hale.

"Guard, remove his binders and escort him to the 'G' level visitor's barracks. Post guards outside the door. See to it he's fed and well cared for. Get him some clean clothes to wear too.

"Chief, I may see a promotion and a Medal of Honor in your future."

The guard released Jake's binders. Jake rubbed his wrists and stood up. He snapped to attention. Saluting the Admiral, he smiled, "Thank you, sir."

The Admiral stood and returned the salute then offered Jake his hand. "Thank you, young man, for saving the Commonwealth."

Jake shook the Admiral's hand and followed his escort out.

• •

Late that afternoon in a flurry of activity, Supreme Executor Luciano Hale arrived with Defense Minister Hamilton Payne.

Later that evening, Admiral Deacons, Admiral Garcia, Commodore Vardin, Defense Minister Payne, and Supreme Executor Luciano Hale met in a conference room on the Romajin CIF Base.

"So, you believe I should honor the agreement with Chief Petty Officer Holden," Executor Hale queried.

Admiral Garcia nodded. "Yes, Executor, I believe we should. He has no real loyalties to Pateras. He's loyal to the Commonwealth. I have a couple concerns about him, but I think we can fix those in short order. He trusts and admires Captain Alexander, although he adamantly opposes the Captain's choice to follow Pateras."

Executor Hale wasn't so optimistic. "What concerns, and how do you plan on fixing them?"

"He mentioned some discrepancies in the *Evangeline*'s reports. I propose we turn him lose then ask him if he would mind going through every report. He can file corrected reports while he waits for his wife to be screened and retrained. We can keep an eye on him, and he will get a chance to see the consequences of the Captain's actions. Once he sees his Captain groveling on the ground, begging for mercy, he won't feel so appreciative of his Captain."

Admiral Deacons winced. He tried hard not to, but the picture Admiral Garcia painted was too vividly painful. His pain was evident to everyone in the room.

No one was going to broach the subject with the Supreme

Executor present. Executor Hale addressed the matter himself. "Robert, are you alright? How are you handling all this?"

Robert straightened up in his chair. He sighed. "I apologize, Executor Hale. I'm surviving. Naturally, I am caught up in an array of emotions. I'm disappointed in my nephew. It's going to be hard to watch him go through the pain of retraining. I'm also embarrassed for myself and his mother. I keep wondering what I could've done differently. We've had security breaches on all twelve teams. I've failed you, sir. Please forgive me."

Executor Hale seemed overly cordial. He stood up and walked over to Robert. Robert stood when the Executor approached him. Luciano put his hand on Robert's shoulder. "Robert, I know this has got to be painful for you. I don't know how you have handled this so well. Please don't blame yourself. There's nothing you could have done. You *will* let me know if you need to step away from this, won't you?"

Robert gave the Executor a curt nod, "Of course, sir. I'm a Commonwealth soldier. I'll do what needs to be done."

Executor Hale studied the Admiral's face for a moment. His resolve seemed firm enough. Luciano released his grip on the Admiral's shoulder and moved to a nearby table to pour himself a glass of water. "You're a strong soldier, Robert. I appreciate your dedication. Edgar, go ahead with your plan for Chief Holden. Don't give him access to the prisoners though. I might have use of him later, to help break them."

Edgar smiled. He was pleased the Supreme Executor approved of his plan. He was hoping to impress the man enough to take over this project from Robert. Edgar and Robert weren't rivals, but with such a poor outcome, something needed to change. Admiral Garcia thought he could improve the situation and win the Supreme Executor's favor.

Defense Minister Hamilton Payne had been quietly listening and taking notes to this point. He glanced up from his data pad. "How do you plan on handling the rest of the crew, Mr. Executor?"

Spurred on by the inquiry, Executor Hale moved back over to the conference table. Setting his glass down, he leaned over and planted his hands on the table. "Gentlemen, bring me up to date. What's been done so far?"

Admiral Deacons jumped in quickly. He knew his comrade wanted to take over this project. Despite being the superior officer, Edgar couldn't legitimately remove Robert from the project without sufficient provocation. Robert didn't want to give him any reason to take it from him. "The crew have been processed into the system and given prisoner numbers to begin the dissolution of their identities. I put them on bread and water rations, and initiated sleep deprivation protocols. They are still in whatever clothing they were arrested in. The temperatures in their cells are being rotated to extremes frequently. I didn't want to proceed too quickly until you arrived. I wanted them lucid, in case you intended to interview any of them. I also authorized Commodore Vardin to work the Captain over. His injuries are minor. He's in pain, but his life isn't in danger… yet."

Minister Payne looked at Admiral Deacons suspiciously. "Admiral Deacons, where are the members of your family right now? I personally sent troops to collect them, only none of them could be located."

Robert had a strong dislike for the Defense Minister. Minister Payne enjoyed witch hunts far too much. "I sent ships to pick them up the instant I knew my nephew was alive. They are on their way here on a Pacification Ship as we speak."

Minister Payne stared hard at the Admiral. "What made you choose to do that, Admiral?"

Robert glared at the Defense Minister. "Why were *you* trying to collect my family, sir?"

Minister Payne held his tongue and returned the Admiral's

glare with equal voracity.

Seeing his refusal to answer, Robert finally responded. "I had a number of reasons. I didn't want my nephew dragging the family into this mess he's made for himself. I thought perhaps his mother could reason with him. I also didn't want David to have a place to hide, or anyone thinking my family had anything to do with this. I would never harm Jessica, but if David discovered she was missing, it could make him a little more *co-operative*." Robert had other reasons for his actions, but they were not reasons he cared to share.

Luciano smiled. "You see, Hamilton. Robert is right on top of things where he should be." Luciano sat down in his seat again. "You were right to move slowly with the crew, Robert. I do want to interview them myself. I want to start with the Captain. Let him suffer through the night, then early tomorrow, run him through the infirmary. I want all his wounds healed."

Admiral Garcia and Minister Payne looked confused. Admiral Garcia questioned, "Sir? You want his wounds healed?"

Commodore Vardin looked down at his own hand remembering the pain he suffered inflicting the Captain's injuries. He wasn't amused either.

Admiral Deacons leaned in. "My nephew is a trained Commonwealth captain. He's going to take whatever you dish out. He can handle physical pain and torture. A captain feels an overwhelming responsibility for his crew. The thing that will hit him the hardest is watching his crew suffer in his place."

Executor Hale smiled again. "You're on it again, Robert."

Seeing Robert was making forward progress, Admiral Garcia proceeded to ask, "What about the rest of the crew? If you're going to hit him through his crew, what are your plans for them?"

Executor Hale held back the information for now and asked, "What's the status of Chief Holden's wife?"

Admiral Deacons didn't want to appear weak despite his less aggressive treatment of the young lieutenant. He took full responsibility for his actions by answering quickly and decisively. "She's sequestered in barracks housing under guard getting full meals. Considering our agreement with the Chief, I wanted her to remain in good condition until I talked to you. I had her given a thorough physical as soon as she was processed. She's had no contact with anyone for several hours. The doctor reported her and the baby to be perfectly healthy. She has not been interviewed yet. How would you like to handle her?"

Executor Hale leaned back in his chair to consider his answer. "Keep her sequestered for now. We need to find out how committed she is to Pateras. Keep the Chief confined to base. You can give him normal base privileges except for access to the other prisoners. If he even attempts to visit or contact any of the prisoners, place him under arrest. Get the Chief started on his new project in the morning. Admiral Deacons, conduct Lt. Holden's interview tomorrow morning while I talk to the Captain. You and Edgar continue conducting the other interviews. I'll expect a full report tomorrow evening."

Defense Minister Payne objected, "Is it really safe for them to be conducting interviews? Shouldn't we just execute them all and start over with a fresh crew? You know what happened to some of those who interviewed previous prisoners. We had to put them all down. We can't afford to lose two Admirals."

Executor Hale gave a disarming smile. "The previous men who conducted those interviews were weak. They had little to lose by following Pateras. The Admirals are strong men with strong minds. They won't fall away."

Defense Minister Payne didn't look very convinced but held his peace.

The Executor moved on, "What about the ship?"

Admiral Garcia returned a blank stare. "The ship? It's here

at the base. Why?”

Before the Executor could reply, Robert volunteered. “The shuttle was on the west coast when we arrested the crew. I had a team ferry it back and dock it in the *Evangeline*’s shuttle bay. I have teams working now to download all logs and computer files. I also have a team conducting a physical search for used data crystals. The crew’s bracelets, equipment, and weapons were confiscated and returned to the ship’s stores for use by the next crew assigned to the *Evangeline*.”

Admiral Garcia was clearly perturbed at missing such an important detail. “Robert, your diligence is commendable, but are you sure you shouldn’t have left this for someone less interested in this case?”

Robert raised up. He placed his hands down firmly on the table and pushed himself upward. “So, there it is. I knew my loyalty would come into question sooner or later. Yes-s-s,” The Admiral hissed, “Somehow, I screwed up and this is definitely my fault. I admit that! I don’t know how it happened, but it did! I’m making every effort to fix this! This is an enormous embarrassment for me. Do you really have to make it worse? I know where my loyalties lie. I set the trap bringing my own nephew to justice. If I haven’t proven my loyalty by now, perhaps it’s time for me to retire!”

Admiral Garcia was taken aback by Robert’s vicious rebuttal. He had never seen the man so angry. Executor Hale watched the exchange closely. Satisfied by Robert’s stalwart claim, he leaned in. “Robert, please… sit down. We’re not questioning your loyalty, only the appearance of conflict of interest. If this had been any other crew, your actions would be absolutely on target. In truth, your actions are the absolute correct response. I believe Edgar only meant in order to maintain the appearance of impartiality, someone else should have issued the orders.”

Before sitting down, Admiral Deacons clarified one more

point. "First of all, the men conducting the searches work for Commodore Vardin. They aren't *my* men. Second, I ordered them to send copies of everything recovered to you, to Admiral Garcia, and a copy to me. Will that be enough to maintain the veracity of the investigation?" The Admiral continued to glare at Edgar as he slowly eased back into his chair.

Admiral Garcia knew he was guilty of trying to win the Supreme Executor's approval at his friend's expense. He tried, unsuccessfully in Robert's eyes, to backpedal. "I'm sorry, Robert, I didn't mean to suggest you were guilty of anything. It is, as the Supreme Executor said. I merely wanted to maintain all appearances of impartiality. Please forgive my insensitivity."

"I can assure you, my forgiveness will be commensurate with your sincerity," Robert spoke coldly.

Minister Payne interrupted, "It's getting late, Supreme Executor. Perhaps tempers will flare less after we have all had some sleep and put a little distance between us and this situation."

Executor Hale glanced at the nearest clock. He seemed surprised at the hour. "Perhaps you're right, Hamilton. Let's adjourn for now. I'll return to my ship for tonight. Commodore Vardin, if you could see to it the Admirals and I have office space available tomorrow. Have Captain Alexander healed and ready for me tomorrow morning at 0800 hours local time. Get some sleep, gentlemen. Hamilton could you remain a moment longer?"

Commodore Vardin and the two Admirals gave the Defense Minister and the Supreme Executor a curt acknowledgment and left the conference room. Commodore Vardin kept a discreet distance from the two Admirals, although he was still close enough to hear more than he wanted to. Robert stepped directly in front of Edgar. Their faces were only inches apart. "Don't you ever try to discredit me in front of the Supreme Executor! You ever try that again, I will take you down so hard and fast, you will never *even* see it coming."

Admiral Garcia stood his ground. "Robert, I just think you're too close to this situation. I think you need to step back and let someone else handle it. It's not that I'm questioning your loyalty. I know you're loyal to the Commonwealth. The thing I'm most concerned about is, your emotions may cause you to miss something. I could just reassign you. You do remember that I am your superior officer, don't you?"

Robert knew Edgar was right. "Admiral Garcia… I have included you in *everything* I've done. You've been involved with my activities, every step of the way. If I am missing something, then feel free to reassign me." Robert backed away and headed for his shuttle.

Edgar watched him go. His own temper was beginning to flare.

• •

Once Executor Hale was alone with Minister Payne, he confided in him. "Hamilton, I have a highly classified project I need to bring you in on. I need you to go to Ahnak III. I've been working on a new special program designed to create a better stronger warrior. There is a large training camp and scientific research facility working on the creation and implementation of these "super" soldiers. I want you to get over there and get them prepared for integration into our regular troops. If this has spread as badly as I think it has, we're going to need everything we can to fight it."

Minister Payne blinked, "Super Soldiers?"

Executor Hale smiled. "They're genetically engineered using very carefully chosen DNA. We – I have created soldiers that are bigger, faster, smarter, and deadlier than have ever been seen before. Because of their increased size, I had to have ships and equipment built to accommodate them. I'd like you to get them ready for utilization. They are already being trained in combat. It's time to get those ships loaded and spread them out to strategic locations. Don't send them on any missions until you hear from me. I want to introduce our enemy and our secret weapons to the general public at the same time."

Hamilton looked like he had just swallowed his own tongue. "Just how big are they, and why am I just now hearing about this?"

A shadow fell over the Executor's face. "I have reason to believe there will be an attempt on my life soon. I'm taking all possible precautions. I wanted you to know about this project so if someone does succeed in… in their attempt you would have the weapons necessary to fight back. You will be my last chance to protect the Commonwealth from Pateras."

Hamilton wasn't quite sure how to respond. He had seen the Executor take chances with his safety in some rather unorthodox ways, yet no one had ever even tried to harm him. He wondered if it was Pateras' forces he was now concerned with. He had a million questions suddenly crowding his thoughts.

"I know you have a lot of questions, Hamilton. Get to Ahnak as fast as you can and be ready. If something happens to me, use those troops. I'll forward my files to you as soon as I get back to my ship."

Hearing the urgency in his voice, the Defense Minister gathered his things and headed for the door. Before he could exit, Luciano gave him one more piece of information, "Nine feet."

Hamilton gave the Executor a puzzled look, "sir?"

"You asked just how big they were. They average nine feet in height."

Hamilton had a dazed look on his face as he hurried out. Commodore Vardin was giving his chief aide some last-minute instructions in the hall. He watched the Defense Minister rush past him mumbling something about nine feet. The Commodore and his aide just shook their heads at the strange man.

• •

Late into the night, Robert was having difficulty sleeping. He finally got dressed and went to David's cell. He stepped in quietly and found David sleeping. He didn't want to interfere in the one moment of rest his nephew was getting, so he stood there and quietly surveyed him while he slept. Each bruise served to only increase Robert's own discomfort. His conscience was no longer pricking him but stabbing him outright. He wanted nothing more than to pick his nephew up and carry him out of there. He knew such an action would serve to only get himself placed in an adjoining cell. When Robert could watch his nephew moan through his sleep no longer, he turned to leave.

David opened his eyes and lifted his head. "Did you come to see your handiwork?"

Robert stopped and glanced up at the camera watching and listening to every action. "Davie, you know I didn't want this to happen to you."

"Commodore Vardin said you ordered it." David said flatly.

Robert stepped over near David and squatted on the floor beside his mattress. He hoped David could see well enough to read the pain and sorrow in his eyes. "I'm just doing what any good soldier would do. You know I would have taken this beating for you if I could have."

David worked his way into a sitting position leaning against the wall at the edge of his mattress. He stared hard into his uncle's eyes. The swelling in his eyes had gone down just enough that his vision was no longer severely impaired. He could see the regrets in his uncle's face. Before he could respond, Robert pointed at the camera in the corners of the cell. "If you should decide to reject Pateras and return to the Commonwealth, all you have to do is wave to the camera and tell the technician to fetch me. I'll get you out of here as fast as I can. You understand that don't you?"

David's eyes followed the direction his uncle pointed. He stared at the camera then looked back at his uncle. "I understand. Do you understand why I can't do that?"

"Don't expect me to sympathize with you, David. Things are not as simple as you think they are. I love you as though you were my own son, but I can't help you. This is one of the hardest things I've ever had to deal with. Don't make me watch you die again."

"I'm the one who's bruised and broken, but you want me to sympathize with you. Nice." David looked around his sparse accommodations then back to his uncle's face. "Uncle Rob, I'm sorry you have to face this again, and I know you're only doing what you have to. Perhaps you should leave and go back to Raesii. Leave us in Pateras' hands. You won't have to watch. No one would blame you, not even me."

Robert stood back up. He carefully cloaked his words. "I'm not going back to Raesii. I have to stay here and see this through to the end. If you won't listen to reason, then all I can do is leave you in the hands of Pateras. You better hope he helps you get out of this… because I won't."

Robert started towards the door, his heart was breaking a little more with each step. "Uncle Rob… whatever you have to do… I understand. I won't hold it against you. I'll still… love you." David said as much as he dared.

When the two went their separate ways on Tudoren, David had insisted his uncle remain in place as a loyal soldier of the Commonwealth despite his true loyalty to Pateras. Robert looked one more time at his nephew. He was seriously regretting that decision now. He was proud of his nephew's strength. The boy he knew had developed into a strong man of honor. Robert gave David a curt nod then left him alone in his cell.

• •

The next morning Robert and Edgar met at Chief Holden's assigned room. Admiral Garcia explained to the Chief what was being asked of him. "Chief, I have a job for you while we are trying to get your wife cleared. I'm afraid if she has a strong loyalty towards Pateras, it may take time to change her loyalty. She'll have to be put through the re-education process."

"Re-education? That isn't going to harm the baby, is it? Will we have to wait until she gives birth?"

Robert and Edgar glanced at each other. Robert spoke up. "I have no idea. I'll have to check with the doctor on base and ask some more questions. I'll get back to you with that information."

Jake felt his tension level peak sharply then slowly come back down. "What job do you have for me?"

Edgar went on to explain his new responsibility. "Chief, you will be confined to the base until you complete this one task. You will also be restricted from accessing any of the prisoners or the prison facilities. That includes your wife. If you attempt to leave the base or access any of the prisoners, you will be arrested on the spot. While you are waiting on us to clear your wife, you will review all the *Evangeline*'s reports and correct any misinformation for us. We do understand you were not present for every single activity and may not be able correct everything. Do the best you can. You may do them at your own pace. You will be getting paid during this time at the rate of a Lieutenant, Junior Grade."

Jake grinned. "I'm officially a Lieutenant JG? That's several ranks above my previous rank. Why did I get such an advanced promotion?"

Admiral Garcia smiled in return. "You've earned it, son. You facilitated the capture of the enemies of the Commonwealth, namely your own crew. Consider it a reward for a job well done."

Admiral Deacons wasn't smiling. Jake didn't like the somber look on Admiral Deacons' face. "Admiral, I'm sorry about the Captain. I did my best to stop him from committing treason."

Admiral Deacons didn't flinch. "Mr. Holden, if you have anything important that needs to get done today, get it done quickly. I will need to use you to evaluate your wife. When I send for you, do NOT mention your own freedom or our agreement. I also expect you to be scared to death, literally."

"Uh, I'm not sure I understand, Admiral."

"I don't really want to give you a full explanation. I need you to *trust* me for one, and I need you to say nothing to your wife except to convince her to disavow her loyalty to Pateras. Do you understand that much?"

"Yes… sir…" Jake didn't sound convinced. He did know how to follow orders though.

Jake set to work as ordered. He did inquire about getting some personal items from the ship. Admiral Deacons temporarily denied the request. He also insisted the chief remain unshaven and put on the clothing he was arrested in. "Lt. Holden, I may have to be horribly cruel to your wife and to you. Forgive me in advance. I have to be certain she can be trusted if we are to allow her to leave here."

Jake was obviously concerned. "Admiral, what are you going to do?"

"This is the part where you're going to have to just trust me. This won't be pleasant. Don't believe everything you hear though. Stay here until I send two guards for you. React as though you are still a prisoner. I won't hurt you… much."

The two Admirals left an unhappy new lieutenant behind as they stepped into the hallway. Admiral Deacons kept two guards posted outside Jake's door giving them a very specific set of instructions.

Edgar listened to Robert's orders and instructions curiously. Once the two were alone, Edgar asked, "Robert, what are you planning to do?"

"My job. Don't you have some interviews of your own to conduct?"

Edgar gave Robert an annoyed stare. Moods had not improved this morning. Realizing his attitude could be construed as a lack of control, Robert clarified more calmly. "I'm sorry, Edgar, you know cruelty is not my forte. In determining this young woman's resolve, I'm going to have to be incredibly heartless. I'm not looking forward to it. Forgive my poor attitude this morning."

Edgar gave a reluctant nod. "I think I understand. We'll talk about it more later. I hope you get the information you need quickly and easily. Maybe you won't have to go to such extremes."

Robert agreed and thanked his companion for his understanding.

• •

Robert moved down the hall alone to Marissa's room. He politely knocked on her door and only entered after she responded.

He stepped inside the small room. The room was divided into two rooms by a small privacy wall. The far room contained the bedroom and bathroom along with a desk. The area closest to the door housed a kitchen/dining area adjoining a living area.

Marissa had moved to the middle of the room when the Admiral pushed on the buzzer requesting entrance. She snapped to attention when he entered.

"As you were, Lieutenant."

Marissa relaxed her stance, although she wasn't sure what to expect from the Admiral, so she kept her position in the center of the room.

After an awkward moment of silence, the Admiral asked, "Is it alright if I have a seat?"

Marissa was pale from worry and fear. "Yes, Admiral, be my guest. I… uh… apologize for my rudeness."

The Admiral waved to another seat. "Please, have a seat, Lieutenant."

Marissa sat down gingerly on the edge of the chair opposite the Admiral. The Admiral pored over a file on his data pad. An agonizing eternity later, he looked up. "Lt. Holden, you have an impressive service record up until recently."

Marissa fidgeted nervously. "Uh – Thank you, sir." She wanted desperately to ask about Jake and the crew. She sensed now was not the time. Her growing belly was beginning to affect her comfort. Adding tension to her physical changes made the fidgeting worse. She was finally forced to sit further back in her chair.

Admiral Deacons was running a program to scan Marissa while he talked to her. The program had lie detector capabilities along with stress monitoring. It also recorded her voice and visual image. The one thing the Admiral didn't want to do was put Marissa under too much stress. The Admiral sat back in his own chair. He propped his left ankle up on his right knee then placed his data pad strategically on his left thigh, so he could view the display casually as needed. "Lt. Holden, you've been arrested for high treason. There's a chance I could make this go away. What are you willing to do to make that happen?"

Marissa stammered, "I'm sorry, s – sir, I don't think I understand."

Admiral Deacons noted a small fluctuation on her stress level. "You've betrayed the Commonwealth have you not? What can you do to repair the damage you've done?"

Marissa stared blankly at the Admiral. "I – I'm not sure there's anything I *can* do. What do you expect me to do, sir?"

"Let me be blunt, Lieutenant. Who are you loyal to, the Commonwealth or Pateras El Liontari?"

Marissa fidgeted again. She swallowed hard. She knew her answer would not be well received. Her mouth went dry. "P – Pateras El Liontari."

Admiral Deacons studied his readout. Lt. Holden's stress level was increasing. "Just how committed are you to him? You know Executor Hale has authorized the death penalty for treason of this nature. Are you planning on following Pateras El Liontari all the way to your own execution?"

Marissa closed her eyes for a moment mentally asking Pateras for strength and courage. She took a deep breath and reached down to touch the bulge in her belly. She spoke with a new confidence, "I am totally committed to Pateras. Do whatever you have to."

"You're willing to give up your life and the life of your child?"

Marissa sat up straighter in her chair. "Yes, Admiral, I am. I can no longer serve the Commonwealth."

The Admiral observed the peaks come down on his data pad. Marissa was calmer than when he had walked through the door. Robert changed tactics. "Why? What makes Pateras so special? Why risk your life for him?"

"That's hard to explain."

"Try. What caused you to choose to serve him?"

Robert watched Marissa's eyes dart back and forth as her thoughts replayed memories in her mind. "When I died on Medoris, Arni Sotaeras Liontari brought me into the presence of Pateras. Pateras showed me who he is. No – that isn't quite right. I didn't actually see him. He showed me the creation of the universe and the first humans. It was so beautiful. I'm not sure I can explain the awesomeness of what I saw. I realized then how powerful he was. He also showed me who Supreme Executor

Hale really is. He used to be this magnificent being, the most powerful being ever created by Pateras. The Executor tried to overthrow him. Pateras banished him. Pateras was so angry, I don't know why he didn't destroy him immediately. He said a day of reckoning is coming when all those who oppose Pateras will have to pay their debt to him. Pateras showed me the debt I owe him. He – He said - He said he loved me and all those he created. He doesn't want to punish those who oppose him."

A faraway look crossed Marissa's face as she continued to talk. The Admiral had intended to pick apart her words nearly as soon as she spoke them. His own subversive fidelity to Pateras made him innately curious. He wished more than anything he could assure the young woman he was trying to find a way to protect her.

"Pateras showed me the day Arni was born as a human. I saw his hand. He pointed to the baby and told me the death of his son would pay the debts owed by all. The day of his son's death was the beginning of the reckoning. Pateras asked me to trust him, but also told me he knew it wouldn't happen today. He promised Arni would take me back to the ship. I don't think I fully realized I was dead at the time. He also gave me one more promise. He said he would give me the one thing I desired most… a family. I saw a day sometime in the future. I was with Jake, our baby, the Captain, and the Commander. I've been dead once already, so has the Captain. Do whatever you have to, Admiral. Pateras runs this universe, not Executor Hale."

Admiral Deacons glanced at his display again. The squiggle on the graph in front of him settled to an all-time low. "So, you've been loyal to Pateras since the day you died on Medoris?"

"No, Admiral, I still served the Commonwealth. I didn't choose to follow Pateras until I saw the things he told me start to unfold. I came closer when I found out I was pregnant. I took another step in his direction when Arni died on Drea. I nearly lost my footing when I thought you killed the Captain on Tudoren."

"You believed I killed the Captain on Tudoren, despite my explanation to the contrary?" The Admiral shifted slightly in his seat. He wasn't sure if this was good or bad insight.

"I wasn't sure. It crossed all our minds."

"What caused you to turn the corner and join Pateras?"

"The day Pateras restored the Captain. I knew if he was capable of that much power and control, I would be safe in his hands."

The Admiral looked down at his pad again. His subject was still calm. Robert wasn't sure he could rattle her enough to prove his efforts were genuine. He decided to change tactics slightly. "Very well, if that is your wish so be it. I will warn you though. The Supreme Executor will be informed of your determination. He may order your execution, or he may attempt re-education. Despite our previous reports, re-education has been marginally successful." Robert stood abruptly and headed towards the door. He held his data pad to continue recording Marissa's actions.

Marissa jumped up. "Admiral, wait. Could I see my husband and the Captain one last time?"

"I can give you a moment with your husband. I can't let you see the Captain."

"Please, Admiral, just let me thank the Captain for trying to protect me. I owe him that."

"That's not going to be possible, Lieutenant."

"Admiral, please, can you at least tell him for me?"

The Admiral still had his back to the young lieutenant. He steadied his own nerves for what he was about to say. "I said that isn't *possible*, Lieutenant. The Captain and Commander were executed this morning! I gave the order myself! If Executor Hale orders your execution, you can tell him yourself." The Admiral turned and shuffled his data pad casually back and forth between his hands. "Do you now understand what you are up against? It's a nice idea to think a supreme being is going to swoop in here and rescue you. How do you know what such a being's plans are? Does he *really* love you? Did he have the same feelings for Captain Alexander and Commander Alexander? Are you even on his radar? Are you sure he didn't tell you what you needed to hear just to win your trust or break your trust with the Commonwealth?"

Marissa was frozen in place. Her thoughts were scattered. Was the Admiral telling the truth? If he was, how could he do that to his own nephew? What about the rest of the crew? Pateras didn't deceive her, did he? The Captain said something to her, something important, just before they got separated at the shuttle port. What was it? She couldn't remember right now. Wait! He said to trust Pateras, no matter what. She would honor the Captain and Commander's memory by following the Captain's last wish. Was it too much to hope Pateras would restore them again?

The Admiral glanced at his data pad. The stress monitor peaked again. He saw it settle back in. It wasn't as low as before. She *could* be rattled. Robert sighed. He opened the door to speak to the two men guarding Marissa, "Gentlemen, fetch the Chief." He stepped back inside and closed the door. In a swift move, he paused the recording on his data pad then pressed a button on his bracelet. "Lt. Holden, do you know where your husband's loyalties truly lie?"

"We – we don't talk much about it. He supports the Captain for my sake, but I'm not sure he cares for Pateras."

"Listen carefully, I only have a moment. I lied to you. The Captain's alive, so is the Commander. I'm afraid I'm going to lie to you again and it's going to frighten you, badly. Forgive me in advance. Don't believe what you see, no matter how terrible it appears. Not everything is as it seems. Trust Pateras, no matter what."

Admiral Deacons pressed the button on his bracelet turning off the signal jammer he turned on seconds ago. He turned it and his data recorder on in time for the guards to escort Jake into the room.

Marissa blinked. She wasn't sure she understood what the Admiral was trying to tell her. He had said the exact thing the Captain had before they were captured. Was this some kind of trap? He just told her not to forsake Pateras. Why would a loyal Commonwealth soldier tell her that… unless…? Where did the Admiral's loyalties lie? She did recognize the Admiral's precautions for what they were and refrained from asking questions. She quickly discerned what part she needed to play. "Admiral, Pateras has the power of life and death in his hands. I'm proof of that. He can bring me or the Captain and Commander back from the dead if he so desires."

The guards brought Jake into the center of the room. Marissa called out, "Jake!" She jumped into his arms the second the guards released him. The Admiral allowed them a moment together. Despite the presence of four guards and an Admiral, Jake and Marissa were preoccupied with each other. Jake made sure Marissa and the baby were fine. He caressed her face and kissed her, then reached down and firmly touched her belly. His son, not appreciating the intrusion into his territory, kicked his father's hand. Marissa laughed through her tears of relief at seeing Jake alive and well. She embraced him tightly. The couple talked softly to each other for a minute. Jake continued to assure her everything was going to be fine.

The Admiral ordered two of the guards to retrieve Jake and put binders on him. The men pulled Jake away from his wife and bound him as ordered. They moved him to an open area on the floor and forced him to his knees. Jake was suddenly confused. "What's going on? Admiral?"

The Admiral backhanded Jake. "You would do well to hold your tongue."

Jake tried to come off the floor. His guards assured his posture remained unchanged.

Marissa began to get nervous again. "Admiral, what are you doing?"

The Admiral folded his arms across his chest. "Lieutenant, I told you. If you want to stop this, all you have to do is recant. Give up your loyalty to Pateras and rejoin the Commonwealth."

"Stop what, Admiral?"

"You said Pateras could bring the others back from the dead if he wanted. We took steps to prevent that. We incinerated the bodies of your Captain and Commander. There's nothing left to bring back. Recant and I'll spare your husband's life. I've already interviewed him. He has no great love for Pateras."

Marissa's pale skin went a shade whiter. "Admiral, I thought he would be spared if he denied serving Pateras. I don't understand."

The Admiral stared coldly at Marissa. "The Supreme Executor believes you are worth saving. Navigators are highly sought after. We've put a lot of effort into training you. Security officers are easy to acquire. I can get new ones from anywhere. We can't afford to waste a navigator. I don't care who he serves. He's expendable. You aren't. I will execute him, right now, in front of you if you don't recant."

Marissa was having trouble processing. She was getting so many conflicting messages.

Jake struggled again, unsuccessfully, to get to his feet. "Admiral, you can't do this! We -"

The Admiral punched Jake in the mouth, busting his lip. "I told you to hold your tongue unless you plan on pleading with your wife." The Admiral addressed his comment to remind Jake of his task.

Jake anxiously looked back and forth between Marissa and the Admiral. "Marissa? Please… don't let him do this."

Marissa, also being a trained security guard, started to move to a more strategic place and stance. Admiral Deacons, having familiarized himself with her file, anticipated her actions and sent the second guards to restrain her. The two guards grabbed her arms, pulling her off balance. They jerked her backward into the chair furthest from Jake and the door. Jake nearly made it onto his feet this time. His guards quickly pushed him back down.

The Admiral quickly cautioned the two men restraining Marissa. "Careful gentlemen. Don't hurt her, just hold her. Put binders on her, for her own safety." The guards complied despite Marissa's attempts to thwart their efforts.

Marissa still struggled, "No… Jake! Admiral, I can't do this. It's not possible. It's like saying water isn't wet. I can't! Please Admiral, don't do this!" Tears began to run down her face.

The Admiral pulled out his weapon, adjusted the weapon's setting. "Give me a reason to think there's hope."

Marissa heard a voice whisper to her. "Trust me."

A quiet peace settled over her. Tears flowed quietly down her face. She stopped struggling. Her eyes had been darting back and forth between Jake and the Admiral. Her eyes settled on Jake and stayed there. "I'm so sorry, Jake. I can't abandon Pateras. Forgive me."

"NO… Marissa, don't do this! They'll re-educate you or they'll execute you!" Jake pleaded with her. He wasn't sure if his own life was actually in danger or not, but hers might well be.

Marissa heard the Admiral's weapon power up. She looked back at the Admiral, with tears streaming down her face, she made one last plea, "Please don't do this Admiral, PLEASE!" Her eyes focused on Jake's once again.

The Admiral stepped closer to Jake and took aim. He

glanced at Marissa. Seeing her make no move to stop him, the Admiral waved the guards away from Jake. If he fired his Tri-EMP while the guards were touching him, they could be caught in the pulse.

Jake looked more lost than scared. His wife had refused to save him. "Marissa?"

"I love you, Jake."

Jake looked even more confused. "Then save me…"

Marissa shook her head, "I can't do what he asks. I'm sorry."

Robert swallowed hard, took aim at Jake, and fired. Jake's body convulsed repeatedly, fell onto the floor then stopped moving.

Despite the calming voice asking for her trust, Marissa cried out, "JAKE!" She tried to go to his side. Her guards pushed her back into her seat. Tears blurred her vision. She cried outright.

The Admiral holstered his weapon. He motioned to the guards, "Get him out of here." Jake's guards hoisted his body off the floor and dragged him out. He wanted Jake's body removed before Marissa realized he was still breathing. The Admiral hit him with a heavy stun setting. The guards had been instructed earlier to take Jake directly to the Infirmary. They were to release him from his binders and issue an apology to him from the Admiral.

While Marissa sat there crying, Robert stepped into the bathroom. A minute later he brought her a cloth to wipe her face. He ordered the guards to release her binders and wait outside. Marissa took the cloth from his hand and wiped her face. As soon as the guards were out of sight, Marissa stood up and promptly slapped the Admiral across the face. Admiral Deacons knew she would. He felt so bad about what he had done, he let her do it. He simply looked at her and asked, "Feel better?" He knew the answer.

Before leaving her barracks, he addressed her one more time. "Lt. Holden, you will henceforth be known as prisoner number 7145. Tomorrow morning you will be moved to a regular prison cell and begin the re-education process. You have the rest of today to mourn. I suggest you start with a hot bath. It will probably be the last bath you get for quite some time. I already started the hot water running for you. If you decide not to take a bath, then be sure to go in and turn the water off. If it overflows, I'll have the guards come in and bathe you themselves. The doctor will come to check on you in two hours. Let him know if you need a sedative. Are we clear, prisoner 7145?"

"Yes… Admiral, I understand." Her voice was soft and low. She appeared to be in shock.

The Admiral left the barracks but continued to monitor her movements on his data pad through the in-room computer system. Marissa cried for a few more minutes. She finally pulled herself up and moved slowly to the bathroom. She could still hear the water running. When she walked in, the room was full of steam. She shut off the water then turned to leave the room. Marissa gasped. Written in the steam on the mirror were the words, "Jake lives." She stood there staring at the words. Her mind raced replaying the events of the last hour. The Admiral was giving her mixed messages. Was this his way of trying to break her and start the re-education process? Dashing her hopes then giving them back to her? One monumental thought crossed her mind, had the Admiral changed sides? Was he playing both sides for the Captain's sake? Marissa shivered despite the oppressive heat and steam now saturating the bathroom. She came to two possible conclusions; either the Admiral had changed sides in which case this message would need to be destroyed to protect him, or he was playing mind games. If he was playing games, wiping it away would tell him she believed him. Leaving it in place would tell him, she didn't trust or believe him. Marissa decided to take the safest course of action. Using her hand, she wiped away the message, then for good measure she used soap and a cloth to clear the mirror completely.

Marissa was fairly certain the Admiral's suggestion to take a bath was a smoke screen and having just showered earlier, she really wasn't interested in taking a bath. She drained the tub. Feeling very lost and alone, she went and sat on the foot of her bed. She stared at nothing trying to sort everything out. What if the Admiral was really being as cruel as he seemed? What if the Captain, Commander and Jake were truly dead? What were they going to do with her and her baby? What about the vision Pateras had shown her of the four of them with her baby? Was it just a dream? Marissa crawled to the top of the bed. Laying down she grabbed the extra pillow and hugged it tightly. Tears began to escape her eyes again. She spoke out loud, "Arni, I need you. Please help me." She cried for a few minutes then a drowsiness overtook her. By the time the doctor came to check on her, she was sound asleep. The doctor did a casual scan of her, then slipped back out quietly to report her condition to Admiral Deacons.

"Good Morning, Captain, I trust you are feeling better."

David was ushered into an office currently occupied by the Supreme Executor and his staff. His escorts shoved him roughly into a chair facing the Executor's desk. David was glad his head was no longer pounding in light of being thrown so roughly into the chair.

Executor Hale stood up and frowned at the two men. "Gentlemen, this man is my guest. Please remove his binders and apologize for treating him so roughly."

The two guards gave each other puzzled glances, then did as they were instructed. They took their orders to heart. Their apologies sounded nearly genuine. David looked at the two men as they waited for him to accept their apologies. David didn't push his luck by attempting to stand or offer a handshake. "Apology accepted. Don't believe everything you hear about me, and we'll call it good."

The two men moved to stand guard at the door. Executor Hale waved them on out. They were not amused at his decision to be unguarded with a prisoner guilty of high treason.

Executor Hale smiled cynically at David, "Nicely played, Captain. You planted a tiny seed of doubt in them. If those seeds take root, I'll have to dig them out. You know that, don't you?"

"Therein lies the question, which one will take root and how far will it spread until then? You don't know the answer to *that* question, do you?" David taunted the alien being he knew was before him.

"Perhaps not, but neither do you. It may go nowhere. I could always execute every guard you speak to or speak in the presence of. Would that be more to your liking?"

"Why am I here, Executor Hale? Why haven't I been executed? Is it because my Master hasn't granted you permission to act against me yet?" David glanced around at the personnel in the room. Everyone's eyes were fixated on David until they heard his peculiar question. The group began giving their superior curious glances.

Executor Hale's face clouded slightly then he smiled sardonically again. "Nice try. I answer to no one. You are still alive because I *allow* it. I have kept you alive to see for myself if you are beyond hope. I want to know why a man of your stature would give up his career, his family, everything he's ever known, and commit treason." Executor Hale looked around the room. "Ladies and Gentlemen, I need to spend some time alone with this young man. Would you please excuse us? I'll send for you later."

His administrative assistant, Stuart Jacobs, declined to obey. Mr. Jacobs spoke softly to the Executor, "Sir, he's guilty of high treason. He's not guarded or wearing binders. It's not safe. What if our enemy uses him to get to you?"

Executor Hale smiled. "I do appreciate your concern, Stuart. I know more about the enemy than even the Captain does. Captain Alexander can't harm me, even *he* knows that."

The man started to object again. The Supreme Executor dismissed him in a more forceful tone.

The last man left the room creating an awkward silence. David massaged his wrists for a moment. The urge to attack the Supreme Executor began to build. David tried hard to suppress the urge. He reminded himself, this was no mere man.

The superior being in front of him was seriously more powerful than David. David knew Arni guaranteed him a certain amount of protection, but how much? How far could the Executor go?

Although unable to read his mind, Luciano could read David's face. "I can see you have lots of questions. Perhaps, I can answer a few for you. I would assume you want to know what I plan on doing with you. You were right about Pateras. He *has* limited my options – *for now*. I may be able to change his mind later, unless I no longer need to."

"And… what is that supposed to mean?"

"Captain, I can give you… well… pretty much anything you want. I can make you the youngest Admiral in history. I can give you an entire planet to rule, or even half the galaxy if you wish. Tell me what you want, and I will give it to you in exchange for your loyalty."

"Ah… I see. In which case, you would no longer need to ask Pateras for permission to harm me."

"I could even set you and your beautiful Commander up on an abandoned planet in exchange for certain considerations."

David wasn't sure how to respond. He had no intention of cooperating with Executor Hale. What did Arni expect of him? He said the only thing he could. "I am loyal to the household of Pateras El Liontari. That isn't going to change. I realize you could give me a lot. You can't give me the things that matter the most. You don't care about me; you care about hurting Pateras. I know Pateras *does* care about me. Even if I had everything imaginable in this reality, I would still face the wrath of Pateras in the Reckoning. You can't protect me or even yourself from him."

Luciano moved to the front side of his desk. He leaned back against the desk and folded his arms across his chest. "That sword cuts two ways, Captain. I may not be able to protect you from the Reckoning, but I can create a reckoning of my own making for you. You are quite right. I care nothing for you or your kind. My interest is in breaking my maker's heart. I was the most powerful being ever created by him. I was a fantastic creature. All others are beneath me. Pateras decided I was full of pride. He rejected me. He created me and then threw me out like a piece of garbage."

"And you did nothing to provoke it, right?" David goaded the man.

Luciano's smile was completely gone now. "You think I can't touch you? Bribery was my first choice, not my only choice. Pateras refuses to allow me to kill you or your crew. He didn't stop me from inflicting a wide variety of pains and tortures on all of you. You can accept a bribe or face *my* wrath." The Executor stood to his full height. A dark shadow displayed on his character. He leaned over into the Captain's face. His physical features morphed into his natural state. His physique dwarfed the Captain.

David thought to himself, if he had run across this creature a year ago, it would have terrified him. It still made his heart pound. A calming presence kept him from panicking.

Luciano continued his tirade. "I will make you and your companions suffer dearly for the trouble you've caused me. You will *beg* Pateras for death by the time I'm done with you." Luciano stopped his tirade and resumed his previous human visage. His tone changed slightly. He spoke aloud, but not to David. "You don't belong here, Arni! Your father put them in my hands." There was a moment of silence. Luciano appeared to be listening for something. Luciano turned his back on the Captain and slammed his fist on the desk angrily. "NO!"

David grinned. He wasn't sure what he missed, but if it angered the Supreme Executor, so much the better. At least he hoped it was better.

The Executor took a minute to compose himself. He turned around to face David again. The anger was gone, but a coldness remained. "I hope that quiet little voice is enough company for you because that's the only source of comfort you're going to get."

"In light of what we know isn't going to happen, what *do* you have planned for me? You had my injuries treated. Why?"

"An advance on my bribe. Since you have refused my bribe, I guess I will need to recollect that advance… with interest."

David sighed, "Of course, you will."

"Oh, that isn't going to be the end of it, Captain. You see, I can have you beaten every night and get your wounds healed every morning. Imagine it, Captain. You can look forward to a beating every day for the rest of your life or until you reject Pateras. Your life is going to feel like a never-ending time loop. You may not know this, but time loops are theoretical and not possible. I love listening to the foolishness of the scientific community arguing back and forth about their theoretical calculations. Time is sealed shut by Pateras. Only he can transverse those lines. The icing on the cake is this, Captain. I'm going to send the doctor in every night to give you a neural stimulant to enhance your pain receptors. You'll feel every little pain several times over. I'm also going to let you watch the audio/video feeds of the pain and torture inflicted on your crew. Then I'm going to repeat it over and over until you beg for mercy."

David tried to steady himself. He wasn't fast enough. Luciano saw him flinch and grinned sadistically. David wanted to plead for mercy for his crew. He was quick to realize anything he said would only make things worse for them. Instead, David grinned. "You convince me to change, I'll convince my crew to change. They followed me out of the Commonwealth, they'll follow me back in."

"Captain, I'm no fool. I know you're just trying to protect your crew. Do you really think you're the Defender of Mankind spoken of in the Ancient Texts?"

"Yes, I'm trying to protect my crew. What Captain wouldn't?

It's what you trained me to do. I'm sure you know if you harm them, you'll lose me *permanently*. As for the Defender of Mankind, I don't believe I've gotten to that portion of the Ancient Texts. I don't know what you are referring to."

"Then I suppose it's not currently relevant. We will see how lost you are to me, though. I'll give you every chance to change your mind. I also have a few surprises planned for you."

The Supreme Executor moved back around behind his desk and sat down. "Captain, do you know how you were captured?"

"I have a pretty good idea. Arni filled in some of the gaps. Admiral Garcia and Admiral Deacons were working with my security chief to set a trap for us." David was fairly certain Luciano wouldn't know exactly what Arni had told him.

The Executor studied David carefully looking for any hint of hidden truths, deception, or fear. David started to tell the Executor he had willingly walked into the trap. He decided to keep the information to himself. It was enough of a thought to show up on his face. Luciano couldn't discern the meaning of what he saw. He decided to test the Captain in the presence of the Security Chief. He pressed a button on his console, "Escort Security Chief Jacob Holden to my office, please." A voice affirmed the order on the other end.

While they waited, David stood up and walked over to a nearby window. He stared out it and mentally begged Arni to keep his crew safe. The Supreme Executor seemed unconcerned with David's freedom of movement. He came up behind David. "Would you like something to drink? It's not a bribe, and it isn't poisoned or drugged. I wouldn't want to be a bad host."

David glanced at a pitcher of water on a nearby table. He wanted it badly. He forced his eyes to look outside. Luciano walked over and poured a glass of ice water. He set it down in front of the Captain. David started to reach for it, the voice softly instructed, "Take nothing from his hand." David hastily closed his hand and turned away from the window and the glass of water.

Luciano scowled when he saw the glass sitting undisturbed. There truly was nothing wrong with the glass of water. It merely represented the Captain's willingness to cooperate no matter how small of a cooperation. His thoughts were interrupted by a hail. He answered the call. The voice from before spoke to him, "I'm sorry, Supreme Executor, Chief Holden is currently unavailable."

Executor Hale scowled. "What do you mean he's *unavailable*?"

The voice hesitated. "He's – uh – He's in the Infirmary. Admiral Deacons shot him with a Tri-EMP. It was a heavy stun setting. He can be made available in about an hour."

David saw the Executor clinch his jaw. He couldn't help feeling a small amount of satisfaction. Jake deserved to be shot. David's lip twitched slightly.

"Then bring me Admiral Deacons. NOW!"

Admiral Deacons was interviewing Lt. Commander Flint when a soldier rushed in. The man whispered hastily to the Admiral. Robert got up just as quickly. He ordered the guards to keep Braxton in the interrogation room as he rushed out. Braxton had only been allowed to sleep two of the last twenty-four hours. As soon as the guards left the room, he put his head down to catch a nap.

The Admiral reached the door to Executor Hale's temporary office. Commodore Vardin had assigned a receptionist to assist the Supreme Executor and his staff. The receptionist escorted the Admiral into the office and announced him.

David said nothing when his uncle entered the room. He watched the Admiral greet and address the Galaxy's most powerful leader. Executor Hale demanded to know why Chief Holden was in the Infirmary.

The Admiral glanced at David before responding. He knew his nephew would not be happy. "Forgive me if I inconvenienced you, sir. I needed to be certain of the loyalties of the Chief's wife. I shot him… in front of her. Despite the threat of losing her husband, she didn't waver. Her loyalties lie firmly with Pateras. I'm going to move her to a regular cell in the morning and begin the re-education process so we can fulfill our agreement with the Chief. The Chief was heavily stunned, not killed. I seriously doubt he's going to like me very much when he wakes up. Make sure you blame it all on me, so he doesn't have any reason to be angry with you."

David moved closer to his uncle, "What did you do? Are you trying to cause her to miscarry? That much stress could kill the baby." David's mind was racing. Surely his uncle wouldn't have gone so far to protect himself. Was this just a story for the Executor's benefit? Was he wrong about his uncle's loyalties? David did the only thing he could. He took a swing at his uncle. Robert dodged the swing and caught David's arm. He twisted expertly bringing his elbow down on the young man's shoulder. The move threw David off balance. Robert swept David's leg putting him on the ground. He twisted David's arm behind his back and pinned him down. Despite David's current pain, he was impressed by such a move coming from a man closing in on sixty years of age. David knew he had underestimated his uncle. He wouldn't do that again.

Robert held David on the ground and leaned over him. "Captain Alexander, not that this is your concern any longer, but I was monitoring the Lieutenant carefully. If the baby were in any danger, I would have stopped immediately. Do you think I am a complete idiot? We have an agreement with the Chief. His wife and child were part of that agreement. I'm not going to put our agreement in jeopardy. Now… if you think you can control yourself, I'll let you up."

David had been struggling to free his arm and push the Admiral off him. As his words sank in, David stopped fighting. He relaxed his fists and placed his free hand flat on the floor. Robert got up carefully making sure the fight had completely left him. David got up slowly still glaring at his uncle. The Admiral ordered the young Captain to return to his seat. David stood there a moment debating whether to comply or resist. Admiral Deacons addressed his insubordination bluntly. "I know you aren't concerned with a charge of insubordination in light of your treason. If I want you to sit down, I can order you to sit and enforce it myself, or I can call security to come in and enforce it. You decide. Is this what you want to waste your energy on, or do you want to use it planning a useless escape attempt?"

David decided his uncle's reasoning was sound. He sat down as ordered still glaring at the two men.

The Admiral and Supreme Executor continued to discuss the Admiral's approach to handling Marissa. Robert glanced at David again. "Are you sure you want to discuss this in front of him?"

Executor Hale smiled as sadistically as he had earlier. "Definitely. I promised the Captain he would know what kind of suffering he's causing for his crew. I want him to know every sordid detail."

"Then he should know something else. I didn't want to mention it to you while he was in here, but since you're alright with it. During my interview with the Lieutenant, I told her the Captain and Commander had been executed this morning."

Executor Hale frowned, "Oh, Robert, I wish you hadn't done that. I had some plans involving the Captain to dishearten his crew. If she believes he's dead…"

"Don't worry, sir. She doesn't know what to believe. I turned my recording off and a jammer on. I told the young woman I had lied to her. I told her the Captain was still alive. After I shot

Jake and left her alone, I left a hidden message for her, telling her Jake was alive. I yanked that girl back and forth so many times, she's definitely on shaky ground."

Luciano's eyes danced gleefully back and forth between the Captain and the Admiral. "Robert, I didn't realize you were capable of such treachery. After your reaction to my orders concerning Galat, Julley, and Strabothon, I wasn't sure you were cut out for this."

Robert winced, "I'm sorry Supreme Executor, I'm not sure I *am* cut out for this. I still object to killing innocent civilians. The Captain and his crew aren't innocent civilians. I'm doing whatever I can to keep them alive. I just might be too soft for your purposes. This wasn't an easy task for me."

The Supreme Executor smiled, "You did an excellent job though. I support your actions. It will get easier the more you do it. I *had* intended on questioning the Captain with his Security Chief present just to keep him honest. I suppose it will have to wait a little longer. What did I pull you away from?"

"I was questioning Lt. Commander Flint. We hadn't gotten very far. Would you like me to return to the interview, or do you have further use for me here?"

"I do have one more request. I think Captain Alexander should talk to his mother. Can you hail her for me?"

"Of course, Supreme Executor."

David stood abruptly. "Leave my mother out of this. She thinks I died a hero's death. Let it stay that way."

Robert and Luciano stopped and looked at David. This time the Supreme Executor ordered David to return to his seat. The Executor stepped aside from his desk to allow Admiral Deacons access to initiate the communication. "Place the call."

David held his ground. His uncle reached down to press the controls. David reacted swiftly. Having nothing else, he grabbed the chair he had been sitting on. He swung it forcefully through the air, smashing the top of the desk. "I SAID NO! Leave my mother out of this!" The desktop shattered loudly. The Supreme Executor and the Admiral jumped back momentarily.

Hearing the noise, two guards, weapons drawn, burst through the door. David turned hastily and slung the chair into the nearest guard taking him to the ground. The second guard seeing the flying chair and the plight of his companion, hesitated. It was enough. David rushed the second guard forcing his weapon upward and pinning the man against the door frame. He and David wrestled for the weapon. David thrust his knee into his opponent giving him the upper hand momentarily. His opponent reacted instinctively to protect himself by pulling his limbs into a more crouched posture. David managed to point the weapon at the first guard, who having recovered his footing, was rapidly encroaching on the skirmish. David slid his finger into the trigger guard forcing the weapon to fire. The first guard writhed and dropped. His companion went from fearful, to apologetic, to highly motivated in less than a second. He brought his own knee up into the Captain causing him to double over. David didn't let his own discomfort overrule his efforts. He continued to wrestle the guard for the weapon until a dizzying blow and a searing pain ran through his skull. He lost his grip and sank to the ground. The Admiral had stepped up behind him and struck him with the butt of his own weapon. Once they had the Captain under control, they pulled him to his feet and looked to the Supreme Executor for additional instructions.

"I think the Captain has enjoyed his freedom long enough. Put his restraints back on him then take your companion to the Infirmary. The Captain won't cause any more trouble, or I'll order his own mother to be executed. Are we clear?"

David's head was spinning again. He looked up at the Supreme Executor whose form kept jumping back and forth in

David's sight. David managed a breathless, "Yes sir, got it!" His stomach was now slightly nauseated. David tried to get his eyes to focus on his Uncle Rob. He had underestimated him a second time. It was obviously a weakness he needed to work on.

Robert gave David a look of pity. There was no malice or disgust in his uncle's gaze, only sorrow. "David, what were you thinking? There's no way you could have gotten off the base."

David tried again to focus on his Uncle's face. He gave the Admiral a smug smile. "It's pointless to call my mother, if I get myself killed. If I…" David's speech was slurred. He finally succumbed to the blow to his head and lost consciousness.

The Supreme Executor scowled. "I suppose we can put him in touch with his mother a little later today. I underestimated him. I won't let that happen again. Get him to the Infirmary. Let me know when he's ready to continue our exercises in futility."

The Admiral called for two more guards to lug the Captain to the Infirmary. He gave the Medic on duty and David's guards a very specific set of instructions. He let them know, the Supreme Executor wanted David alive and in top condition as soon as possible. The medic looked at the other occupied beds around him. The medic was confounded. "Admiral, what's going on? I haven't had this many moderate level injuries at one time since I was posted here. I'm used to treating minor abrasions, twisted ankles, stress related headaches, you know, annoyance injuries. This man has been on base for twenty-four hours and I've treated two Tri-EMP injuries, treated him twice now, did a full exam on a pregnant woman, and I treated some minor injuries on the men who – uh – interrogated him last night. Who is he?"

The Admiral squinted at the man. He wanted to give him the whole story, but knew he needed to answer carefully. "This man is my nephew. He's formerly the Captain of the *Evangeline*. This is also what happens when you reject the Commonwealth."

"Should I expect more of this?"

"I don't think so. I think we all know where the lines are drawn now, although you should expect to treat more of *his* injuries."

• •

Admiral Deacons returned to his interview room. He found Braxton sound asleep. He hated to wake the man. The retraining protocols stipulated extremely minimal amounts of sleep. The Admiral knew he should have instructed the guards to keep their prisoner awake. He was fully aware of his omission when he left. He neglected giving the order purposefully. The Admiral was still trying to work out a way to rescue the captain and crew. He had been kept so busy, escape plans were eluding him. The Admiral wondered if allowing Braxton to catch a brief nap was his own subconscious way of compensating the Lt. Commander for the inability to help him escape. The Admiral stood there a minute watching Braxton sleep. He sighed. It was time to put on his heartless suit of armor again. He leaned over near Braxton's ear and shouted. "PRISONER NUMBER 7140! WHY ARE YOU SLEEPING?"

Braxton jumped. He sat up bleary-eyed. He managed to mumble a halfhearted, "Sorry, Admiral." He wasn't sorry in the slightest. He was grateful for anything he could get. He was sorrier about getting caught.

The Admiral ran Braxton through a gamut of questions. None of his answers were good Commonwealth indoctrinated answers.

Three hours later, Admiral Deacons was again summoned by the Supreme Executor. David was awake and alert. This time the three, along with two guards, met in the conference room. David was wearing binders and the disciplinary collar placed on him when he was arrested. The guards dropped him into a chair at the far end of the table. His reputation appeared to be growing. The two stood warily by the door. David looked around the room and grinned. The panels of the enclosure were thick glass walls with privacy screen capabilities. At the press of a button the walls would go from clear to a milky white. If he wanted out badly enough, it was still breakable glass. He knew his collar would stop him from getting very far, although he liked to know what his options were. He also liked the idea of gaining a reputation.

Executor Hale instructed Admiral Deacons to again contact David's mother. Admiral Deacons hailed the ship carrying his family. As he waited for the hail to go through, he thought back to two months ago when he told their family about David's death.

• •

He had sent for David's sister Abigail and her family. He contacted David's mother, Jessica, her husband, Steven, and David's half-brother, Stevie Jr. The group met at Jessica's home. The Admiral picked up his own mother and brought her with him. He remembered everyone's tenuous behavior as the two walked into the house together. Jessica offered everyone something to drink as any good hostess would. She stayed as busy as she could. She knew Robert had news she didn't want to hear. It didn't take long for him to decide he needed to corner her first. Jessica disappeared into the kitchen four times within ten minutes of his arrival. That last time he glanced around the room addressing the rest of the family, "Give us a moment alone in the kitchen please." Robert met Jessica before she could leave the room. He firmly took her by the arm. Escorting her out to the patio, he led her to the table and chairs. He sat her down then pulled a second chair up close.

Jessica's hands were shaking as he took them in his own. She looked up with tears in her eyes and begged, "Robert, please don't do this. Please don't say what I know you're going to."

Robert remembered looking around the garden as though

the right words were somehow written there. His eyes came back to hers. It was a risk, but he had to tell her the whole truth. "Jess… when I go back inside, I'm going to have to lie to the rest of the family. I want you to know Pateras is real, and he saved David's life. Well, actually he didn't. David died in my arms, but Pateras restored his life."

Jessica jerked and grabbed tightly onto his hands as though he were her lifeline. She looked up with tears in her eyes. "Robert… you aren't making sense. Is my son alive or not?"

Robert squeezed her hands tightly. "Jess, you can't tell anyone, *not anyone*, what I'm telling you. David was alive when I left him and to my knowledge, he's still alive. He died in my arms. He took an arrow in the chest to save me. The CIF now thinks he's dead. If they find out he's alive they'll hunt him down. He'll be arrested for treason and either re-educated or executed. If the CIF finds out I knew about it, the same thing will happen to me."

Jessica still had trouble processing the Admiral's message. "Pateras can't do that. He's not real."

The two were so focused, neither heard their mother, Kay Deacons come outside. "Jessica, Pateras can do anything he wants. He is the Timeless One, the creator and maker of all things. He gives life and he can take it away. I was afraid to continue teaching you about him when you were a child. After you were grown, your father and I were afraid to bring the subject up again. We did a great wrong. Just before your father died, we vowed to set things right. When Saul was killed, I got scared again. Forgive me. I lost your sister because I served Pateras and I lost your father for the same reason. I've been afraid of losing anyone else, so I remained silent. I'm done being afraid. Robert, has Pateras cost me my first grandchild?"

Robert smiled. "No, Mom. I must report him as dead to the Commonwealth and the family, but he's alive and well. Mom, he serves Pateras… and so do I."

Kay's eyes welled up with tears. She clasped her hands over her mouth and wept openly. She wrapped her arms around her two remaining children and held them tightly. "Pateras, thank you!" She cried. "I didn't know how to put right what we had done wrong."

Jessica, still confused by the mayhem of the situation, stopped crying. "Mom, you're okay with this? You know what the Commonwealth teaches about such things. Gods are for the intellectually undeveloped and the weak-minded."

Her mother's eyes snapped angrily at her daughter. "I was a well-educated physicist on Drea and I served Pateras since childhood. The Commonwealth kidnapped me, forced me to work for them, and forced me to deny Pateras. My weakness was in wanting to protect my children, so I rejected Pateras. I should never have rejected him. Robert and David have found their way back to Pateras despite my best efforts to the contrary. I am neither weak-minded nor intellectually undeveloped."

Jessica, upon hearing the stories with fresh ears, began to recall the suppressed memories of Drea and life with Pateras. She came to understand what was at stake. She mourned as much as David's sister, Abby, because she knew the chances of ever seeing her firstborn again were infinitesimally small. She doubted he would ever be able to contact her in any way again, although deep inside, she carried a sense of satisfaction. Her oldest son would be heralded as a hero.

• •

Robert sighed as the call went through. Now he was going to have to tell her David was now known as public enemy number three, behind Pateras and Arni Liontari. Jessica's face finally appeared in front of him. Robert glanced one more time at his nephew before speaking. David's face was completely blank. Robert heard Jessica speaking to him and realized he intended to take a strong lead in the conversation to prevent her from saying something she shouldn't. "Robert, what's going on? Where are we going? Why did you spirit us all away like this? Robert, are you listening to me? Robert?"

"Jess, I'm sorry about this, really I am. Jess, I'm here with Supreme Executor Hale. I'm afraid I have some news that's going to be difficult for you to hear. I need you to just listen and let me get through this. It's not going to be any easier for me to say than it is for you to hear." Robert gave his words a moment to sink in.

Jessica sat back in her chair. The last time they had a conversation like this, it wasn't pleasant. "What's wrong? The last time we talked like this you told me my son was dead. This somehow sounds worse. What could you possibly have to tell me? What could possibly be worse?"

Robert sighed. "Jessica, this will come as a shock to you, but David isn't dead."

Jessica's eyes darted back and forth nervously. He wouldn't say this in the presence of the Supreme Executor and on an open channel unless it was now common knowledge. Jessica gripped the arms of her chair tightly. "Why are you saying this? You said he died in your arms. You said he gave his life to save yours. I don't understand."

Robert glanced up at Luciano. His eyes asking how much he could say. Executor Hale gave him an approving nod. "Jessica, Supreme Executor Hale has authorized me to tell you a little more about David's mission. We've been pursuing an enemy of the Commonwealth known as Pateras El Liontari. This enemy has extremely advanced technology. He was able to restore David's physical functionality after I left him. In the process, he corrupted his mind. David is no longer loyal to the Commonwealth. He's loyal to Pateras. I gathered the family for your own protection. Once I learned David was alive, I didn't know what he might be capable of. He's here with us now. In dealing with previous situations, sometimes relatives have been able to bring the corrupted back to reality. We wanted you to talk to him. Remind him of what he's allowed to happen and where he's come from."

Jessica stared blankly at her older brother. All she could hear was her own heart pounding. She knew the stakes. "My son's – alive?"

Robert was relieved. Jessica understood – everything. "Yes, he's alive, but he's not himself. We need you to talk to him. Convince him to reject Pateras."

"How? What am I supposed to say to him?"

Robert glanced at David again. "Tell him… Tell him how much you love him. Do whatever you can to remind him of who he was." Robert knew this could be the last time she ever saw her firstborn son. He wanted to give her a chance to say farewell without letting her know he may be executed for treason soon. "Just be prepared, Jessica. He will likely lie to you and reject you. Don't take it personally."

Jessica nodded weakly, "I understand. Let me speak to him."

David was no longer angry. Seeing the look in his uncle's eyes, he knew his uncle hadn't deceived him. His uncle served Pateras. His uncle was walking a fine line between Pateras and the Supreme Executor. Again, the look on his face was blank. There were hints of emotion though nothing discernible.

The Admiral pressed a control on the table. The monitors in the rest of the room lit up with Jessica's face. Although Robert told her two months ago David was alive and in hiding, seeing his face was still a shock for her. Tears began to stream down her face. "Oh, David, I never imagined I would ever see you again. Are you alright, son?"

David glanced at his two captors. "I'm fine, mom. In fact,

I've never been better. I really don't know what all the fuss is about. I was doing the job I was trained to do. I guess they don't appreciate my methods. They wanted me to locate Pateras. I found him. I've visited his home, twice. I can't really give anyone any coordinates because I'm not sure how I got there. I'm still working on that part."

"David, please, this situation is serious. Don't make things worse. Is it true that you died? Did you die trying to save Robert's life?"

"Yes, Mom, I couldn't let him die, no matter what… you didn't tell her that part did you, Uncle Rob?"

Jessica had her screen split so she could see her son and brother simultaneously. A look of guilt briefly crossed his face. Jessica started to ask him what David was talking about, but decided it would wait, for the moment. "Robert, we will talk more about this later," Jessica said icily. "David, I love you and I'm so proud of you. You worked so hard in the Academy and Officer's school. I knew you'd make us all proud. I know this isn't your fault. Please son, please make this right. I need you to come back to me."

David smiled. "I love you too, Mom. I hope you can forgive me if I can't fix this. I'm sure you're dying to ask me why I did this. I'll save you the trouble. Let's just say my version of the truth and the Supreme Executor's version arc not in agreement. I won't bother giving you the details because Uncle Rob already tried to convince you I was going to lie to you."

Tears still ran down his mother's face. She was scared to ask too many questions and scared she wouldn't ask enough questions. "David, please stop this – this nonsense. I'm begging you."

David forced a smile. "Give Gramma, Abby, and Stevie my love. If you hear from Dad, give him my love as well. Be sure and tell my new nephew about how his uncle died a hero's death. You don't need to tell him about that pesky treason charge."

"David, what are you saying? You sound like you're about to die again."

David shrugged. "Whether they execute me or re-educate me, I'll be dead to everyone anyway. What does it matter? I'm not going to willingly reject Pateras. The person I am right here, right now, will probably never see any of you again."

"Execute? David? You're alive?" Abby's voice came across the transmission. She leaned in over her mother holding a sleeping infant. "What's going on?"

David smiled without thinking at the sight of the baby in Abby's arms. "So, that's Joshua."

Abby went from startled to proud then back to startled in an instant. "Yes, this is your nephew, Joshua Aiden. David, what's going on? Uncle Rob told us you were dead."

David smiled. "It's just a matter of time, Abby. I really didn't want to burden you with grieving twice. This was Supreme Executor Hale's decision. I'm guilty of treason against the Commonwealth, and he's trying to get me to rethink my position. It's not working."

Abby started to rattle off a litany of questions, but the distress in her voice and body woke her sleeping baby. Aiden began to cry loudly. Abby tried unsuccessfully to quiet him. Jessica abruptly asked her to take the baby out of the room. "David, what about Brynna? Have you considered what might happen to her?"

David sighed. "She faces the same things I'm faced with. She chose willingly to follow Pateras, just like I did."

"And the rest of your crew? David, you're responsible for your crew."

"I know, Mom. I'm taking care of my crew in ways you couldn't possibly imagine." David saw his response get a reaction from Executor Hale. "I think our time is up, Mom. Love you." The screen went blank. David looked up at Executor Hale.

"Well, *now* you've done it. You upset my mother *and* my sister. Was that the reaction you were hoping for? I got the distinct impression you were trying to upset *me*."

Executor Hale quietly dismissed the Admiral to return to his interviews. Executor Hale sat down at the opposite end of the table. He stared at David for a long time. David met his gaze with equal voracity. The Executor finally asked, "So, how is this taking care of your crew? You seem awfully self-assured."

David answered without hesitation, "As long as the crew serves Pateras, they are protected from the Day of Reckoning. You know that already. Why ask stupid questions, or are you just testing my knowledge of the Ancient Texts?"

Luciano bolted to his feet. "You are far too cocky for the position you're in. What makes you so sure you're going to make it out of here alive?"

"Pateras makes me sure."

Luciano couldn't argue with his logic. He sat back down slowly and grinned. "Well then, we'll have to at least make your stay as memorable as possible. I noticed the attention you gave to your nephew. This is the first time you've seen him, isn't it?"

"I've seen video of him, but nothing in real time until now."

"Your family are on their way here. I'd hate to see anything happen to such a tiny helpless baby."

David's heart skipped a beat. Fear for his sister and her baby gripped him until he heard a voice inside him whisper. "Your family are my concern, just like your crew."

David closed his eyes and took a deep breath. "You harm any member of my family, and you win nothing. My loyalty to Pateras will reach new heights. You would also risk alienating my uncle. Is the reward worth the risk? Why do you even care about me? I'm one man. Why not stick me in a jail cell and forget about me?"

"Because Pateras has something in mind for you. If I can

turn you or destroy you from the inside, he'll no longer be able to use you. I could stick you in a cell, but Pateras will only get you out." Luciano let David consider the idea for a moment. He waved the guards forward. "Take him back to his cell and soften him up again but see that he stays conscious. I'll have the Doc come by later to give him something for pain. I mean… something to *enhance* his pain."

David gave his tormentor one last cocky smile. "No need to go to all that trouble for me."

Luciano returned an icy stare until David was out of sight. The most powerful man in the Galaxy lost his cool, again. He picked up a nearby vase and smashed it against the door David had just exited. He shouted into the air, "You can't keep him totally protected. I may not be able to touch him, but I'll find a way to get at him. I'll wipe that cocky smile right off his face! He'll be begging to get back in my good graces." There was no response.

• •

Late that evening, Admiral Deacons and Admiral Garcia returned to Executor Hale's borrowed office to report their findings from the interviews. Every member of the crew were firm followers of Pateras. They weren't just following their Captain. Each one would rather die than reject Pateras. As each man reported off on the crew's strengths and weaknesses, Executor Hale sat there sullenly listening. The Admirals finished their reports and waited for their superior to speak. The Executor got up and paced a moment longer. An idea finally hit him. "Gentlemen, did you tell me you authorized a promotion for our Security Chief?"

Admiral Garcia nodded. "Yes sir, he's been promoted to lieutenant junior grade."

"Well, invite LTJG Holden to join us. It's time for him to start earning his new pay grade."

A few minutes later, a guard escorted Mr. Holden into the room. Jake approached the Supreme Executor cautiously and reported as ordered. "I apologize for my appearance and civilian attire, sir. My uniforms are aboard the ship."

"It's perfectly alright, Chief… or rather, Lieutenant. Congratulations on your promotion."

"Thank you, sir. What can I do for you?"

Executor Hale invited Jake to have a seat at the table. "I understand you've been assigned a project to work on while you wait for your wife's release."

"Yes sir. I'm verifying the accuracy of the reports filed by the Captain and crew."

"Well, Mr. Holden, I might need you to put that project on the back burner for a while. I need your assistance. Your Captain gives the impression he's untouchable. I need to hurt him, badly. I don't want to execute him, but I need to shake his foundation. Can you help me do that?"

Jake glanced at the Admirals before answering. The two gave him no clue what he was about to face. "I'll do my best, sir. What do you need from me?"

"I need to know what it would take to rattle him. What are his strengths and weaknesses? What do I hit him with?"

Jake thought for a moment. "If you hurt the crew, you hurt him. I assume you already knew that."

"Yes, we knew that. Pateras has assured the Captain he'll get out of here reasonably unharmed. So, what can I do to him? Admirals feel free to jump in at any time."

Admiral Garcia was losing patience. "Why don't you just execute him and save us all some trouble?"

Executor Hale wasn't about to tell Admiral Garcia Pateras refused to allow it. Supreme Executor Luciano Hale chose to look shocked and hurt. "Edgar, I'm doing whatever I can to preserve the life of Robert's nephew, not to mention the lives of an expertly trained crew. Would you feel this way if it were your family member in question?"

Admiral Garcia glanced at Admiral Deacons, "I'm sorry Robert, Executor Hale. I didn't mean to be so insensitive. He just seems to be a lost cause. I guess I'm just ready to be done with this."

Jake sat there quietly listening to various ideas being tossed about. Suddenly a thought crossed his mind. "Um… Supreme Executor, Admirals, I just had a thought. I don't know if we can make it work or not, but it's worth considering."

The three men turned their attention to the junior officer in the room. Admiral Garcia jumped in impatiently, "Well spit it out, Lieutenant."

Jake nodded and started laying out his idea. "What if we could convince the crew that the Captain and Admiral Deacons conspired to get them arrested?"

The men weren't ready to get on board with the idea. Still impatient, Admiral Garcia asked, "What good is that going to do? They already know you betrayed them."

Admiral Deacons could see the damage it might cause. "How are you proposing to sell that idea?"

"You want to rattle the Captain, convince the crew he betrayed them. He saw how rattled the crew became after our time on Drea. Perhaps he realized they were weak and decided to test them. He purposefully led them astray."

Admiral Garcia interrupted, "Commander Alexander said Arni came to her on Tudoren to tell her the Captain was dead but would live again. How do you explain that?"

Jake looked perplexed. How could he explain that? "Pateras' power is so great, perhaps it warped his mind. He couldn't handle a second exposure. Maybe he saw something so terrifying, it caused him to run away from Pateras."

A smile slowly spread across Executor Hale's face. "That's

brilliant. We can use that."

Edgar and Robert exchanged questioning glances. "We can? How?" Robert asked.

"The Ancient Texts refer to a Day of Reckoning when all debts to Pateras will be settled. Maybe he caught a glimpse of the massive destruction that will happen on that day. Destruction brought on by Pateras, not by the Commonwealth."

Robert swung his chair around to face Jake, "Lieutenant, was the Captain behaving oddly after his second encounter with Pateras? We'll have to have something to hang this on."

Jake thought back to the past two months. "Not particularly, but he did take a backseat to the point of almost being reclusive. He said he was studying the Ancient Texts. That first time he went on a tear like that, he was a mess. He was short-tempered like none of us had ever seen. He even shot me with a Tri-EMP. He later checked himself into the Infirmary with a case of exhaustion and malnourishment."

Admiral Deacons grinned for the first time in days. "He shot you?"

Jake winced at the memory. "I might have deserved it. It – It's possible I disobeyed a direct order."

Admiral Deacons continued grinning. "You *possibly* disobeyed a direct order."

Jake shifted nervously in his seat. He grinned sheepishly, "Is it considered disobeying a direct order if the order was issued by a traitor?"

Admiral Deacons continued to eye the young man with amusement. He enjoyed the thought of his nephew shooting his betrayer.

Admiral Garcia was not as amused. "You're splitting those hairs pretty thin, Mr. Holden."

Executor Hale was motivated. "I *like* the way you split hairs, Lieutenant." The man jumped to his feet and began to pace excitedly. "The Captain didn't have to go off the deep end to sell this. We just have to make them question any little aberration from normalcy. I think we can do this. We need to weaken them a little more before we introduce the idea. Mr. Holden, I'm afraid you're the only one who can sell it, though. It's going to mean you go undercover as a prisoner. Can you handle that?"

Jake felt his anxiety level climbing. He really hated undercover work. "Me? They aren't going to trust my word."

Admiral Garcia began to get on board with the idea. "We would have to get a couple guys to work you over to make it look like you've been treated the same as the others."

Jake gave a wry, "Great. How is this going to work if everyone is being kept isolated? What about Marissa? Does she still think I'm dead?"

Admiral Deacons volunteered, "We'll keep her isolated and give you a cover story to hide her absence."

The four men discussed their options and laid out a course of action. It was starting to sound plausible, even to Jake.

Executor Hale moved excitedly over to Jake's side. "So how about it, Lieutenant? Do you think you can sell it? It's possible we could use the guards to push the idea, but it would be more believable if you did it. You ready to earn your new pay grade?"

"Do I get hazard pay? If they don't buy it, I could get killed by my own shipmates."

Executor Hale laughed and slapped Jake on the back. "I'm sure you can do this, Mr. Holden. You break the Captain and stay in the CIF, and I'll give you your choice of assignments."

Jake wasn't thrilled at the idea, but his choice of any assignment in the galaxy? He couldn't turn that down. "Yes sir. Can I make a suggestion? Since we want to weaken them a little more before totally introducing the idea, have the guards propagate the idea by talking about Commodore Vardin getting transferred and Commodore Alexander taking his place. They can talk about how this guy walks in as a prisoner and now he's about to be running the place."

"Good idea, Mr. Holden. Anything else we need to cover? My administrative assistant is about to have a fit. He thinks the galaxy is about to go belly up if I don't sign off on some documents." Hearing nothing else, Executor Hale returned to his ship to take care of galaxy business. The Admirals went their separate ways.

• •

Admiral Deacons headed for the Infirmary. Jake chased after him. "Admiral, may I ask you a question?"

The sight of the traitor made the Admiral sick. It was getting late, and the Admiral feared his control was nearly gone for the day. If he made one wrong comment, it could prove disastrous. "It's late Mr. Holden, what do you want?"

"Did you have a chance to talk to the doctor about Marissa and the baby?"

"It's where I'm headed now, Chief… uh… Lieutenant. Perhaps you would like to accompany me."

Jake fell into step beside the Admiral. They said nothing until they reached the door of the Infirmary. "Admiral, are you upset with me?"

The Admiral felt all control leaving. Mentally he reached out to shut his own mouth to no avail. He asked for Pateras to guide the ramblings he was about to give way to. "Am I upset with you? What would give you that idea? Would it be because it's late and I'm exhausted? I'm sure that's part of it. Would it have anything to do with you betraying the entire crew of your ship? No, it wouldn't be that! Would it be because I've had to deal with the presence of my boss, my boss's boss, and his boss's boss. You know, the most powerful man in the galaxy? No, that's not it. Would it be because you have forced me to do things I find repulsive by your actions?"

Jake looked stunned. He expected to be applauded for his actions not berated. "I'm sorry, sir. What was I supposed to do?"

"Anything would have been more admirable than what you did. You lied to your shipmates and you betrayed them."

"They committed treason! I stayed true to the Commonwealth, and you're mad at me? I reported them. I did my job!"

The Admiral's sanity slowly began to return. "You're right. They betrayed the Commonwealth. Jake, what you did wrong was you lied to a crew who trusted you. You should have reported them… openly. You make the call, then report to the Captain what you did, or you maroon them on a planet and take the ship. I'm not saying what you did was wrong. I'm saying your method was wrong. When you're in space, you depend on your shipmates to keep you alive. No matter what they do wrong, you don't subvert them! It would have been far more honorable if you had just executed them outright. Before you ask, no, I didn't want you to shoot my nephew. I just expected a Commonwealth soldier to act more honorably. What do you think David would have done if you had gone to him and told him you reported the crew for treason?"

Jake huffed. "He would have thanked me for my honesty."

"So, you're saying he wouldn't have thrown you out the nearest airlock?"

"No, he might have confined me to quarters or even stuck me in a stasis chamber. He wouldn't have harmed me."

The Admiral nodded. He breathed a sigh of relief. His mood was under control once again. The young man was beginning to understand the consequences of his actions and he no longer was worried about the Admiral's foul mood.

Jake looked at the Admiral. "I'm sorry, sir. I won't make the same mistake twice. I'm also sorry for what's happened to the Captain."

The Admiral acknowledged the young man's apology.

"Shall we go talk to the doctor?"

Jake followed the Admiral into the Infirmary. The two sat down in the physician's office to discuss Marissa. The doctor reviewed numerous files before answering their questions. "Gentlemen, I'm afraid any method other than straight up hypnosis is going to put the baby at risk. Hypnosis would only be partially and temporarily effective. It would have to be reinforced regularly and there would be no guarantee she wouldn't manage to circumvent her programming. We could keep her under control here on the base, but I wouldn't trust her to stick with the program. Even if we tried reprogramming without drugs, the stress on the body alone would put the baby at risk. I'm afraid if you want to save the baby, we would have to wait until after the child is born. We could deliver the baby prematurely. I would prefer to wait another four weeks before doing even that. I don't have the equipment for dealing with a baby born this early. There's a facility west of here that could handle it."

A sullen Jake shook his head. "This is not the way I wanted our baby to come into the world."

The Admiral stood up to leave the room. "Doctor, I appreciate your help. Lt. Holden, we need to go. We'll let the Supreme Executor know the situation tomorrow. At least we know what our limitations are."

● ●

The two left the Infirmary and Jake looked like he had lost his best friend. "Lt. Holden, you want to join me in the Officer's Club for a few minutes?"

Jake started to decline, "I can't go in the Officer's Club. I'm not an… wait, I *am* an officer now."

The two sat down in the club which was winding down from the nightly activity. The Admiral ordered a coffee and Jake followed his example. The two talked for the next hour about whatever Jake wanted to talk about. Robert was reminded of some of the talks he and David had, just after his nephew finished the Academy. As Jake's mood lightened, he finished his now cold coffee and expressed his appreciation to the Admiral for listening to him. The young man stood to excuse himself and get some sleep.

The Admiral looked up angrily. "I'm glad you feel better, Mr. Holden. Sit down and listen to me for a little while. Do you want to know what I feel? Do you?"

Jake sat back down slowly. He was both startled and afraid to answer. "Yes sir?"

"David didn't tell you about our family history, did he?" Admiral Deacons watched Jake slowly shake his head. "He probably didn't trust you with that information, and I suppose I shouldn't either. You and I talked about this on Tudoren. Let me tell you a little more about it. My father and mother were Drean citizens. The Commonwealth yanked them off Drea, forced them to work for the Commonwealth by killing my older sister in front of me and David's mother. Do you know why my sister is dead?"

Jake sat there stunned. "You said the Dreans killed her, didn't you?"

"As a boy, I blamed the Dreans. My family served Pateras. The Commonwealth ordered us to reject him or die. My father and mother refused until they watched my sister die in front of them. I stopped trusting Pateras that day. I embraced the Commonwealth because it seemed the safest option. I chose not to have children because I didn't want anyone to EVER have that kind of power over me. You know I sat in a room similar to this one listening to my father tell me he made a mistake by rejecting Pateras. Do you know what I *heard* him say? This isn't what he said, but it's what I *heard*. I heard him tell me I should've died that same day. I was so angry. I went to the Officer's club on Raesii, got drunk, and told everyone who walked in my father wanted me dead and he was praying to an Ancient Deity. My father died in a car accident the next day. His vehicle developed some sort of programming error. I never told my mother I got my own father killed."

"Why are you telling me this, Admiral?"

"I'm telling you this because you can't trust that Pateras will spare the lives of those you love, and you can't trust the Commonwealth to be any better. I denied myself and my wife children and all the joys associated with them, just to see my nephew go through the same things my family went through fifty years ago. Don't be so sure your wife and child are going to make it through this. I hope I'm wrong, but if your wife really has been in the presence of Pateras, I can't see the Supreme Executor letting her live."

"We have an agreement, Admiral. He wouldn't go back on that agreement."

"Are you sure about that, Mr. Holden?

Jake wanted to get up and storm out. His fear, that the Admiral was right, kept him from moving. The waiter came by and refilled their coffee cups leaving them in an awkward silence. Jake pulled his cup close to him and cradled its warmth in his hands. "I'm not sure what you want from me, sir."

The Admiral looked around the room before responding. "I'm not sure I want anything from you. I suppose I just want you to go into these next few days with your eyes wide open. Not everything is as it seems. As a boy, I studied the Ancient Texts. I knew Pateras, and I walked away from him. It's possible, I made a mistake, but now we'll never know."

"Admiral, could you return to the service of Pateras? I mean, would Pateras take you back?"

"The Ancient Texts say he will accept any who ask in earnest. The question is, could I ask in earnest? David said he had blood on his hands. I have a lot more blood on my hands, older blood."

The Admiral got up, took another gulp of his coffee. "The coffee's on me, Mr. Holden. Good night." With that, he was gone.

Jake sat there and nursed the rest of his cup for a few minutes. He took a few more contemplative sips before heading to bed himself. As he walked back to his quarters, he wondered if the Admiral were serving Pateras or not. He hadn't said one way or the other, only that it was possible. The things he had seen the Admiral do the last two days, he couldn't be serving Pateras. Could he? How could he serve Pateras and allow the crew to remain in custody? It just wasn't adding up. Maybe it would make more sense after a good night's sleep. Jake wasn't lucky enough to get a good night's sleep. What little sleep he got was littered with haunting dreams. His lucid moments were filled with worry about Marissa and the baby.

CHAPTER FIVE – DAY THREE

The Captain had little sleep, and morning came far too quickly. The Supreme Executor had been true to his word. The Doc had given him a neural stimulant designed to enhance nerve function. In his case, it caused every pain stimulus to increase exponentially. At least, it felt exponential. He doubted he would survive a medicine as strong as this one felt. The medication wore off around what David guessed was three or four in the morning. The guards roused him shortly after 0600 hours. He caught site of a clock as they dragged him back to the Infirmary. This was going to get old, fast. Getting beaten every night then having his injuries healed every morning. David did his best to be as annoying as possible. "Morning, Doc! I've been looking forward to seeing you this morning. Do you think I could get a breakfast tray while you work on me? Glass of juice maybe?" The doctor returned a scornful glare. David smiled again. "I guess not. You know, you might want to find out the facts before judging me so harshly." David settled in for his daily tissue regeneration, nutritional supplement injection, and rest on a bed more comfortable than the one in his cell. He managed to get another hour's sleep, despite the Doctor's attempts to keep him awake. The guards finally came to escort him out.

As he neared the door, the Doctor finally spoke to him. "You're guilty of treason. That's all I need to know."

David turned as far as the guards would allow. "Really? I must have slept through my trial."

The Doctor watched him go, then stared at the closed door. The man hadn't had a trial. Why not? With the presence of Executor Hale on the base, maybe that wasn't the best question to be asking.

David was planting seeds of doubt whenever he could. He tried to be careful not to react violently, except for the incident with the chair. That wasn't really violent, though. He attacked a desk, not a person. He didn't want to give them any reason to think he was a violent criminal. He figured at this point they all thought he was insane.

The guards met Admiral Garcia on the way back to David's cell. "Escort the prisoner to barracks housing. See that he showers and shaves. I'm having a clean uniform sent for him to wear. Run him by the barber shop to get a haircut too. Oh, and gentlemen, despite his uniform and rank insignia, he's still a prisoner. Don't let your guard down."

David wasn't sure what today's game was all about, but he decided to start playing. "Admiral, surely you don't think I would try to escape. You know I'm not leaving without my crew. Arni told me I was walking into a trap. I came anyway." David grinned smugly.

Admiral Garcia turned three shades of red. "If it weren't for the fact you just came from the Infirmary, I'd deck you here and now." The Admiral looked away for a moment.

David saw it in his eyes. He wasn't going to let it go. To duck or not to duck, that was the question. He decided quickly, DUCK!

The Admiral muttered something profane under his breath and swung at the Captain. David ducked. For once, he stopped someone from hitting him in the mouth. His escort was not so lucky. David's movement pulled the man off balance bringing him into the path of the Admiral's fist. The Admiral clocked him in the chin. The Admiral let out another expletive. He apologized emphatically to the guard. Admiral Garcia instructed the guards to escort David to the barracks as ordered, then once he was secured, get to the Infirmary. He issued one last instruction, "Captain Alexander, you have thirty minutes to shower, shave, and get dressed. If you can't accomplish it on your own, I'll send some men in to *help* you. Are we clear?"

David gave the Admiral another annoying smile. "I think I can handle that, Admiral."

Admiral Garcia made a hasty exit leaving the Captain to follow his orders.

• •

The Captain did exactly as he was told until he got to the uniform over-shirt. All uniforms began with a plain shirt which could be worn in a more casual setting, and trousers. The shirt was a mock turtleneck made of a ribbed fabric. Rank insignia could be placed on the neck in the casual setting although it wasn't present on this occasion. The over-shirt displayed the rank and specialty insignia. David froze when he saw the rank. It was the insignia for a Commodore, a step above his own rank. He wasn't sure he liked the direction this game was going. He wondered how he could sidestep this and what the ultimate goal was? When the guards came for him, he still hadn't put on the over-shirt. Their attempts to force the issue resulted in a stalemate. The guards escorted him roughly to the Supreme Executor's office and carried the shirt with them. The Supreme Executor's eyes followed David and the guards as they entered the room. It was obvious he noticed David's lack of an over-shirt as his eyes landed on it.

Executor Hale motioned the men to place their prisoner in a chair at the conference table, then continued with his business. More guests arrived and quietly took their places at the conference table. David's eyes followed his uncle as he entered with Admiral Garcia. The fear that his uncle might have truly abandoned and betrayed him still haunted him. He couldn't be certain. He wanted to talk to his uncle privately… badly. It pained him to be so unsure.

Moments later Lt. Jake Holden, Commodore Vardin, and the base's Chief Medical Officer, Dr. Grayson Rhodes joined them at the table. Luciano completed his business and dismissed his personal staff. Joining his new entourage at the table he began without hesitation. "Gentlemen, as per our discussion last night, we have decided to add a new aspect to the Captain's developmental plan. Captain would you like to guess what it is?"

David looked at the over-shirt lying on the table in front of him. Despite his nutritional supplements in the Infirmary, he was nearing total exhaustion. He searched his mind frantically for a smart remark. He hoped his catty comments helped hide his poor condition. He didn't want to offer even the smallest satisfaction to his captors. David looked up. The best he could come up with was, "Costume party?"

Executor Hale grinned. Self-satisfaction welled up within him. "Captain, you sound tired. You wouldn't want to reconsider your position in exchange for a good night's sleep, would you?"

David felt a slight surge of energy. "Probably not. I have a job to do, and I have no intention of quitting until it's done." David's eyes landed on Jake who shifted uncomfortably in his seat under the Captain's stare.

A cloud fell over Executor Hale's face. He saw the Captain's eyes focus on Jake. "A job… uh-huh… Dr. Rhodes, as you can see my prisoner is slightly delusional. I'm not concerned with curing his delusions. I do need something to keep him compliant, just for the day. I want him conscious and basically functional, but completely obedient. He needs to be able to walk and talk unassisted."

Still feeling the energy surge, David jumped in, "and dance.

I can't go to a costume party and not dance."

Jake gave the Captain a bewildered stare. Why was the Captain acting like this? David met Jake's gaze again. Jake sensed there was an indiscernible message in the Captain's gaze. He hated seeing him like this. He knew the humor must be an attempt to hide pain.

Dr. Rhodes perused a list of medications on his data pad. "I believe I can create the perfect cocktail for you, sir. How long do you want it to work? I can create a formula that works for anything from ten minutes to twenty-four hours."

"Prepare several two-hour doses. I don't want the Captain to be gone for too long. As the man said, he has a job to do." The Executor's tone was cold and harsh. "How long will it take for you to prepare the cocktail and how quickly will it take effect?"

"It will take about ten to fifteen minutes to prepare it, and once injected, he'll be quite docile within two to three minutes."

"Perfect. Get on that as soon as we're done here. My next question is also for you, Dr. Rhodes. Mr. Holden's wife, what can we do about her re-education?"

Dr. Rhodes frowned. "The doctor on duty last night left a log notation that he discussed it with Admiral Deacons and Lt. Jake Holden late yesterday. His conclusion was formal re-education would not be feasible until after the baby delivered. The baby could be delivered now if she were transferred to a more appropriate facility. We don't have the equipment to deal with it here. He also informed them, we could deal with it here, if we waited a few more weeks. The only other alternatives are re-educating her slowly and take chances with losing the baby or just wait until the baby is born at term and re-educate afterwards."

Executor Hale glanced at Jake and Robert. "Why were you discussing this with the physician last night?"

Fearing they had done something wrong, Jake turned his gaze to Admiral Deacons. Robert gladly accepted the responsibility. "The Lieutenant asked me about this a day or two ago, but I hadn't had time to pursue it until last night. I transferred his wife to a regular holding cell yesterday to begin the re-education process, although I was unsure how safe it would be for the baby. So far all we've done is isolate her, begin identity degradation, and repetitive indoctrination. She's the only one receiving meals although they're only emergency rations."

Executor Hale nodded thoughtfully. "I see. I trust there are no foreseeable problems with using compliance enhancing medications on the others?"

"No sir, no problems barring an unknown medication allergy. When did you plan on starting those?"

"Either tomorrow or the next day at the latest. Is there anything else you need to add, Doctor?"

"Yes sir. For the dose to be effective, I need to have extra staff available to monitor each one carefully. If the dose is too strong, they'll mentally just shut down or fall asleep. If it isn't strong enough, they'll be able to maintain enough control to fight back against the programming. I would like at least a twenty-four-hour notice to be ready for this. If it were only two or three patients, I could handle it alone. Starting on so many patients, all at once, would be difficult."

Luciano didn't blink. "Consider this your twenty-four-hour notice. Get the Captain's cocktail ready then start your preparations for the crew. I suppose if I decide to wait the extra day, it won't cause any problems?"

"No sir, I can work with that. Will that be all, sir?"

"I will have one more issue to discuss with you later. Go ahead and start your preparations. The rest can wait."

Dr. Rhodes left the meeting and started working. He got his medications mixed then started scheduling extra personnel for the next few days. He ordered his staff to prepare the monitoring equipment and medication dosages based on the crew's weights.

Since David's daily trip to the Infirmary took care of his aches and pains from his nightly beatings, the comfortable air temp and softness of the chair compounded his drowsiness. He knew he needed to pay attention to gather whatever information he could. He wanted to lean his head back on the back of his chair and sleep so badly. Knowing Pateras would hears his thoughts, he called out to him mentally. "Pateras, I'm tired. I need sleep. Help me stay awake and alert." Pateras said nothing.

"Well, Captain, I suppose you're wondering what my plan is for you today."

"The question had crossed my mind." David replied blandly.

"You seem to have an agenda. I'm putting an end to your agenda. Today, you become the traitor instead of Mr. Holden. Your crew are going to be led to believe, you betrayed them. Two of your crew will see you appearing to move about freely." Executor Hale watched for David's reaction.

The fog in his mind still slowed his reactions. "Good luck with that. My crew followed me even before they were willing to follow Pateras." Then it dawned on him. Executor Hale hoped the crew would think he abandoned Pateras and continue to follow his lead. David felt his spirit sink within him. If the crew were suffering the same sleep deprivation, physical and mental abuse he had been suffering, they might just believe the lie.

Executor Hale's smug smile reappeared when he saw the pain in David's eyes. Admiral Deacons avoided looking at anyone just now. Executor Hale turned back to Jake, "Mr. Holden, which two crew members should we let see the Captain?"

Jake scowled as he considered the question. "If they could be convinced, the Doc, Lt. Flint, or even the Commander would be the most influential. They would also be the hardest to convince. They know the Captain's behavioral patterns the best and if he isn't acting like himself, they'll be the first to see it. Lt. Commander Dominick is an engineer and not a people person. He's influential among the crew because of his rank. The other possibilities are Lt. or Ensign Ryder."

"What about Ensign Dominick? She seems fragile."

"Don't let her frailty fool you. She has a degree in sociology and might realize the Captain's been drugged. She's stronger than she appears. If you can convince her, it would probably break her spirit. I'm just not sure you'll convince her."

David flexed against the binders securing his wrists. He wanted very much to put a stop to what was happening to himself and his crew. Anger began to well up within him. Surely the crew would see through this ruse. What if it put doubt into their tired minds? David cast one more pleading look at Jake who looked away. When Jake avoided his gaze, David knew his former security chief was going to offer no hope. David looked down at the over-shirt on the table. He was too tired to think anymore. He simply stared at it.

The Supreme Executor watched the exchange between the two men curiously. Robert watched David as well. He knew David was strong, but the Supreme Executor seemed to be pressing all the right buttons to hurt his nephew in the worst possible ways. Robert hated seeing his nephew hurt like this. He decided he would take matters into his own hands. If he couldn't find a way to rescue his nephew, he would execute him with or without the Executor's blessing. He hoped Pateras would forgive him. He also hoped Jessica would understand. It would be the most merciful thing he could do. He might suffer some harsh wrath himself. He was ready to deal with it.

Executor Hale set up two scenarios to put David on display. He decided Lt. Commander Dominick and Ensign Dominick were the two he wanted to use. His reasoning was not what anyone expected. Luciano suggested having someone being supportive of the Captain might strengthen the supposition, especially since it pitted husband against wife. He sent Admiral Deacons and Admiral Garcia to get them organized. He asked Commodore Vardin to locate an attractive young woman to adorn the Captain's arm. Commodore Vardin didn't have far to go. One of his own staff came to mind immediately. He left to track her down and offer her the assignment of entertaining the handsome young Captain for a couple hours.

Aside from the security guards, Jake was now alone with the Supreme Executor and the Captain. Jake was getting used to being in the presence of the most powerful man alive, however being alone with him brought on a new wave of nervousness. "D – Did you have something else for me, sir? I thought I could get in a little more work on editing those reports. I should be able to get in several hours work before rejoining the crew."

The Supreme Executor sighed. "There's one thing I'm concerned about, Lieutenant."

"What is it, sir?"

"I'm sure you know I can't particularly trust what the Captain says."

"Yes sir, I understand that."

"He said one thing, I do believe. When he said; he had a job to do, he looked at you, Lieutenant."

Jake glanced over at the Captain who was once again paying attention. "Me? I'm not sure I'm following."

"I have reason to believe, the Captain's so-called *job*, is to recruit you, Mr. Holden." Executor Hale put on his most serious and concerned face.

Jake glanced nervously at the Captain. Was the Supreme Executor accusing him of something? "Recruit me? That's not going to happen. Supreme Executor, I can assure you my loyalty lies with the Commonwealth. Have I done something to cause you to doubt me? What can I…"

The Executor leaned over and placed a reassuring hand on Jake's shoulder. "Relax, Mr. Holden, I trust you. What concerns me is the Captain is holding out hope and it seems to be aimed at you. I need you to do everything in your power to destroy that hope he's carrying around."

Jake looked over at the Captain. Something in the Captain's face told him the Supreme Executor was right. He looked back at Executor Hale. "What do you want me to do?"

Executor Hale squeezed Jake's shoulder firmly. "Do whatever *you* think it will take to convince him where your loyalties lie and crush that hope he's carrying. His re-education won't progress if he has something to hold onto. Find a way to make your point before rejoining the crew. Can you handle this assignment?"

"Yes sir. Anything for the good of the Commonwealth." Jake gave the Captain a wary look. He wasn't entirely sure what this assignment would entail, although it did sound unpleasant.

• •

Over the course of the next hour, everyone who had left the conference table began to return. The Admirals reported placing the two desired prisoners in separate observation rooms strapped into the training station. The couple were given stimulants to keep them awake along with a mild drug to make them suggestible without putting them to sleep. Their heads were strapped into position, preventing them from looking away and a small device kept their eyes in an open position. Their senses were assaulted with indoctrination feeds disparaging Pateras and praising the Commonwealth and its Supreme Executor.

The doctor returned with his cocktail for the Captain. He explained the delicate balance of medications to the assembled group. "I have included a drug to relax the Captain. He will seem at ease. The medication will make him completely suggestible. He won't do anything except what he's told although he'll be enthusiastic about whatever we tell him to do."

Executor Hale smiled. "Are we ready to proceed?" He scanned everyone at the table for problems or questions. Jake looked apprehensive, but eager. Admiral Garcia and Commodore Vardin exuded sadistic glee. Admiral Deacons face was cold, hard, and emotionless. Executor Hale expected his reaction and fully understood it. Dr. Rhodes was simply conducting business.

The young woman, Heather Shields, recruited by Commodore Vardin was a new addition to the meeting. She looked almost terrified. She was excited at the prospect of helping the Supreme Executor of the Commonwealth. Her case of nerves surfaced when she found out she was expected to flirt with a dangerous criminal accused of treason.

Seeing her fear, Executor Hale decided he better address it before moving forward. "Miss Shields, are you alright with this?" Her discomfort was obvious. Executor Hale didn't give her the opportunity to respond before continuing. "Miss Shields, I can assure you this man will not harm you in any way. His crimes were not violent. His crimes resulted from an opposing ideology. He could even be called a complete gentleman. As a precaution, he's wearing a behavioral modification collar. If he gets out of line at all, I will bring him instantly to his knees."

The young woman nodded nervously, "Y – Yes sir."

Executor Hale could see she wasn't entirely convinced. He waved at the Captain, "You can see the Captain is a handsome man, surely this won't be a terribly unpleasant experience. The drugs the doctor is about to give him will make him very suggestible. I don't expect excessive displays of affection, although you might get a decent back rub out of him. I expect you two to flirt with each other as though you are about to go out on a first date. If the Captain can be re-educated and you find you enjoy his company, there's every chance you could win him over for a longer time, if you so desire. This should be an easy and pleasurable assignment."

The woman glanced at the Captain. David locked his eyes on hers. In his attempts to thwart the Supreme Executor, his first inclination was to threaten to choke the life out of the young woman, a threat he had no intention of carrying out. He knew she was frightened and a threat of that nature would likely push her over the edge. David decided the Supreme Executor would continue with or without the girl. He decided to put the girl at ease. "I have no intentions of hurting you or trying to escape. I'm sorry for whatever they force me to do and for your discomfort."

The woman's eyes grew wide. Something certainly wasn't adding up. She was expected to cozy up to a hardened criminal… why? She decided to address her questions. "S – Sir, I'm not sure what the goal is here."

Executor Hale smiled warmly at the young woman. "I want the other prisoners to give up on the hope their beloved Captain is coming to their rescue. I need to discredit him in their eyes. They need to view him as a traitor to *their* cause. This will strengthen the Commonwealth's position. Your contribution to the Commonwealth would be extremely valuable. I'm not asking you to sleep with him, just make it look like you *might*. Can you handle this?"

Heather glanced at the Captain. He *was* an attractive man. His apology and assurance, that he had no intentions of harming her, had a surprisingly profound impact on her. Something in her trusted him. She gave the Executor a small smile. "I think so, sir."

Executor Hale took it as a complete victory and moved on. "Great! Let's get started. Guards, make sure the Captain can't resist. Dr. Rhodes, give him his injection."

David resisted the urge to resist. His fight or flight instincts kicked in. Despite his efforts, he found himself stiffening when the guards approached him. The guards roughly forced his head and torso down on the table. The doctor moved in behind the guards and pressed the hypo-spray against David's neck. A silence filled the room permeated only by the hiss of the pressurized hypo-spray forcing the medication into the Captain's tissues. The doctor stepped back and watched David's reaction visually and on a scanner. The guards felt him relax. The two released their grip on him slowly, half expecting him to jump them at any moment. In a minute, the doctor spoke to David. "Captain Alexander, could you sit up in your chair please?"

David began to feel like he was watching somebody else. His body complied with the instruction. His brain felt disconnected and crowded as though someone or something had shoved him into a dark corner. A numbness seemed to set in. He heard the doctor speak again. "Captain, how do you feel? You seem like you're in a great mood today. You've been laughing, talking, and joking with everyone. Are you in a good mood?"

The Captain heard a voice answer, "Oh, yeah. I'm having a wonderful day." It was his own voice. Why couldn't he silence his own voice? The drug… yes, that was it. The drug was too powerful. He couldn't fight it.

Another voice spoke, in his head. "You can fight it. Wait for the right time." Everything was so foggy, he would wait as instructed. Fighting was just too hard right now.

"Captain, I have good news for you."

"Really?"

The doctor continued testing his subject. "Your promotion just came through. You are now a commodore."

"It did? I don't remember putting in the request for a promotion."

Executor Hale gave the doctor a concerned look. Dr. Rhodes gave the Executor a slight shake of his head. "The drug acts slightly like a truth serum. We just have to provide the appropriate guides and covers. Commodore Alexander, you're right. You didn't put in for the promotion. Admiral Deacons put it in for you. Your tunic is on the table in front of you. Don't you want to put it on?"

"Absolutely. I don't want to get caught *out of uniform*." David smiled then tried to reach for it only to find he was wearing binders. His smile faded. "Okay, who's the wise guy? Why am I wearing binders?"

The doctor nodded to the guards to remove the binders. The guards complied but stayed close in case the Captain's dosage wasn't strong enough. With the binders off, David enthusiastically put the tunic on and proudly displayed his new rank to everyone in the room.

Following the doctor's example, Executor Hale continued to guide the Captain. "Congratulations, Commodore Alexander. I understand you've been through a challenging time recently, your entire crew committing treason and trying to kill you. I understand you've suffered some amnesia resulting from that attempt."

David's smile faded. "I guess I – I don't remember. What happened to me?"

Admiral Deacons picked up the tale. "When you turned the crew in at the shuttle port, they used a Tri-EMP on you. The charge was very high. You almost died."

His brain was processing slowly. He searched his memory then smiled. "Oh, yes, I think I do remember that day. It is a little fuzzy though."

Executor Hale got up and moved around near David. He spoke in a soft tone. "Listen, Commodore, your marriage annulment went through as well. I have it on good authority the young lady across the table finds you very attractive. Would you like me to introduce you to her? Perhaps the two of you could go out to dinner tonight, my treat."

A piece of David's brain balked. This wasn't Brynna. Where was Brynna? His marriage was annulled? Wait, she was a traitor? "I'm not sure. Isn't it a little too soon after the divorce?"

"No, Commodore, you need to get out there again. An unscheduled marriage dissolution can be quite painful. The best way to get over it is to start dating again. You will be a complete gentleman with the young lady, won't you? She's very intimidated by your rank."

David hesitated again, and Luciano added one more boost. "I would consider it a personal favor."

"Sure, okay. Make the introductions."

Luciano waved the woman over. As Heather got up and moved around the table. Luciano leaned over and whispered to David. "She's one fine looking woman, isn't she? I bet you'll have trouble keeping your hands off her won't you."

David looked the woman over and smiled at Executor Hale. "Absolutely."

Executor Hale smiled at David's response. "Be warm, friendly, cozy even, just don't move *too* fast." Executor Hale stood upright and turned to introduce Heather to David. David stood up for a proper greeting. The security guards tensed again. Executor Hale scowled. "Gentlemen, return to your posts by the door."

David looked at the guards and their proximity to him. Why were they so close? The fog neglected to allow any clear answers through. He remembered his head being down on the table. He glanced at the doctor and Executor Hale. "Did I pass out?"

Executor Hale gave the doctor a look of concern. Dr. Rhodes quickly filled in the gaps, "I'm afraid you're still suffering from the side effects of your injury. You should be good as new in a few days. I do suggest you hire a car for your date tonight instead of driving yourself."

David smiled enthusiastically, "Good idea. I'll do that."

Executor Hale moved on quickly knowing he only had two hours before the medications wore off. "Commodore David Alexander, I would like to introduce you to Miss Heather Shields. Heather, this is David. Heather is a civilian employee here on the base."

Heather gave David an anxious smile, "Commodore, it's a pleasure to meet you."

In his suggestible state, the Captain behaved in a most charming manner. He offered his hand to shake hers. When she reached out to shake his hand, David took her hand. Leaning forward he raised her hand to his lips and kissed it. In her skittish state, a flustered giggle escaped her lips.

David smiled warmly. "The pleasure is mine, Heather. Please call me, David." He wasn't quick to release her hand. David admired the pretty young woman in front him. Looking at her blond hair, he kept thinking she might look better as a brunette. No, something wasn't right with that idea. She was pretty just the way she was.

David offered her the empty chair next to him. Heather sat down, still smiling. A two-hour assignment with a drugged up, nonviolent, good-looking criminal wearing a behavior modification collar, on a secure military base, maybe this assignment wouldn't be so bad after all. He was interesting.

Executor Hale and the doctor returned to their seats. "Commodore, I'd like you to observe a couple of the prisoners during their re-education. I want them to see you as well. It will give us an idea how they are progressing. It's up to you if you interact with them. I would just ask you not to give them any reason to think you might have pity on them. Right now, they are your enemy. Treat them as such. Miss Shields can accompany us. Perhaps she will provide a pleasant distraction for an unpleasant task."

David looked over at Heather and smiled. "Would it be too much of an imposition?"

Heather smiled back at him. Heather was a liaison from the governor's office to Admiral Vardin. She was accustomed to smiling even if she didn't feel like it. This situation was very different. She knew about re-education techniques, although she had never seen them in action. She hoped it wouldn't be too frightening. "It's not the kind of setting a girl expects for a first date, but I'm willing to give it a go. I'm just excited at the prospect of spending time with you, Commodore." She grinned like a school girl with a crush.

David reached over and squeezed her hand. A voice, his own voice, cried out when he reached out and touched the young woman. His eyes grew distant for a moment and the memory of the Executor telling him he was no longer married to Brynna offered a small amount of solace.

● ●

Executor Hale got up and led the group, except for Jake, out of the office. Commodore Vardin took the group to the detention facilities. The two prisoners were in separate rooms. The group entered the observation area which was more of a wide external hallway extending down three of the four sides of the internal training room. The area was cordoned off by glass walls capable of being one-way or two-way glass. The glass was currently two-way. As soon as they entered the dimly lit external walkway, Heather grabbed David's hand. Seeing her anxiety David pulled her close to him. He wrapped his arm around her waist. His programming was kicking in. Cozy, he had been told to be a gentleman, and be cozy. This felt cozy.

Heather put her arm around him in turn. She looked up into David's eyes and smiled. David smiled back at her and gave her a gentle squeeze. Yes, this was not a bad assignment at all.

Maybe there were future possibilities here.

Commodore Vardin led the entourage through their tour. The group proceeded slowly up the first side across the back of the room to the far corridor. A technician sat at a control panel wearing a dark visor and a headset. He was monitoring the prisoner's vital signs, stress levels, and brain waves. Seeing the substantial number of high ranking officials entering, he lowered the intensity levels of the programming by fifty percent. Once the levels were lower, he was more comfortable standing up and snapping to attention. Commodore Vardin took the initiative, "As you were, Chief." The man returned to his duties. With visitors not wearing protective gear, he didn't bring the intensity back up just yet. Commodore Vardin began to explain the process to his guests. "As you can see prisoner number 7141 is restrained. He's been given medications to keep his mind suggestible and compliant. The technician monitors the prisoner's physical and mental status. He floods the prisoner's mind with a careful balance of gamma and beta waves to keep him awake, alert, and able to take in the indoctrination information as effectively as possible. The subject's eyes are kept open by a small device that periodically sprays a saline mist into the eyes to avoid damage to them since blinking is not possible."

The Commodore's voice droned on. His words were not penetrating the fog in David's brain. He stared at the prisoner in the center of the room. The man was familiar. Lt. Commander… Dominick, yes that was the man's name. He's a prisoner, a traitor to the Commonwealth, my enemy. David wondered why the man would commit treason. He just didn't seem like the type to do that. Someone spoke to him. David forced himself to face whoever just spoke. "I'm sorry, sir. What did you say?"

Executor Hale repeated his question. "What are you thinking, Commodore?"

"The prisoner was a good officer. Why would he commit

treason?"

Executor Hale glanced at the prisoner. The prisoner didn't appear to have noticed the Captain. "Why don't we go ask him? Chief, suspend the program."

The chief's headset filtered out external noise. Commodore Vardin tapped the man on the shoulder to get his attention. The man looked up to see Commodore Vardin point to the prisoner and make the sign for "cut it off." The man shut down the program then removed his own protective gear. "The Supreme Executor and the Cap – uh Commodore, would like to speak to the prisoner."

The Chief replied, "Yes sir." He reached down and pressed a button opening a door to access the inner room. He pressed another panel which released the head and eye restraints.

As the restraints released, Lazaro visibly relaxed. He immediately closed his eyes. David slipped back to holding Heather's hand. He started to leave her behind in the observation room. Knowing what the Supreme Executor wanted from her, she grabbed tightly onto David's hand. David stopped to look at her face. Seeing her intention was to stay with him, he led her into the inner room. Executor Hale nodded for David to proceed.

David extricated his hand from his attractive escort. He stepped up beside Lazaro's head. He glanced at the display to see the identification code. "Prisoner number 7141, open your eyes."

Lazaro's eyes rolled back and forth under the lids as he attempted to comply with his orders. He took a deep breath and forced a small crack in his lids. He blinked heavily a couple times then pushed them further open. His head rolled back and forth. He still couldn't pull himself together. He mumbled something unintelligible.

Executor Hale stepped forward. "Perhaps you need to be more aggressive to get his attention."

David reached over and slapped Lazaro's cheeks roughly. "Wake up prisoner! No one gave you permission to sleep. Open your eyes and look at me!"

It suddenly clicked in Lazaro's mind whose voice he was hearing. He pushed harder to get his eyes open. His eyes were still not seeing clearly, somehow, he finally forced them to focus on the Captain's face. He blinked several times. Lazaro's dry mouth produced a vicious cough when he tried to speak. David looked around. Spotting a pitcher of water and cups sitting nearby, he poured a small amount and offered it to his former crewman. Lazaro drank as much and as quickly as he could. He coughed and sputtered another time or two then spoke. "C – Captain, are you okay? Can we go home now?" His words were slurred.

David ignored the question. "It's Commodore Alexander, not Captain. Prisoner 7141, can you explain to me why you committed treason against the Commonwealth?"

Lazaro stared at David and tried to make sense out of the situation. He slowly shook his head. He didn't understand what was wrong with the Captain. He finally managed a response. "You – You know why." His eyes landed on Luciano Hale. "He's a murderer. He killed in – innocent civilians. He d – destroyed Galat."

David looked over his shoulder at the Supreme Executor, he was willing to believe anything. His mind started to head down the trail indicated by Lt. Commander Dominick. Executor Hale shook his head. "It appears he hasn't made much progress. I did send the Pacification Fleet to destroy the home base of Arni Liontari and yes, I'm sure innocent civilians died. He's twisting the facts. I would never attack a civilian population. I'm an honorable man."

David left the previous train of thought and now followed this one. He looked at Lazaro again. The voice inside his head

screamed to get out again. One sentence escaped the fog. "He's
l – lying." David couldn't make sense of his own utterance. He
was looking at Lazaro when he said it, but it didn't apply to
Lazaro. Who did it apply to?

David turned to leave. He reached over and took Heather's hand. Lazaro's eyes followed David. "Captain! What's wrong
with you? He's the one lying. He's not an honorable man. He's
not even human."

Heather gave Lazaro a bewildered stare.

Executor Hale shook his head. "Poor man is delusional.
That happens sometimes. Perhaps we should go."

David placed his arm around Heather's waist again to escort her out of the room. The Supreme Executor watched Lazaro carefully. Lazaro saw David leave without looking back.

As soon as the two cleared the room Executor Hale leaned
over Lazaro and pressed the knuckles of his fist firmly into the
man's rib cage. "You might want to keep that part to yourself
about my background. It could prove extra painful if you repeat it to anyone else." Lazaro groaned and twisted against his
restraints in vain. Luciano pulled his hand back and joined the
others in the observation corridor.

Lazaro watched as his Captain continued to walk away.
He strained against his bonds once more. He began to wonder
about his decision. Had he made a mistake? No, the Captain
had been right. Pateras cared about humanity, Luciano Hale
didn't. Lazaro looked into the realm of Pateras. "Pateras, help
us, please. Help the Captain."

• •

The tour moved on to the second prisoner's training room.
The group walked in and moved to the control panel. David
brazenly stepped over and instructed the technician to suspend
the training program. The technician glanced at Commodore
Vardin who nodded his approval. David walked into the train-

ing room. Heather sensed he would again offer the prisoner a glass of water. She went for it first and handed it to him when he was ready. David smiled appreciatively at the attractive young woman.

Glass in hand, David turned his attention to the female prisoner in front of him. Like Lt. Commander Dominick, this prisoner was in a semi-reclined chair and strapped down. The chair was designed to restrain prisoners through interrogation, re-education, or even torture and execution. David stepped over to the female prisoner. Cheyenne had also shut her eyes the second she had the chance. "Prisoner 7148, I have a drink of water for you."

Cheyenne blinked heavily several times as she tried to keep her eyes open. Her eyes focused first on Executor Hale's face. Seeing him so close rattled her. She squirmed in her seat and strained against her restraints. David spoke again, "Prisoner 7148, take a drink. It'll help."

Cheyenne's eyes moved from Executor Hale, to Heather, then to the Captain. Seeing he was the one offering the water she took several large swallows. She drank too fast and got choked. David pulled the glass back, allowed her to recover, then offered another drink. Cheyenne took another couple of careful swallows then looked up at the Captain. She wasn't sure what to make of the situation. She wondered why the Captain was in the company of the Supreme Executor. Her eyes fell on his rank insignia. She looked back into David's eyes. There was something hollow and empty about them. Her eyes went immediately back to their nemesis. "What have you done to him?" Cheyenne demanded.

The Captain handed the glass back to Heather. "Prisoner 7148, I am asking the questions here not you. I can make all this end for you if you would consider rejoining the Commonwealth. Pateras can't help you here."

Cheyenne shook her head at him. "Captain, please tell me you're still in there somewhere."

David tapped his rank. "It's Commodore Alexander, Prisoner."

Cheyenne glared at the man addressing her. "I'm not talking to you. I'm talking to Captain Alexander. I know he's still in there somewhere. Captain, please tell me you're okay."

"Why did you abandon the Commonwealth, Prisoner 7148?" David stayed the course of his programming.

Cheyenne was very tired and needed rest badly. Her mind still followed a natural progression. "Why did you?"

"I ask the questions. Answer me, Prisoner. You had a promising career ahead of you and you threw it all away. Why?"

Cheyenne steadied herself. "I did it for the same reasons you did. Why did you abandon the Commonwealth?"

Executor Hale stepped closer to intervene. He knew David's programming was shallow and short-lived. "Your Captain never abandoned the Commonwealth. He learned early on the crew was weak. He just didn't realize *how* weak until he provided the vehicle necessary for all of you to reveal your true natures. Your Captain was outnumbered, so he did the only thing he could. He turned you in."

Cheyenne looked for a moment as though she had been punched in the stomach. Caught in a horrified stare at the Supreme Executor, Cheyenne had to force her eyes to look away from him.

The Captain turned towards Luciano while he spoke. He brought his gaze slowly back to Cheyenne. "Tell me your reasons for your treason, Prisoner."

Cheyenne set her jaw stubbornly. "I'll tell you my reasons if you tell me what my name is."

"Prisoner 7148," David responded flatly.

"No! Say my name and I'll answer your question."

David stared at her with his hollow eyes. "You no longer have a name. You are prisoner 7148… unless you choose to reject Pateras and rejoin the Commonwealth."

Cheyenne's eyes teared up from sorrow as she heard his words. "Then you'll get no answer from me."

David shook his head. "We should let them resume the reprogramming. They aren't ready to give up yet. I'm sorry I couldn't be of more help, Supreme Executor."

Executor Hale sighed. "Well, it's a little early to expect much progress. So where are you going to take Heather on your date tonight?"

Sensing their business was complete, Heather slid back up under David's arm, wrapping her own around his waist. David's sleeve brushed against Cheyenne's hand. Instinctively, she grabbed it. "Captain, please don't do this."

David stopped. His eyes landed on his sleeve caught in her hand then worked their way up to her face again. The voice of David's own persona cried out. This time it escaped his lips. Looking at the tears running down her face, his voice quietly broke through the fog, "no… satisfaction."

Cheyenne began to cry outright. Executor Hale and Admiral Garcia incorrectly identified her tears as tears of sorrow. Admiral Deacons remembered David's message of "no satisfaction" given to Cheyenne the day they were arrested. Robert had taken care to stay out of Cheyenne's sight to avoid being compromised. As the elite group began their egress, Robert's eyes locked on Cheyenne's. He gave her a curt nod. Her tears were tears of joy and relief.

• •

The group returned to the Supreme Executor's office. Jake was no longer in the office. He had returned to his quarters to work on the report corrections as requested by Admiral Garcia.

Executor Hale dismissed Heather to return to her duties

and thanked her cordially for her help. He assured her there would be a sizable bonus in her next stipend. Luciano followed David's example and tenderly kissed the young woman's hand. Heather blushed. She was an attractive woman and as such was accustomed to male attention, but never so much by so many high-ranking individuals. Heather thanked Executor Hale. Before she departed she asked for one favor. "Sir, if he is properly re-educated, I might be interested in pursuing a relationship with him. Call me anytime if you need to."

Executor Hale smiled. "I may have one other small job for you, if you're interested."

Executor Hale escorted Heather out of the room to speak to her privately. He carefully revealed his plan, "As part of his re-education, I need to destroy him completely. Please don't misunderstand what I'm asking and feel free to decline. I would like you to get him into a compromising situation. He's drugged right now. I can program him to behave himself or render him completely unconscious. I would like him to wake up with you in bed with him. I'm not asking for you to be intimate with him, just make him *think* you were. I'll have guards close by monitoring the situation, so things don't get out of hand. I can also assure you they won't be watching directly."

Heather's heart began to beat faster and stronger. She wasn't sure how to react to this request. The Captain was a very good-looking man. He was still a stranger and a criminal. This was also a request from the most important and powerful man in the galaxy. "H – How will they be watching?"

"I'll arrange for you to stay in the guest barracks and turn all computer terminals except for the bedroom to monitor mode. If you make even one cry for help, the guards will be there in seconds. I seriously doubt he'll do anything inappropriate. He'll be too angry with himself."

Heather shifted back and forth nervously. "Wh – When do

you need an answer?"

Executor Hale clasped his hands behind his back, turned around, and walked away from her for a moment. He wanted to give her a moment to consider her options without his watchful eye. He presented the appearance of considering his own options. Luciano heard her breathing relax. When he heard her take a deep breath, he turned around slowly and moved back to her side. "Miss Shields, I don't want to put undue pressure on you, but I'm seriously pressed for time. I would like to get this done in the next few hours. I can give you up to one hour to give me an answer."

Heather's skepticism displayed on her face. "Supreme Executor, I don't think…"

Before she could finish, Executor Hale added. "Do you remember the bonus on your stipend I mentioned?"

"Uh… yes, sir."

"The bonus for what you have already done is two hundred credits. I know what I'm asking is a great deal more difficult. I would gladly give you an additional two thousand credits for this job. Please, please, don't think I am disrespecting you in any way. You seemed to have an interest in the Captain, and this will work towards breaking down his mind and putting him back on the right path. I could hire a – uh – professional, but I would rather have you do this. You understand the value of discretion. If you are afraid your reputation will suffer, I can also offer you the chance to move into a new position wherever you'd like, even on my staff if you're interested."

Heather began to feel intensely pressured. Her thoughts raced, two thousand credits and a new job anywhere she wanted. The Captain's handsome face popped into her mind again. One nagging thought kept pulling at her. This was a *cheap* way to get paid and move up in the galaxy. Another voice in her head rebutted, if the Supreme Executor wants this, it must be alright.

The Supreme Executor cares about people. He's a good man. The Captain also seemed like a good man. Was this really fair to him? He's a traitor. Exactly what kind of fairness did he deserve? "Executor Hale, I need to consider your offer for a few minutes if you don't mind. I'll have your answer shortly."

"Of course. I will await your response." Executor Hale gave the young woman a slight bow and watched her walk away. Staring at the back of her head, he whispered a suggestion into her mind, "He'll never remember. What's it going to hurt?" Luciano smiled when Heather stopped walking. He stepped over to the receptionist's desk.

Before he could address the receptionist, Heather interrupted him, "Excuse me, Supreme Executor, may I ask you another question?"

Luciano took the young woman's elbow and escorted her away from the desk. "Of course, what is it?"

"Will he remember anything?"

"I can arrange for him to remember as little or as much as you desire. I can even create the false memory of your choice, such as a pleasant dinner date and a tearful good-bye. You can include a promise to stay in touch if you wish. We've got time to work out the details, his retraining will take several weeks. You'll have time to consider your job options while he's being retrained." Executor Hale stopped speaking to watch her reaction. He was very good at reading faces and body language. He couldn't read her thoughts, but he was very good at making suggestions. One hint of doubt on her face and he was prepared to flood her mind with convincing thoughts and images. Anxiety continued to cloud her face. "You seem to have more questions. I want you to be as informed as possible. Ask me whatever you like."

"It's not exactly a question. I just don't want you to think badly of me. I'm not a loose woman. I don't want to get ahead by unscrupulous means."

The Executor's face fell. He began to fidget. "Miss Shields, I apologize. I never meant to suggest such a thing. This – uh assignment is an intelligence type of assignment. I suppose I should have brought in an operative who was trained for this. I did not mean to insult your reputation. As I said, you are quite free to refuse my request." The Executor looked away nervously giving his words time to sink in. He stroked his chin thought-fully. "I'm just in a bind. I need someone I can trust, and it must be today. I don't want to delay his re-education. I'm going to tell you something I probably shouldn't. This is classified informa-tion, if you discuss it with anyone, you could be charged with treason. Do you understand, Miss Shields?"

"Y-Yes sir."

"Miss Shields, the Commonwealth is on the brink of war with a new enemy. The Captain and his crew have been compro-mised against their wills. I can save them and bring them back to our side, but I need help. I put a lot into training this crew and it hurts me to see what's happened to them. The Captain is Admiral Deacons' nephew. I want to do everything I can to save him. Unfortunately, I will have to put him through some rather uncomfortable processes to do that. To achieve my goals, I need soldiers and intelligence operatives who are willing to put their lives, their reputations, everything they are, on the line. In order to bring them back into the Commonwealth, I must break their personalities down from the inside out. This enemy is insidious. This job isn't simply an attempt to discredit him or ruin his rep-utation. This goes much deeper. This enemy calls for complete voluntary celibacy from his followers. If he believes he's broken his vow, it will open the door for us to loosen the grip the enemy has on him. He will begin to doubt himself." Luciano laid his lies down thicker and thicker. He knew soon she would be begging to volunteer.

The Supreme Executor's words buzzed in Heather's mind. It was a lot to take in. Certain phrases seemed to reverberate in her mind. Intelligence Operative? He meant spy. He was asking her to be a spy. Spies weren't looked at as having a bad reputation. They did what they had to in order to get the job done. Was this a career she wanted to explore? Her heart began to beat faster again. Maybe she could handle this.

Executor Hale summed up his persuasion, "If we can't turn these people back, the Commonwealth itself could fall. This job is crucial for all of mankind. Forgive me. I seem to be putting a lot of pressure on you. Time is short, but perhaps I *should* just enlist the nearest female intelligence operative."

Heather's face went from tense to excited. "I have one more question. What if I fail to convince him?"

The tension in Executor Hale's face melted away. "Then we haven't lost anything. If you succeed, we are ahead. If you even plant a slight doubt, we're a step closer than we were. If he doesn't believe you at all, then we are in the same place we are now. You will still be paid for your work. Perhaps you would consider more work as an intelligence operative. I could set you up in a training program, if that's what you would like to do."

Heather smiled. "I'd like to give it a try, sir. Are you going to do the same thing to all of the crew?"

Executor Hale spoke apologetically, "I'm afraid so. I won't ask you to participate in any of that. Your service to the Commonwealth and to me has already gone to extremes. I wouldn't think of putting any more on you until you've had the appropriate training. I feel like I have asked far too much from you as it is."

Having reached an agreement, Executor Hale discussed the specifics of his plans with her then sent her on her way to prepare herself. Executor Hale returned to his receptionist to make arrangements for the VIP suite in barracks housing to be prepared as quickly as possible. The receptionist got busy ordering a bottle of champagne and a tray of fruit, cheese, and crackers delivered to the suite.

• •

Despite his assurances to Heather, Luciano ordered the receptionist to program audio/video surveillance to be recorded in all rooms of the suite. If Heather decided to carry her assignment to its furthest possible conclusion, he could use the footage to taunt the Captain later or to break down Commander Alexander. Even if Heather stopped short, it could still be used to provide a haunting reminder.

Executor Hale returned to his office to handle the debrief. He glanced at the Captain who sat there staring blankly at a spot on the wall. Having no new instructions, he had nothing to do or think. Executor Hale asked each one their opinion of how the exercise went. Everyone believed damage had been done to the Captain's credibility with his crew. Executor Hale turned to David and asked, "Commodore Alexander, do you think your crew believes you were the one who betrayed them?"

Robert jumped in before David could formulate his answer. "Is that wise, sir? In his current state, isn't he going to tell you just what you want to hear? I'm not sure he knows his own mind right now."

Luciano looked to the doctor. "Dr. Rhodes?"

Dr. Rhodes brow knit itself together tightly. "I'm not sure. It's possible you may get a little information from him. I can't verify accuracy. You can ask the question. Don't put a lot of trust in the answer. As Admiral Deacons mentioned, he's suggestible. If he believes you want a specific answer, that's what he'll give you."

Luciano scowled and studied the Captain for a moment. Taking a deep breath, he asked, "Commodore Alexander, in your honest opinion, did the two prisoners believe you betrayed them?"

The Captain's eyes darted back and forth as he replayed the images in his mind. The piece of his consciousness pushed down into the deepest darkest recesses of his mind lashed out again. His voice uttered a halting, "Yes… No… Yes… No."

Fearing for Cheyenne's safety, Robert wanted to jump in with an "I told you so." The doctor beat him to it.

"I was afraid of that. He can't process the information. It's probably useless to pursue this with him.

Executor Hale decided to move on. He laid out his plans for Heather and David for the afternoon and the potential extended plans. He explained the potential best and worst-case scenarios. There were certain parts of his plan, he *didn't* reveal to them. Luciano was planning an attack on David he couldn't share without revealing his true identity.

The longer Robert sat there listening to Executor Hale, the sicker he became. David was a man of strong character. He didn't deserve this. Brynna didn't deserve this either.

Executor Hale dismissed the group, with the exception of Dr. Rhodes. He discussed a matter with him briefly then sent him on his way with strict orders to discuss their conversation with no one. Dr. Rhodes completed his task, and a few short hours later he dropped a small vial off with Executor Hale. The doctor was confused as to why Executor Hale needed the vial, but he didn't want to question the man. The substance preserved in the vial had only one use and there was only one reason it would be needed. Executor Hale clearly expected Captain Alexander to live well past this week. This was a weapon to use against the wayward Captain months from now.

CHAPTER SIX – DAY FOUR

David began to stir. He felt a head on his chest and a warm body snuggled up against him. He inhaled deeply. A hint of perfume gently stimulated his senses. He kept his eyes closed to savor the moment. The last few days… the last few days must have been a dream. He slowly reached up and stroked Brynna's hair gently. A contented sigh reached his ears and the woman beside him began to wake up as well. David opened his eyes and twisted to kiss his beloved wife. His eyes focused on the blond hair just beneath his chin. David froze. Brynna was a brunette. He searched his memory for answers. He needed them – fast. They were captured. He endured two beatings and his injuries were healed each time, then… what? Vague images of Executor Hale, the Admirals, three of his crew, and a blond woman permeated the fog. David's heart began racing. What had he done? He glanced around the room. There was a half-eaten tray of fruit and cheese, an empty bottle of champagne and an array of clothing on the floor. David attempted to slide gently out from under the woman resting on his chest. The woman groaned softly from being disturbed, but rolled over the other direction and settled back in. David discreetly looked under the covers. He still had his underwear on, that was a plus. He rolled quickly out of the bed and grabbed his clothes from the floor. He headed for the bathroom to get dressed. What was the Supreme Executor trying to accomplish? Again… what had he and the young woman done? Had they done anything? He couldn't remember. David looked at himself in the mirror. Lipstick smudges adorned his neck and face. David decided he needed to shower, a long hot shower to clear his head. If he was still a prisoner, he didn't know when he might get another one. He did remember the so-called shower in his cell was lukewarm at best. David's mind was a jumble of images of Cheyenne, Lazaro, and Jake. He remembered hearing laughter and crying. Who was the woman in the other room? What was her name? Why were they in bed together? Well, that part was slightly self-explanatory. The shower wasn't helping. He needed to talk to the woman in the next room. He shut off the water and dried off hastily. Dressing as quickly as he could, he slid his trousers on then pulled his tank style undershirt on. No sooner had he tucked it in when he heard a knock on the bathroom door. David picked up his uniform undershirt, over-shirt, socks, and shoes. He started to leave the bathroom, so the young woman could get in. Just short of the door he looked at the items in his hands. Why was he carrying a Commodore's uniform? He stood just inside the door staring at his clothing. A memory returned. He had been escorted to base housing, ordered to shower, and given this uniform.

Heather knocked on the bathroom door again, "David… Commodore… Can I come in?"

David continued to stare at the rank insignia on the overshirt. Why was it the rank of Commodore? He was clueless. He needed to talk to the young woman. Realizing she was still waiting at the door David responded, "Coming."

Opening the door, he found Heather standing there in a short, pale blue satin gown. The gown flowed softly along her own curves. David kept his eyes on her face and avoided looking down her form. Heather attempted to wrap her arms around his waist. Seeing him half dressed, she pursed her lips into a pout. "You're already dressed? I was hoping to join you in the shower,"

Heather whined.

David pulled her arms gently back from around his waist. "Why don't you hurry and get dressed. We… uh… need to talk."

Heather's face changed. She gave him a look that said she was about to unleash a venomous wrath on him. "It had better not be one of those, 'It was nice while it lasted' talks. I didn't think you were that type." Her attitude was now definitively cold towards him. Heather started to close the bathroom door on him.

David blocked the door with one hand and reached up to touch her face gently. "I'm not that type. This is slightly embarrassing, but I apparently had too much to drink. I just need some events clarified. We can talk when you're dressed."

Heather smiled seductively. "Are you sure you wouldn't rather go back to bed and talk?"

David worked harder to keep his eyes on her face. "As enjoyable as that might be, I'm fairly certain I have some appointments coming up."

Heather looked puzzled. She knew he was a prisoner and his dose of mind altering medications should have worn off by now. What appointments could he be talking about?

David started to close the bathroom door again when he realized Heather's clothing was still scattered on the floor. He turned around and quickly collected the pieces. He hastily handed them off to her and closed the bathroom door. Now alone in the room, he pondered his next move. He decided to finish dressing first. He put his socks and shoes on and then pulled the uniform shirt on over his undershirt. He laid the Commodore's over-shirt aside. He wasn't about to put that back on. He decided he and Heather would do better to talk out on the balcony, away from prying eyes and listening ears. He asked the computer to play some soft music. As he suspected, his access was denied. David picked up the tray of food and moved it out onto the balcony. Going to the kitchen, he retrieved a pitcher of ice water along with two glasses. In his search, he realized the kitchen was fully stocked, including knives. David grabbed several knives and tucked them into his boots and waist band. He carried the pitcher and glasses back out onto the balcony.

He decided his best option for dealing with the situation was to play along, for the moment. He went back inside and made the bed but turned the covers down to appear ready to use again. His eyes fell on the Commodore's over-shirt. He didn't want to put it on, but reason suggested he needed to present the command presence. He slid the jacket on and went back out to the balcony. He sat down at the table and looked out at the view. He felt the warm sunshine on his face and hands. The images of Cheyenne and Lazaro flashed through his mind again. Most of the previous day was missing from his memory. David looked down at his wrists. There should have been binders there. He was supposed to be in a cell, not a luxury suite. What had happened to him? Unable to stay seated any longer David jumped up. He paced back and forth on the balcony. He finally spoke aloud, "Arni, what's happened to me? What did I do? Please tell me. Forgive me if I did something I shouldn't have."

Heather stepped out onto the balcony, "Who are you talking to?"

David turned around and forced a smile. "Oh, hi, I didn't hear you come outside. Do you suppose you could put on some music?"

Heather smiled, "Sure." She stepped back in and got some music playing loudly enough to be heard outside as long as the door to the balcony remained open. David moved around and pulled out a chair for Heather to sit in. Heather smiled pleasantly at David and sat down in the chair he offered. As soon as she was seated, David pulled the balcony door nearly closed. The young woman looked at him quizzically. "Why did you shut the door?"

David sighed then launched into their *discussion*. "First, I need you to forgive me if I did anything inappropriate."

Heather giggled. "We did all kinds of inappropriate things, but I wouldn't say they needed forgiveness. I enjoyed them all."

This was accomplishing nothing. David leaned in and smiled. "It sounds like you wouldn't mind repeating them."

"I wouldn't mind at all and maybe some new things." Heather absentmindedly reached down and picked up a piece of fruit. She sensuously caressed her lips with the fruit then took a bite of it.

"My memory is a little fuzzy. Perhaps we should start at the beginning again and this time stay away from the champagne."

Heather looked tenuously at the Captain. She wasn't sure where he was going with this. "Sure, if that's what you want."

David stood up. He poured a glass of water for Heather and for himself. Setting the pitcher down he reached his hand out to her. "Allow me to introduce myself. My name is David Alexander. I'm new around here. Perhaps you could help me get acclimated to my new surroundings."

Heather smiled nervously. She wondered what he was up to. She reached out and took his hand. Shaking his hand, she giggled, "My name is Heather… Heather Shields. I am the governor's liaison to Commodore Vardin. It's a pleasure to meet you, sir."

David breathed a sigh of relief. At least he didn't have to go through the embarrassment of telling the young woman he didn't know her name. He still had to somehow find out what he missed during his memory loss. David softly kissed her hand to smooth over what he was about to say. Sitting back down in his chair, he casually picked up a cracker and slice of cheese. "Heather, please forgive me for asking. I really must have enjoyed myself far too much. What is the date and time and what all have we done together. I'm afraid I blacked out completely." David shoved the cracker into his mouth to provide a distraction from any embarrassment he might be causing.

Heather laughed. "Are you serious? You really can't hold your liquor, can you?"

David took a sip of his water to wash the cracker down. "It's not something I'm practiced at. In my position, I've found it's best to keep a clear head. Really, please tell me what I missed."

"We were introduced yesterday morning in the Supreme Executor's office. We hit it off right away. Commodore Vardin took us to the detention area where you checked on the progress of your former crew's re-education. After the debriefing, Executor Hale gave us the rest of the day off to celebrate your promotion. I got this suite for us and we've spent the last several hours taking advantage of it."

David's demeanor took a new turn. "Okay, that's the cover story. What's the truth?"

Heather's eyebrows raised. "Excuse me?"

David picked up some fruit and nibbled on it casually and smiled. "I know Executor Hale has something really ugly in mind for me. What really happened? I wouldn't black out from one bottle of champagne. What else was I given, and what happened between us?"

Heather blinked. His questions caught her off guard. She replayed his words in her mind. She latched onto one thing. "Did you just call me ugly?"

David didn't allow the conversation to get sidetracked. Popping the last piece of fruit in his hand into his mouth. He scooted his chair over closer to her. He grabbed her wrist before she could pull away. "You definitely aren't ugly. You know exactly what I'm referring to. I am a traitor to the Commonwealth. Traitors don't get beautiful women at their beck and call. What's he trying to do to me? I have a gap in my memory for a reason.

What is it?"

Heather tried to jerk her arm back. David's grip tightened on her. He slipped his free hand down into his left boot and pulled out the knife. He laid it gingerly on the table. Heather's eyes focused on the kitchen utensil, now turned weapon.

David held out his left hand. "Give me your other hand."

Heather pulled back. His grip tightened on the hand he already had control of. Heather cried out in pain. Tears began to run down her cheeks. "Please don't hurt me."

"Give me your other hand, and I won't" he insisted.

Heather moved her shaking hand close enough for him to grab it. Once he had her second hand in his, he loosened his grip on the first. From a distance, they appeared to be having an earnest discussion. David knew Executor Hale would have guards watching the exchange. He didn't want them to think this was anything more than an intimate conversation. The tears on Heather's face suggested he was breaking off their relationship. He hadn't threatened her with the knife. He had simply laid it on the table. Her guilty conscience suggested he had reason to threaten her with it.

Heather looked at David with tears in her eyes. "All I have to do is scream, and they'll be in here."

David smiled again. Heather shivered. He smiled at the strangest times. "If we're going to start threatening each other then consider this. Will they be able to get to you before I could snap your neck or slice your throat? And that's assuming they hear you scream over the music. You know they're probably watching and recording from the terminal in the bedroom. From this viewpoint, I'm just giving you the 'been nice knowing you' speech."

Heather looked toward the bedroom. "He said they wouldn't watch the bedroom. He guaranteed us privacy."

David nodded. "I see. I don't recommend you ask him

about it. He won't like it if he thinks you don't trust him. Did you know he threatened to kill everyone I talk to or even anyone who overheard my conversations?"

Heather looked stunned. "You think Executor Hale would kill me? Why?"

"He'll destroy anyone he can't control. He wants to control me, and he wants to hurt the one I sold out to. It would give him far greater satisfaction to destroy me. I can't give in to him. I won't give in to him, no matter what it costs me. If he thinks you mean anything to me, he will try and use you against me."

Heather stared at him. "Why are you saying this?"

"I need to know why you were here… in bed with me."

"He said an enemy had control of you. He said if I… if we…" Heather was embarrassed. "He said it would help break the enemy's hold on you. He said the enemy you serve demanded celibacy of his followers."

David smiled again. It was still unnerving to her when he did that. "I serve Pateras. He is the true ruler of this galaxy, of the entire universe. He doesn't require celibacy, at all. He does suggest it as an option to prevent distractions. My wife would not be happy about such a practice."

"Wife? He said you were divorced."

David shook his head. "Not by my desire, nor by hers. I suppose Executor Hale has the authority to nullify our marriage, but that doesn't change the devotion my wife and I have for each other. We are staying together, permanently."

"Permanently? Are you insane? Nobody does that."

"Heather, I need to know. Exactly how far did we go?"

Heather's eyes landed on the knife again. She didn't know what he would do with either answer.

David saw her staring at the knife. He had placed it on the table purely for intimidation. It had done its job, now it seemed to be interfering. He now assigned the knife a new purpose, it's job was now to build trust. He released her right hand then reached for the knife. David, still holding her left hand in his right, felt her tense up. With his fingertips, he turned the knife around, so the handle was facing Heather. He slid it slowly across the table. Before releasing her left hand, he added an explanation. "Heather, I just want to know if I betrayed my wife or not. Pateras doesn't demand celibacy. He does require us to honor our agreements. If I betrayed my wife, I owe her an apology and I need to ask her forgiveness. I also need to ask your forgiveness. That's all I want to know. Just so you know, if you pick up the knife, the guards will rush in here and you'll get no more information from me." David slowly released her other hand. He scooted his chair back and walked away from her.

Heather looked at the knife. She wondered if this were some sort of trick. The Captain had his back turned. The words of Executor Hale rang through her mind. He just needed some hint of doubt. She could still do this. She was scared to death, but she could still do this. "M – May I leave?"

David didn't look at her. "Yes." He leaned over the handrail and rested his forearms on it.

Heather got up and moved to the door to the bedroom. David glanced over at the table. The knife was still laying there, untouched. It had done its job well. "Heather, please… I need to know."

Heather wasn't sure who to trust. The Captain could have harmed her, but he hadn't actually threatened her. She decided to hedge her bets. "Perhaps you should apologize to your wife."

David turned his head away. Tears formed in his eyes. He didn't want Heather to see his grief. David heard the door open. He called out, "Miss Shields?"

Heather hesitated again. "Yes?"

"Thank you for being honest with me. I'm sorry for everything I did to you. I hope you can forgive me." He turned to face her. As ashamed as he was, he couldn't offer the apology without looking her in the eye.

Heather stared at him in disbelief. He was crying? Over something this mundane? "Yeah, sure. Think nothing of it. Sorry." She hurried away. This situation was just too strange.

• •

Heather hurried straight to the Executor's office. The man was in a meeting, but he sent everyone out the instant she showed up in his reception area. Once the two were alone, Executor Hale asked, "How did it go?"

"I – I think he believed me. It was strange. I thought he was angry and going to hurt me, but he didn't." Heather fidgeted nervously. "You said he only needed a hint of doubt. I, at least, gave him that much. He was clearly upset. I hope you got what you needed."

"I dare say it was enough. You have earned your bonus and whatever job position you desire. Take whatever time you need to decide on your job choice. I'm sure I could find a spot for you on my personal staff if you wouldn't mind the travel. I can provide you with whatever training you desire."

"I think I would like that, sir. I was afraid for a few minutes, yet I was exhilarated. This situation is fascinating. I want to help the Commonwealth fight off this new enemy." Heather was indeed fascinated by this new enemy, although not quite the way she indicated.

Executor Hale smiled. "Very well then, I plan on leaving here in a few days. Get your affairs in order and you can leave here when I do. I will arrange for a stateroom aboard my flagship. I have need of people like you."

The two shook hands on their agreement. Heather turned to leave. She stopped at the door and gave the Executor a puzzled look. "Executor Hale, I don't know if this information helps or not, but Captain Alexander was… um… crying when I left.

He wasn't *crying* crying, but there were tears in his eyes."

Executor Hale smiled. "Yes, that helps. Thank you."

Heather left his office and started making plans to leave. Executor Hale left orders not to be disturbed.

• •

David leaned on the railing for a long time. He pictured Brynna's face. He wanted desperately to see her face again. David called out, "Arni… Pateras… please forgive me. I didn't mean for this to happen. Help me please."

A voice whispered into his mind. "Pateras will never forgive you for this. Brynna will never forgive you."

David folded his arms on the rail and lowered his head onto them. He felt so alone. Arni promised not to leave him alone. Where was he now? Why wasn't he answering? "Arni… please…" David wasn't even sure what to ask for.

The voice whispered in his mind again. "Pateras has abandoned you. There's only one way out. You should jump. Jump off the balcony."

David lifted his head. He looked over the edge of the balcony. He was twenty stories up. David entertained the idea. He felt like a failure. He'd failed himself and the young woman who'd just left him. He'd failed his wife, his crew and Pateras. If he continued to live, his days would be filled with more failure, pain and suffering. He had disgraced his family. Why should he remain alive? Was his life good for anything now? He'd promised to protect Marissa and her baby and the rest of the crew. He'd failed everyone. Arni spoke briefly to refute the attack on David's mind. "How can you have failed? The crew is mine. All I asked from you is to stay strong."

David considered the words. Did he need to die so Arni could bring him back? He had been told six days. This was only the beginning of the fourth day. Perhaps his failure meant an end to his days. The words from one of the prophetic books in the Ancient Texts came to mind.

The Dark Lord will be cast from his throne among the stars to roam, unseen. He will whisper evil to the hearts of all who might listen to him to entice them away from the light of Pateras.

He began to wonder why he was being told to jump. Who wanted him dead? He raised his head and looked around. He was still alone. There was only one who wanted him dead, one who was prevented from killing him. "Luciano, I'm not giving up, not this easily."

Luciano materialized in front of him. "Very well then, we'll see how you feel this time tomorrow. What, may I ask, gave me away?"

"Ancient Texts," was David's minimalist response. Giving too much information could reveal his own weaknesses.

"When the guards come for you, you won't have another chance to end your suffering."

"I've been ordered to stay strong by my commander. I'm done with the idea of suicide."

Executor Hale stiffened visibly. "We'll see about that. I'll make sure you have reason to wish you *had* committed suicide. The guards will be here for you shortly." He disappeared as abruptly as he had appeared.

David pulled the Commodore's jacket off and hung it on the back of a chair. He also pulled the knife out of his waistband and tossed it on the table. He still had one knife in his right boot which he left in place. Sitting down in a chair, he swallowed a few more crackers and cheese as quickly as he could. As promised, minutes later four guards came to retrieve the Captain. They placed binders on him then scanned him for weapons. They quickly pulled the last knife from David's boot. The guard who removed the knife stood up. He gave his prisoner an annoyed look. Holding the knife in front of him, he asked, "Really? Did you think we would miss this?"

David shrugged, "It was worth a shot." The guards escorted him back to his cell and left him alone for a time.

Executor Hale headed to the prison facilities after David had time to consider his predicament again. A guard brought a chair in for the Supreme Executor to sit down for a casual conversation. David remained seated on his mattress on the floor. Executor Hale spent a few minutes repeating his offer to give the Captain a high-ranking office and position before resorting to his faithful standby of threats. David declined as expected. Executor Hale was slightly disappointed at David's refusal to accept the offer; however, he wasn't surprised. "Well, Captain, let me know if you change your mind. In the meantime, let me tell you what the price of your stubbornness is. First, I'll send the doctor in to give you your daily neural stimulant. Next, I'm sending someone very special in to see to your daily beating. Once you've had a chance to catch your breath, I'm going to send teams in to beat every man on your crew. I'm going to make sure the feed is broadcast on all four walls of this cell. You will be able to see and hear every blow, every cry of pain. I'll make sure my men work your crew over one at a time. I wouldn't want you to miss anything. The last thing I'm going to do is send men in to entertain the women of your crew, starting with Commander Alexander. They'll be sure to tell her how much you've been enjoying Heather's company."

David's anger and helplessness began to build. "She'll never believe your thugs," He spat.

Executor Hale stood up to leave. The Captain, while continuing to glare at the man, stood as well. Executor Hale stood at the door between his two guards. His smile dripped with evil as he responded. "You're right. She probably won't. Do you think she'll believe your own crewmen? You were seen just yesterday morning by two of your crew in your Commodore ranks being escorted by Miss Shields. Your crew are well on their way to believing you were the one who betrayed them, not Mr. Holden. Perhaps I'll bring Commander Alexander to my office, let Heather tell her all about your time together. Despite my assurances to Miss Shields, I did record the two of you. I can show those to her as well. Do you think she'll believe that?"

David's anger reached a head. He launched himself at the Supreme Executor. In the back of his mind, he knew his move was pointless. He couldn't help himself. The two guards were on him before he could lay a finger on the Supreme Executor. The guards pinned him against a wall and pummeled him with several blows to the ribs and abdomen. When it was clear to them David was no longer capable of advancing, they withdrew. David slipped down to his hands and knees trying to catch his breath. He looked up through his pain and sweat. "Pateras… will… set this… right. He will… end you."

Executor Hale studied the anger on David's face. He stepped closer to him. "You think you're the one, don't you? You think you're going to be the one from the twelve twelves who ends my human existence."

David was beginning to catch his breath. "It would be a genuine pleasure, if it were. If it's not, I'd at least love to shake the hand of the one who does. You should be careful though. You don't want your guards to hear you say too much."

Executor Hale glanced at his men who stood there ready to pounce again. "Those two know exactly who I am and who you are, Defender of the followers of Pateras." Executor Hale saw the blank look on David's face. "You really haven't read that part yet, have you? No, you haven't. Interesting."

David made a mental note to search the Ancient Texts for

the reference Luciano mentioned. He watched Luciano leave the cell. As the door closed behind him, he heard the Executor instruct the guards, "I will be sending a feed from my office shortly, make sure he's able to see it." David struggled to his feet. He made his way over to the sink and splashed some water on his face. Anger still seethed within him. He had nothing to take his anger out on. Punching a wall would undoubtedly result in broken bones in his hands. He had no furniture to kick or throw except the one chair left behind by the guards.

David toyed with the idea of taking his frustrations out on it. He thought better of the idea since it was the only thing, other than the floor for him to sit on. Despite the presence of the chair, David walked back over to his smelly mattress. Sinking to his knees, he called out again, "Pateras, please talk to me."

A presence filled the room. A voice spoke to him. "I'm here."

David looked around. He saw no one in the darkness of his cell. "Arni? I can't see you."

"I know. I'm here, just like I said I would be."

"Arni, forgive me for… for everything I did with Heather. I have no memory of my time with her. I don't know what I might have done to the crew either."

"It's forgiven. David, you didn't succumb to the temptations put there by Luciano. You've resisted his temptations to the point he's had to resort to trickery to accomplish his goals. You were drugged."

The memory of the guards forcing his head down on the conference table flashed in David's mind. He remembered feeling the warm stinging sensation of a hypo-spray on his neck, then nothing.

"Does the crew think I betrayed them?"

"The crew is my responsibility, not yours. Whatever they believe will be set right when this is over."

"Arni, did I go too far with Heather? She said we did. I have to know."

"David, my father has forgiven you because you asked him to. Whatever you did or didn't do is no longer relevant. Why do you need to know? Will you hate yourself if you did go too far? Will you be relieved if you didn't, glad you won't have to tell Brynna?"

David searched the darkness again, wishing he could see Arni's face for himself. "I – I don't know."

"Let me say this again. You were drugged. You have been forgiven. You still need to talk to Brynna about it. I know the answer to your question, but you need to talk to her about what you remember, not what you don't.

"Isn't there something else you need to be concerned about?"

David's eyes blurred with tears again. "He's going to hurt the crew. Can you stop him?"

"A great battle will occur over this. Ask my father for help. Don't stop asking. You won't see the battle. It will occur in what you've called the realm of Pateras. You will need to join this battle. They will come for you, this cannot be stopped. While they seek to harm you, call out to Pateras for your crew. Do you understand?"

A peace settled on the young Captain. "I don't understand everything. I do know what you are asking of me. I'll do what you ask."

The walls of David's cell lit up with a view of Executor Hale's office. He saw Brynna being escorted in. Her steps were uneven and off balance. Her eyes were bloodshot, and her hair was un-combed. Despite her disheveled appearance, she was the most beautiful woman he had ever seen. David got up and walked over to the wall. He reached up to touch her face. His fingers felt nothing but the cold hard wall of his cell. His memory of touching her face overwrote the sensation of the wall. David watched as the drama unfolded in front of him.

• •

"Prisoner 7139, sit down," Executor Hale commanded.

Brynna sat down in the chair facing Executor Hale's desk. She stared coldly at him. "So, how did some one of such a lowly rank as mine rate the attention of the Supreme Executor?"

Executor Hale responded just as coldly, "It wasn't your rank, but your crime that got my attention."

"So, what do you want from me?" Brynna wanted to get this pointless conversation over with.

"I wanted to give you the opportunity to rejoin your husband. You see, David chose wisely. He serves the Commonwealth."

"David would never rejoin the Commonwealth."

Executor Hale leaned back casually in his chair. "That's where you're wrong, dear lady. He never left us. He's responsible for your capture. I'm only willing to spend a small amount of time and energy on retraining all of you. I have scheduled you and the rest of your crew for executions in two days if I don't have reason to believe you're making progress."

Brynna scoffed at him. "I don't believe anything you say."

David smiled and touched the image of her face again, "Good girl."

Executor Hale gave the appearance of a man with an ace up his sleeve. "I didn't really expect you to, at least not without proof. Let's get to the heart of it. David has been promoted to Commodore. He's asked to have his marriage contract dissolved, although he has indicated if you recanted, he might reconsider your marriage. I've given him his choice of command positions. If you consider rejoining the Commonwealth, you could join him. If not, dissolving your marriage contract won't be an issue in two days."

Executor Hale gave his words a moment to sink in before continuing. "Now, about that proof, I recorded these images over the last two days." He pressed the buttons to reveal audio-visual recordings carefully spliced together and the sound turned off.

Brynna saw David parading about in his Commodore's uniform, his flirtatious introduction to Heather, and the trip through the detention area. Brynna saw David compassionately offer his crewmen a drink of water. That was David. The man touching and caressing the mysterious blond woman, that wasn't David. Something in his eyes was wrong. His eyes were cold and empty. There was a smile on his face, but not in his eyes. Brynna decided to keep her thoughts to herself. She chose to voluntarily play into his hands.

"Who's the Bimbo?" Brynna's eyes flashed with jealousy. "A hired professional, I presume?"

"She's a local civilian. She works as a liaison between the governor of this province and Commodore Vardin. She's a professional, but not in the sense you're thinking. I did find it quite helpful to record their activities though."

The images had frozen on the screen. Executor Hale pressed a button and a snippet of the couple in bed appeared. Brynna looked away from the screen. Executor Hale locked the image in place. He zoomed in on David's face. "Look! Look at his face! I can't make that up. I can't force that emotion."

Brynna looked despite not wanting to. Tears began to form in her eyes. This had to be a trick. David wouldn't do this. She couldn't come up with a satisfactory explanation.

• •

David watched Brynna's face on the screen. She was believing the Supreme Executor. David's hand folded into a fist. He pounded it on the wall. "No! Brynna! Don't listen to him!" He relaxed his fist and caressed her image on the wall again. "Arni, please don't let her believe this. Brynna, please… I thought it was you!" The image had stopped just short of David opening his eyes to discover Heather. If Brynna could see just a minute more, she would understand. Anger welled up in him again.

The door to his cell opened. Two guards walked in at just the wrong time. David grabbed the chair and swung it at the nearest one taking him down. He reversed his thrust and tried to launch a kick to the second guard's face. The second one reacted quickly. He backed off, pulled his weapon, and fired. David convulsed and fell to the floor. His anger still propelling him, he managed to roll over onto his hands and knees. He was still in no condition to fight back. Two more guards entered the room. One pulled the injured man from the room. The second pinned David down. The guard still brandishing a weapon walked over and kicked David in the side. "That's for my partner." He kicked him again. "That's for me."

The doctor walked in just in time to stop the guard from continuing. "Knock it off! You know the Supreme Executor wants this done in a specific manner. You mess this up you'll face *his* wrath. You want to end up like him?" The guard backed off angrily. The doctor knelt and scanned David for any life-threatening injuries. Seeing only bruising, he reached down and injected David with his promised neural stimulant. The throbbing in his side escalated. The guard released his hold on David.

David moaned and grabbed his side. He looked up at Brynna's face. The image of her tears was now frozen on the wall. Luciano timed everything perfectly. The doctor and guards made a wary departure. "Pateras! Take care of my crew!"

A couple minutes later the door opened again. Jake stood in front of the Captain. The burst from the Tri-EMP caused residual twitches throughout his body. The neural stimulant forced the twitches to fire more rapidly. David was shaking from the effects. The pain in his side was searing. David tried hard to look at Jake. His eyes were having trouble focusing. "J – Jake …"

"That's Lt. Holden to you, Prisoner 7138."

"N – not on m – my sh – ship, it's n-not."

The guards laughed at their prisoner. "He's losing it. He still thinks he has a ship."

"And a crew," the other one added.

"Prisoner 7138, Executor Hale seems to think you're holding out some hope that I'm going to rescue you. Is that true?"

David pushed himself into a sitting position and tried to slow his breathing. He forced his muscles to relax. "N – no Ch – chief, I'm here to – to r – rescue you."

Jake's befuddled look was almost amusing. The two guards laughed again loudly. Jake waved the guards forward. "Get him up."

The guards hoisted the Captain onto his feet in front of Jake. David worked hard to pull himself together. "So, you're my s – surprise guest. He s – sent you in here to d – drive a rift between us?"

"He didn't send me. I volunteered."

David's twitches were fading away. The pain in his side had eased and his speech came more easily. "That's what he wants you to think. He manipulated you. Just so you know, I'm not going to hold this against you."

Jake tried to stay detached. The Captain's words were still hitting too close to home. "Prisoner 7138, are you prepared to rejoin the Commonwealth or face the consequences?"

David took a slow deep breath. "Let's go to war, Chief."

Jake was totally confused by the Captain's comments. He did the only thing he could. He punched the Captain roughly in the stomach forcing him to double over. The guards, still holding David's arms, forced him upright again. David took a gasp of air and called out, "Pateras… please…" Jake landed another blow. He assumed David was asking for mercy from Pateras until he heard the next few words between blows. "Protect…

protect… my… my crew."

Jake continued to pummel the Captain. Each blow enhanced by the neural stimulant. He heard the Captain asking Pateras to hide the crew from Executor Hale. He was begging for mercy, but not for himself. He invited more pain if it would save the crew. When the Captain was finally too weak for words and too weak to stand, the guards dropped him on his mattress and left the cell. Each one seemed visibly shaken. Jake was probably more shaken than the others. He had never seen anyone take that much of a beating and not once ask for mercy or help.

Jake reported back to the duty physician who swung by David's cell to verify his injuries were again non-life-threatening. The doctor even came away shaking his head. He concluded David must be delirious. He reported his own findings back to Executor Hale. The Executor had finished with Brynna and sent her back to her cell promising to send her some company of her own later.

• •

Executor Hale received an emergency call and returned to his ship in orbit. The call was from a messenger of his own about the battle commencing in the realm of Pateras. Luciano sequestered his physical self in his quarters leaving orders not to be disturbed. He changed to his alternative form and joined the skirmish. He was the strongest of all those created by Pateras, but he was still outnumbered.

• •

Commodore Vardin was facing a crisis of his own. He sent his men to carry out their orders against the crew. The first group of men approached Braxton's cell.

Braxton heard them coming for him. He thought it was too soon for his next re-education appointment. When three men entered the cell, Braxton realized they were entering the next phase of re-education. He sighed. This was not going to be fun. He wondered what the men were waiting on. The guards were looking anxiously around the room. They quickly left, closing the cell door behind them. Seconds later an alarm went off. Braxton wanted to look out into the corridor to see what was happening. He started to roll over to get to his feet when a voice spoke softly inside his head. "Get some sleep while you can. You're safe for tonight."

Braxton hesitated then laid back down and mumbled, "Okay." Seconds later he was asleep.

The guards checked cell after cell. The panic increased. Commodore Vardin walked into the control room of the detention area. "Report!" He bellowed.

The Duty Officer quickly reported, "Commodore, our surveillance feeds show each prisoner from the *Evangeline* as being in their cells. When I sent parties to carry out the Supreme Executor's orders, the cells were empty. The only prisoners we can confirm as being in their cells are prisoners 7138 and 7145. They aren't showing up on any other scans of the base. Their identification chips, implanted when they were arrested, are still showing them in their cells."

Commodore Vardin had not been briefed on the powers of Pateras. He scowled at the displays in front of him. In a moment, he began to bark orders. "I want each of the scanners and a/v monitors rebooted two at a time. Reroute the feeds through secondary and auxiliary feeds. Get two teams with manual scanners chasing down those identification chips. Put the entire base on lock down. I don't want anyone entering or leaving this base. Find me Mr. Holden."

The room was a buzz of activity. Teams took off in multiple directions. Minutes later Jake was unceremoniously dropped into a chair in front of Commodore Vardin. The Commodore glared at the man, although he addressed his guards. "Where did you find him?”

“In the Officer’s Club, sir. He was drinking himself into a stupor, I think.” The guard replied.

“Mr. Holden, how many drinks did you have?” Commodore Vardin wanted to know just how drunk Jake was before he attempted to question him.

“One, sir. I didn’t even finish the one. What’s wrong?”

“Your crew are missing from their cells. Where are they?” The Commodore demanded.

Jake stood up slowly. “First of all, sir, they are no longer my crew. Second, I just finished working over my former Captain alongside two of *your* guards. They can vouch for my whereabouts and my activities. The surveillance in the Officer’s Club can tell you what time I entered there. In between, I reported to the Medical Officer on Duty, so the Captain’s wounds could be checked. I don’t know anything about the crew. My orders were to stay away from them or my clemency would be revoked. I have followed my orders, to the letter, sir.”

Commodore Vardin glanced at a technician, “Verify that.”

A long minute later, the technician replied, “The information is accurate, sir.”

Jake displayed the bruises and broken skin on his hands. “I didn’t even stop to get myself patched up.”

Commodore Vardin glared at the man. A hint of distrust still haunted his thoughts. “So, help us find them.”

Jake followed the Commodore to the nearest screen. The Commodore explained the situation. Jake stared at the screen for a minute. “Give me a combat helmet and let me go look for myself.”

“Why do you need a combat helmet?”

“Executor Hale plans to throw me in with the prisoners tomorrow to convince them the Captain was their enemy. I need to see inside those cells myself, but I can’t be identified.”

Commodore Vardin was uncomfortable with the idea of turning Jake loose near the prisoners. He contemplated his request.

"Commodore, you should probably send a couple men in combat gear with me, so I don't draw unwanted attention. It would give me some back-up, just in case."

Commodore Vardin stood directly in front of Jake. "Just what is it you think you'll find?"

Jake glanced around at the others in the room. "Just how much has Executor Hale told you about the power of Pateras?"

"Are you saying Pateras is here on my base?"

"Perhaps we should talk privately." Jake's skittish behavior was noticeable.

"You'll tell me what I need to know right now!" Commodore Vardin snapped.

"Not without permission from one of the admirals. Our mission was classified. We were ordered not to discuss it with anyone outside the chain of command. You may outrank me, but you're outside my chain of command."

Commodore Vardin glared at Jake. Without taking his eyes off the defiant young lieutenant, the Commodore addressed the Duty Officer, "I need to talk to Admiral Garcia or Admiral Deacons immediately."

The Duty Officer hailed the two men who were having dinner in the Officer's Club together. The Officer's Club had been sequestered from the turmoil caused by the base lock down. The two men were not even sitting in a position to see Jake escorted out minutes earlier. Commodore Vardin requested the assistance of the Admirals in the Detention Control Center. He hastily explained his situation and Lt. Holden's reluctance to share his information. The two men arrived minutes later. Their moods clearly affected by the abrupt end to their meal and the severity of the situation. Commodore Vardin went into further detail about the situation including Jake's plan of action and refusal to share information. The two men exchanged silent knowing glances.

Admiral Deacons finally asked, "Lt. Holden, what is it you think you'll find in those cells?"

"I think the crew are right where we left them. I think Pateras is concealing them. I didn't want to explain it without clearance, sir."

Admiral Garcia scowled. "You were right to keep this quiet. Commodore, clear the room."

Commodore Vardin was in the middle of a crisis and clearing the control room didn't seem like the right course of action. Nevertheless, he complied. "Everybody listen up! I need the room cleared right now! Wait out in the hall! Move it, people!"

The personnel in the room were of the same mindset as the Commodore. Leaving the Control Center during a crisis seemed quite counter-productive. Some seemed to have trouble comprehending and acting on the orders.

The second the door closed behind the last man, Commodore Vardin quickly and respectfully demanded answers. "So, what's happening to my base?"

Admiral Garcia began the explanation. "You know we are searching out and destroying the forces held by Pateras El Liontari. The twelve crews we sent were supposed to be the advance scouts searching out the footholds of the Liontari followers. What you haven't been told is this: Pateras El Liontari is a superior alien life force. He has powers we don't really know how to fight. Lt. Holden is probably our leading expert on the subject. He's seen and interacted with Arni Liontari on numerous occasions."

"Superior alien life force, you're joking." Commodore Vardin managed to avoid rolling his eyes at the Admiral. "This entire galaxy has been explored from stem to stern. The only intelligent life forms are human. We've found every kind of animal imaginable and humans in various shapes, sizes, and colors. There are human societies of varying technology and intelligence levels, but they're all still classified as human. There aren't any superior alien life forms. It's a myth."

Admiral Deacons chimed in to back Admiral Garcia. "It's no myth. The Liontari forces can manipulate matter, energy, and space. They can be anywhere and everywhere. This crew isn't just under some sort of hypnosis. They chose voluntarily to join Pateras El Liontari, the most powerful being in the universe. That's what makes them so dangerous. They are driven by their own desires to stay loyal to him. He can see and hear everything, including individual thoughts. The more people who know about him, the greater the chances his influence will spread."

Commodore Vardin was having greater difficulty controlling his anger. "And you brought this onto *my* base?"

Jake stood up slowly to add to the briefing. "Admirals, I think I know why the crew can't be located."

Jake glanced anxiously at Admiral Deacons who gave him an annoyed, "Spit it out, Lieutenant."

Jake nodded, "Yes sir, forgive me, sir. Executor Hale had me work the Captain over earlier." Jake hesitated, knowing his information must be painful for Admiral Deacons.

Admiral Garcia pushed the lieutenant to hurry and alleviate Admiral Deacons discomfort. "Get to the point quickly, Lt. Holden."

"When I was working the Captain over, he… uh… he was calling out to Pateras, but not for himself. He was asking for Pateras to protect the crew. From what we know about Pateras, he can move his people around unseen, including humans. The Captain said he has a job to do, and I heard him tell Marissa this would be over in six days. I believe the crew are in their cells, right where you left them. He's protecting them from the assaults Executor Hale ordered."

Admiral Deacons nodded thoughtfully at Admiral Garcia. "It makes sense. It would explain why they show up on the scans but can't be seen."

Admiral Garcia considered his theory. "So why not hide them from the scanners? And how do we confirm it?"

"Run a portable scanner in each of those cells. If the location of the identification chip matches the exact spot these monitors show the crew to be, it's not likely to be a computer reprogramming job. The portable scanners can be operated separately from the main computer banks. If we can alter the location of the chips within the cells, it verifies the voracity of the scan."

Commodore Vardin was struggling to grasp all the information. "What do you mean by alter the location of the chips?"

Jake pointed to the monitor showing Thane sleeping on his mattress in his cell. "Pick up the back of Thane's mattress and dump him in the floor. If the scanner follows it and the guards can't visually locate the chip, then you've dumped Thane in the floor and the chip is still in his body. I would caution you though. Don't make any attempt to harm the crew. If Pateras plans to keep the crew protected tonight, any attempt to harm them could invite worse disasters."

Admiral Garcia wasn't convinced. "I see how this can help locate the crew, but why can't we use this information to our advantage. Why can't we follow the Supreme Executor's orders by just attacking the space around the chip?"

Jake shook his head. "I've learned that when Pateras says, 'No,' he means it. Commander Alexander put herself in harm's way on Tudoren. Two of the locals had a grudge against her. She went into a dungeon full of prisoners without back-up. The two saw her come in alone and thought they were going to get their chance at some revenge. Pateras sent in two guys to protect her. These two guys were invisible to everyone, except the two local guys."

Admiral Garcia shook his head. "What are you saying?"

"I'm saying, you don't know who else is in those cells with them. I don't see anybody else, but that doesn't mean they are alone. I'm suggesting a way to confirm the crew is still present. I'm also suggesting you call off carrying out the Supreme Executor's orders for tonight. Consult him again in the morning."

Admiral Deacons continued to scowl. "Why do you want to be the one to do this scan?"

"I don't have to be the one to do the scans. I just want to see inside the cells. I'm not under orders to harm the crew. If they truly are still in their cells, they *might* be visible to me."

The anger and frustrations had been building in Admiral Deacons for days. Finally reaching a head, he grabbed Jake by the front of his uniform and pinned him against the nearest wall. "You just callously beat my nephew. Do you really think Pateras is going to believe you mean the rest of the crew no harm?" He shouted.

Commodore Vardin was frozen in shock. Admiral Garcia calmly stepped over to Admiral Deacons' side. "Robert… let go of him. He didn't volunteer. He was following orders."

Robert slowly released Jake. Jake certainly didn't look pleased with himself. If he had shown any hint of being satisfied with himself, Robert would've decked the man.

Jake thought it was probably best if he kept his mouth shut, but his own guilty conscience wouldn't allow it. "Sir, you may not believe me, but I respect the Captain. I didn't want to be the one to do this to him. The Supreme Executor thought it was too important. I hope you can forgive me, someday."

Unable to stomach the sight of Jake, Robert kept his back to Jake. "Maybe someday, if David can forgive you."

"This is going to sound crazy. I think he already has, even before I hit him."

Robert froze in his tracks for a moment. He turned slowly. His eyes focused on Jake's face. The young man's face reflected a certain genuineness along with some inner conflict. Robert stepped closer to Jake. Edgar braced himself to move in between the two men again. Admiral Deacons stared at Jake long enough to make Jake very nervous. "I believe you, Lieutenant. Edgar, I suggest we conduct the search as Lt. Holden recommended with one exception. Lt. Holden, I don't want you to enter any of the cells. You can look in through the door only. I don't want to take the chance you'll be recognized. They may not see your face, but they could recognize your walk or mannerisms. You can lead the scan teams yourself, just don't enter the cells for any reason. Are we clear?"

Jake nodded, "Yes sir! I'll get some men and gear and head in right away."

Jake disappeared out the door as quickly as possible. He was anxious to clear up Commodore Vardin's distrust of him and wanted away from Admiral Deacons' angry stares. Jake grabbed the necessary troops and escorted them to the armory to gear up.

Commodore Vardin was clearly disturbed by the entire situation. "So, what now? Should I let my people back in here?"

Admiral Garcia took the lead. "Bring in the Duty Officer and a technician. Keep the base on lockdown and full alert. Perhaps Lt. Holden is right. We should hold off on the Supreme Executor's orders until we can talk to him. Have you had any luck reaching him?"

Commodore Vardin shook his head. "I have hailed his ship several times. He is currently unavailable."

Admiral Deacons added, "I agree. We dare not attempt to touch the crew until we get new orders from the Supreme Executor. Call a minimal number of staff in here and give them strict orders to discuss none of it, ever."

Admiral Garcia nodded in agreement. Commodore Vardin stepped outside to give the appropriate orders. He allowed three personnel back into the room, posted two others at the door to refuse entry to anyone without express permission, and sent the remaining men and women to other posts with strict orders to not discuss the situation. The promised penalty was quite high.

• •

Jake put on his combat gear and helmet and hooked his comms up, enabling him to direct the teams from outside the cells. He assigned each member of the team a pseudonym. Unit A was the team member conducting the scan. Unit B was the backup, Jake claimed the title of Unit C as he was in command of the activity and Unit D was Jake's backup.

The first cell he chose was Brynna's. Brynna was still upset from her meeting with the Supreme Executor and moving around anxiously in her cell. Jake peered into the cell. He could clearly see Brynna leaning over the sink. Jake sent Units A and B into the cell instructing them to only advance on his orders. Jake closed the door to the cell and stepped back. Looking at his data pad, he directed the two guards. "Unit A, advance your position to within three feet of the sink. Unit B stay near the door."

The guard advanced as ordered. Brynna could see the guards, however she was unaware they couldn't see her. When the guard approached her position. She moved aside. She no longer had the strength for a fight as her bread and water rations were lacking in nutritional value. As soon as she moved the guard turned towards her again, although he didn't advance. She heard the guard report.

"Unit C, this is Unit A. The target has moved. I repeat the target has moved. Sending coordinates."

Brynna was confused, exhausted, and annoyed. "What do you want?" She demanded.

The guards never heard her question. Unit A moved closer to Brynna without Jake's instruction. Brynna was standing in the back-left corner of her cell. As the guard came towards her again, she moved to the front-left corner near the guard standing by the door. The guard continued to follow the signal.

Seeing their movements on his data pad, Jake called out over comms to the guard. "Unit A, stop pursuing the signal."

Unit A returned a confused comment and failed to follow orders. "Sir, the signal keeps moving. If the tracker was removed, it should be stationary. The signal shouldn't be bouncing around like this."

The guard continued to chase Brynna in circles in her cell. He finally managed to pin her into the front right corner of the cell. She continued to demand to know what the guards wanted. Despite Jake's orders to back off, the guard reached out to the exact spot in Brynna's shoulder where the chip was implanted. Before he could touch her, the guard was thrown across the room. Brynna was caught as much by surprise as the two guards. She hadn't touched the guard. She couldn't help but smile when she realized who had.

Jake called out to his troops, "Unit B, get Unit A up and out of there immediately."

As soon as the group were well clear of the cells, Jake took off his helmet and gave the group a strong dressing down. "This is no ordinary situation! I am running this op because I know a little bit about what we're up against. You go against my orders again, I'll have you scrubbing toilets for the rest of your military career. That's assuming you survive disobeying my orders. Are we clear?"

The guard who had been thrown across the room was still clearly shaken up by the event. He acknowledged his orders then asked if he could go to the Infirmary to get checked out. Jake quickly denied his request. "As soon as we've looked at everything I want to look at, you can get checked out. I want this finished first. I will allow you to swap places with Unit D for the next one and assume his call sign."

Unit A mumbled a weak, albeit thankful, "Yes sir."

The group moved randomly from one section of the prison to another. Thane's cell was the next one they chose to investigate. The group were far more cautious this time and heeded Jake's instructions to the letter. Jake ordered Unit A to move to the head of Thane's mattress. He ordered the second guard to the foot of it. "Units A and B, slowly lift the back side of the mattress up off the floor. I said slowly, people!"

The two men struggled just a bit. They expected to be lifting an empty mattress. Thane had been sleeping on it and when the two guards began to move the mattress, Thane rolled off it and onto his feet. He moved as far away from the two as he could and crouched in a defensive posture. Jake ordered the two men to drop the mattress, aim the scanner in the direction of the identification chip for one more scan, then exit quickly. This time the men complied.

Thane watched the two men leave his cell then laid back down slowly. He didn't have any idea what just happened nor why. He knew he did want to get whatever sleep he could since they seemed to be allowing it for the first time in… how many days? Three? Four? Being on the run the last day before they were captured hadn't helped his sleep deprivation either.

Jake peered into the cell. He could see Thane, plain as day. In the back of his mind, he wondered why Pateras allowed it. Was it because of the Captain?

The group made a brief pass through each cell scanning for the chips and any other unidentified signals. This time, Jake made no effort to disturb the crew's positions. All he needed to do was confirm for himself where they were and get the logs to match up. Having collected all the data, he disposed of his combat gear, sent his ailing team member to the Infirmary, then reported back to the Detention Control Center.

Jake reported his observations and findings to the Command staff. He pulled the logs from the scan of Commander Alexander's cell. "As you can see by the scan, Commander Alexander still has her chip implanted. Every time she moves, the location of the chip moves. No one could predict those movements to put them into an algorithm. I can also attest to seeing every member of the crew in their cells. My biggest question is, why did Pateras actually allow me to see them?"

Admiral Deacons suggested it was exactly as he mentioned earlier. Pateras knew Jake meant the crew no harm.

Commodore Vardin had another theory. "I suppose that's a possibility. Another possibility is, you could be lying about seeing them in their cells."

"While my pregnant wife sits alone in her cell? I don't think so. If you'd like more supporting evidence, I can provide it."

"Commodore Vardin, why are you so quick to blame Lt. Holden for this? We've told you what you're up against. Why haven't you blamed me? My nephew is one of the prisoners just like his wife is."

Commodore Vardin wasn't about to accuse his own superior without some solid proof. He was slightly conflicted by the Admiral's question. "I suppose because he's the only member of a treasonous crew running around freely on the base. When the crew disappeared, he's the first one who came to mind. Maybe I'm just having trouble getting off that train of thought."

Admiral Garcia tried changing the subject. "Now that we know where the crew are, it would be awkward, but we could still carry out the Executor's orders. We can use the scanners to locate the prisoners. Let's send some men in to carry out the orders even without being able to see them."

Jake balked quickly. "You can't do that, sir. You'd fill up the Infirmary faster than you'd cause harm to any of the crew."

Edgar scowled, "Explain yourself."

"I can't see anyone else in those cells except the crew, but they are *not* alone." Jake was clearly unnerved by the suggestion. Seeing Admiral Garcia's unmitigated resolve, Jake continued with his explanation. He called up the surveillance video from the Commander's cell. Pulling it up to the point where she had been cornered, he started moving the record forward frame by frame. "Watch this closely. The Commander's stance changes to a defensive posture. Computer, freeze frame. Her hands are pulled inwards. She's preparing to strike in self-defense."

Admiral Garcia continued to scowl. "What's your point?"

Jake shook his head in disbelief. "Look at the Chief Petty Officer. He's already been hit by something or someone and it wasn't the Commander. Computer advance video, two frames per second. Watch, even the Commander's startled by what's happened. She didn't hit him. Somebody else did. If you send troops in there, you're going to start losing people."

Admiral Garcia was mesmerized by the image unfolding in front of him. "Computer, replay video same time frame and speed." The computer backed the image up and moved forward again. After seeing the images a second time, his anger and frustration gave way to acceptance. "He's right. We can't send men in those cells. We risk making the situation worse. We have to wait for the Supreme Executor. I'll put another call in to him. Keep everything locked down for tonight. Nobody goes in or out."

Commodore Vardin put troops in key positions and kept his people on high alert. Jake and the admirals retired to their quarters for the night.

• •

Admiral Deacons stopped by to look in on David before retiring. David was moaning and twitching from the effects of the neural stimulant enhanced beating. Robert stepped into the cell and placed his hand gently on David's head. David looked up at the Admiral through swollen eyes. He managed to ask, "Th-The c-crew... s – safe?"

Robert nodded. "Yes, they're safe. Pateras wouldn't allow us to touch them. I hope whatever you're doing is worth this."

David writhed and shivered, "M – Me t – too. I'm s – sorry."

Robert shook his head. "What are you sorry for?"

"F – For putting you th – through this." David's insides felt like they were on fire with neurons firing from all directions. He grabbed his sides and rolled back and forth trying to find some position that didn't hurt.

"I think you got the worst end of this, son. You know I would help you if I could." Robert's heart was breaking as he watched David suffer.

"N – No, d – don't help. Stay out of th – the way. Pateras... is in... control. He'll take c-care... of us."

Robert felt like he was watching David die in his arms again. The painful memory resurged in his mind. Tears began to form in his eyes. "David..."

David grabbed the Admiral's shirt. "NO! Pateras... he's got this. I'll... unh... be okay. P – Please go."

Admiral Deacons stroked David's head gently one more time then got up to leave. His heart ached for his nephew.

Admiral Deacons spent a rather sleepless night silently begging Pateras to intercede on David's behalf.

Chapter Six – Day Four

Moods were not good for anyone this morning. When Executor Hale finally contacted the base, he wasn't happy his orders hadn't been carried out. He didn't sound surprised though. The guards reported the crew were in their cells as they were supposed to be. Executor Hale returned to the base and ordered the Captain to the Infirmary again. While awaiting his pending healing, he met with the command staff and Lt. Holden.

"Gentlemen, what happened last night cannot be allowed to happen again. I know none of you are to blame. I expect the fault is my own."

Admiral Garcia looked confused. "How is this your fault, sir?"

Executor Hale got up and began to pace. "I made the mistake of telling the Captain my plans for the crew. He, in turn, begged Pateras for help. If the Captain hadn't done that, perhaps Pateras wouldn't have intervened."

Commodore Vardin was just beginning to wrap his brain around the concept of Pateras. "So how do we fight this… being?"

"If we can't hurt them physically, then I'll have to work on them mentally. Lt. Holden, it's time for you to go in and add to the lies I've already told them. I'm going to have the crew moved to two large holding cells in the temporary holding area. We can attempt to cause a few painful accidents as we move them. It won't be as much as I wanted, but it's something. Since the crew may have trouble believing Mr. Holden, I'm going to need you to keep a close eye on him, Commodore Vardin. Lieutenant, I trust you can take as much as you can dish out."

"Yes sir, I can take it."

"I hope you haven't cleaned the civilian attire you were captured in?" Executor Hale queried.

"No sir, they are in the same condition they were on the day we were arrested." Jake was pleased at the chance to prove his worth to the Supreme Executor, although he wasn't in a hurry to face the possible wrath of his crew-mates.

"I suggest you put them on and hit the gym for a little while so you, and the clothing, start smelling rather rank. Dr. Rhodes, I also need something to make his eyes look bloodshot. The others have been sleep-deprived and going through the indoctrination sessions. The lieutenant needs to have the same appearance."

Dr. Rhodes acknowledged his orders. He also pointed out that the new lieutenant had been eating regularly. The crew had been on bread and water for the last four days. Dr. Rhodes was concerned his bathroom schedule could give the young man away as well. Executor Hale ordered the doctor to take whatever precautions he deemed necessary as soon as they were dismissed. The group went over Jake's story again to make sure there were no holes in it. Seeing none, Jake and Dr. Rhodes were dismissed to prepare for Jake's infiltration of the crew. Jake was not amused by Dr. Rhodes methods of preparing him. The doctor gave him something to empty his stomach and his bowels, quickly. Jake spent the next hour in misery in his bathroom. Once the doctor was satisfied, he gave him an antidote to settle his stomach and bowels back down then sent him to the gym. He left instructions for another medical officer to treat Jake's eyes when he returned from his workout.

• •

Dr. Rhodes returned to the Supreme Executor's office as ordered. He slipped in quietly and sat down at the table. He came in just in time to start answering more questions.

"Dr. Rhodes, what is the Captain's condition this morning?"

"He's exhausted, dehydrated, his electrolytes are seriously compromised, he has two fractured ribs, but no actual broken bones. He's suffering from numerous bruises and contusions, all non-life threatening. The neural stimulants exacerbate his dehydration and electrolyte imbalances. He has access to water in his cell, but his ability to reach it and drink it are impaired by his pain. If I do nothing else, I need to treat the electrolytes. That's the one life threatening issue he's dealing with now."

Executor Hale sat back in his chair contemplating his options. Glancing at Admiral Deacons, Executor Hale came to a decision. "Admiral Deacons, do you think when the Captain's family arrives, they could talk any sense into him?"

Robert shook his head. "I seriously doubt it. I stepped in to check on him personally last night. Despite his pain, he was more concerned about how this was affecting me. He wasn't concerned about his own suffering. I… uh… I was tempted to do whatever I could for him. He knew that and ordered me not to help him."

Luciano leaned forward in his chair. "And just what would you have done to help him?"

"I thought about smuggling an antidote to the neural stimulant to him or…"

"Or what, Robert?"

"I wasn't going to help him escape if that's what you're thinking." Robert's pain and annoyance blatantly displayed on his face.

"What *were* you considering, Robert?" The Executor demanded.

"I considered ending his suffering myself. Alright? Are you satisfied? Perhaps it's time for me to recuse myself." Robert reached up and pressed a button on his data pad. The pad went black. Robert stood up to excuse himself. "I'm sorry if I've disappointed you, sir. I've reached my limit where my nephew is concerned. Do you have any additional orders?"

Executor Hale stood up as well. Concern showing on his face, he approached the Admiral. "Robert, let's step over here and talk for a moment."

Robert laid his data pad down on the table and stepped to the other side of the room. The two began to talk quietly. "Robert, I know how much this young man means to you. I am doing everything in my power to bring him back to us. I know this is painful. If it makes things easier, I'll keep you out of the loop where he's concerned. You are a very talented man and I really want to keep you on this project. I could use your help retraining the others and directing Lt. Holden. Please don't do anything rash where your nephew is concerned. I don't want you to have to tell his mother what happened to him. I know you, Robert. You would have to confess what you had done to his mother, even knowing she'd never forgive you. Can I count on you?"

"What do you want me to do?" Robert wanted to stay involved to protect his nephew and the crew. Although the amount he had helped them so far was mostly nonexistent. He was still near his own breaking point.

"Keep an eye on the surveillance of the crew once Lt. Holden goes in. Just remember to call him Chief Holden not Lt. Holden. Do whatever you think is necessary to perpetuate the misinformation we are feeding them. You might also want to question the Commander and Lt. Ryder about what happened last night."

Robert nodded. "Understood, sir. Shall I start moving

them into their new cells?"

Executor Hale gave his approval and sent Robert on his way. The second he was gone, Luciano reconvened his meeting. "Actually, I'm glad he decided it was time to step away."

Admiral Garcia leaned forward on the table. "Is there a problem with Admiral Deacons, sir? Is there reason to doubt his loyalty?"

"No, of course not," Executor Hale responded. "The problem is I don't think he's going to be able to stomach what I have to do next."

"Which is what, Supreme Executor?" Edgar was eager to step in and replace his obviously weak counterpart.

"Lt. Marissa Holden and Captain Alexander have both been in the presence of Pateras. They *can't* be retrained. I must do whatever is necessary to see that they don't survive. I don't want to execute them openly. It could alienate Lt. Jake Holden and Admiral Deacons. It has to look like an accident, or suicide."

The room grew deathly quiet. Executor Hale finally asked, "Does anyone *else* have a problem with this? I am within my rights to *order* their executions. I *am* ordering their executions, I simply need a better method. Suggestions?"

Admiral Garcia leaned back in his seat. "Are we going to try to save Lt. Holden's baby? It could serve to placate him over the unfortunate loss of his wife."

Executor Hale nodded. "Possibly, or it could saddle him with a constant reminder of what he lost. Is it possible to save the baby and lose the mother, Doctor?"

"Not without raising all kinds of red flags. On a backward world, yes, it's possible, probable even. Here and now, it's just not possible. The chances are greater for saving the mother and losing the baby. Losing them both is easy enough."

"How would you go about it?"

Dr. Rhodes sighed. "You know that cover story we fed Mr.

Holden? That's exactly how I would do it. Give her something to cause her to abort the baby along with a blood thinner and a sedative. She'll bleed out alone in a cell at night."

"What about the Captain? Suicide might be the best option."

Admiral Garcia appeared contemplative, "What if we got Mr. Holden to offer him a lethal dose of a sedative? We could get him to leave it in the cell for the Captain to use if he so desires. Send someone else in later to use it on him and leave it in the floor to be found. It'll end up looking like an assisted suicide. The doctor could even claim to feel sorry for the Captain and offer it to him."

Executor Hale took a deep breath. "Based on a conversation I had with him, I seriously doubt the Captain will take his own life willingly… unless…" The Executor began to smile.

Admiral Garcia leaned forward again. "Unless… what?"

"Let's step up the program. Shorten his days by four to six hours. Increase the number of beatings he's taking. Add a hint of a hallucinogenic drug to the mix and he won't know how many days he's been here. If he's counting the days by the number of beatings he's taking, getting him to the seventh or eighth beating might be enough to do it."

"Seventh or eighth, why seventh or eighth?" Admiral Garcia asked.

"According to Mr. Holden, the Captain believes he will be here enduring this torture for six days. If he thinks he's reached day seven. He'll start to think Pateras has abandoned him. He might be willing to commit suicide at that point."

Commodore Vardin looked confused. "But sir, didn't you try to talk Admiral Deacons out of that not ten minutes ago?"

"Yes, I did. If Admiral Deacons euthanizes his own nephew, he would never be the same. If he takes his own life, *without my knowledge*, the Admiral is relieved and remains loyal."

Admiral Garcia joined Commodore Vardin in his confusion. "I don't understand, sir. You said you weren't concerned about his loyalty."

Executor Hale was slightly annoyed with the two men. He hated explaining himself to these pitifully finite creatures. "Perhaps you are unaware of Admiral Deacons' history."

"Sir?" Admiral Garcia added concern to his confusion.

"Admiral Deacons is a second-generation conscript. His parents were taken from a world deemed unready for admission to the Commonwealth. He was a boy when his family was recruited. The world he came from had a Liontari presence and his parents served Pateras. They were able to be convinced to change their loyalty. I want to be sure Pateras gets the blame for the Captain's death, not me."

Commodore Vardin swallowed hard. "Forgive me for asking, but how did someone with such a questionable background reach the rank of admiral? Why have you trusted him this far?"

Executor Hale glowered at the impertinent man. Admiral Garcia stepped in to calmly smooth the ruffled feathers of his superior. "Commodore Vardin, the Supreme Executor knows what he's doing. You would do well to keep your questions to pertinent matters."

Executor Hale nodded appreciatively to Admiral Garcia. He didn't, however, want to leave the Commodore doubting him. "His family, until his nephew came along, have been model Commonwealth citizens. When the question of his promotion came up, I decided it would work best to keep him on the offensive side of the upcoming conflict. I have kept him under close surveillance for several years. He has not given me cause to doubt him. I intend to keep it that way."

Admiral Garcia was glad to hear the Supreme Executor's explanation, although his concerns weren't unilaterally relieved. "What's our next move?"

"Commodore Vardin, start running him through the new program. I'll set up a timetable for you. You'll need to put all shifts on standby. If we're going to convince him two days have passed, we'll need all shifts to show up earlier and earlier. Instruct the guards of their role in convincing the Captain he's losing track of time. Don't let them get caught up in any casual conversations about their schedule being screwed up. Are we clear?"

Commodore Vardin nodded. "Yes sir."

As the man stood to leave, Executor Hale added one more word of warning. "Make sure he isn't seen by his crew while being transported."

The man nodded and hurried out to set to work. Dr. Rhodes stood to leave with him to prepare the Captain for his new treatment. Executor Hale had one last set of instructions for the doctor. "Dr. Rhodes, keep the Captain on a very low level of hallucinogens constantly. Use the neural stimulants for his beatings. Stay attuned to the timetable I send out as well. If the Captain is used to seeing certain personnel at certain times of the day, see that they are present. That includes you. Prepare whatever you need for Lt. Marissa Holden. I'll let you know when I'm ready to use it. Any questions?"

Seeing none, he dismissed the rest of the meeting. Luciano moved over to the window and looked out across the base. As he stood staring out the window, his body coursing with hatred for Pateras' precious humans, two figures materialized behind him. Luciano turned around. The two figures dropped to one knee and bowed their heads in front of him. Luciano smiled. He so enjoyed having others at his feet. It was what he desired and what he felt he deserved. "You may rise."

The two stood although their posture remained contrite. "My Lord," the first one spoke. "We don't understand what you're attempting to accomplish. If Pateras has refused to allow you to harm this man, how can he be harmed by anyone?"

"If he chooses to kill himself, I have obeyed Pateras. Pateras doesn't interfere with the free will of men. He may talk to him. He might beg him not to kill himself. He might even heal him. He might *not*. This is the best chance I have of stopping this man. It might be the only chance I have."

The second creature spoke, "Yes, My Lord. What would you have us do?"

"Keep him company. Suggest whatever you can to cause him to believe Pateras has abandoned him. Keep his mind so occupied, he can't hear Pateras."

The two nodded. "Yes, My Lord," they answered simultaneously then vanished.

• •

As David began his own gauntlet, Jake was about to face one of his own making. The crew were placed in the temporary holding cells as ordered. Brynna and Thane were together in an interrogation room. Admiral Deacons questioned each of them about the previous night. The two were confused by the questions and offered little insight. Brynna finally asked, "Admiral, why are you asking about last night? Why were the guards chasing me in circles?"

The Admiral continued to ask questions about Arni. He finally appeared to get angry. He wanted to tell them what happened. The only way to give them the information was to appear to angrily *say too much*. The Admiral slammed his fist on the table. "You think Pateras has you under his protection, don't you? That little invisibility act is not going to work again. We're taking steps to see that none of you disappear like that again!"

Thane and Brynna glanced warily at each other. It certainly explained the guards' behavior. The Admiral continued his rant. "If I have to, I'll chain every one of you to your beds! You'll have to *beg* the guards to escort you to the toilet! If you know what's good for you, you'll stop asking Pateras for help. Every time you ask him for help, I'll make your lives ten times more miserable! Are we clear?"

Thane and Brynna wearily replied, "Yes sir." The two were only partially clear on what had happened. Their minds were so tired, they could only make partial sense of the situation. The Admiral had the two escorted to their new quarters in the temporary holding cells.

These cells were larger and designed to hold up to eight prisoners. From the cells they had previously been in, this was a clear step up despite the increased number of occupants. Their previous cells had an open shower in the corner with a weak stream of cold water and no privacy wall. The toilet sat next to the shower and a small sink beyond that. All were in the same room as their mattress on the floor. This cell had actual beds with an opaque wall separating the bathroom facilities from the rest of the room and offering a small amount of privacy. As it turned out, the shower even offered hot water. The five women were placed in one cell and their husbands were placed in a cell across from them.

Seeing their comrades for the first time in days energized the crew. The front wall of the cell was designed in old style bars. The sides and back were the more modern thick opaque polymer. The husbands and wives spent several tearful minutes reconnecting as the last crewman joined them. Jake was brought down the hall in cuffs and tossed roughly into the men's cell. No one greeted him. Although no one had any proof, each one believed Jake was responsible for their plight.

Thane could finally stand it no longer. "What's the matter, Jake? Did you do something to tick off your master?"

Jake didn't respond. He sat there on a bunk in the back of the cell and avoided eye contact with anyone.

Thane went to stand directly in front of the dejected security chief. "C'mon Jake, we all know you're the reason we're in here. What gives? Why did they throw you in here?"

Jake looked up at Thane, then got up and moved slowly away from him. Thane's rage overtook him. He shoved Jake face first into the wall and gave him several sharp jabs in the back. Reflex took over for an instant, and Jake reacted. He pushed off the wall enough to twist free. He grabbed Thane by the shirt to throw a punch of his own. Thane had his own fist ready to go again. Jake slowly dropped his fist and released Thane. Thane, surprised by his reaction, hesitated. His hesitation didn't last long. He threw Jake against the wall again holding him there with his hand firmly around Jake's throat. Jake grabbed his hand to protect his own throat. He knew how to get out of the hold and had the strength to do so. He forced himself to remain in place. Thane punched Jake with his free hand. "Let's hear it, Jake! I want to hear you confess! Tell us why you betrayed us! Was it worth it? Was it?"

Jake looked angrily at Thane as Thane punched him a couple more times. The crew watched in shock. No one was quite sure how to react to Thane's outburst. His strength was fueled by his anger, although his weakened physical condition severely diminished his ability to maintain his grip on Jake. Jake felt Thane's grip waning and managed to finally address his accuser. "I – didn't – report – you. The Captain did."

As soon as the words were out of his mouth, Jake felt Brynna's eyes on him. Thane's grip tightened again. Braxton approached Thane. "Stand down, Lieutenant. That's an order."

Thane protested. "But sir, he just accused the Captain of lying to us and betraying us."

The Lt. Commander was the ranking officer in the cell. He ordered the lieutenant once again to release the security chief. Thane slowly released his grip and backed away. His eyes never moved off his target. As Jake started to relax slightly, Braxton put him right back in the same spot he had been in. "Alright, Chief, you've got about thirty seconds to explain yourself before I make Marissa a widow and your baby an orphan before he's born."

The drops put in his eyes by Dr. Rhodes were quite irritating to Jake's eyes. They had made his eyes bloodshot as intended. They also caused his eyes to water easily. Jake looked Braxton in the eye and lied to him. "I don't know what you want me to explain. I didn't do this. I've been locked up in a cell for five days except for trips for my re-education and… and… two other times."

Braxton wasn't giving in so easily. "So, how can you tell me the Captain did this if you've been locked in a cell like the rest of us? None of us has seen him, how could you? Talk fast, or I swear I will squeeze the life out of you here and now."

Jake forced tears out of his eyes. "Then do it! I don't have anything left to live for anyway. It's too late to make Marissa a widow. She and the baby are already dead. Admiral Deacons shot me in front of her. He convinced her I was dead. It caused her to miscarry during the night. She bled out. She and my son are dead! They let me see her and the baby before they shipped the bodies home. On the way back to my cell, I saw the Captain in the hall with some woman. He was wearing a Commodore's uniform. The woman was – was all over him. I'm sorry, Commander." Jake twisted as much as Braxton's grip would allow to try and see Brynna's face.

Lazaro cast a guilty look towards Brynna as well. As soon as her eyes met his, Lazaro looked away. Brynna moved her eyes slowly back to Braxton. "Lt. Commander Flint, release him."

Braxton didn't let go, yet. "Commander, you can't believe this traitor! The Captain would never do that to us."

"I understand that, Braxton. I'm not ready to trust Jake and believe his story either. He's telling me roughly the same things the Supreme Executor did yesterday. Either Jake was planted in here to try and convince us the Captain betrayed us, or he's telling the truth. What's it going to look like to the general public if we start killing each other? They'll know for sure Pateras is to be avoided. If you kill him, you're betraying Pateras."

Lazaro looked up at Jake then Brynna. "Commander," he started slowly, "I saw the Captain as well. He came in wearing a Commodore's uniform. He was in the company of the Supreme Executor, some blond woman, the Admirals, and a couple others. Jake may be right."

Cheyenne jumped in. "No, he's not right. I saw the Captain with those same people. There was something strange in his eyes. He wasn't himself. It was like he was drugged or something."

Cheyenne bit down on her lower lip. Brynna could see she wanted to say more. "You see and hear things the rest of us don't catch. You tend to have a sense about these things."

Cheyenne nodded slowly. She hoped Brynna had seen her hesitation and knew she was guarding some other piece of information.

Brynna looked back at Braxton whose patience was running out. "Braxton, personally I believe he and the Supreme Executor are lying. I still would like you to let him go. Please, Braxton."

Braxton clenched his jaw. Jake felt his hand tighten on his throat. He had two options, try and talk his way out of it or break Braxton's hold on him. If he broke the hold, he might reveal his physical strength as being unimpaired by hunger and sleep deprivation. He decided to go with talking his way out of it, although not the way one would expect. "You're right! I lied. I did it. I turned you in. So, finish it. Finish me! Do it!"

Braxton froze. This was not what he expected. Doubts crept in. Why would Jake confess like this? Did he want to die?

Why would he want to die? Was this a dare? Was Marissa really dead? She hadn't been brought in with the other women. From across the cell he heard Brynna still asking him to release Jake. Braxton slowly conceded. He released Jake's throat. He grabbed Jake's shirt and swung him around off the wall. "Alright Chief, you get to stay alive, for now. I don't trust you and I don't believe you. Stay out of my way and Thane's if you want to live."

As Braxton's hands released Jake's shirt, Jake moved back over to the bunk he'd been sitting on. He sat down and again avoided eye contact with the others.

Braxton, Thane, and Lazaro moved to the front of the cell to talk to Brynna. Jason stayed sitting on a bunk where he could easily hear the conversation while keeping an eye on Jake. He had trouble concentrating on the conversation. His thoughts kept lingering on his inability to stop Braxton or Thane from harming Jake. He was a physician, sworn to heal and protect others from harm, yet he had just stood there while Jake was attacked. He caught himself wondering why he still sat here, doing nothing to check on his crew mate. Jason finally pushed himself to go check on Jake while the others talked.

Braxton and Thane were still full of anger and bitterness. Braxton began to spout off. "Commander, why did you stop us? You know he's guilty. I don't know what's going on with the Captain, but I trust him more than I trust Jake. If Marissa is dead, it's Jake's fault. You know it is."

Thane quickly followed. "We may have committed treason and deserve to be punished. Jake's betrayal is far worse. He knew what the Commonwealth was guilty of. He knew what they would do to us, and he turned us in anyway. I would rather he had executed us himself than live like this. He doesn't deserve mercy, Commander."

Brynna's shocked face greeted Thane. "Gentlemen, have you forgotten Drea? We were all guilty of betraying Galat III to the Commonwealth. Arni died to save us all, including Jake. We didn't deserve mercy, not one of us."

Thane wasn't ready to give up. "Jake knows all that and he still betrayed us. His guilt is worse than ours. We didn't know what was going to happen to Galat. He knew what would happen to us."

Brynna sighed. "Mr. Ryder, I don't know what Arni's plan is. I do know this is a part of it. We need to wait and see what his intentions are. That means we leave Jake to face whatever Arni intends."

Thane gripped the bars in front of him tightly. "What if Arni intends him to face justice at our hands?"

Brynna shook her head. "Is that justice or revenge? Gentlemen, give me your word. None of you will lay a hand on him. He's Arni's responsibility."

Each one gave the Commander their word including Jason who was giving Jake as thorough of an exam as he could without a scanner.

Jason was cautious in his examination of Jake. After the reaction of the first two men, he doubted Jake would trust him very much. "Jake, let me check you out."

Jake glared at the doctor. He had more reasons than his shipmates' violent reception to distrust the Doc. Jason had nearly forced an abortion on Marissa several months ago. "I'm fine. Go away."

Jason held up two fingers and began to wave his hand back and forth at a fast pace blurring the image. "So how many fingers am I holding up?"

Jake didn't smile, but he stopped glaring. "Very funny."

"I know my bedside manner hasn't always been the best. I'm trying to improve. Let me know later how I did, okay?"

Jake was skeptical. "Why later?"

Jason gave Jake an apologetic look. "Because right now I'm

going to have to press on your ribs and your back and belly. It's not going to feel good. I just don't want you to hold that against me. Why don't you lie down?"

Jake did as he was told. As predicted, Jake didn't care for the Doc's poking and prodding. Jake had a gash above his eye from being shoved into the wall. Jason tore a piece of cloth off his own shirt and dampened it from the sink. He cleaned the wound as best he could. Normally he would have checked a patient's vital signs first using a scanner. Since he had no such access, he resorted to checking them last. Jason picked up Jake's wrist and held onto it while looking across the room. "Doc, what are you doing?"

"I don't have a scanner to check your vitals. I'm using a clock down the hall."

"You can see through walls now?"

"Don't be ridiculous, Chief. There's a reflection of a clock from down the hall on the back wall of that cell over there."

Jake started to sit up. "Seriously?"

"Lie still, Chief. Oh great, you made me lose count. Now I've got to start over."

"Well how long is this going to take?"

"It's going to take an entire minute. I can't make out the seconds well enough to use them. I can only make out the hours and minutes. So, you saw the Captain?"

"Yes." Jake replied as succinctly as possible.

"He's alive and healthy?"

"Yeah, … why?" Jake wondered where this was going. "I thought you were counting."

"Not until the clock minute changes again. It'll take one minute after I start counting. I also have to count your respiratory rate at the same time. You know… I expected the Captain to be executed, or if he was a prisoner, I expected him to be in bad shape by now. I really didn't expect this."

"Me either." Jake tried to look anywhere other than the Doctor's face.

"Admiral Garcia actually shot you in front of Marissa? That's cruelty beyond measure."

Jake immediately brought his gaze back to Jason. "It was Admiral Deacons, our beloved Captain's uncle." Jake's bitterness was apparent in his speech.

Jason simply nodded. He had started counting again. Jake stopped talking. He didn't want Jason to lose count again. This old-fashioned way of practicing medicine was not pleasant. In a minute, Jason was done. He laid his arm down gently and encouraged the young man to get some sleep. He assured him his injuries were painful, not lethal.

Jason moved back over to his own bunk and stared into space. After a long time, Lazaro wandered over by him. "What's going on, Doc?"

Before he could answer, five guards approached. "Prisoners, lie face down on your bunks with your hands behind your backs. Turn your faces towards the wall."

The crew moved slowly into position. Once they were in place, the guards entered the cells. Two stood guard just inside the men's cell, one stood guard outside with his weapon drawn, the last two made their way from one prisoner to the next. One would hold each prisoner down while the second would administer a hypo-spray of some type of medication.

The women watched in horror, fearing the worst. They demanded to know what the men were being given. The guards ignored their pleas.

The guards reached Jake and plunged the hypo-spray into a thickly folded cloth placed discreetly near Jake's shoulder. They quickly made the rounds. When they reached Braxton, they injected him then put binders on his wrists and pulled him out of the cell. "Prisoner 7140, it's time for your re-education session."

Braxton's eyes began to glass over. "Yes sir," he meekly replied.

The guards pulled out of the cell. They turned their attention to the women. Giving them the same instructions, they began to administer the same drug to the women. Brynna was taken from the women's cell for re-education as well.

As soon as the two were gone, Lexi moved to the bars in the front of the cell. Her eyes were just as glazed as Braxton's had been. "Jason… Jason… what – uh, what did they give us? I feel strange."

Jason sat up. His eyes and his mind were unfocused. He knew he heard someone call his name. "Laurel? Did you call me?"

Laura was already sitting up staring at the floor. "No… Lexi called, I think Lexi called you. I don't feel right either."

Lexi repeated her question. She began to pace. It seemed to keep her brain working. When she realized the pacing helped, she encouraged Jason to get up and walk too. Jason stood up slowly and paced artificially at first, then more purposefully. Lexi tried again once he looked more ready to answer. "Jason, what did they give us?"

Jason stopped pacing to answer. "I would… I think it was something to… to make us more suggestible. It… It seems to be a mild dose." Jason started to pace again. His brain was having trouble processing. "They can't give us anything stronger… because… If it's too strong, we'll just shut down."

Lexi continued to pace. "How do we fight this? The pacing seems to help."

"Increased… increasing the metabolism will get it out of your system faster. I don't know how long the drug is designed to last. We may not be able to keep it up long enough to… uh… to stop it… counteract it."

"We've been subjected to sleep deprivation to try and break

us. Why would they give us something that might put us to sleep?"

Thane slowly rolled into a sitting position. "I think Pateras hid us from them last night. The Admiral said – he said something about stopping us from disappearing again. The guards came in my cell last night. They rolled me out of bed then looked around like they were searching for something. They never looked at me directly. He said not to call on P-Pateras."

Jason nodded. "That makes sense. If they think we might disappear again, drugging us would – would – it might interfere… I think. We can't think well enough to – to call on him."

Lexi looked at Lazaro. "Lt. Commander, it's making me sleepy. Do we lie down and get some sleep, or do we fight this?"

Lazaro and Jason were the ranking officers present. Jason got Lazaro up and moving. The two then ordered the rest of the crew to get moving. The crew were already so exhausted, they were more inclined to give in to the drug. Jason insisted they spend one hour in increased activity.

Cheyenne wasn't even slightly interested in obeying orders. Lexi and Laura pulled her up by her arms and dragged her into the shower. They doused her with cold water until she reacted as desired. Lazaro didn't handle it well when he heard Cheyenne scream as the chilly water hit her. Cheyenne rushed out of the bathroom crying. "Stop IT! Laz, please get me out of here. I can't do this anymore! I just want to sleep!" She reached her arm as far as she could through the bars. Lazaro reached as far as he could from his side. It wasn't nearly enough.

Lazaro tried to reassure her. "Cheyenne, you're strong. You can do this."

Cheyenne dropped slowly to her knees with her face still pressed to the bars. Tears still streaming down her face. "No, I can't. I'm not strong. The Captain knew I wasn't. He keeps telling me not to cry, because he knows I'm not strong."

Lexi stood still watching Cheyenne and Lazaro talking. Things started to get fuzzy again. She resumed pacing as soon as she realized what was happening. In a minute, she was clear enough to encourage Lazaro to keep Cheyenne engaged. Cheyenne's crying was keeping her metabolism elevated.

Lazaro had knelt to stay at eye level with his wife. "Cheyenne, call on Pateras. Use his strength. You have to keep moving to get this drug out of your system."

Cheyenne stood up slowly, tears still streaming down her face. She began to pace with the others. As soon as she calmed down, she began to audibly cry out to Pateras for help.

• •

The guards made another pass by the cells. Seeing the increased activity, they reported to the Chief Medical Officer. Minutes later, Dr. Rhodes came to see what was going on for himself. He folded his arms as he stood there observing the crew. He finally dropped his arms back down to his sides and abruptly left, muttering under his breath. Twenty minutes later, the guards returned with a second dose of the medication and bracelets with medical scanning capabilities which were placed on each prisoner. The doctor was with the guards this time. He placed a neural inhibitor patch on the back of each crewman's neck. He left each one immobilized until every prisoner had been treated. He waited until everyone had been immobilized more than long enough for the second dose to take effect. He removed the neural inhibitors and left the area once he was satisfied none of the crew were in danger from the drug.

The second the coast was clear, Jason popped his head up and looked directly at Lexi. "What just happened?"

Lexi gave Jason a wary look. "Did you suffer from memory loss?"

"No…" Jason made a face. "I remember what happened. That second shot, accompanied by the neural inhibitor, should have put us under the table. We should be babbling idiots. Is everybody else clear-headed?" Jason made eye contact with every member of the crew. Each one gave a calm clear reassuring nod.

Lexi seemed as perplexed as Jason. She felt fine, better than she had minutes ago. No one was quite sure what to do or say. They sat there quietly considering their circumstances.

Cheyenne broke the silence with a giggle. The group looked to her curiously. She stared at the floor and began to quote from the Ancient Texts:

> **The weapons of the Dark Lord will fail when the children of Pateras call on their Father's name.**

Lazaro looked at his wife in awe. "How do you remember this stuff?"

Thane sat up slowly, still paranoid his head would be woozy. When nothing happened, he smiled for the first time in days. "Who cares how. I'm just glad she does."

The others echoed Thane's sentiments. Jake said nothing. He continued to play the part of the grieving husband and father. Jake looked around at the others. He didn't like seeing the very crew he had protected for months suffering, yet he knew he needed to report the medication failure. The conflict within him was growing. The crew agreed to take the time to get some non-drug-induced sleep. It was the second time in two days they were allowed unexpected sleep. When they had been alone in their cells previously, one hint of sleep brought on an onslaught of deafening squeals broadcast through the audio-visual system or the guards coming and forcing them to stand or march back and forth in their cells. They were given only about two hours of sleep per night.

Thirty minutes later, the entire group was sound asleep except Jake. Assuming the crew were now sufficiently drugged the guards came through looking rather smugly at their prisoners. They stood outside the door to the women's cell discussing the orders given for the previous night. They had heard the rumors about the crew's disappearance. The two thought this was a perfect time to carry out the lapsed orders since the women were drugged. One guard entered the cell while the other stood watch at the door. The first walked slowly past each bunk trying to decide which woman appealed the most to him. He stopped at Cheyenne's bedside. Looking over at his co-conspirator he grinned maliciously.

Jake was lying on his back with his hands behind his head. His eyes were closed the entire time, yet he heard every movement and the entire discussion. As soon as he heard the guards discussing Cheyenne, Jake gave them a subtle warning. "I wouldn't do that if I were you."

The guards looked towards the men's cell. Jake raised his head and rolled over to watch the events he knew would quickly unfold. "Shut up, Prisoner," one guard barked.

"She's not nearly as helpless as she seems," Jake grinned. He really hoped the man would try. He enjoyed watching Cheyenne retaliate in combat. She was petite, but she packed a wallop.

The guard standing watch moved over to the men's cell. "Don't make me come in there and shut you up."

Jake laid back down. "Don't say I didn't warn you." He continued to grin as he heard the uncertainty of the guards reflected by their hesitation.

Jake finally heard one say to the other, "Hurry up, get on with it."

Jake took a deep breath and yelled, "CHEYENNE! Watch out!"

Cheyenne's eyes opened to see the guard standing over her, reaching for her. The other women stirred as well. Cheyenne had been sleeping in the perfect position to kick her assailant in the side of the head. She caught the man completely off-guard, despite Jake's warning. The man failed to dodge her kick and managed to hit his own head on the bunk above her. Cheyenne twisted around quickly and planted both her feet to his chest and abdomen. He stumbled backwards and fell over a bench in the center of the cell.

Hearing Jake's warning and the commotion across the hall, the men roused. They quickly got out of bed. The women heard emphatic shouts of instruction for themselves and useless threats for the guards.

The guard standing watch was so shocked, he was unable to react. By the time he was able to move, his partner was on the floor. He pulled his weapon and fired at Cheyenne. Knowing his probable intent, Cheyenne ducked just as the man fired. He missed. The other women came to Cheyenne's aid. Laura attacked the guard at the door preventing him from aiming his weapon a second time. She couldn't overpower him, although she could disturb and distract him. Aulani went to the aid of Laura while Lexi joined Cheyenne in kicking and stomping the guard on the ground.

The guard on the floor recovered enough to grab Cheyenne's foot before she stomped him again. He shoved her backwards onto the ground. The break was enough to stop Lexi's next attack and force her off balance as well. The guard managed to roll over onto his hands and knees. Lexi regained her balance and bloodied his nose. The man got to his feet and shoved Lexi to the floor. Cheyenne launched herself at him. He caught her and tossed her aside like a sack of laundry. He'd had a belly full of this. Heading for the door, he grabbed Aulani around the waist. Tossing her back into the cell, he reached for Laura who wisely withdrew. The guards hastily secured the cell and retreated.

The women caught their breath for a moment before answering the men's entreaties as to their well-being. Except for a couple bruises and additional exhaustion, the women reported being in good condition.

Thane looked over at Jake who was still lounging on his bunk. "Are you comfortable, Chief?" His tone dripping with sarcasm.

Jake looked over at Thane. Sitting up slowly he responded, "I warned him not to do it."

Thane's temper flared again. "You warned them… the guards? You…"

Aulani quickly interrupted. "Thane! He also warned Cheyenne they were coming for her."

Cheyenne walked to the front of the cell. "Thanks, Jake, I appreciate the warning. I owe you one."

Jake nodded to Cheyenne. "No thanks necessary, I was just doing my job."

Thane glared at Jake. "You really tried to protect the women?" The frustrated pilot was still not convinced Jake had the crew's best interests at heart. He sat back down on his bunk. Glancing up at Aulani he asked, "Are you sure you're okay?"

"I'm a little bruised, Thane, but thanks to Jake, I'm fine and so is Cheyenne."

• •

The guards who were trounced by the women reported a modified version of their story to their superior. The one guard who was injured was sent to the Infirmary. Word quickly got back to Dr. Rhodes. Dr. Rhodes questioned the guard in the Infirmary then reviewed the surveillance footage. It was clear these prisoners weren't affected by their injections. A new briefing in the Supreme Executor's office ensued.

• •

The crew settled back down quickly to get back to sleep.

Braxton and Brynna were returned to the cells. The routine generally included an exchange of one set of prisoners for another. This time no one was taken for re-education. The crew was both relieved and unsettled by the alteration in procedure.

Before Braxton and Brynna were able to get much rest, several guards entered the facility. This time the crew was ordered to kneel in front of the bench in the center of the cell and place their hands behind their backs. A device was placed around the neck of each prisoner. The crew had seen this device the day they were captured. One had been placed around the Captain's neck to insure the cooperation of the crew. Once each crew member had been harnessed with the devices, the guards quickly left the area. Most of the crew moved back to their beds, although this time they didn't settle in.

A cold heaviness filled the air. The crew scooted up onto the edge of the bunks sensing something was about to happen. Supreme Executor Luciano Hale strode slowly down the corridor. The anger and hatred etched firmly across his face. He'd been unable to hurt the crew nearly as much as he wanted. His goal had been to stop Pateras' message from spreading and his own people had furthered it. He wanted revenge, badly.

The Executor's appearance did not bode well in the crew's minds. Brynna already knew from experience his attention meant unwelcome news. Being the senior officer, Brynna stood up carefully and approached the front of the cell. She was still shaky from her visit to the re-education chamber. "What can I do for you Executor Hale? Are you here to bring more bad news?"

Luciano grinned smugly. "I do my best where traitors of your caliber are concerned."

"What is it this time?" Brynna no longer felt compelled to call him, *sir*.

"It appears I made a mistake putting all of you together.

It seems you have gained strength by seeing each other. I hope it's enough to sustain you because it is the last time you will ever see each other. I'm moving you back to your original cells. We don't have a large re-education facility here, so I intend to change the game plan, again. You will begin re-education in your own cells."

The Supreme Executor held up a small remote. Pointing to it, he continued to boast of his new plan. "Guards will be assigned to watch you with a remote like this. We won't force your eyes open the same way we do in the re-education chamber. What they *will* do, is press this button every time they see your eyes close." Executor Hale pressed the button on the remote in his hand. Brynna's collar illuminated. She cried out and grabbed for her neck. The Executor released the button and Brynna relaxed. "That was the lowest setting. The highest setting could kill… eventually. Just so we're clear on some things. This is not a simplistic device. If you try to break it or remove it, the device will deliver an incapacitating charge to your body. An alarm will be sent to the guards, so they can hopefully save your life before the charge becomes lethal. I only hope for your sake, they can reach you in time. I'm having you all moved in a few days to Mara where your training will be completed. If your re-education is unsuccessful, you will live out the remainder of your days in the prison there. I'm not expecting you will live long lives. As soon as the restraints are lifted from me, I plan on executing any of you who can't be turned back to the Commonwealth."

Executor Hale gave his words a minute to sink in. He looked from face to face. The looks of fear and hopelessness fed his cruelty. "Furthermore, your families are going to be taken into custody, questioned, and possibly imprisoned as well."

The crew erupted in anger and objections. Brynna took control quickly. "Executor Hale, you know our families know nothing about our mission or our treason. We took great pains to protect them by keeping them in the dark. What do you expect to gain from harassing them?"

Executor Hale moved directly in front of Brynna and folded his arms across his chest. "I expect to motivate you to change your position. The transport ship taking you to Mara will be here in three days. If I must put any of you aboard it, the orders will immediately go out to have your families arrested. You can stop this yourselves any time between now and the day you're put aboard the transport. Declare your allegiance to the Commonwealth again, and this will all be an unpleasant memory."

Braxton stood and approached the front of his cell. "Even if we did declare allegiance to the Commonwealth, you wouldn't trust us. What would it prove?"

Executor Hale smiled sadistically. "That's true. I *wouldn't* trust you. You would have to prove yourselves to me. You would still have to complete the re-education process although it would be less painful. You would be allowed to eat regular meals, and you would receive medications to help ease you through the process. I might even consider allowing you to stay under house arrest in the base housing. You do know I wouldn't trust you to resume this mission. You would be reassigned to a nice safe, protected facility. Someplace where you aren't bombarded with questionable influences. Of course, I would also expect you to update your previous mission reports. I seriously doubt the veracity of what was previously submitted. Your Captain has been kind enough to give me alternative versions of his previous submissions."

Brynna grabbed the bars in front of her. "What makes you think anything you can do to us in the next three days is going to cause us to change our loyalty? Pateras has -" Brynna's collar lit up again and began to shock her more violently this time. Her muscles contracted refusing to allow her to release the grip she had on the bars in front of her. The shock only lasted about three seconds, although it felt longer.

Executor Hale snickered mockingly. "Did I forget to mention, if you call upon the name of Pateras or Arni or use any of the names they are known by, your collar will deliver increasingly larger and longer charges? You will learn to despise the name of Pateras… or you will join him."

Brynna's knees had nearly given way under her. Laura and Aulani jumped immediately to her side to keep her from hitting the floor. The two helped to steady her as she gave an appropriate riposte. "Do whatever you think you have to. I will call on his name from now until the day I die. I don't have to speak it aloud. Unlike you, he hears my very thoughts. Nothing you can do will change my loyalty or stop me from calling on HIM."

The smirk was wiped from the Dark Lord's face. It was quickly replaced with anger and hatred. "Just so you all understand. For the next three days, you will no longer be on a diet consisting of bread and water. You'll get nothing, no bread, no water. I'm having the water to your cells turned completely off. You'll get no sleep, you'll be punished for inappropriate words or actions and inundated with re-education. If you are still alive and resistant to returning to the Commonwealth in three days, then you'll be put in a stasis chamber and moved to Mara where you can be reunited with your families. If you come to your senses, let the guards know. They'll be glad to welcome you back to the Commonwealth. Any questions?"

Executor Hale was met with silent angry stares. Seeing he had made his point, he walked away feeling rather pleased with himself. The Executor returned to his office and sent for Commodore Vardin.

Once alone, Jason advised everyone to drink as much water as they could immediately. He also suggested they wash up and even soak their clothing to carry at least a small amount of water with them.

"Soak our clothes? What good is that going to do?" Thane balked.

Jason sighed. "This is going to sound crazy, but it has a two-fold purpose. You can squeeze or suck the fluid out of your clothing after leaving this cell. The water in your clothes will evaporate quickly so you'll have to ingest it quickly.

Aulani hesitated. "Jason, what if they take the temperature in our cells way down again? We'll end up with a case of hypothermia."

Jason nodded. "That is a possibility. That is the second reason I told you to soak your clothes. What I don't think you understand is, we can't survive even a week without water. The average time to live without water is three to five days. We're already in bad shape. When Supreme Executor Hale said, if we were still alive and fighting him, it was a very large *if*. A lowered body temp might prolong our lives."

Cheyenne stopped drinking to ask, "The Captain said six days. It's been five. We only have to survive one more day."

Lazaro gave his wife an apologetic look, "Unless he's been lying to us all this time."

Cheyenne gave her husband a look Lazaro had only seen one other time. Lazaro hung his head. He shouldn't be having these doubts and he knew it. His wife's disappointment in him was all too obvious.

Brynna backed the doctor's advice. "Drink up people, and get those clothes soaked. Whatever his plans are, be strong and be ready. He will get us out of this. I trust him, and I trust the Captain." Brynna was careful to avoid calling Pateras' name. She hoped the crew understood her full meaning.

Brynna soaked her clothing in the shower and drank what she could from the shower. Jason jumped quickly into the men's shower and soaked his own clothing. Braxton jumped in next. To continue perpetuating the myths spun by the Supreme Executor, Jake moved to drench himself as well. Lazaro and Jake moved towards the shower at the same time. Jason pulled Lazaro back. "Commander Dominick, let me take another look at that bump on your head."

Lazaro stopped. Sensing Jason was trying to say something, Lazaro tried to play along. "Hunh? Oh, okay sure. I feel okay though." Lazaro sat down on the bench.

As soon as Jake stepped behind the wall in the shower. Jason grabbed Braxton and whispered. "Make a little noise to cover my conversation."

Braxton nodded. He gave Lt. Ryder a noisy reprimand for not obeying his orders promptly earlier and not trusting Jake as he should have. Thane played along and argued back briefly before managing a hostile, "Yes… sir!"

Jason stepped quickly to the bars and whispered loudly, "Commander, Jake was lying. I was checking his pulse while he was talking. He was lying about the Captain. I just thought you should know."

Jason finished just in time for two guards to arrive to move Brynna back to her original cell. The guards were not amused at moving the ten drenched prisoners. Jake stepped out of the shower soaking wet allowing Lazaro to take his turn. Thane continued to glare at Jake. Hearing Jason's evaluation only served to strengthen what Thane already knew to be true.

The prisoners were moved out from highest rank to lowest leaving Jake and Cheyenne as the last two to be moved. Jake knew he wasn't being moved to a cell, although he continued to play his part to the very end. He saw Cheyenne watching him. Her face shrouded in fear and sorrow. "Cheyenne, are you okay?"

"I'm afraid, Jake."

"You could always change sides. The Captain seems to be doing well for himself." Jake offered nonchalantly.

"I'm not afraid for myself, Jake. I'm afraid for you. I know who's got my back. Who's going to have yours when Executor Hale turns on you? You betrayed us, and he'll betray you."

Jake started to argue with her then decided against it. "Why are you so sure the Captain didn't betray us? You said you saw him, yourself."

"He was drugged, Jake. I could see it in his eyes. I saw the real Captain reach out to me. He wasn't the one who betrayed us. You were the one, and we all know it. I only hope the others can forgive you for what you've done to them."

Jake sat down on the bench. "If you think I'm guilty, why do you care what happens to me? You're potentially facing your own death or life in prison, and you're worried about me? Cheyenne, that's insane."

"I care about you, Jake. It's not as insane as you think it is." Cheyenne saw the guards coming for her and stopped talking. She turned around to prepare for being cuffed. She didn't want them to have any excuse for roughing her up. The guards escorted her out without incident.

As soon as Cheyenne was gone, two more guards came and released Jake. Jake wasted no time in getting back to his room to get his wet clothes off. After getting cleaned up, he headed to the Supreme Executor's office.

CHAPTER EIGHT - LIONTARI

Pateras El Liontari slowly, quietly infiltrated the galaxy currently governed by the Commonwealth under the oversight of Supreme Executor Luciano Hale. His plan had been in the works since man's beginning. Pateras was the original ruler of the galaxy and beyond the edges of the universe. The crew and Luciano Hale both knew Pateras to be a Supreme Being, the ultimate Supreme Being.

Luciano had once been a trusted servant of Pateras. He was the second most powerful being in the universe. His abilities far surpassed human capabilities yet could not remotely touch the abilities of Pateras El Liontari.

Pateras foretold his plans hundreds of years before in the Ancient Texts. The Texts were given to hundreds of worlds to prepare the people for his return and the dreaded Day of Reckoning. The plan set in motion by Pateras took root on Galat III when his son Arni Sotaeras Liontari was born. Arni traveled to other worlds teaching them about his Father, the eventual fall of the Dark Lord, and the fulfillment of the Ancient Text prophecies.

The Ancient Text prophecies spoke of twelve groups of twelve dispatched by the Dark Lord, now known as the Supreme Executor of the Commonwealth Luciano Hale. The twelve groups of twelve were the first members of the Commonwealth touched by the movement of Pateras. Pateras spoke softly and lovingly to each of the twelve crews, turning them slowly into allies instead of the spies Luciano intended.

The *Evangeline*'s crew met Arni on their first mission stop on Galat III. Arni warned the Captain not to report his presence on Galat III or there would be blood on his hands. Not seeing the true danger, David followed his Commonwealth orders. Executor Hale ordered the Pacification Fleet to destroy every human life on Galat III. The *Evangeline*'s crew were not aware of the results of their actions. Pateras continued to send his son, Arni, to aid the crew during their missions to Medoris IV, Drea III, and Tudoren III.

The crew's apparent ability to resist the advances of Pateras earned them broader latitude in dealing with the Liontari influences. Unlike the backward planets previously encountered, Drea III was an advanced non-space faring society with a tumultuous history with the Commonwealth. Drea had earned the Commonwealth's wrath by refusing to give up certain primitive beliefs and uniting as one government under the Commonwealth. The planet was promptly punished by being blockaded by four satellites designed to shoot down any space craft attempting to leave their world. The *Evangeline* lacked the appropriate intelligence reports about the fifty-year-old satellites and was nearly shot down in Drean space. Being unable to develop space technology, Drea developed a wormhole technology allowing them to transport themselves from one planet surface to another. A demonstration of the technology took the crew back to Galat to discover the town littered with bodies of people the crew had befriended. The bodies included the mother of Arni Liontari.

The crew's broader latitude concerning the Liontari influence also came with an odd set of instructions. The crew was in no way to allow Arni Liontari to die. The orders were quite peculiar, considering the impending war between the forces of Pateras El Liontari and Luciano Hale. Those orders and Pateras' plan came to a head on Drea. Arni Sotaeras Liontari held the esteemed position on Drea as a religious leader known as the Intercessor. The crew discovered the deaths on Galat were attributed to an attack by the Commonwealth. Commander Alexander admitted to the Dreans, the Commonwealth's responsibility in the deaths on Galat. The Drean officials promptly arrested the crew, tried and convicted them of mass murder. Arni interceded on the crew's behalf by taking their death sentence on himself. Captain Alexander attempted to take the death sentence, but Arni surreptitiously took his place. Pateras restored Arni's life opening the door to a release from the coming reckoning.

Arni gave his continued support and guidance to the crew. Although his appearance was that of a man around thirty years of age, he treated the crew like beloved children. Arni prepared the crew and Admiral Deacons for the next stage of his plan. The crew didn't expect being captured, imprisoned, and tortured to be part of that plan. Soon, they would become aware of the intricacies of Pateras' plan.

• •

Before reaching the Supreme Executor's office, Admiral Deacons grabbed Jake and escorted him outside the building.

"Admiral, where are we going?"

"I'll tell you when we get there." The two walked quietly out of the building past a hangar and onto the tarmac. The Admiral began to explain his actions. "I'm taking you to see the ship the Supreme Executor brought in for you. If you decide to leave the CIF, the ship is yours. If you decide to stay in the Force, there are other possibilities."

The two moved towards a ship similar to the *Evangeline*. It was slightly smaller and not nearly as tall. The Admiral gave Jake some of the basic specs for the ship. The vessel was brand new and had the same technology and capabilities. Jake was favorably impressed. After touring the outside of the ship, the two started up the steps to look inside. Before stepping inside, Jake ran his hand across the hull lovingly. He was already falling in love with his new ship, his fingers running gently over the tachyon webbing. While the two toured the inside, Jake couldn't help feeling like the Admiral was expecting something the entire time. The Admiral was waiting patiently for Jake as he explored the rest of the ship. They toured the bridge first where Jake anxiously tried out the command chair.

The ship was designed to be for personal use or as a small cargo vessel. It was aptly named the *SS Independence*. Instead of the seven crew quarters, there were only four crew quarters. The quarters were larger and more luxurious. The Infirmary was smaller. It was capable of holding only three patients. The dining hall housed an actual kitchen. The crew recreational areas were reduced in favor of a hydroponics area. The ship's cargo bay held a surface vehicle, but there was no shuttle bay on the ship.

Jake and the Admiral finally ambled into the engine room. The Admiral sat down at the control panel and powered up the engine. Jake gave the Admiral a startled look. He was still restricted to base. Powering up a space ship with him on board might draw some attention. The Admiral looked up purposefully, "What do you think about the sound of those engines? They're so smooth and quiet, you can barely hear them." As the Admiral spoke, he manipulated some controls on his bracelet.

Jake's face moved from concern to outright worry. "What's going on, sir?"

Admiral Deacons moved closer to Jake. "I have to tell you something. It's not going to be pleasant or easy for you to hear. It does need to be quick and above all, you need to keep your wits about you."

Jake's face went slightly pale. "Okay, so now I'm worried."

Robert's gaunt face did nothing to alleviate Jake's fears. A dozen questions began to crowd his thoughts, each one vying for priority in the split second between sentences. Jake forced himself to refrain from jumping to conclusions and asking questions which might slow down whatever was coming.

Robert didn't really want to start this conversation, but time was of the utmost urgency. "Executor Hale has no intention of allowing David or Marissa out of this alive. He means to execute them. I know you heard his plans for the rest of the crew. They are unlikely to survive three days without water. Even if the crew makes it to Mara, David and Marissa won't."

Jake bristled. His face began to turn red. "We had a deal. My wife is supposed to go free. Do you have any proof of this?"

Admiral Deacons pulled out his data pad. He played a recording of the meeting he had abruptly left earlier that day. Once the pertinent portion was over, Robert shut it off.

"Admiral, how did you get this recording?"

"I was upset when I left that meeting this morning. Perhaps I hit a wrong button, then accidentally left my data pad behind. I retrieved it when the Supreme Executor went down to address the prisoners with his new plans for them."

Jake's heart began to pound. His face now blood red, He started to bolt. Admiral Deacons quickly blocked his path. "Jake, you can't react like this. You'll only get yourself killed along with the others."

"Admiral, with all due respect, get out of my way. We had an agreement. I'm going to make sure he keeps it."

The Admiral didn't budge. "With all due respect, Lt. Holden, I'm trying to at least save your life. There's nothing you can say or offer the Supreme Executor to change his mind. He's a superior being, not a mere mortal like us. Just how do you plan on stopping him?"

Jake backed down. He turned away and leaned wearily against a bulkhead. "What do you want me to do?" he asked meekly.

The Admiral swallowed hard. "I'm not entirely sure what the answer is. I know you can't let *anyone* know you're aware of this, especially not Executor Hale. The only other course of action we can take is to depend on Pateras to handle it."

Jake turned around quickly. Another dozen questions popped into his head, each one again vying for priority. "You want me to commit treason? Pateras knows everything I've done. He knows I don't *deserve* his help. Why would he help me?"

"Jake, do you really think any of us deserve his help? We're all guilty of something, some more than others. Whether he chooses to rescue the crew or not, he's all you have." Robert paused then added, "He's all I have."

The realization of the Admiral's change in loyalty began to sink in. Jake hung his head and paced around aimlessly. "When did you change sides, sir?"

Robert's heart was pounding loudly. He knew he had just placed his own life in the hands of a known traitor. His own life might now be forfeit. Robert forged ahead. "I knew Pateras as a boy and rejected him. I returned to him on Tudoren the day David died. David begged me to keep my alliance quiet. He didn't want me to risk my position to save him or the crew. He fully believes Pateras will take care of him and the others."

"You knew he was alive when you left Tudoren, didn't you?" Jake raised his eyes to look at the Admiral.

The Admiral nodded.

Looking like a lost little boy Jake asked, "Is Pateras going to save them?"

Admiral Deacons shrugged. "I honestly don't know."

"What am I supposed to do? How do we save them?"

Robert shook his head. Responding in a more desperate tone he replied, "I don't know. I can't fight Executor Hale. He's beyond human capabilities. I'm really not the one you should be asking."

Realizing he had no other options, Jake sank slowly to his knees. The anguish of his situation etched on his face. Tears began to flow. Jake called out, "Arni… Arni can you hear me? Please help me. I screwed up, badly. I made a mistake, a lot of mistakes. I shouldn't have remained loyal to the Commonwealth. Please forgive me. Arni, please help me." Jake lowered his head and sobbed openly. His guilt and desperation overwhelmed him.

Arni appeared standing next to Robert. He was wearing a simple Drean business suit. His dark brown hair just touched the top of his shoulders as it had on Galat and Medoris. He placed a reassuring hand on Robert's shoulder for a moment then moved over to Jake. Arni dropped to one knee and placed a hand on Jake's shoulder. Jake tried to look into Arni's face. His tears were coming so large and fast, his vision blurred. Jake's shoulders slumped in defeat.

With compassion displayed prominently on his face, Arni gently squeezed Jake's shoulder, "Jake, it's forgiven."

Jake looked up and tried again to focus on Arni's face. "Everything? I've made so many bad choices and hurt some really good people."

Arni nodded. "All of it - is forgiven."

"I got the Captain and crew in trouble. I don't know how to fix this. Arni, please tell me what to do to make this right again. I don't want them to die for my mistakes. Please, I'll do anything you ask, even if it costs me my life. I'm willing to give my life if it saves theirs."

Arni stood up and pulled Jake to his feet. "You're willing to die, to save the men and women you betrayed?"

"Yes, I'm willing to do whatever it takes to set this right." Jake continued to plead.

Arni shook his head. "Your death isn't what I want from you, Jake."

"Whatever it is, I'll do it. All you have to do is ask." Jake looked into Arni's face. Arni's face still reflected the compassion he felt for Jake, Robert and the rest of the crew. Jake waited anxiously for Arni's request.

"Jake, I've already provided for the crew's safe release. No matter what you do, the crew and your son will escape to safety. The only thing I've ever wanted from you is your trust. I want your *life*, not your *death*. I want you to trust me to always be there for you."

"It's yours. My life is yours. I serve you and Pateras from now on. Just tell me what you want me to do." Jake affirmed his allegiance and desire to serve his new commander.

Arni looked intently at him. He felt as though Arni was peering into his very soul. "Jake, I need you to trust me. Can you do that?"

Jake's brow furrowed as he repeated his affirmation. "Yes, I trust you. What do you want me to do?"

Arni smiled. "I'm going to ask you to do the hardest thing possible. No matter what, you must do exactly as I ask."

"I'll do it, whatever it is." Jake emphasized his decision anxiously.

Arni put his hand back on Jake's shoulder. "I need you to wait until I send a messenger to escort you out."

"What?" Jake blinked. "I don't understand."

Robert laughed ironically. "Jake, he's saying his plan is already in the works, and it always has been. He just needs you to wait for it. Waiting is always the hardest part of any plan."

Jake looked back and forth at both men. "Wait? Wait for what?"

Arni smiled again. "This is where you have to trust me. Consider it a test of your loyalty. Everyone will get out of here safely. You have my word. They will need water, and the Captain will need help walking out of here. Plan for it. Robert, I will need something from you."

"What is it?" Robert was anxious to do what he could as well.

"I will talk to you about it later. Right now, I need both of you to go on about your day and rest assured that I have everything under control. Jake, you're going to have to take command of the *Evangeline* when the crew gets aboard. They won't be capable of functioning as a ship's crew. I'll protect your escape. My messenger will stay with you and help you until you are out of the star system. He'll handle your navigation. Marissa can pilot the ships. Her condition is considerably better than the others."

Jake looked confused. "Ships?"

Arni smiled. "I'll link the controls of this ship to the *Evangeline*. We're taking both ships. Marissa will need to fly them in tandem."

Jake's confusion was not appeased. "You know how to do that?"

Arni's smile grew even larger. "My father designed every atom in the entire universe. I think I can handle some basic computer programming coupled with a little geometry and logistics."

Jake blinked. Having things placed in perspective made a dramatic difference in his finite mindset. He felt like Arni was oversimplifying the concepts, although maybe not, considering the larger picture.

"Okay, so why are we taking both ships? Are we splitting up? Using the second ship for cover?"

"The second ship will contain civilians. You'll need to protect both ships. I can't tell you everything right now. You'll have to wait and trust me for the details. The more you know the greater the chances you'll say or do something to give away my plan. You need to go now. They're getting nervous about the ship being powered up."

Jake offered Arni his hand, "Thank you, and thank Pateras for me. Everything I have is yours. You have my word."

Arni shook his hand. Placing his left hand on Jake's shoulder, Arni smiled, "Welcome to my father's house."

Jake hesitated to release his grip on Arni's hand. He knew Arni would disappear again in a moment. He felt safer knowing Arni was with him. He finally released his grip knowing Arni expected him to follow through on the trust requirement. Arni looked at both men seriously. "I've limited Luciano. I have not limited the men on this base. They can still make things more difficult, although I will not allow them to harm the crew. Robert, go into town for dinner. I'll see you there." With that Arni disappeared.

The Admiral shut off his jamming device and powered down the engines. "We should head back. I think the Supreme Executor will expect a report from you. I trust that won't be a problem?"

Jake twisted and winced. The blows Thane had landed that morning were taking their toll on him. Robert stepped closer to him. "Lt. Holden, are you alright?"

Jake braced himself against a bulkhead and tried to twist and stretch to relieve his discomfort. "Thane landed a couple good punches earlier. I didn't think he could do any damage in his weakened condition. I guess he was angrier than I gave him credit for."

"You need to get to the Infirmary and get fixed up. You need to be ready for the next few days."

"I'll be okay. I told the Supreme Executor I could handle it. It might not look good if I went to the Infirmary."

"Let's head back. If you don't go to the Infirmary, then I am at least ordering you to get some rest as soon as you report in to Executor Hale. Are we understood, Lieutenant?"

Jake nodded and started moving toward the exit. As soon

as they emerged from the ship, they were met by five guards. The lead officer stepped forward. "Admiral Deacons, the Supreme Executor would like to see you and Lt. Holden in his office immediately."

Jake looked nervously at Admiral Deacons who maintained eye contact with the guard in front of him. Admiral Deacons appeared annoyed. He glanced around before answering. "He wants to see us immediately, and you didn't bring a vehicle? Just how long ago did you make the rank of Ensign, Mister? If you don't do better than this, you might not keep your rank very long. I suggest we hustle. Come along, Lieutenant. Let's not keep the Executor waiting. I'd hate to cause this man to lose his rank because of us."

The man swallowed hard and turned to lead the men hastily back to the Supreme Executor's office. Jake asked as casually as he could. "Admiral, what are you going to say to the Supreme Executor?"

Robert gave Jake a sideways glance. He knew Jake was trying to see to it the two of them had their stories in agreement.

"The truth," Admiral Deacons replied casually knowing their conversations would be overheard.

"The truth?" Jake echoed.

"Of course, the Supreme Executor will completely understand our dismay for the crew's reluctance to submit to reason. They are our friends and family. They brought this on themselves, of course. We don't like it, but we know it had to happen. It's hard to talk about and no one else can understand what we're going through. He knows that. He won't have any trouble understanding our need to share our heartbreaks. I'm the only one who can understand what you're going through and you're the only one who can understand what I'm going through."

"Yes sir" Jake replied nervously.

● ●

The group walked into the Supreme Executor's office. The Executor looked up from his computer briefly. "Ensign, did you have any problems to report?"

The Ensign stood at attention, "No sir, no problems, sir."

Admiral Deacons interrupted irately. "I would like to report a problem."

The Ensign suddenly looked frightened. "This *officer* said you wanted to see us immediately. We were all the way out on the tarmac. I want to know if something was so urgent, why he didn't bring a vehicle out to get us. He wasted precious time in getting us here." Admiral Deacons didn't want to appear to be hiding anything or afraid of being *found out*.

Executor Hale stopped what he was doing and studied Admiral Deacons face. Without taking his eyes off the Admiral, he addressed the Ensign. "Ensign, could you and your men wait in the outer office please?"

"Yes sir!" The Ensign turned to leave and motioned his men to follow him out. His face was flushed from embarrassment and anger.

Executor Hale watched to see if Admiral Deacons flinched when the guard detail wasn't summarily dismissed.

Admiral Deacons ignored the guards entirely. He continued with an apology. "I'm sorry if we kept you waiting, sir. What seems to be the problem?"

Executor Hale left the two standing without an invitation to have a seat. He wanted to keep them on edge a little longer. "I'm sure you'll forgive my paranoia. The two of you were observed entering the ship promised to the Lieutenant and his wife. The engines powered up and you were out of communication for several minutes."

Admiral Deacons folded his arms across his chest. "I see. You think we were conspiring against you in plain sight." Admiral Deacons gave an amused huff. "I suppose I was conspiring, but it was against the Lieutenant, not you. You see, the Lieutenant and I share a common bond. We both have loved ones acting foolishly and suffering for their mistakes. It pains us both to see this. I'm a seasoned veteran. I know the signs and symptoms of battle fatigue. I know when to throw in the towel. The Lieutenant doesn't. He prefers to hide his pain. I took him on a tour of his new ship to distract him then I blocked all communications, so he would be free to discuss his feelings."

Executor Hale leaned back in his chair. "And what did you learn?"

"Some things were obvious. He misses his wife. He was quite uncomfortable in the presence of his former crew-mates. He's also hiding information from you."

Executor Hale leaned forward and stared intently at Jake who was now looking pale and nervous. Jake swallowed hard. Arni wouldn't betray him. Admiral Deacons couldn't fool Arni either. What was the Admiral about to say?

The Executor squinted at Jake. "What are you hiding from me, Lieutenant?"

Jake looked at Admiral Deacons again. "Nothing, sir. I don't know what he's talking about."

Admiral Deacons turned slightly to face Jake. "Sure you do, Lieutenant. You told me Lt. Ryder got in some pretty good hits when you were in the cell with him. You're in pain, and you're afraid the Supreme Executor is going to find out about it."

The look on Jake's face changed from fear to guilt and irritation. "I thought that conversation was privileged, sir."

It was Executor Hale's turn to be annoyed. "Were you injured by your own crew-mates, Lieutenant?"

"It's just some bruising, sir. I expected a little bruising when I went in." Jake answered wryly.

"And why were you afraid to let me know about it?"

Admiral Deacons picked up again. "He's afraid you'll think

he's weak and unable to take a little beating. I personally think Lt. Ryder got in more than a lucky hit. I think he got in some vicious hits because of his anger. Mr. Holden needs to visit the infirmary and get checked out. He was more interested in giving you his report."

Executor Hale sighed. "Mr. Holden, I truly hope your report is worth whatever pain you've continued to put yourself through. Please, sit down and report." Luciano waved both men to the chairs sitting across from his desk.

Jake reported his progress to the Supreme Executor. He reported Cheyenne's refusal to believe the lie the two attempted to propagate. He mentioned there seemed to be some doubts, although no one was decidedly convinced.

Executor Hale nodded thoughtfully. "You warned me she might be hard to convince. I should have listened to you. Why do you suppose she was so hard to sway?"

"Ensign Dominick notices details. I also think the Captain said or did something to reach out to her. She didn't say what." Jake found it difficult to sit here in front of the Supreme Executor. Thoughts of his wife constantly rolled around in his mind. He couldn't help thinking about the times he had laid his hand on Marissa's belly and felt his son kick him. Would he ever see his son's face? Arni's presence on the ship made this moment easier. For the first time, Jake felt Arni's presence with him now.

"Admiral Deacons, perhaps you're right. I believe the Lieutenant does need to visit the Infirmary. He seems to be out of sorts. Lt. Holden, report to the Infirmary and get checked out. I may have something to discuss with you later. I'll be in touch. You are a good soldier, Lt. Holden. I appreciate your efforts."

Jake stood up to leave. Executor Hale and Admiral Deacons both saw him wince as he stood up. As soon as he was gone, Luciano looked back to the Admiral. "Is he standing as strong as he appears?"

"He's a little hard to read sometimes, but I think he's doing better than I am. Maybe it's because he's still got hope for his wife. I don't see any hope for my nephew. He doesn't seem likely to come to his senses. I don't relish facing his mother tomorrow."

"What time will your family arrive, Admiral?" The Supreme Executor's tone and demeanor were so cold and businesslike.

Admiral Deacons face clouded as the painful thoughts of dealing with David's family manifested themselves in his mind. "The ship will enter orbit around 0300 hours local time. I've arranged for a shuttle to bring them down at 0900 hours. I thought that should give us enough time for the morning briefing." Robert yawned and rubbed his face. It was the middle of the afternoon, but the Admiral was drained.

"My word, Robert, you look like death warmed over. Are you sure you're okay?"

"I've been putting in some pretty long, hard days and I'm not as young as I used to be. I guess I've gotten soft. I'm used to working business hours. I'm going to try to get some rest before the family arrives in the morning. You've been putting in some long days yourself. I realize the dynamics of the situation don't weigh on you the same, but you seem to be in great shape. How do you do it?"

Executor Hale had no reason to think Admiral Deacons knew who he was, unless the crew had told him. The Admiral's comment called the issue into question. Executor Hale shut down his computer. "I don't understand. What do you mean?"

Despite the Admiral's knowledge of Luciano's true nature, his comment was addressed to the human Supreme Executor. "You aren't caught between your nephew's regrettable actions, your family's distress and the obvious disapproval of your co-workers. To you, it's an unfortunate incident to be dealt with. I realize you have the weight of the entire galaxy on you, but it's not personal for you. This is personal for me. The stress is different."

The piercing look began to fade from the Supreme Executor's eyes. "I see. I hate to tell you this, Robert, but you're wrong. This is more personal for me than you could imagine. It hurts me to see the pain you're going through. You are a good man, a strong man. You don't deserve this. You're right about the weight of the galaxy being on my shoulders. The good thing about my situation is, I have excellent people working under me. I don't have to carry such burdens alone. You're one of those people and I appreciate all your hard work. After we're done here, I want you to get some rest and relaxation. Go a few rounds with the punching bag in the gym or run some laps, whatever you prefer, to work out some stress."

"Thank you, sir. I appreciate your patience with me. I know I've put you in a difficult situation."

Luciano got up and walked over to the chair next to Admiral Deacons. He sat down and turned the chair to face the Admiral. "Robert, I realize I've put you in a very difficult situation. For that, I apologize. When we talked early this morning, I asked you not to take matters into your own hands regarding your nephew's life. I'm thinking I may have been asking too much of you. I know it's got to be incredibly hard for you to see him like this. It's hard for me. I'm within my rights and responsibilities to order his execution. I haven't done that because I had hoped we could bring him back to us. Robert… I am authorizing you to euthanize him if you wish. If you aren't comfortable with that, I have another option. I talked to Dr. Rhodes. He has a lethal dose of a sedative he can put in a hypo-spray. Take it to him. Let David make this choice himself. If he wants to end his own life, he can, and your hands will be clean. You won't have to tell his mother you had to execute him."

"Are you ordering me to do this?" Robert asked sullenly.

"No. I'm merely retracting my earlier request. I don't think we can save him. He's too strong. His suffering is going to go on indefinitely from what I can tell. I don't want to see you, or him, continue to hurt. All I'm saying is, no questions will be asked if you want to offer him a way out. If he doesn't take it, that's his choice. Leave the hypo-spray with him. He may decide later, he wants to use it. You know he won't do it if I offer it to him. He won't accept anything from me, not even compassion or mercy."

Admiral Deacons contemplated how to respond. He wasn't sure if David would be able to resist. Perhaps he could pass a message to him discreetly to encourage him. He looked up at the Supreme Executor. "When do you want this done?"

Luciano put on his most compassionate face. "I have no time in mind. I just thought I would offer it before his family arrived, so they wouldn't see him in such bad shape."

"You're going to let them have contact?" The Admiral was shocked at the prospect.

"I thought perhaps it might encourage him to come to his senses. The choice is yours of course. I'm not ordering his execution. You can put him down yourself or you can offer him the option of taking his own life… or… leave him as he is. Do whatever you think is best, except set him free." Executor Hale offered a sympathetic smile. "I wish I could set him free. I really do. The peacc of the entire galaxy depends on stopping Pateras' influence. I'm sorry, my friend."

"I'll let you know what I decide." Robert was obviously troubled.

Executor Hale stood up and moved back around behind his desk. "I have one other idea. If you want to end his suffering, but you aren't comfortable being this close to it, I can ask Lt. Holden to step in. I think he could do this, if you want it done."

"I'm going to go into town for dinner this evening. I'll let you know what I decide after dinner," Robert said with an air of finality.

Robert left the Supreme Executor's office to work on relieving stress as ordered. He was also very much in need of some air.

• •

An hour or so later, the Supreme Executor took a walk down to the Infirmary to check on Jake. Dr. Rhodes was just finishing up. He was recording data on his data pad when Executor Hale approached the two. "So, Dr. Rhodes how's the patient? Is he going to live?"

Jake was lying face down on the exam table. Dr. Rhodes tapped Jake's arm. "You can roll over now.

"Yes, Executor Hale, he'll survive… this time. He suffered some deep bruising and slight kidney damage. It probably would have healed on its own, although there was a chance of some complications. I feel much better having treated it."

Executor Hale scowled. "Are you sure he isn't going to need surgery or genetic reconstruction?"

Jake bolted upright looking concerned. "Surgery? For what?"

Dr. Rhodes looked up curiously. Jake was perfectly fine according to the displays on the scanner. He wondered where the Executor was going with this.

"Lt. Holden apparently has a *stubborn* growth that needs to be removed." The Executor gave the doctor a sly wink.

The doctor looked back down at his data pad. "I'm sorry, sir. I thought you were referring to his injuries. I'm afraid his condition is congenital and unfortunately, it's terminal."

Jake looked alarmed. "What stubborn growth? A congenital what? Terminal?"

Dr. Rhodes finally lowered his data pad and began to grin as he spoke. "You have a stubborn growth or growth of stubbornness. Congenital means you were born with it and it's probably the thing that's going to get you killed someday if you don't see your doctor when you're supposed to."

Jake looked annoyed and gave a meek, "Yes sir." His eyes turned to focus on Executor Hale. He expected a surge of anger to rise within himself. Surprisingly, he remained calm.

Executor Hale escorted the Lieutenant from the infirmary. The two ended up back in the Supreme Executor's office.

"Lt. Holden, may I ask you a question?"

"Of course, sir." Jake shifted uneasily in his seat.

"Do you have a full understanding of who I am?" Executor Hale studied Jake's reaction carefully.

"I think so, sir. I haven't read any of the Ancient Texts, but I heard the others discussing who you really are. I don't quite know what it means. What I mean to say is… I know you aren't human. You are a superior being and the enemy of Pateras. You're referred to as the Dark Lord. I don't know what your actual capabilities are. I've seen a little bit of what Pateras can do. I don't really have much information about you. I know you've given me a serious promotion and could probably offer a good deal more." Jake tried to seem as nonchalant as possible. The conversation unnerved him.

Executor Hale nodded. "That's an accurate though vague description. You know these things and you remain loyal to the Commonwealth?"

Jake's eyes narrowed. "I'm not sure I understand the question. This galaxy was a disaster three to four hundred years ago. You've brought us to a point of peace. I came from a rough planet. It was one of the places the Commonwealth had to step in and police. If it hadn't been for that action, I would be dead or in prison. The Commonwealth gave me a chance to make something of myself. I lost two older brothers to the pack skirmishes. My mother was shot when one of the packs retaliated in our neighborhood. She thought she was going to die and begged me to leave the planet and stay away from the packs. I gave her my word I would make something of myself. The second a recruiter showed up for the Commonwealth Interstellar Force, I jumped at it. My mother survived being shot, and she's extremely proud of me. I really don't want to disappoint her by committing treason. My mother's life has been hard enough. I'm not about to make it harder. I owe the Commonwealth, not Pateras."

"What about your wife and child? Pateras restored your wife and made it possible for her to have a child." Executor Hale leaned back in his chair and casually fingered the ornate molding on the edge of his desk. His intent was to put the former security chief at ease.

Jake's eyes flashed with anger. "According to the Captain, Pateras could have prevented the whole thing from happening. Every bone in her body was broken. He didn't stop it. He put her through all of that to make a point. He knew our orders and he set her up to get pregnant. He knew she wanted to have children. It made her vulnerable to him. Pateras may have allowed her to get pregnant, but he's also responsible for putting her and the baby at risk. It was a power play, a bribe. He thought he could use our deepest desires to manipulate us. I'm grateful Marissa's dream of having a child is a reality. I'm not grateful for everything he's putting us through. I'm done being a pawn in somebody else's game."

Executor Hale looked up again. "I'll keep that in mind, Lieutenant. What do you expect from me?"

"From you, sir? I'm not sure I understand."

"You know I have every resource imaginable at my disposal. Are you loyal because you know what I could give you or truly because of a promise you gave to your mother?" The Executor seemed to stare straight through him.

Jake weighed his question. He knew the Executor had already lied to him and broken his agreement. If he thought Jake was fully a man of integrity, he might view him as a threat. If he thought Jake had a price the Supreme Executor would be sure to own him. Jake answered cautiously. "The promise I made to my mother is important to me. I don't want to disappoint her. I'll do whatever it takes to keep from breaking her heart. Being public enemy number one is not the way to do that." Jake fought the urge to grin as soon as he said the words. He was certainly about to become just that. "Executor Hale, I – I have no desire to try and take advantage of you. I did what I did because it was the right thing to do. I'm not opposed to improving my station in life. I'm just not seeing that I have earned anything more than what you've already promised me. If I can do more, I'm open to the idea. If you have no further need for me then I'm satisfied to take my wife and son and disappear."

"I'll consider your offer. I believe I have at least one more job for you. I know you haven't had much of a chance to update your ship's mission logs. I'll try to let you get back on those in a couple days."

"Of course, sir. What would you like for me to do?" Jake leaned forward on the arms of his chair. He tried to appear interested and eager.

"Your Captain is very stubborn. He's taking everything we're throwing at him. He's suffering. I don't want to order his execution for the Admiral's sake." Executor Hale leaned forward to match Mr. Holden's posture.

Jake leaned back slowly in his seat. "Are you asking me to put him down? I'm not sure I can do that. I couldn't execute him on board the ship."

"No, of course not. What I'm suggesting is you provide him with the means to do it himself and maybe the motivation. Tell him how much his uncle is suffering seeing him like this. The doctor can provide you with a lethal dose of a sedative. Just offer it to him and leave it tucked under his mattress in case he chooses not to use it now. His mother and family will arrive in the morning. He may not want them to see him like this."

"Should I tell him what it is, or should I tell him it's just to counteract the neural stimulant?" Jake's intent was not to let the Captain kill himself.

"Be honest with him. If you aren't, he'll be uncertain what's in the hypo-spray. He may choose not to use it as a defense mechanism." Luciano leaned forward a tiny bit further. "I've offered this option to Admiral Deacons. If he is unable or unwilling, can you help me with this?"

"Yes sir, I can. I do have one question though. Will he trust the syringe coming from me? I would think his uncle bringing it would be more expected?" Jake didn't want to seem reluctant, but it really didn't feel like a good idea. "The Captain isn't going to trust anything I give him at this point."

Executor Hale leaned back in his chair. "That's possible. I'm hoping the Admiral will do it, but if he can't, will you?"

"Of course, I will. I'll go in all apologetic and tell him I'm sorry for what he's going through. I'll tell him I owe him this one small mercy for trying to protect Marissa. He might believe it. I hate to say it, but I'm getting a little too good at lying." Jake frowned.

Executor Hale stood up indicating their discussion was at an end. "I trust you haven't been lying to me."

"Ha! That would certainly be an exercise in futility, sir. I know where my loyalties lie. I owe you a lot and that's no lie."

Jake acknowledged his orders then headed to the officer's club to grab some dinner. He strongly suspected he wouldn't be welcome in an officer's club for much longer and wanted to take advantage of it while he had the chance.

• •

Jake sat alone at a table on the balcony overlooking the horizon. It was a relaxing view and the food was excellent. He sat there looking at the full plate of food. His appetite just wasn't there. He felt guilty for eating when his crew-mates, his captain, and his wife were slowly dehydrating and starving to death. As he stared at the plate he felt a reassuring hand on his shoulder. A voice whispered near his ear, "You should eat. You're going to need your strength."

Jake turned to see who had spoken to him. The voice was familiar though it felt out of place. As he turned, he recognized his driver, Adam Franklin, from their west coast cottage stay. His presence startled Jake. "Mr. Franklin? What are you doing here?"

The man was wearing the same uniform as the club's wait-staff. He smiled. "I go wherever I'm needed. Right now, you needed me to tell you to eat your dinner."

Jake looked unsettled. "Do you work for the Admiral? How did you know I was having trouble eating? How did the Admiral know?"

Mr. Franklin smiled, "You ask too many questions. Eat your dinner and get some sleep. You've got lots of work to do." The man started to walk away. He stopped and said the one thing Jake needed to hear. "Oh… and… welcome to the Liontari household."

Despite the worries plaguing his mind, Jake smiled and breathed a sigh of relief. He watched the man walk away and back inside the building. He picked up his fork. He still felt guilty for enjoying such a delicious meal, but he did as he was told and finished every bite.

● ●

Another invisible observer watched Jake eat then reported back to the Supreme Executor. "Master, I have watched Mr. Holden as requested. I don't believe his conscience is bothering him at all. He just ate a large meal at the Officer's Club. He didn't seem interested to begin with. He may have been engrossed in the scenery, though. It took him a few minutes to get started, but he ate his entire meal, somewhat aggressively."

Executor Hale nodded. "Thank you. His behavior earlier was questionable. I just wanted to be certain. If he were having doubts or regrets, his appetite would have suffered. You may return to your previous duties.

• •

Admiral Deacons got a vigorous workout in the gymnasium. His thoughts were jumbled to the point he felt himself going numb. He finished his work out, showered and picked up a car to leave the base. He declined the offer of a driver as he preferred the solitude of driving himself. He drove an hour out to the coast, to a quaint seaside restaurant. He went inside and requested a quiet table near the waterfront. He sat down and ordered. He expected Arni to arrive first, but his food was delivered to his table while he remained alone. He looked down at the plate in front of him so long that the waiter returned to find out if there was something wrong with his food. The Admiral assured him the food was fine. He offered some light humor regarding his mindset being the problem instead of the food. The waiter gave him a polite laugh and moved on to his next table. Robert decided he should go ahead and eat to keep the waiter at bay. He found himself having the same difficulty eating Jake had faced. Robert finally finished most of his food. He settled his bill and took a walk down to a nearby pier.

• •

Another observer reported back to the Supreme Executor. "My Lord, I came to report on Admiral Deacons as you requested. He does seem conflicted, although he was able to eat his meal. He has been alone, and no one spoke to him other than the waiter. He went for a walk on the docks. No one had joined him when I left to report back to you."

Executor Hale scowled. "I'm not sure you should have left until he was returning. Arni could be appealing to him even now."

"Do you want me to return?"

Luciano shook his head. "No, it's pointless. If Arni wants to hide his contact with any of them, there's nothing we can do about it. At least I know he's still functional. You may return to your duties."

• •

Robert sat down on a bench on the pier and watched as the sun began to set. He finally muttered softly, "Arni, where are you?"

"I'm here, Robert."

"Arni, I know Pateras has everything under control, but I'm still scared. I'm about to lose my entire family. I'm afraid David's going to hate me for everything I've allowed him to go through. I ordered some of those things." Robert finally unloaded all the pain, anger and frustrations which had reached a crescendo. Robert was a strong man. It took a great deal to shake the man. The last few days had taken their toll on him. Arni's presence was the key to unlocking all his pent-up emotions. Robert confessed all his heartless behaviors and his feelings of helplessness.

"Arni, these people should hate me for the things I've put them through. My nephew and his wife have suffered horrible things. They're my family and the things I've done to them… What're Jess and my mom going to say when they find out what I've done? Will they ever be able to forgive me? It's a wonder I *didn't* cause Mr. Holden's wife to miscarry." Admiral Deacons got to his feet and paced on the dock.

"Arni listened intently. "Robert, you did what had to be done. You protected them from the Dark Lord. I protected Marissa and her baby. They're grateful for your help."

"My own behavior has made me sick to my stomach. I haven't slept well for days. What am I going to tell my wife? The only way I can protect her is to send her into hiding. I'll probably never get to see her again. Is she going to forgive me for sending her away?" The Admiral finally leaned over the dock railing and propped his arms on the edge. He lowered his head and stared into the dark water ebbing below him. He wasn't one to cry. He had cried the day his father died. He didn't remember crying before that day since his sister died on Mara. Slow quiet tears began to flow down his face. "Arni, I don't know how much longer I can do this. I feel like I'm watching my sister die all over again only much more slowly."

Arni moved over beside Robert. "David isn't dying. He will recover, quickly. Your family may not understand why you're sending them away or why you allowed David to be in this situation. They will accept David's explanation, and they will forgive you because David won't hold any of this against you. He's going to have the hardest time forgiving Jake. He will forgive him far more quickly than trusting him again. That's going to take some time."

"This doesn't excuse me. I did horrible things."

"Robert, according to your orders, you should have executed them all. Right?"

Robert looked hard at Arni. "Yes, that's right."

"You saved their lives. You kept yourself in a position to be able to protect them. You followed your orders which kept Luciano from finding out where your true loyalties lie. You made good choices. Not one of the crew has recanted from following me. Yes, they are in pain. Their pain will cease, soon. They have to make it through one more day then we'll free them."

Robert nodded silently. The compassion in Arni's eyes spoke volumes. He decided Robert needed to hear one more thing. "Robert, I forgive you. I thank you for all you've done. Luciano's days appearing as a human are nearly at an end. He will be restricted very soon. A new Supreme Executor will take his place. You will be there to guide the new Executor. A great rift will develop and split the galaxy. Your presence will be crucial in the days ahead." Arni paused a moment then continued, "Robert, we need to talk about the plans for tomorrow."

Arni gave specific instructions to Robert to insure the crew's escape and to lay the groundwork for the future. By the time Robert was ready to leave, his spirit was greatly lifted.

"Don't worry about David. I won't leave him alone.

Robert looked confused. "But, you're here with me. Doesn't that mean you've left him alone right now?"

Arni smiled kindly. "No, I gave him my word I would not leave him. Physically, yes, I am here with you, but my father and I are not alone. The comforter is with him. A day will come, very soon, when I will no longer be with man. When that day comes, the father will send the comforter to always reside with those who desire him. In terms you would better understand, he is a non-corporeal being that can inhabit corporeal beings, but he only goes where he is welcomed. He is a part of the father like I am. It's a complex relationship. I am in the father and the father is in me. The three of us are one."

Robert gave Arni a peculiar look. "I assume this will make more sense later?"

Arni smiled again. "It will."

The two finished talking and Robert began his drive back to the base.

• •

When he arrived, the Supreme Executor had not yet returned to his ship. Robert went in to give him his answer. "Supreme Executor, you may consider it weakness on my part, but after much contemplation, I cannot euthanize or assist my nephew with suicide. I'm sorry if that disappoints you. I must hold out some hope for him and give him every chance. I really think his mother, or the rest of the family may get through to him." Robert's words were guarded. The hope and the chance he referred to were hopes and chances for survival away from the Executor. He knew the Executor wanted David dead. He knew Jake would be called upon to provide that option. The Executor appeared to be understanding, although he wasn't surprised.

After escorting the Admiral out of his office, Luciano returned to his seat. "Computer, hail Lt. Jake Holden."

Jake's face appeared on the screen. "Yes, Supreme Executor?"

"Lieutenant, I need you to drop by the Infirmary and pick up the hypo-spray we talked about. Admiral Deacons has declined to offer his nephew a way out. Pick it up tomorrow afternoon. I want his family to see him first. They have a history with Pateras. I want to be sure they know the price of serving him."

Jake nodded. "Just to be clear, I'm not supposed to use it on him, just offer it to him."

Executor Hale nodded his approval. "Do not force his hand but give him any reason you can to use it himself. The later in the day, the better."

"May I ask, what you're thinking, sir?" Jake asked tenuously to avoid sounding suspicious.

His attempt was only marginally successful. Executor Hale eyed Jake cautiously. "What does it matter, Lieutenant?"

Jake responded confidently, "I'm a soldier. I'll do whatever you ask whether I understand or not. I just thought I might be more effective… and more useful, if I understand where you were headed with this."

Executor Hale studied Jake for a moment longer. Deciding he was worth the risk, Luciano answered the inquiry, "Well Lieutenant, I have reason to believe Pateras plans to help Captain Alexander and his crew escape sometime around midnight tomorrow night. If I wait until the last possible moment, when the Captain is at his weakest, he may give up hope. Whether he recants or decides to kill himself, he'll no longer be a follower of Pateras. I can do whatever I want to him."

Jake nodded thoughtfully. "Wow… that's… well thought out. I think I can work with that."

"Good, I will expect some positive results, Mr. Holden." Executor Hale ended the call then returned to his ship satisfied with himself.

• •

Lying alone in his cell, or seemingly alone, David shivered from the cold temperatures, the excruciating pain, and the drugs coursing through his veins. He could no longer cry out verbally to Pateras. The collar around his neck saw to that. The beatings and trips to the Infirmary were coming in endless cycles now. The drugs in his system would begin to wear off just in time to have his wounds healed followed by a new dose of drugs and yet another beating. Arni had assured him, he would be there. As David struggled to find a less painful position to lie in, he cried out. "Are y-you here? Y-You said y-you'd be here."

For a few minutes there was nothing but the sound of his own labored breathing. Two dark figures circled menacingly around him. Their voices answered his cry.

He lied to you.

        He's not as powerful as you thought.

You failed him.

        You aren't strong enough for him.

If you had just been stronger.

        You betrayed your marriage vows.

He can't use you anymore.

        He said only six days.

It's been more than six days now.

        It's been eight days, or is it nine?

267

Your crew is dead.

You failed your crew.

Jake hasn't turned.

Your mission is a failure.

Surrender to Luciano.

Luciano will stop this.

You can finally be at peace.

David covered his ears. The voices continued their endless taunts. Their voices spoke into his mind, they couldn't hear *his* thoughts, but he heard *their* words. After a time, he could bear to hear them no longer. He did the only thing he could. "Arni!" His collar released a painful charge. Combined with his current pain and the drugs in his system, the electrical charge was more than his mind and body could handle. He lost consciousness and silenced the voices.

• •

When Captain Alexander came to later, the drugs were working their way out of his system again. He opened his eyes to see the two dark figures standing in the corner of his cell glaring at him. David waited for them to continue assaulting him with their whispers of doubt and fear. The two said nothing. David looked around the cell once more. He asked the question he knew he could get away with. "Father… did you stop them?"

A strange silence was all he could hear. It was a silence that outweighed the normal prison noises. He could still hear muffled voices in the hall, a dripping faucet, and occasional footsteps. Something about the silence told him, he wasn't alone. He had grown accustomed to a sense of calm when Arni was around. This was somehow different. All his doubts, fears and regrets continued to haunt him. The two figures in the corner weren't speaking, but they shook their heads at him sorrowfully. They appeared to be having a silent conversation between them.

They began to point at him and laugh silently.

There was something about the silence. He knew Pateras heard his cries. His own pain and sorrows refused to leave, but Arni had promised to always be there. What was it he was supposed to do? Oh yes, stay strong… for six days. Something about the silence was comforting. David followed his survival instincts. He forced himself to crawl to the sink and drink a cup of water. He crawled back to his mattress and collapsed again. He allowed himself to fall asleep in the heavy silence until the guards rousted him for his next trip to the Infirmary.

Day Six of captivity started with a flurry of activity. The ship carrying David's family had arrived during the night. The family members who were able to sleep got up early and prepared to take the shuttle down to the surface. Those who had slept little, got up slowly. Each step was taking them closer to a frightening encounter they desperately wanted to avoid. The ship's galley provided an excellent breakfast, although most of his family had difficulty eating. David's Grandma, Kay Deacons, ate a minimal breakfast and stayed busy trying to make sure everyone else ate. David's mother, Jessica, was the hardest one to convince to eat. She complained about her stomach being tied in knots. Her mother finally pulled her aside, gave her a harsh lecture, and forced her to eat a small, but balanced, breakfast. Steven, David's step-father, slept restlessly. He was able to eat but brooded the entire time. Stevie, David's half-brother, was a high school student and not fully aware of the implications of everything going on around him. He simply knew the adults were all on edge. Stevie just did the best job he could to eat, sleep, and stay out of the way. He tried to help his sister, Abby, with baby Aiden. David's sister was named after Robert and Jessica's older sister Abigail. Her husband, Caleb, wasn't as emotionally vested in the situation as he was barely acquainted with David. His concern was more with the anguish his wife was going through. David's father had not been located and was unaware of any of the happenings over the recent months. Due to the shocking nature of David's situation, his family kept a low profile on the trip out.

The morning on the surface started with more activity than the ship. The Supreme Executor began the day with his usual staff meeting. Jake was beginning to get accustomed to being part of the Command Staff. Despite his new rank of lieutenant, he still felt like a Chief Petty Officer amid so many high-ranking officials.

Executor Hale explained his plan for David for the day. He conveniently left out the part about Jake bringing the lethal injection to his captain. He intended to take his family one or two at a time in to see David at his worst. Commodore Vardin reported one other minor problem. With the Supreme Executor parking himself and his ship in one port for so long, it got the attention of the press. Executor Hale didn't usually stay in one place more than a day or two unless it was Commonwealth headquarters. The press was anxious to know what held such a powerful man on such a low-profile planet this long. Executor Hale told Commodore Vardin to hold the press off-base and keep them at bay until he was ready to make a statement.

David's beatings had gone from daily to twice a day, and now they were three times a day. His trips to the Infirmary were becoming shorter and less effective as the medical staff began to realize, healing the young Captain's injuries was a waste of time. Word of David's treason had gotten around the base causing the medical staff to see little reason to treat him as adequately as possible. Everyone seemed to know the prisoner would be dead soon. David was currently in the Infirmary getting healed before his next scheduled beating. The guards were unaccustomed to beating prisoners. Such behavior was normally frowned upon. As their exhaustion increased, the guards began enlisting the use of batons like the disciplinary rods used on him on Drea. The batons could be used to incapacitate or inflict pain with an electrical charge or as an instrument of brute force. The introduction of the batons seemed to infuse the guards with new energy in their cruel task.

Executor Hale affirmed Admiral Deacons' plan to meet his family and spend some time with them before meeting with Executor Hale. Admiral Deacons was both anxious and dreading to see his family.

The imprisoned crew's morning didn't differ from their night. Every time their eyes closed, a shrill alarm sounded keeping them from gleaning any significant sleep. The temperatures in their cells vacillated every couple hours, from frigid to sweltering. Their mouths grew drier with each passing hour. By the end of the day, their lips would be cracked and bleeding. Jason and Laura were the most distressed. Their medical training caused them to be even more painfully aware of their deteriorating conditions. Jason found himself obsessing over his own pulse. He checked it frequently, although without a clock, the count was merely an estimation.

The advancement of their re-training meant the crew was continually bombarded with the Commonwealth propaganda both in the re-education room and in their cells. It was less effective in their cells, just more annoying. Lexi became so tired and annoyed, the next time the temperature began to cycle to the cold side, she grabbed her thin floppy mattress and rolled it up around her head and upper torso. The mattress blocked enough of the noise she was able to get a brief nap. The alarm was programmed by the computer to sound when the scanners picked up a prisoner sleeping. The alarms usually sounded for a minute or two then shut off. Two guards making their rounds noticed the alarm going off for a considerably longer time and went in to investigate. Finding Lexi asleep, they rousted her roughly then removed her mattress from the cell. Lexi yelled angrily at them, "You might as well turn your sirens off! Pretty soon, we'll be too weak to move! What difference will it make then?"

The guards had one brief moment of pity. It lasted only long enough for them to pause to consider her words and feel just a *little bit* bad about what they were doing. They didn't feel bad enough to leave her the mattress or turn off the siren. It did continue to gnaw at them periodically throughout the day.

The crew's redundant cycle of sleep depriving sirens, blaring repetitive Commonwealth mantras, extreme changes of temperature, lack of food or water, and the roughness with which they were handled was nothing compared to David's days. The guards were still quite spooked by the invisible beings protecting the crew. The guards might cause small slips, trips, and falls, but they weren't going to cross the line of open assault.

• •

The Captain's days and nights were now a blur. The hallucinogenic drugs injected into him caused his sense of time to become totally lost. He never knew whether it was day or night. The Supreme Executor had failed to turn off the water in his cell, although it would have made little difference. The neural stimulants and hallucinogens made reaching the water, mere feet from him, a tremendous ordeal. Since the guards started using the batons instead of their fists, his bruises were spread from his trunk and face to include his extremities. As soon as the neural stimulant would wear off, he would have his tissues regenerated and the cycle would start over. A small sane part of his mind knew he needed water. As his drugs began to wear off each cycle, he would move slowly and painfully to the sink and manage to drink whatever he could.

The guards began feeling a discomfort of their own with each passing cycle. This prisoner should have been fighting back, cursing the ground they walked on and begging for mercy. He didn't do any of those things. He called out to some invisible or imaginary person and asked for protection for his crew, never for himself. The incidents of men showing up late for work and having altercations among themselves began to increase. Tensions on all sides were reaching critical levels.

• •

Precisely on schedule, the shuttle carrying Admiral Deacons' family arrived at 0900 hours. The Admiral waited just off the landing pad until the shuttle door opened. He stepped forward. The first person to meet him was his own mother. He reached his hand up to her to help her down the steps. The woman was now eighty-two years old. Although being quite agile and active for such an age, the recent events seemed to have slowed her down. Her heavy heart kept an ache in her bones and gave her pain with every step closer to the Romajin surface. Reaching the bottom step, she collapsed into Robert's arms. Robert lovingly hugged his mother for what seemed like a very long time. He started to release her and pull away to greet the others when she pulled him in even more tightly. She quietly whispered, "How bad is it?"

Robert held onto her more tightly. "I'm sorry, mom. It's not good. David's in bad shape. He expects Pateras to get him out of this somehow. Knowing what I do about Pateras, he will free him, I just don't see how."

Kay gave her son one more squeeze then released him. Jessica was in his arms almost immediately. "Robbie, I think I preferred our conversation the day you told me David had died to the one we're going to have today."

Robert hugged Jessica just as enthusiastically as he had his mother. When she called him Robbie, he stiffened slightly. She had called him Robbie while they were children. When he reached high school and college, he asked her to stop. She couldn't seem to break herself of the habit. It had caused numerous arguments between the two. It wasn't important today, though the instinct remained.

Robert shook hands with Steven and his other nephew Stevie. He gave Abby a one-armed embrace as she was carrying Aiden in her arms and used his free hand to shake Caleb's hand. Caleb offered little more than a polite greeting. His eyes darted from Robert to Abby then back to Robert in a questioning manner. Robert said simply, "We'll talk inside."

Robert's wife was the last to step out of the shuttle. His face brightened as she appeared. Even after being married for so many years, she was still a bright spot in his life. Unlike most marriages of the Commonwealth, the two had been married for over twenty years. She was also Robert's first and only wife. "Hannah!" Robert wrapped his arms around her and kissed her tenderly.

Hannah was surprised the Admiral was willing to offer so much physical contact while in uniform. He had always been clear about no public displays of affection while in uniform. "Robert, what's going on?"

Admiral Deacons put his command presence back in place and gathered the family in closely. "Before we go any further, you need to know something. This situation has gotten the Supreme Executor's personal attention. He's concerned about treasonous conspirators. He's aware of our family's history and concerned about possible negative influences. Be aware that you will be monitored and recorded at all times. Don't say anything, even in jest, that could be misunderstood. I would prefer none of us get arrested. Are we clear?" Everyone nodded soberly. Robert looked over at Stevie, "Stevie, are we clear?"

Stevie wasn't as clear as he wanted to be. He was uptight before. Now, he was downright scared. "Yes, Uncle Rob."

Robert went on. "We're going to a conference room to talk for a little while, and I will explain the situation to you in more detail. The Supreme Executor wants to meet with you."

Jessica was more frightened than anyone. The news of the Supreme Executor's presence nearly sent her over the edge. Her face went white. "Supreme Executor Luciano Hale is here? Why does he want to talk to us?"

Robert reached out and took Jessica's hand. "Jess… let's go inside and sit down. We can talk there. We put the past behind us. We're safe now. He's just trying to save David. Come on. Let's go inside."

• •

The group followed Robert into the complex. His comments sparked numerous questions in their minds, but no one voiced them yet. They anxiously settled into the conference room. A petty officer supplied the group with glasses of water. Robert was the only one who touched his immediately. Once the family was alone, they waited for Robert to offer his explanation.

Robert sat down at the head of the table and stared into his glass of water for a moment. It was time to do the thing he didn't want to do. He took another sip of his water then a deep breath. "Executor Hale has authorized me to give you the basic information about David's mission. "David's ship was one of twelve ships sent out to undeveloped worlds to create new Commonwealth allies. The purpose of this mission was to harness these worlds as allies before they fell under the control of an enemy known as Pateras. The rough truth of the matter is, they were sent out as spies. David's crew located the enemy right off. They were able to resist him, at first. As the months passed, David succumbed to the influence of Pateras. His crew fell in line right behind him, except for one. If it weren't for the one crewman, there's no telling what could have happened."

Steven began to lose patience with the generic cover story. "Get to the point, Robert. You told us months ago, David died a hero. So, is he alive or dead? What did you mean about the family's history?"

Robert winced from the mental anguish. "David did die. That much is true, and he died saving my life. He died in my arms just like I said. This Pateras I am referring to… he's… well… he's not human. He's a superior being… a supreme being… a god if you will. Pick whichever term suits you. He's capable of manipulating matter and energy. Pateras brought David back to life. David rejected the Commonwealth and chose to serve Pateras."

Steven was old enough to have heard a good many strange things in his lifetime. He stopped to ponder what Robert was saying before responding. Caleb was still young enough to be impetuous, "A god? You've got to be kidding me? There's no such thing."

Kay looked up slowly. "Caleb, you're wrong. Fifty years ago, I served Pateras along with my husband and children. Pateras is real."

Robert was suddenly on high alert fearing his mother would say too much. He jumped in quickly. "She's right. He is real. He's powerful, and we walked away from serving him to serve the Commonwealth. He is a superior being, whether he's a god or not. What I didn't tell you about David's death is, he admitted to me his loyalty had changed. I drew my weapon thinking I would test his loyalty to know for certain. He didn't waver, even faced with his own demise. When he died, I thought I could spare the family this embarrassment. I told everyone, except the Admiral's board, he died a hero's death. He did save my life by sacrificing his own. According to the one crew member who remained loyal to the Commonwealth, David was restored to life shortly after his funeral."

Abby fidgeted nervously with a squirming baby in her lap. Aiden seemed to sense his mother's anxiety. Caleb reached over and took the baby from her. Abby was now more capable of listening and comprehending what her uncle was trying to say.

"Davie's really alive? Can we see him?"

Robert shook his head. "Not yet. We'll discuss that in a few minutes. Steven, you asked about our family's history. Our home world was one who served Pateras when the Commonwealth approached us. My father and mother chose to reject serving Pateras in favor of joining the Commonwealth. The Supreme Executor is afraid our rejection wasn't complete. His concern is that somehow, knowledge of Pateras was passed down within the family."

Steven scowled. "That's ridiculous. I'd never heard of this Pateras before today. Jess, you don't know anything about this either do you?"

The look on Jessica's face said considerably more than what she wanted to verbalize. "I – I remember a little about him. I was pretty young when we joined the Commonwealth. I never taught David anything about Pateras though. Robert, please, what's going to happen to my son?"

Robert glanced at Stevie. "Perhaps, Stevie could take Aiden out into the hall?"

Stevie began to realize the true unpleasantness was about to come out. "No, I'm not leaving."

Jessica jumped in quickly. She stood up and moved over by Stevie. Kneeling by his chair, she politely asked for his cooperation. "Stevie, I know you are old enough to handle this. Aiden's not. He's a baby. He isn't going to understand why his mother is upset."

Abby interrupted. "Mom, you're scaring me."

Jessica ignored Abby's interjection. "Stevie, I will speak to you privately a little later. I promise I will tell you everything you want to know. I won't hold anything back. Please wait outside with Aiden, entertain him a little longer. I'll send for you the second I can."

Stevie glanced at his dad hoping for a second opinion. Steven nodded to his son to cooperate. Stevie realized he was hopelessly outnumbered. He grudgingly scooped Aiden up from his father's arms and headed for the door. He grabbed the baby's bag from a chair by the door and went into the hall.

As soon as Stevie left the room, Robert activated the privacy screen causing the walls to go from clear to milky white and a sound barrier to activate. He took another sip of his water. "David and his crew are considered traitors to the Commonwealth. They are subject to the penalty of immediate execution. Executor Hale has graciously not carried out that sentence. He's giving them as many chances as he can to reconsider their positions. He's attempting to re-educate them. The re-education process is not pleasant. David is not showing any signs of recanting his position. His re-education is being pushed to its furthest limits, or perhaps I should say, he's being pushed to his limits. Executor Hale wants to spare David and his crew. I just don't know if that's going to be possible. David's…" Robert's voice trailed off as words began to fail him.

Everyone in the room was riveted as the Admiral leaned down over the table. His hands were planted firmly on the tabletop. His eyes stared at his half-empty glass of water. Tears were beginning to form in Kay, Jessica, and Abby's eyes. Abby finally prodded. "Uncle Rob, please… what's happening with my brother?"

A voice from the opposite side of the room spoke up to answer. "Your brother is unfortunately being retrained rather vigorously."

The tension had been so high in the room, no one had noticed the Supreme Executor and Admiral Garcia enter. Executor Hale had entered in time to hear and answer Abby's question. Luciano took over the briefing to put his own spin on the situation. "Each of these teams we sent out were warned about the dangers of too much exposure to the Liontari influence. I made the mistake of giving Captain Alexander some expanded latitude in dealing with the son of Pateras, Arni Liontari. I never should have done that. This whole situation is my fault. I'm trying my best to redeem him. The re-education protocols are not deadly. They are, however, painful and unpleasant. If he doesn't respond to these protocols, we'll have to revert to a total mind wipe. Genetically, he will remain alive. He won't be David Liam Alexander anymore. My other two options are a lifetime of solitary confinement or execution. I *really* don't like those options. What I've been forced to do to him is… painful, sickening, and upsetting for *me*. I hope you can forgive me for what I've had to put him through. I *swear* to you all I'm doing this to try and *save his life*." Executor Hale began to look tortured and persecuted. The man was obviously a good liar. By the time he finished his emphatic speech, Robert was *almost* feeling sorry for him.

Jessica wiped tears from her eyes. "Supreme Executor Hale… what have you done to my son?"

Executor Hale appeared to blink back tears of his own. "I tried to reason with him to begin with, and even later, I tried again. Reason didn't work. I'm afraid my psychological mapping experts said the only way to save his personality was to begin a course of negative reinforcement. He's been subjected to re-education stimuli up to and including… torture. I'm so sorry it had to be this way."

Jessica cried out and clasped her hands over her mouth. Abby began crying. She grabbed onto Caleb's hand. Caleb scooted his chair closer to her and pulled her into his shoulder. Hannah sat there looking at Robert saying nothing. Her face was pale.

Kay stopped crying. She was sitting nearest the Supreme Executor. She slowly got to her feet and slapped Executor Hale across his face. Robert wanted very much to do the same thing, although his current fear, was for his mother's safety. He moved quickly to her side. He grabbed her and encouraged her to sit back down while apologizing profusely to the Supreme Executor. "I'm so sorry, Executor Hale. My mother hasn't been herself since this started. Please excuse her actions, she doesn't know what she's doing."

Admiral Garcia stood there in shock. He had never seen anyone even get close enough to the Supreme Executor to slap him.

Executor Hale rubbed the place on his face where she had slapped him. "Don't be concerned, Robert. I deserved that and much more. The safety of the entire Commonwealth is at stake. I'm afraid I can't just look the other way. I'm doing the best I can for everyone involved."

Steven had moved closer to Jessica to try to comfort her as well. He looked up from her face to ask, "Just how dangerous is this Pateras Liontari person?"

Executor Hale's face grew sober. "Very dangerous. He intends to destroy anyone who doesn't declare loyalty to him. One of the reasons he's so dangerous is he isn't human. I understand Robert explained the nature of this alien being?"

The group nodded. Luciano continued his skewed viewpoint. "He has the ability to regenerate human cells. He is telepathic so hiding things from him is pretty much futile. The one advantage we have is he wants to work through his human conscripts. If we can prevent this one part of his plan, we can control his access to this galaxy."

Steven looked nervous now. "Is it safe to be around David then? Can this influence us?"

Executor Hale was pleased with Steven's reaction. "If you spent any significant time with him, it's possible. You won't be allowed to spend that much time with him. You will be allowed in to see him long enough to try and reason with him. He's wearing a special collar which prevents him from speaking the very name of Pateras… well, it doesn't stop him from saying it. It… I'm sorry, again… it punishes him for saying it. It also prevents him from saying anything else for a few minutes. Be careful about touching him. If you touch him when he speaks, the charge from the collar can pass into you as well. I'm so sorry about this, really I am." He was sorry, just not remotely like it sounded. He was genuinely sorry David was still alive. His preference was to execute him and his crew the minute they were arrested.

Jessica was shaking with the realization of the situation. "How bad is it? What shape is he in?"

Executor looked at Admiral Garcia and nodded as he moved away from the table and the distraught family. Admiral Garcia stepped forward. Typically, he would have been proud of his handiwork. This time he toned himself down and gave a clinical report of the sleep deprivation, beatings, drug induced pain enhancements and psychotics, the brainwashing, and the lack of food. As Admiral Garcia spoke, Executor Hale looked like a man beaten and downtrodden. His demeanor truly emulated a man experiencing regrets. After he finished his explanation, Executor Hale suggested the family needed a moment alone. Admiral Garcia followed Executor Hale out of the room.

For a few minutes, the only sounds heard were those of quiet sobs. Jessica pulled herself together enough to confront Robert. When she came face to face with him, she was ready to slap him the way her mother had slapped the Supreme Executor. She looked into his eyes and saw pain greater than her own. She knew how close David and Robert had been. Robert had been more of a father to him than his own father or his stepfather were. Instead of slapping him, she grabbed him and hugged him tightly. "I'm sorry I doubted you," she whispered to him.

Robert held her tightly as tears of his own flowed silently

down his face. "I'm sorry I couldn't stop this from happening. I'm sorry I couldn't protect him. Can you ever forgive me?"

Jessica laid her head on his shoulder. "I forgive you. What's going to happen to him next?"

Robert pulled away to answer so everyone could hear him. "A ship is coming in two days to take the crew to the prison facilities on Mara. If he shows any signs of recanting, they may leave him here to finish his training. If he shows no signs of ever recanting, he may not…" Robert couldn't finish the sentence.

Steven sat there contemplating the situation carefully. "Robert, who was the one crew member who didn't fall? It wasn't Brynna was it?"

"No, it was their security chief. Brynna is being re-educated with the others. She'll be shipped to Mara in two days until her training is complete."

Jessica moved back to her seat while asking. "Is there any chance of seeing her?"

Robert shrugged. "I don't know. I have reason to believe the Executor won't allow it though."

Caleb was clearly annoyed at the entire situation. "Why didn't this security chief keep his crew secure? The man ought to be flogged for this."

Robert scowled at Caleb's callousness. "The chief was under orders to execute any crew member who changed sides. He nearly carried out those orders on David. He had too much respect for David and felt he owed him a debt for saving his own life. He did the only thing he could. He got the crew arrested without anyone getting killed. Is that what you would have preferred? They were in space when the truth came out. He should have spaced David. Do you know what kind of death spacing is? It isn't instantaneous, and it isn't pleasant."

Caleb backed down. "I'm sorry. I guess I don't have a handle on all this yet."

Abby looked up with tear stained eyes. "Can we see him now?"

Jessica composed herself. "Not yet. I need to talk to Stevie first. Robert, is there someplace Steven and I can talk to him privately?"

"Of course. I have a temporary office just down the hall. Let me escort you down there." Robert escorted them to the door.

Abby took charge of Aiden again. She began to hold him tightly as she thought of her mother about to lose her own first-born son. Somehow being a mother changed her perspective on some things.

When the group returned to the conference room a few minutes later, Stevie looked more somber than anyone had ever seen him. His confusion was still evident on his face. Stevie admired his older half-brother to the point of planning on entering the CIF Academy after high school. David had gotten in much earlier on a scholarship, but Jessica and Steven didn't want Stevie heading to the Academy as early as David had. If the thoughts of the Academy crossed their minds at this juncture of their lives, they would have done anything in their power to stop Stevie from pursuing it at all now.

Robert conferred with Executor Hale. He wanted to be sure he was done meeting with the family and their visitation with David was approved. Executor Hale entrusted the rest of the situation to Robert's hands. Robert discussed the security protocols they would face when entering the prison facilities. He also covered one last thing. "The pain enhancing medications or neural stimulants used on David means any small painful stimulus is greatly increased. He's going to feel excruciating pain every time you brush up against a bruise. It's best if you touch him as little as possible. Are we clear on that?"

Abby looked like she was ready to cry again. "Are you saying we can see him, but we can't even touch him? This may be the last time we ever see him, and we can't hold him, or hug him, or …"

Robert walked over to her and placed a loving hand on her shoulder. "I'm saying be extra gentle or you will add to his pain." In truth, he *was* saying don't touch. He knew David would be better soon enough, but he couldn't tell her that, not yet.

• •

Robert led the group into the detention area. He didn't really want to take the entire group in, either in part or in whole. Executor Hale wanted every member of the family to see David. The Admiral opted to take them in two or three at a time starting with Jessica and Steven. He ordered the indoctrination feed stopped before entering David's cell. Before opening the cell, he gave Jessica one last reminder, "Remember not to stimulate him in any way. Noises will seem several times louder, touch far more intensely painful." Jessica looked like she was about to rip the door off at any moment. Robert wasn't sure she was getting the message. "Jess, don't run in there, grab your baby boy and hold him. You'll hurt him. Tell me you understand."

Jessica's eyes pleaded with Robert to open the door. "I understand, Robert. I understand."

The Admiral nodded to the guard who opened the door. Steven kept hold of Jessica's hand and escorted her cautiously into the cell. The lighting was exceptionally dim. It took a minute for their eyes to focus on the small room. As soon as Jessica's eyes adjusted and focused on David she gasped. He was lying face down only halfway on his mattress. She quickly pulled away from Steven and dropped to her knees. Remembering Robert's warning, she gently reached down and touched his right shoulder. David recoiled and groaned loudly. He wiggled and rolled away from her.

Jessica's eyes teared up again. "David… David, I'm sorry. I didn't mean to hurt you."

David's eyes couldn't focus. His mind was clouded by the drugs in his system. Robert knelt beside Jessica. "David, it's your Uncle Rob. Your family's here. I brought your mother and Steven to see you."

Robert gently lifted David's head and shifted him until he was sitting slouched against the wall. David pushed himself up higher with his left arm. He continued to focus on Robert's face. "My shoulder's… my shoulder's… out of joint." He winced and moaned as he tried to find a position that didn't hurt. He wasn't sure there was one. His head turned and finally focused on his mother's face. "Uncle Rob, is my mother really here, or am I dreaming again?"

Jessica reached down and touched his leg gently. "I'm really here, David."

David's eyes continued to go in and out of focus. He grinned. "That's what you said the last time and you weren't really here. I'm not f-falling for that one… again. Besides, my uncle would never let you see me like this. He knows b-better."

Jessica looked helplessly at Robert. "What do I do?"

Robert reached over and grabbed David's jaw. Getting down in his face Robert responded, "David! The Supreme Executor ordered your family be brought in to see you. They are here to convince you to recant!"

David had taken several blows to his face. When Robert grabbed his jaw, he felt like it would splinter and crack at any moment. It wasn't nearly as bad as it felt. When the truth of the situation hit his consciousness, David grabbed Robert's lapel with his left hand. "No… Uncle Rob, don't do this to them. Pa – Pa – te – ras … UNNNNHHHHHHHH." A jolt of electricity shot through his body. His body convulsed and his back arched. His teeth clinched together tightly. Jessica had pulled her hand off him just before the collar fired. Steven instinctively jerked Jessica backward. The jolt caused David to fall back down onto the mattress. Robert decided a sitting position might have been an ill-conceived idea. He carefully maneuvered David into a more neutral position lying flat on his mattress. "David." Robert spoke softly to the young man again. "Son, are you okay?"

David's eyes opened again. They were still jumping slightly, and his body still twitched. Remembering what was happening around him, David forced himself to take a deep breath which caused him to be racked with a series of painful coughs. Jessica glanced around the cell and spotted a cup on the edge of the sink. She started to step over to pick it up when Steven tried to pull her back. Jessica gave him an angry and determined look then jerked away from him. She filled the cup halfway with water and knelt beside David. Robert helped her lift David's head enough to drink. He coughed and sputtered, but slowly finished every drop. Jessica moved to refill the cup when Robert grabbed her arm. "Jess, don't give him anymore just yet. He should only drink a little at a time. Wait a few minutes."

Steven stepped forward. "We should go. I don't think there's anything we can do here."

Jessica cast another angry glance at him. "Would you leave so quickly if this were Stevie?"

Steven stepped back. He knew they would have to drag him out of here if this had been Stevie. His concern was Stevie's idolization of his older half-brother. What was this going to do to him? Knowing Jessica needed his support more than his fear, Steven stepped forward again. "What can I do to help?"

David caught his breath and looked up at his Uncle. "You held me like this b-before… wh-when I d-died on T-Tudoren. I – I'm not dying. Th-they want me to k-kill myself. Th-they keep t-telling me P-Pat -"

Robert quickly interrupted him. "Don't speak his name. We know who you're talking about."

David cast an angry glare across his small cell. "They keep

telling me, HE has abandoned me. I know they're liars. His son is with me. I feel him. He p-promised he would never leave me. They c-can't stop him." David smirked. His eyes still focused on the other side of the cell.

The three looked in the general direction David was looking. Seeing nothing, Jessica asked, "They who? The guards?"

David looked at his mother then back at the figures standing on the other side of his small cell. "You d-don't see them, do you? They're s-servants of the Dark Lord." David twitched and coughed again.

Steven picked up the empty cup and refilled it with water. He handed it to Jessica. His eyes were filled with pity. "He's delirious." Jessica helped David drink some more.

David rolled his head around to look up at his uncle. "You don't see them either, do you?" He looked and acted as though he was drunk.

Robert looked concerned. He remembered Arni's words in their meeting the previous night. He wasn't sure if David was hallucinating or if there really were superior beings standing in the room with them. He knew he needed to choose his words carefully. "Maybe… or maybe not. We're dealing with non-corporeal superior beings. I don't see anything over there either, but there may be something there. I wouldn't completely discount the idea."

Steven looked more annoyed than anything. He was having trouble accepting all of this. "David, the Supreme Executor will stop all of this if you recant your position. Surely this isn't worth all the pain you're going through."

"Steven… Steven, you don't understand. He's l-lying. He'll never willingly let me out… out of here alive. If I recant… he'll kill me outright. My father… won't let him kill me. My father is protecting me." David continued to twitch, jerk and moan between words. His skin felt like there were insects crawling all over him. The bruising on his back, ribs, and abdomen made deep breaths insanely painful. He took frequent shallow breaths until the lower part of his lungs objected to being ignored and forced him to take a slow deep breath. As soon as he did, he would cough causing his pain to reach an unbelievable crescendo.

Steven looked confused. "Your father? I thought no one had been able to locate your father."

Jessica glanced at Steven. "He's speaking of Pateras. He can't say the name of Pateras so he's using one of the roles Pateras claims."

Steven shook his head. "I don't understand. Just how much do you know about Pateras?"

"Only what I learned as a small child. I was taught he considered himself to be the Father of all mankind. It's an easy thing for a child to understand and remember." Jessica gave David a little more water and gently squeezed his hand. "David, are you sure about this? Isn't there anything you can do, or we can do? Tell me what to do. How can I help you?"

David looked her squarely in the face. "Tell me one thing and answer quickly. How many days has it been since I talked to you?"

Before anyone could stop her Jessica answered, "Four days."

David laughed as he looked at the empty spot he had been staring at before. As soon as he laughed and took another deep breath he wrenched and coughed again. "They didn't want me to know that. My father will free me soon. Mom… Mom… they'll try to use the family against me. Be ready to run. You have to be ready today." David wrenched and coughed again uncontrollably.

Jessica gave him the last of the water then set the cup down. Robert gently laid David down on his mattress. "We should go. He needs to rest."

Jessica leaned down and gently kissed David's temple and ran her hand gently across his head. "I love you, son. I'm sure we'll see you again soon." She stood up and quietly followed Steven out of the cell.

Once in the hallway, everyone looked at her expectantly. Her tears were gone. Her countenance was quiet and stoic.

Abby broke the silence. "Mom, what is it? Is David okay?"

Jessica looked up slowly. Robert caught her eye and rubbed his ear discreetly. "He's… uh… he's either delirious or… I don't know. He's not changing his mind. He thinks he's going to get out of this somehow."

Abby started to hand Aiden off to Kay then changed her mind. "I need to see him."

Jessica stepped in front of Abby and gently took hold of her shoulders. "Abby, I really don't think that's a good idea. He's hurting, badly, and he doesn't need to be disturbed."

"I'm going in!" The young woman replied defiantly. "Uncle Rob, please let me see my brother."

Robert wanted nothing more than to deny her request. He knew Arni would have everything fixed by tomorrow. If they had come one day later, they would never have seen David like this. He also considered one day later might mean never seeing him again. He didn't know where David and the crew would go after leaving here, but they would be on the run. Denying her request would also bring his own alliances to light. The Supreme Executor wanted the entire family to see David to gauge their reactions.

Robert steeled himself again. "Are you sure you want to do this? It's not going to be pleasant."

Abby nodded resolutely.

Robert glanced at the others. "Are you coming in alone or do you want someone with us?"

Jessica glanced at Caleb. "Caleb, why don't you go with her?

I don't want her dealing with this alone. Let me hold Aiden."

Abby teared up. "No, I'm taking him in with me. This might be the only chance David will get to meet his nephew."

Jessica realized it was pointless to argue with her. Her heart began to break all over again at the prospect of losing David a second time. She turned and buried her head in Steven's chest. She knew Pateras was capable of freeing David. She just wasn't sure he would.

Robert escorted them into the cell. Abby immediately started to cry when she saw David lying on the ratty mattress. He had tried to suppress his pain while his mother was present, but the magnified aches, throbbing, and burning from the baton searing his flesh returned the second she left. He was now moaning and groaning as his limbs twitched and tried to find a position not causing excruciating pain.

Robert moved over by David's head and raised him up gently allowing his head to rest on Robert's lap. David opened his eyes again. He looked up at his uncle. The temperature in the room had been dropping rapidly over the past few minutes. David began shivering, adding to his pain. "I th-thought you l-left."

Robert glanced over at Abby and Caleb. "Abby insisted on seeing you."

"N-no, p-please d-don't -" David reached up with his left hand and grabbed his uncle's arm. He twisted awkwardly to see Robert's face. He realized his objection was coming too late. David turned painfully towards the room. He saw Abby's strained face appear in front of him. He gritted his teeth as he turned to face Abby and Caleb. His emotions were conflicted at the sight of her. He didn't want her to see him like this. He didn't feel much like dealing with more company, but he missed her and was glad to see her. His eyes focused on the baby in her arms. "Abbs, is th-this b-baby J-Joshua?"

Abby gave David a weak smile. "Yes, Davie, this is Joshua

Aiden. We're calling him Aiden."

David smiled briefly. He reached out with his left hand and offered his finger to the curious baby. Aiden cooed and grinned back at David. His chubby fingers curled around David's finger. "Hey th-there l-little g-guy. Ab-by, he's b-beautiful. Y-you sh-should g-go. He sh-should… shouldn't s-see me l-like th-this. P-please g-go. C-Caleb, p-please t-take th-them out of here."

Caleb stepped forward and tried to encourage Abby to leave. Abby scooted closer to David. She begged him to change his loyalty back to the Commonwealth. She began to cry. Aiden, confused by the situation started to whimper. He was getting cold and scared by the strange events. Caleb reached down and took Aiden from Abby.

"Abigail, I'm taking Aiden back out. You need to come too." Caleb's eyes locked on David's for a moment. The two said nothing out loud, but the message was clear. Caleb clearly pitied David. He wanted to honor David's wish to be alone. A piece of him wanted to keep his family clear of this whole situation. Caleb was profoundly scared for his family.

David understood Caleb's message, loud and clear. David conveyed his appreciation and understanding with a look of his own. He saw the fear in Caleb's eyes. Ironically, David pitied Caleb and Abby.

Caleb stepped outside with Aiden. Abby was not ready to leave yet. "Davie, please don't do this. Do whatever they tell you. I don't want to lose you, David, please." Abby pleaded. "I don't want Aiden growing up thinking his uncle died a traitor. You have to forget these crazy ideas."

David grabbed Abby's hand. "Abby… l-let's t-talk about it, t-tomorrow. Ev-Every… th-thing's g-going to be okay. I p-prom-ise."

The cell door opened again, Kay stepped in with Hannah and Steven. Abby was beginning to shiver from the cold and from the mass of emotion waging war on her psyche. Robert looked at Hannah. Abby gently picked up David's hand and kissed it. Robert nodded towards Abby, "Help her out." Hannah guided Abby to the door.

Abby stopped and looked back at her older brother, "David… I love you." Hannah put her arm around Abby and escorted her on out. As soon as the door closed behind her, Abby threw herself sobbing into her mother's arms.

Kay held tightly to Stevie's arm. Stevie's eyes grew wider as they moved closer to David. Due to the drugs in David's system, his mood was erratic. The impact of such emotional exchanges, taxed his ability to control his emotions. "Gram… Stev-vie, d-don't c-come in here. P-Please… j-just l-leave m-me b-be. Ahhh! Th-This hurts!" David gritted his teeth and rocked more aggressively. "I c-can't c-call his n-name wh-wh-when you're t-touching m-me. PLEASE GO!"

Robert nodded to his mother and Stevie to leave. He gently laid David back down. The three started to go out when Kay stopped and knelt by David. Putting her hand on his, she leaned over and kissed him gently on his temple. Before standing up she whispered, "You believe Pateras will protect you. You better not be wrong. I want to see you tomorrow."

• •

Jake watched the entire scene with the Captain's family play out on a monitor from his quarters. He knew the Captain was vulnerable right now. If he took him the hypo-spray, it would be easy for him to give in and use it. Jake got up from his computer station and made his way to the infirmary. He picked up the waiting syringe. Sliding it into a pocket he felt sick at the sight of it. Jake left the Infirmary then headed for the prison facilities. When he reached the high security area, he grabbed the standard riot protection gear and helmet worn by prison guards. It was lightweight as well as effective. The helmet had a dark face shield capable of hiding his identity. Jake stopped before leaving the combat staging area to check out the appropriate weapons then discreetly pressed a button on his bracelet. The button initiated a computer program putting the surveillance feeds on a repeating loop in any corridor where Jake's bracelet was detected. The new young lieutenant knew he was kissing his promotion and his freedom goodbye. For better or worse, he was in it now. His first stop was not the Captain's cell.

Jake headed to the re-education suite. He stepped into one of the suites. Walking casually around the outside of the observation area, he made his way around to the control station. He stood there and watched as the technician manipulated the controls indoctrinating Ensign Aulani Ryder. He slowly struck up a casual conversation with the technician. In a minute, he saw the technician yawn. Jake jumped at the opportunity. He offered to watch the man's station while he ran to get a cup of coffee. The man started to decline. Jake yawned and stretched giving the technician a psychological reinforcement of his own drowsy state. He commented on the tedious nature of the task. The man finally relented and took Jake up on his offer. Jake sat down at the station and exchanged his own helmet for the technician's. He did a brief glance at the controls then appeared to settle into a casual monitoring stance. The technician promised to hurry. Jake encouraged the man to take his time, assuring him nothing could go wrong.

The second the man was gone, Jake tagged his comm unit to alert him when the man headed back. He also programmed the doors and security check points to move more slowly than usual. It wasn't enough to warrant a maintenance report, but just enough to slow him down. Jake shut down part of the program and released Aulani's restraints. Aulani still stared blankly at the screen in front of her. Jake shook her roughly. "Ensign Ryder! Snap out of it! I need your help!"

Aulani blinked and roused. Her eyes finally focused on Jake. "Jake! I don't understand. How did you get free?" Her mind began to put things together. His appearance wasn't synonymous with a tortured prisoner. "You really are the one who betrayed us. I'm not going to help you with anything."

"Aulani…" Jake was about to argue with her. Something told him he should just tell her the truth. "Yes, I'm the one who betrayed you. I'm sorry. I'm trying to fix this. Arni has a plan to get the crew out. I'm trying to help you."

Aulani jerked away from Jake. "I don't believe you!"

"Aulani, listen to me! We only have a couple minutes. I need to get the water turned back on in your cells without arousing suspicion. I have a program written to falsify the data for the primary monitoring stations. I'm worried about secondary monitoring stations and other redundancies. I just need to fool the systems for the next few hours. I also need to change the indoctrination feed to include subliminal messages to encourage the crew to turn the sink on." Jake pulled Aulani roughly to the control station and shoved her into the chair. He plugged the program into the terminal computer.

The rubric popped up on the screen. The images correlated with Jake's request for help. Aulani slowly put the pieces together in her mind. Jake's programs did seem to support what he told her. Aulani's head snapped around to face Jake. "How much time do we have?"

Jake glanced at his bracelet's display. "Five minutes, tops."

"I don't have time to do this. Just listen to me. Write a sub-routine to feed the water flow rate discrepancies back into usage for other locations. Change the code for the prison usage to a secondary code. You could also create a leak somewhere unrelated to the cells to cause an expected discrepancy. As far as the subliminal messages, put one frame in per every ten frames. You'd better be legit, or I'll come after you myself."

Aulani headed back to the chair in the re-education chamber. If he really was trying to help, she didn't want him to get caught. She hated this chair. It would have made her much happier to turn and run the other way. Jake fastened her back into the chair. Aulani could see the remorse in his eyes. Some of the tension drained out of her. There was hope, at least a little.

Jake wanted to check to be sure there was nothing he had overlooked. "What about the sewage output? Does it have to balance the intake? Is there anything else I should watch out for?"

"No, the two absolutely should not balance. The only other thing you have to watch for is program tampering detection. You can get around that by creating another sub-routine to report the tamper detection twenty-four hours from now or a year from now, whenever. Jake... be careful."

Jake worked on the programs Aulani instructed him to work on and let the chamber remain idle until he knew his absent technician was nearly at the door. Seeing the technician was returning, he restarted the chamber, closed the program, retrieved his data crystal and erased the log of his activities. He leaned back in the chair, tucked his hands idly behind his head, and swiveled back and forth casually.

The technician apologized for taking so long. He had no real explanation for the delay. He thanked Jake for covering for him. Jake relinquished his seat and helmet and left the room. He moved into the corridor where the Captain's cell was located. He turned off the program hiding his movements. The guards had been told to expect Lt. Holden. They opened the door to the cell and left him alone.

Jake knelt beside the Captain. "Captain... Captain, can you hear me?"

David jerked awake. The programming hadn't been restarted after his family left him, allowing him a small amount of rest. He worked to make his eyes focus on the face in front of him. "What do you want?" His mood had not improved.

"We need to talk. Can you sit up?"

David pushed himself slowly and painfully into a more upright position. Jake scooted over and helped David lean against the wall. "Wh - What do you want… Chief?"

Jake knew the Captain's use of the title chief, was meant to defame him. "Captain, I want to apologize to you. I never meant to put you through all of this."

"Is that… unh… Is that it, Chief? Y- Your apology w-wasn't really what I was l-looking for."

"I know what you were looking for. You were looking for me to change my loyalty. I'm afraid I can't tell you my loyalties have changed. You seemed to think I was worth going through all of this. I'm not worth this, Captain." Jake sat down on the floor in front of him.

"J-Jake, I… unh…" David picked up his right arm with his left hand and gingerly repositioned it. "Are you… looking for… forgiveness? I gave… it to you… already."

"No, Captain. I came to offer you a way out." Jake pulled the hypo-spray gently from his pocket. He held it up in front of the Captain. "This is a lethal dose of a sedative."

"Are you here to execute me, Chief?" David's head was suddenly quite clear.

"No, Captain. This is entirely up to you. I wanted to offer it to you before your family had the chance to see you like this. I didn't get here in time. I'm sorry about that. Captain, if you use this, your suffering ends here and now." Jake studied the Captain's face carefully for signs of weakness or temptation.

David looked at the syringe and at Jake's face. He was trying to assess Jake's true motives. "How d-do I know that's wh-what you s-say it is? Why would you… d-do this? Are you t-trying to… m-make it up to the b-brass for n-not executing m-me?"

Jake's somber appearance did nothing to assuage David's concerns. "Captain, I have nothing to gain or lose by lying to you. If you want to wait to use this, to suffer through another couple beatings, that's your choice. I just don't want to see you suffer any longer. The war is over. I surrender. Executor Hale wanted me to be responsible for your beating the other day to make sure you weren't expecting me to rescue you. This is the only escape I can offer. You want somebody to rescue you. Pateras is going to have to be the one to do it, not me. Do you really want your family to continue to see you like this? What if he decides to try and use them against you? Do you want that? If you're dead, he's got no reason to touch them. What do you expect to gain by putting up with this?"

Jake watched David's eyes. The more his gaze landed on the syringe, the more Jake worried. He was considering using the syringe. Jake decided to push harder. He was hoping to push the Captain to the point of pushing back. "Just what did Arni promise you? Where is he now? Is serving him worth all of this? Do you know what he's put the crew through? The crew are dying. They're going to be dead before you. With that collar on, you can't even call out to him for help. Just take the syringe. No one would blame you. You've proven yourself to be loyal to Pateras. Surely, he doesn't require anything else from you. If you die, you'll join him, right? So, join him. It's where you wanted to be anyway."

A fire began to flicker in David's eyes. Jake saw it. He tried hard to keep his face neutral.

"Give me the syringe," David ordered.

Jake hesitated. That wasn't what he expected. David ordered him once again with more voracity. Jake leaned forward to hand him the hypo. David was holding out his left hand for the syringe. The Captain was right-handed. Why was he reaching with his non-dominant hand? Jake looked at the Captain's physique more carefully. His shoulders were not symmetrical. His right shoulder must be out of its socket. Jake placed the syringe in David's left hand and glanced purposefully at David's empty right hand. "I knew you'd make the *right* choice." Jake made sure David's eyes connected with Jake's on his right arm.

David pushed himself up a little further against the wall. "I w-want to see the S-Supreme Executor before I use this."

Jake hesitated. "Are you sure about that, sir?"

David insisted.

Jake stood up to go. "You'll be here when I get back right?"

The fire in his eyes continued to burn. "I'll be here, and I'll be alive."

"You wouldn't lie to me, would you, sir?" Jake eyed him carefully. He was scared. Security officers weren't supposed to show fear. Jake had the distinct impression his fear was conspicuous.

"No, Chief… I wouldn't."

David saw relief on Jake's face. David's heart skipped a beat. Had Jake finally joined them?

Jake left quickly to report to the Supreme Executor. Hearing his report, Executor Hale wet his lips in anticipation. He moved faster than Jake had ever seen him. Executor Hale was on the cusp of getting the victory he so fiercely desired.

Jake followed Executor Hale into the Captain's cell. He was relieved to see his Captain still alive and the fire still burning in his eyes.

"Captain, I understand you wanted to see me? What can I do for you? Name it. If I can, I will give it to you." Executor Hale smiled that same disarming smile.

"I w-want t-to know why you want… me dead? I know I l-left the Commonwealth, b-but I'm… I'm one m-man. Why – Why is my s-service s-so important?" David fingered the syringe in his hand. It was true, his intense pain made him want to take the dose. The hypo-spray would cause him to fall asleep then stop breathing. It would be a peaceful death. David shook off the thoughts. He had a job to do. His thoughts were jumbled. What could possibly be this important? Stopping an evil tyrant. Yes, he had to stop Executor Hale. Executor Hale was too powerful. How was one mere mortal supposed to stop him?

A calming voice spoke to him. "You aren't supposed to defeat him. I've already done that. You just have to resist him. David, I'm here with you." Arni's voice was as clear as though it had been spoken by someone standing next to him.

David refocused his wayward attention. "Why pay so much attention to me?" His words were clear and unbroken by pain.

Executor Hale looked over at Jake. "Lt. Holden, wait for me down the hall. Take the guard detail with you."

Jake nodded anxiously and left the room. He made quick eye contact with David. He wanted to say something… anything. He was afraid if he spoke right now, it might reveal his change in loyalty. He stepped outside the cell and beckoned the guards to follow him. The three headed to the gated juncture at the end of the corridor. Jake sat down on a bench outside the door. Jake whispered under his breath, "Arni, please don't let him kill himself."

Arni's voice whispered softly to Jake. "He'll be fine."

Jake blinked. Had he actually heard Arni's voice or was it just wishful thinking? He genuinely hoped it wasn't just wishful thinking.

• •

Now alone in the cell, Luciano ventured to answer David's inquiry. "I don't hate you, in particular. I hate this entire human race. Pateras is so *in love* with his precious creation, it makes me sick. I'm far greater than any of you. I know I can't wage war against him directly, but I can destroy everything he cares about."

"It's because you're jealous? That explains the Commonwealth. It doesn't explain why you didn't just ship my crew and me off to prison. You're putting a great deal of effort into trying to turn me back to you."

Luciano pulled himself to his full height. "I am NOT jealous of you pitiful creatures," he sneered. "In your entire short lives, you're lucky to see a dozen worlds. I've seen millions. I have abilities you'd kill to have. I don't *need* a starship to travel on. I can go wherever I please, whenever I please. I have funds beyond compare at my disposal. I have people who kneel at my feet, people who bow and scrape to earn my favor. Your own security chief is *drooling* over the opportunity to earn my favor. Your uncle serves me rather than try to rescue you. I have no *reason* to be jealous."

David nodded. "I see… You aren't jealous of us. That makes sense. We certainly don't have anything to offer you except loyalty and servitude. You *are* jealous of the love and attention He gives us. I may not completely understand the situation, but here's what I think. We fell out of His good graces just like you did. The difference is, you fell out on your own. We were seduced and tricked by you and your kind. He put a plan in place to bring us back into his good graces. You don't have that option. That's why you're jealous! He continues to offer us his love and compassion. Your vendetta is against me because you think I paved the way for it. Ar – His son, died in my place and you want revenge against me for that."

Luciano shifted into his natural state. He grabbed David up off the mattress and shoved him roughly against the wall. He held him mere inches from the ceiling. David's feet dangled well above the floor. Luciano brought his face right up in David's face. "YOU HAVE NO IDEA WHAT YOU'RE TALKING ABOUT!"

David grunted when he hit the wall. He grabbed one of Luciano's hands with his left arm to take some of the pressure off the rest of his body. David used what little energy he had left to smirk and reply, "You're a fool. I didn't let… Ar – his son, take my place. He just took it. You caused all of this. If you hadn't destroyed Galat, if you had left my family on Drea, if you hadn't created this mission, none of this would have happened." David was trying to be careful not to speak the names of Arni or Pateras aloud. He really didn't need to feel the jolt of the collar right now.

Executor Hale dropped David back to the ground. David crumpled roughly in a heap on his mattress.

"You want to know why? I'll tell you why. I know the Texts inside out. You're the one who brings Pateras back into this galaxy. I had nearly eradicated all signs of him. I raised you and groomed you to serve me from two generations back. Pateras didn't create you. I did. He may have created you from a biological perspective, but I prepared all of you for this mission. I took every one of you away from your familial ties to keep you strong and hard. I kept you independent to isolate you from weakness. This was *my* plan. Your crew would never have strayed if you hadn't led the way. I'm punishing you the hardest because you're the Captain."

"So why not kill me yourself?" David realized as soon as he asked the question, Executor Hale was not just forbidden in a verbal sense from killing David. Arni had made sure he was physically incapable of killing him. "You want to, but you can't, can you? He didn't just forbid you from touching me. He's shielding me from you, isn't he?"

Executor Hale returned to his human form. "I'm done with your questions, Captain. Our time is at an end. What would you prefer me to tell your crew and family? I will honor your last request. I can tell them you died from the stress of the situation or I ordered your execution. I can tell your family one thing and your crew another if you wish. I can leave them wondering if that's your desire."

David pushed himself upright again. Picking up the hypo-spray, David positioned it in his hand with his thumb on the plunger. He held it above his left thigh. He looked up and grinned. "Tell them I died of… old age." David quickly plunged the head of the hypo-spray onto his mattress and pressed the trigger mechanism forcing the medication into his mattress.

David saw Executor Hale's temper flare. The man was so accustomed to behaving as a human, it now came naturally to him. His face turned beet red. "That was the last gesture of mercy, you're going to get from me! If you want to be released from your suffering, you're going to have to beg me on your hands and knees to forgive you! I'll see you groveling on the ground before I give you one shred of mercy!"

• •

The Executor stormed out of the room and down the hall. Jake stood up when he saw him coming. From the look on his face, he was wary about asking questions. He decided it was better to ask and get his head bitten off than look like he *expected* a poor outcome. "Supreme Executor, what happened?"

Executor Hale turned his rage on Jake. He grabbed Jake and pinned him against the nearest wall. "Just what did you say to him?"

"Nothing of consequence. He was almost there. I saw him. He was toying with the idea. I wasn't sure he'd still be alive when I brought you back to see him." Jake paused a moment before continuing. "I take it he didn't use the hypo?"

Executor Hale was suspicious of Jake. He debated testing him again then decided it was pointless. If Jake had sold out to Pateras, there was no way to hurt him. He did decide to increase his odds. He slowly released Jake, smoothing out the wrinkles in his uniform, he asked, "If you wanted to take one more shot at causing him to fall, what would you do?"

Jake stopped and thought for a moment. He knew he needed to throw suspicion off himself without the risk of bringing harm to the Captain or crew. "Sir, may I ask why you haven't ordered his execution outright?" Jake already knew Pateras had forbidden it. He also knew he wasn't supposed to have that information.

The Supreme Executor glanced around at the nearby guards. He ordered the Captain's guards back to their posts outside his cell. He motioned for Jake to follow him through the corridors leaving the prison facility. "Pateras has forbidden me to touch his life for six days. You of all people should understand such a limitation. I can't defy him on this. I believe he has a plan to release him and his crew by midnight tonight. I have today and only today to turn him."

"What if you do the same thing to him the Admiral did to Marissa and me? Give him either a weapon with one shot or another hypo-sprayer. Tell him you will kill the crew one at a time until he uses it on himself. I'm assuming you can't kill the crew because of Pateras' protection too, so it would have to be late today, close to midnight. The Captain won't know what time it is. The other option is to shoot the Admiral, just don't tell him I suggested it. The Captain may be too convinced of the crew's protection. He may not have been assured of his family's protection. Besides, I owe the Admiral for shooting me a few days ago. I don't suggest you touch the rest of his family. I'm not sure you want to start shooting civilians with the press so close by."

Luciano stared hard at Jake then smiled. "You have a twisted way of thinking. I like that. I may have further use for you if you choose to stay in the CIF. Tell me again why you couldn't execute your captain months ago?"

Jake sighed. "I may have a twisted way of thinking, but I'm still a man of some honor. The Captain saved my life, Marissa's life, and my son's life. I owed him. I also owed the Common-wealth, which is why I turned him in. I pay my debts."

Luciano started to ask Jake if he was capable of killing his Captain after midnight tonight. He decided it was a waste of time. If he managed to keep the Captain in custody after midnight, he could press the issue later.

• •

The two went their separate directions. Jake had more work to do to get ready for Arni to free the crew. He finished up his water bypass algorithms and the adjustments to the indoctrination feeds. He added the frames at the ratio Aulani prescribed to the feeds and erased the logs indicating the program had been tampered with. He also took the precaution of sending all back-up logs into a redundancy loop to keep them from being accessible for a full twenty-four hours. Almost as an afterthought, Jake created a program initiating a full diagnostic of all systems on the base. He put the program on a data crystal and slipped it into his pocket. He really wished he knew what time Arni was going to break the crew out. He wanted to set the program to go off at a certain time. Jake sat down to think if there was anything else he had forgotten. He shook his head. The only way they were getting out of this alive was with the help of Pateras. The data crystal in his pocket would keep the CIF base from shooting their ship down and it would hinder their attempts to launch ships to chase them. It wouldn't stop the launches, it would only slow them. There were also three large, heavily armed, flagships in orbit around the planet. Jake buried his face in his hands. From where he was sitting, there was no way to get out of this alive.

Arni spoke softly to the young man's mind, "Get some sleep."

Recognizing Arni's voice, Jake bolted to a standing position. "Get some sleep? Are you kidding me? How am I supposed to sleep at a time like this?" He heard no response. Somehow, he had the distinct impression Arni was laughing at him, or at least mildly amused.

Once his gut reaction settled, he heard the same voice lovingly whisper, "Get some sleep. I have the watch. Consider this your first exercise in trust."

Jake sighed and did as he was told. He laid down on the sofa in his quarters. He didn't really expect to get any rest. Five minutes later, he was sound asleep.

● ●

Executor Hale worked on plans of his own. He sent for Commodore Vardin and Admiral Garcia. The three sat down together in the Supreme Executor's office. "Gentlemen, I have received some intelligence reports that require immediate action. I'm going to make this as straightforward and to the point as I can. Asking me how I know is going to be a colossal waste of time and energy, so please keep your questions as functionally related as possible. Do you have any problems with that?"

The two men looked curiously at each other. They both agreed, in short order, to abide by his ground rules.

Executor Hale moved quickly on. "I have reason to believe Pateras plans to infiltrate this base and free our prisoners. Here's how I want to prepare. I want all personnel, all shifts, in here and on duty as soon as possible. Once on the base, no one leaves until this is over. Arrange billeting in base housing if we need to rotate shifts."

Commodore Vardin interrupted, "Sir, I don't know if we have enough beds in base housing."

Executor Hale seemed annoyed at such a low priority issue. "I'm not expecting this to last longer than the next twenty-four hours, probably less. One bunk is good for three shifts if needed. If there still aren't enough beds, put men on couches, infirmary beds unless otherwise needed by the sick or injured, and use the beds in empty prison cells if you need to. I'm sure you can work it out Commodore. If you can't, I'll look into finding you an assignment you are more suited for. I understand the commander on Mara is looking to retire soon."

Visions of the prison facility on the frozen tundra on Mara ran through Commodore Vardin's mind. He had never actually seen the place, but he'd heard about it from colleagues. He decided his next question had better be far more important. "I'll make sure everything works out, sir. What else do you need?"

Executor Hale's stare seemed to bore holes right through him. Thankfully he moved on quickly. "I want every entrance and exit covered. I want everyone armed, the cleaning staff, kitchen staff, receptionists, everyone. No one gets near the prisoners, no one. Every prison door is to remain shut. No one gets through for any reason. I am the final authority for the next twenty-four hours on the opening and closing of every door in the prison. When you need to change people out, move them two at a time reporting in on themselves and their prisoners the second they take up their stations. I want this place locked down so tight, not even an insect could get in or out without my permission."

Admiral Garcia leaned forward. "Do you want me to bring men from my ship down to add to the Commodore's troops?"

"No, keep your men on your ship. If they get past the Commodore's troops, we'll have to chase them down. As a matter of fact, I want you to return to your ship. I want to set up a planetary blockade using your ship, Admiral Deacons' ship and my own. Get all civilian interstellar traffic in orbit, out of the area by 1800 hours local time or ground them. Anyone not observing the blockade will be shot down or arrested."

Admiral Garcia seemed troubled. Luciano cocked his head slightly. "What are you concerned about, Edgar?"

"Are you going to shoot down civilian vessels with so many

reporters watching?" Admiral Garcia seemed more concerned with the bad press than the death of civilians.

"No, of course not. If I do, it's an absolute last resort, and I'll have a good cover story. I just want the warning going out to discourage stragglers. Tell the press I will be conducting a press conference aboard my ship shortly after midnight local time. After you issue the travel orders, invite the press to shuttle over to my ship to await the press conference. Edgar, if you would let Admiral Deacons know I need him to return to his ship as soon as possible. Commodore Vardin, keep the Captain's family sequestered in their suite in base housing. Tell them we have a security issue and it's for their own safety. Let them know I will personally arrange another meeting with the Captain as soon as possible."

Commodore Vardin acknowledged his orders and took some notes on his data pad. "Do you want troops on the tarmac and covering all the hangars?"

"Absolutely. I don't mean to step on your toes, Commodore, so please don't take this personally. I need all security codes changed and transferred to me. Once I'm aboard the *Chimera*, I will coordinate everything from there. Oh, and one more thing, have a firing squad on standby. If the Captain and his crew are still in custody at 0000 hours, I want them executed at 0001 hours."

Commodore Vardin looked confused. "What about the Captain's family? You told me to tell them you would arrange a meeting with him?"

"I just did. I am arranging for them to see him one last time… at his execution." Executor Hale gave the Commodore another icy stare.

Commodore Vardin swallowed hard. "Yes sir. Will there be anything else, sir?"

"Yes, two more things. First, bring Prisoner 7145 to my office. Second, cancel the ship coming to escort the crew to Mara. We won't be needing it anymore. I almost forgot. Please inform Miss Shields I would appreciate it if she would be aboard my ship and ready to depart by 1700 hours."

CHAPTER TEN – THWARTING EVIL

Jake felt a hand shaking him awake. As reality reasserted itself in his drowsy mind, he realized someone was in his quarters. He sat up quickly and opened his eyes. His fight or flight instincts started kicking in. His eyes focused on whoever touched him. His heart raced. He pulled his feet up onto the sofa and poised himself in a squatting position to run or fight as needed. A large humanoid man stood in front of him. A bright light emanated from the being and two fiery eyes stared at him. "Who… What… are you? No… better question… Who do you work for?"

In a strong voice, his celestial visitor answered. "Don't be alarmed. Pateras sent me to be your guide and your guard. Your friends know me as Gabe."

Jake began to relax a little. "Have you freed the crew?"

The figure shook his head. "That job is yours. It's time for us to go."

Jake looked perplexed. "How am I supposed to do that? There are guards all over the place. They aren't going to let us just walk in and escort them out."

"Let me worry about that. I'll take care of the guards. You take care of the crew. Get your things."

Jake still wore a myriad of emotions on his face while he grabbed his over-shirt and a collection of data crystals. He had procured one of the batons used by the prison guards and a Tri-EMP which he stuck in his belt. Gabe stood impatiently by the door. Seeing Jake grabbing weapons, he objected. "You won't need those. I am empowered to protect you and your crew. No harm will come to any of them. Let's go."

Gabe's bizarre appearance was intimidating to say the least. It didn't persuade him to leave his weapons behind. He was really hoping Gabe wouldn't press the issue. He headed towards the door. "It's my job to carry weapons. I'm a security chief. I won't use them unless I need to. Do you really want to wait for me to take them off again?"

Gabe gave him an annoyed stare. He knew Jake's weapons were designed to be drawn in a split second and the man could have disarmed himself in half a second. He let the matter pass and escorted Jake down the hall. The two reached the elevator. Just as the doors opened to reveal two off duty personnel getting off the elevator, Gabe put a reassuring hand on Jake's shoulder. The two officers stepped off the elevator and walked on down the hall chatting about an attractive young woman they had met off base a few days ago. One of them complained loudly about his leave getting postponed by the increased security measures. The two never even looked at Jake or the alien being. Gabe gently guided Jake onto the elevator. The two walked unobserved through lobbies and reception areas. They passed checkpoints unobstructed. As far as Jake could tell, no one could even see them. As they took an elevator up to the appropriate prison level, Jake's curiosity got the best of him. "Are you using some sort of cloaking device to keep us hidden from view?"

Gabe smiled slightly at the concept. "You… could say that. I have no device, but they cannot see us."

Jake considered his answer. "That's why you said I wouldn't need my weapons, isn't it?"

Gabe nodded.

Jake waited for him to expound on the concept. Gabe offered no further information. He appeared to be extremely task oriented.

The first cell they reached was Thane's. Jake pressed his hand against the pad to open the cell. Knowing he was forbidden to access the crew, he feared it would set off alarms or at least refuse him access. The door opened without incident. Jake moved quickly into the cell. The prisoners were currently on one of their brief respites from indoctrination and sleep deprivation. Jake shook Thane who was sound asleep. "Thane, wake up! It's time to get out of here."

Thane was so tired he really wanted to slug Jake for waking him. The only thing protecting him was Jake telling him it was time to leave this horrific place. Thane got up slowly and started to follow Jake as instructed. Jake stopped for a second. "Thane, have you had any water in the last few hours?"

"Uh… yeah, my water got turned back on somehow. I think I'm still a quart low, but I'm functional. I'm not sure why I checked the sink,"

"Good. Let's get moving." Jake led the way out of the cell and moved on to the next one. Thane followed obediently as he tried to shake the cobwebs from his brain. Jake placed his hand on the next pad. Thane watched it scan Jake's hand. His eyes focused skeptically on the pad then visually traced Jake's arm up to the rank insignia on his shoulder. The door opened. Jake stepped into the second cell. The cell was Lazaro's. The exchange was similar to Jake and Thane's moments ago.

Jake hastily stepped into the corridor and pressed the pad to the cell across the hall. As the door opened, Thane grabbed Jake and spun him around. He shoved Jake against the wall. "I thought you said the Captain was the traitor. It was you all along, wasn't it… Lieutenant!?"

Jake had forgotten his attire was a CIF uniform bearing his traitorous rank. He looked down at his shoulder then back up at Thane. "Thane, I'll explain everything later. Pateras has a plan to get us out of here, but we've got to move – now!"

Lazaro looked back and forth, watching for guards. "Thane, this might not be the best time…"

Thane glanced at Lazaro. "I say we throw him into one of these cells and leave him here."

Hearing the commotion outside his now open cell, Jason cautiously poked his head into the hallway. Seeing the drama unfold, Jason moved to Jake's side. "Thane, I'm not sure what's going on here, but can we settle it later?"

Jake swiftly pulled his weapon and shoved the barrel into Thane's ribs. Thane released his grip on Jake and backed away slowly. He raised his hands in a gesture of surrender. As soon as Thane was two arms lengths away, Jake flipped his weapon around and offered it to Thane, butt first. "Thane, once we get everyone free, if you don't like what I have to say, then do whatever you feel is justified."

Thane looked at Jake then at the weapon. He reached down and took it gingerly from Jake's hand. He gripped the weapon tightly and motioned for Jake to stay in front of him. Jake moved cautiously. Pointing at Gabe, Jake added one word of warning. "Just be careful, I don't think he appreciates our weapons."

Jason, Lazaro, and Thane looked at each other and the spot where Jake had pointed. Jason finally asked, "Who doesn't?"

Jake looked at the blank stares of his shipmates then back at Gabe. Despite the creature's assurances no one could hear or see them, Jake whispered loudly. "Are you serious? I thought it was your *job* to protect me. The crew doesn't trust me. They want to do me serious harm and you don't even let *them* see you?"

Jake appeared to be listening for a response from his "imaginary friend," who was apparently a great deal taller than Jake. "Great! Right! The crew's my responsibility. Got it. By the way, I think my weapons have come in handy."

Lazaro gave Jason a sideways glance. "Doc, you think he's

losing it?"

Jason stared dumbstruck. "I'm… going to withhold judgment… for now."

Jake led the three men past a couple cells to a fourth cell. He pressed the pad to open it. Lazaro stepped in and roused Braxton. Braxton hurried out of the cell. "How did you guys get out?"

Thane wasn't pointing his weapon in any particular direction. His gaze was firmly fixed on Jake. "He let us out." Thane gestured Jake's direction.

Braxton wasn't sure whether to slug Jake or shake his hand. An icy stare seemed sufficient for now.

Jake headed towards the last cell past one of the checkpoints. Before they rounded the corner, Jake gave the men very specific instructions. "Guys, my invisible friend is keeping us hidden from the guards. Just walk right through when I get the door open. The Captain has been kept under heavier security and he's been tortured far more extensively than any of you. He's going to need help getting out of here."

Jason stepped forward. "What are we looking at?"

Jake cringed. He didn't want to report it to the doctor, but he knew it was for the best. "He's been given neural stimulants then beaten with a baton like this. He also has several burns from the electrical charge. They've been running him into the infirmary long enough to heal anything life threatening. Once he has a semi-clean bill of health, they start the beatings and stimulants all over again. It started out once a day, then twice, now he's up to six beatings a day. Unless they've repaired it, his right shoulder was dislocated this morning. They've also been giving him a mild hallucinogenic drug to distort his sense of time."

Jason cussed under his breath. "That's barbaric. How is it you know so much about his situation, Chief?"

Jake swallowed his pride, not an easy thing for him to do. "I was one of the ones who did this to him, okay? I'm incredibly sorry and I'm trying to set things right. Can we move on? You can get with Thane when this is over and settle scores with me later."

Braxton, along with the rest of the men, was ready to rip into Jake. The delicacy of their situation kept him from acting on his impulses. "Gentleman, let's get to safety then worry about settling scores with our *security chief*. Jake, you're sure they can't see us?"

Jake looked up at the security cameras then over at Gabe. Gabe gave a reassuring nod. "No, they can't see us."

Braxton gave the order. "Then let's go get our captain."

As the group rounded the corner and headed straight for the barriers and the posted guards, Thane gripped his weapon more tightly. The guards weren't even making small talk. They were standing at attention. The door to the high security area was typically only opened by calling into the control station to request access. The door opened automatically.

Jake glanced at Gabe. "Did you do that?" He asked quietly. Jake smirked a second later, "Awesome, thanks."

Braxton cocked his head oddly. Looking at Thane he asked, "Who's he talking to?"

Thane shrugged. "I don't really know, but he seems to actually be there. I don't know how else we're getting through here."

Jake reached the cell door and silently prayed the Captain was still alive. He pressed the panel to open the door. The door slid open. The Captain lay unconscious on the mattress.

Jason rushed to his side. He rolled the Captain over onto his back. The Captain moaned. He did a quick assessment and determined the Captain's shoulder was still dislocated. He shook his head. "With those drugs in his system and without a pain-killer, I hate to try putting his shoulder back into place. It would also be harder to transport him with it out of joint like this. If I had a stretcher, we could do it."

Jason turned to see if Jake had a plan to deal with this. Jake appeared to be listening to his "friend." A couple seconds later Jake looked back at Jason. "Doc, Gabe says to put the shoulder back into place. Pateras has taken the drugs from his system. It will still hurt, but he's not conscious enough to feel it right now."

Jason stared at Jake for a moment and decided at least the last part was true enough to work with. Jason slowly and carefully manipulated the arm until it was in the correct position then popped it into place. The Captain gave subtle moans and groans throughout the procedure without opening his eyes. The instant the shoulder painfully slid into place, the pain broke through and woke him. He rolled to one side and began to dry heave. Lazaro grabbed a cup of water and brought it to the Captain. The Captain took several short sips. His body attempted to heave again. His muscles were too sore, and his stomach too glad to have the water to lose any of it. Once he was able to sit up, the Captain looked at the men crowded around him. His eyes fell on Jake. "So, it was worth it?"

Jake's face fell. "The goal was achieved, sir. I'm not sure it was worth all of this. I'm sorry… for everything, Captain."

The Captain's eyes moved over to the bright light coming from the door. "Uh… Jake, who's your friend?"

Jake looked puzzled. He glanced at Gabe then back at the Captain. "You can see him?"

"Yes, I can see him. Who is he?"

"He said he was Gabe. I thought you knew him."

David looked at the looming bright figure in front of him. "Gabe? Is that really you?"

Gabe nodded.

David wanted to make a witty comment about Gabe doing something different with his hair. It just wasn't in him anymore.

His pain and exhaustion had nearly consumed him. He finished the cup of water in two swift gulps then Jason and Lazaro pulled him to his feet. David tried to hold his own weight, but his knees buckled. "I don't think I can walk."

Lazaro pulled David's left arm across his shoulder and anchored him there while Jason did the same on the other side. Jason and Lazaro weren't moving very quickly, but their movements were fast enough to be painful for the Captain. David tried hard to keep his pain silent. A few grunts and groans still managed to escape no matter how hard he tried to suppress them. Lazaro gave him one quick reassurance. "Captain, you've protected us more times than we can count. It's our turn to protect you for a change. We've got *your* back this time."

David inhaled slowly and deeply. Every muscle in his chest and abdomen hurt with every deep breath. Despite his efforts to breathe slowly, his body still objected and forced him into an unwelcome bout of coughing. As the coughs subsided, David glanced around at his loyal crewmen. "Thank you… all of you." His eyes landed lastly on Jake, to whom he gave a meaningful nod.

Jake returned the nod hastily. "As much as I appreciate the sentiment, we need to get moving. Let's head for the women's cells." Jake led the way as quickly as the crew could keep pace.

The first cell they reached was Laura's. Jake pressed on the panel to open the door and directed Braxton to go in and retrieve her. He also instructed him to be sure she had resumed drinking water. If she hadn't, he should get some down her quickly. None of the crew had reached a life or death point, but they were quite weak by now. Even a small amount of water would bolster their strength and stamina.

Braxton did as he was told. While he was in Laura's cell, Jake opened Aulani's cell and sent Thane to bring her out. Thane didn't want to take his eyes off the traitorous security chief. The option of seeing his wife again outweighed his distrust of Jake. He moved quickly though, not wanting to leave the chief out of sight any longer than he had to.

When Thane returned to the corridor, Jake was no longer visible. "Where's the chief?" he asked brusquely.

Lazaro nodded to another open cell door. "He's in there pulling Lexi out."

A couple seconds later Jake emerged carrying Lexi. Braxton hurried to take her from Jake. He immediately began barking orders. "Thane, take the Doc's place. Jake, get the rest of the cells open. Aulani, Laura, help him get the other women out while we try to get Lexi squared away. Move it people!"

Thane was reluctant to put away his weapon and restrict the use of his arms by holding the Captain up. He still didn't trust Jake, not even a little bit. He also wasn't in a hurry to let go of his wife. Upon the pressing tone of Braxton's order, Thane moved into position sparking the others to move as well. Jake opened the next cell freeing Cheyenne. Aulani ducked in quickly to bring her out while Jake proceeded to Brynna's cell. Laura grabbed Brynna and pulled her out. Jake hesitated outside her door long enough to give her one quick message. "The Captain is innocent. Don't believe anything Executor Hale told you or showed you." Without waiting for a response, he hastened to his next stop.

Jake moved to Marissa's cell. He opened the door and rushed in. The cell was empty. As soon as he entered a recording began to play on the walls. It was Executor Hale holding Jake's wife roughly by the back of the neck. The message began to play.

"Mr. Holden, at least I assume you are the one freeing the crew, if you would like your wife back, bring me the Captain. I'm guessing Pateras is using you to free the crew since that was what the Captain seemed to be waiting on and hoping for. Now I'm going to use you to turn the tables on him again. I believe you know where my office is."

Jake stood there staring at the frightened face of his wife and the cold evil stare of the Supreme Executor. The message repeated. Aulani stepped into the room when Jake didn't come out. She saw Jake staring at the message on the wall then surveyed the small empty cell. "Jake… we need to go get Marissa," Aulani calmly prodded.

Jake turned around slowly. There were small tears in his eyes. "I can't sacrifice the Captain to save my wife and son. I can't do that. I can't lose them either."

Aulani stepped over and took Jake's hand. "I'm glad to hear you say that, but we need to tell the others." She gently pulled him towards the door.

Jake followed Aulani into the hall. Aulani hastily explained what they found. No one wanted to sacrifice either crew member. With Brynna at his side, David looked up weakly at Gabe. "What does Pateras want us to do?"

Gabe's voiced boomed loudly and his presence became visible to all. "Luciano cannot harm her, and he cannot have you. You are under the protection of Pateras. He knows this. *You*, apparently need to be reminded. Go fetch the woman from his office." Several crew members gasped at the sight of him. Gabe looked around at the others. "I am not the one you need to fear. Luciano is far more powerful than I am, but Pateras has unlimited power."

David looked at Lexi who was now barely conscious on the floor. "Jason, can she travel?"

Jason shook his head. "She'll have to be carried. She doesn't have the strength to stand."

David didn't really want to ask but he needed to know. "What's wrong with her?"

"Extreme dehydration, exhaustion. I can't do very much here except give her sips of water." Jason added a layer of frustration to his own exhaustion.

Jake looked perplexed. "Aulani helped me get the water turned back on without being noticed. Lexi, why didn't you drink any?"

Through the haze in her mind and her dry cracked lips, she mumbled, "A trick… thought someone… was playing games… with my mind."

Jake shook his head. "Someone was… me. It figures. I used subliminal messages to reach everyone except the ship's psychologist." Jake looked over at Gabe. "Can Pateras give her a little boost or something?"

Gabe stepped over beside her. He took her hand and said, "Get up."

Jake wondered what good that was going to do until he saw her get up and reach for Braxton's hand. Gabe turned and headed for the elevator. The crew followed as quickly as they could. The women were taken aback when they walked past numerous guards unnoticed and unhindered.

The now lengthy entourage headed directly for the Supreme Executor's temporary office. David ordered the bulk of the crew to remain outside. He allowed Jake to come with him, along with Lazaro and Thane. The four entered his office unannounced. Marissa was sitting on the far side of the table, bored, scared and tired. She heard the door open quietly. Seeing Jake and the Captain, she started to bolt towards them. Executor Hale was too fast for her. He grabbed her arm pulling her back into the chair. The Supreme Executor picked up a weapon. He pointed it at Marissa. "Mr. Holden, do you care to explain yourself?"

"Not really, I just want my wife back." Jake wanted to grab his weapon, the same weapon now in Thane's possession.

Executor Hale stood up and moved over behind Marissa, still pointing his weapon at her. Marissa was effectively trapped.

She was penned in by the table in front of her, the arms of her chair on either side, and the Supreme Executor behind her. The Executor had forced her chair forward until the arms of the chair were firmly against the table. Instinctively, Marissa grabbed the edge of the table protecting her belly and its tiny inhabitant. Executor Hale grinned slightly. "Well, Mr. Holden, did you come to exchange the Captain for your wife?"

Jake swallowed hard, "No, I came to free my wife. Let her go, NOW!"

Luciano smiled even bigger. "You can't give me orders, Mr. Holden, not in this realm nor the other.

Jake whipped around, jerking the Tri-EMP from Thane's waistband. In one swift move, he had it primed and pointed at the Supreme Executor's head.

David hastily pulled his arm from across Thane's shoulders. His strength was starting to return. Lazaro helped him limp forward. "Stand down, Chief."

"Not until he releases my wife." Jake maintained an inflexible, unyielding posture.

Executor Hale taunted Jake, "Do you really think you have any weapons that can harm me?"

David affirmed the Executor's position. "Chief, you can't kill him. You can't even hurt him. Give me the weapon. I'm the one he wants."

Without taking his eyes off Executor Hale, Jake objected, "Sir, you can't turn yourself over to him."

"That's my call, Chief, unless you now outrank me. Give me the weapon and stand down. I'll get Marissa back safely. You have my word and… well, you know whose."

Jake had not removed the collars from the crew's necks yet. Saying the name of Pateras would have put the Captain on the ground again. Jake knew who the Captain was referring to. He took his first steps towards trusting Pateras. He slowly lowered his weapon.

David took the weapon from Jake's hand. The Captain began to wave the weapon around somewhat carelessly. He hobbled to the table and steadied himself against the edge of it. His wild appearance was amplified by the lack of control of the weapon. "I suppose your terms for releasing her are if I use this on myself."

Executor Hale smiled again. "Captain, you already know I either want you to reject Pateras or kill yourself. I'm fine with either. I would even accept your word that you will voluntarily remain here with me. Let's not play games and get to the crux of the matter. Choose now. I want your life, but I *will* take hers if I have to."

Jake took an anxious step forward. He looked like he was ready to leap over the table. David waved him back.

Gabe materialized in the room catching Luciano's attention. "You have no business here. Get out! This is between me and him. You have no authority over me."

Gabe appeared to bristle. "Any authority I have was given to me by Pateras, who does have authority over you. You are not my concern, they are."

David watched the exchange carefully. When the two finished, Luciano turned his attention back to the Captain. "Well, Captain, what's it going to be?"

David straightened up as best he could. "I'm taking my crew, all of my crew, and we are leaving. Release the lieutenant. We are under the authority and protection of Pateras. You have no authority over us. By the authority and power of Pateras, release her now."

Executor Hale's eyes narrowed. His face went beet red for an instant then faded. Captain Alexander's collar had not fired. Pateras had obviously intervened. He was angry, but regained control. "This isn't the end, Captain. You're going to wish you had agreed to my terms. You and your entire crew are going to be hunted down like rabid animals. Everyone's going to want your blood."

Executor Hale pulled Marissa's seat back away from the table and lowered his weapon. Marissa fled to the other side of the room and into Jake's waiting arms. He hugged her tightly. In between reassuring whispers, he kissed her softly.

The Captain tossed the weapon back to Thane. Thane placed it firmly back in his waistband. He and Lazaro stepped up to help the Captain out. The crew rendezvoused in the reception area and headed for the *Evangeline* without delay. Jake shoved a data crystal into the receptionist's terminal and punched a couple buttons.

David watched Jake's actions, "What was that?"

Jake was in a hurry to get everyone off the base and answered very briefly. "Just a little something to confound their defenses."

• •

The crew boarded without incident and Jake began barking orders. Thane balked. "You're in no position to be giving orders, traitor. I follow the Captain's orders."

The Captain was looking dazed again. The Adrenalin rush that got him through their escape and rescuing Marissa was quickly fading away. The Captain looked up slowly as he realized there was a problem to address. He tried hard to gather his thoughts. "Lt. Ryder, I appreciate your candor, but I'm in no shape to get us out of this. I know… I know Jake has some things to answer for, but this is his op. Let him run it, and follow his orders *to the letter*. That goes for all of you. Understood?"

The Captain was met with halfhearted agreement. The Captain looked at Jake. "What are your orders, Chief?"

Jake gave the Captain an appreciative nod. "Doc, get the Captain and Lexi into the Infirmary and get them back into shape as quickly as possible. Marissa… er… Lt. Holden report to the helm."

Thane balked again. "Helm? That's my station! You don't have a clue what you're doing, do you."

Jake tried not to look annoyed. "No disrespect intended, Lt. Ryder, but *you* don't have a clue what *I'm* doing. I need you, Lt. Adams, Ensign Ryder, and Lt. Commander Dominick to head to another ship five hundred yards in that direction. It looks very much like this ship. It's a civilian vessel named the *SS Independence*. The navigation is already linked between the two ships. Lt. Ryder, I want you at the helm on that ship, just in case. Marissa is in better shape than any of you are. She'll follow the course set by Arni. I'll need you to actively pilot once we're clear of this system and not a second before unless something goes wrong."

Jake didn't bother with asking if Thane understood his directive. He knew it would only open the door to another argument. He quickly moved on with his orders to keep everyone moving. "Lt. Commander, you are there as a command presence and in case there is a problem in engineering. Gabe will still be protecting us as we leave this system so don't panic and do anything rash. Lt. Adams, you are the medical personnel for those aboard the *Independence*. Once the crews are at their stations, provide them with food rations and lots of water. Ensign Ryder, take comms. After we're clear, Lt. Commander, you'll need to be a liaison between the crew and your passengers."

David had not made a move towards the Infirmary as he wanted to hear all of Jake's orders. "Passengers? Who's aboard that ship?"

Jake smiled. "Your family, sir. We have to keep them out of the reach of the Supreme Executor. He'll try to use them against you if he can. We're taking them to safety. Your uncle's not going with them. He's staying in the Commonwealth, and he *will* attempt to fire on us as we leave."

David looked at Jason, "Get me to the Infirmary. Chief, keep me updated." David was now in a hurry to be well enough to command. It was one thing to risk his crew's lives. They were prepared to die. The Captain's family wasn't. They barely had a clue what was going on.

Jake moved on quickly. "Gabe, get the crew safely to the second ship. I want us off the ground in five minutes at the outside. Lt. Commander Flint, go to Engineering. Commander Alexander please get food and water to the crew then report to the Infirmary. Ensign Dominick, report to Comms. Get to your posts or to the infirmary."

The crew headed the directions they were told, still in a daze from the exhaustion and dehydration. As soon as Lt. Commander Dominick's team checked into their stations, Jake ordered the ships buttoned up and instructed Marissa to power the engines. Cheyenne monitored CIF Base activities and relayed them to Jake. "Chief, alarms are going off throughout the base. Troops are scattering everywhere, but none are headed this direction."

Jake quickly barked. "Show me surveillance footage from outside both ships." Troops were racing towards each other, but not towards the ship. Jake took one look and barked. "Get us in the air! Our course should already be plotted. No matter what happens, don't stray from that course setting! Lt. Commander Dominick, did you get that?"

Lazaro's voice came across the speaker, "Understood, Chief and will comply."

The ships lifted slowly off the ground and proceeded to gain altitude as they headed out to sea. Cheyenne reported four other ships lifting off. "Chief, are they trying to force us down?"

Jake looked at the video feed. "No, that's Executor Hale's shuttles and security detail. They should be headed for the CIF

Chimera. Stay on course, build speed as fast as you can."

The ships reached the edges of the atmosphere then took a sudden turn towards the southern pole of Romajin. The three heavy cruisers waiting in space had placed themselves equal distance from each other roughly around the equator. The CIF *Stalwart*, Admiral Garcia's ship, was slightly north of the equator, the second, Executor Hale's ship, the *Chimera* was right on the equator, and the third, the CIF *Valiant* was slightly south of the equator. The two escaping ships emerged from the southern polar region beneath the ship farthest to the north. Admiral Garcia's ship was the northernmost ship. Admiral Deacons ship was furthest south, but it was a third of the way around the backside of the planet. The three ships moved to converge on the two small escaping vessels. The *Evangeline* and her sister ship left the planet's atmosphere. As they reached the area of lunar orbit, the three ships neared firing range. Cheyenne nervously reported, "The cruisers are powering up their weapons."

Jake was just as scared as Cheyenne sounded. Nevertheless, he boldly ordered, "Both ships, stay on course." He swallowed hard then ordered, "Power up the tachyon nets."

Lazaro protested, "Chief, if those ships hit us with the nets full of tachyons, we'll be ripped to shreds or explode in a ball of fire."

Jake tried hard to keep his voice confident and strong. "We'll be fine. They won't hit us. Power up your net now!"

Lazaro hesitated for a second then ordered Thane to power the net. He sat there staring at his display screen.

Thane turned from the helm on board the *SS Independence*. "Are you really going to follow his orders? He's going to get us all killed."

"Power the net, lieutenant. He's gotten us this far. If we don't, they'll either disable us, board us, then drag us right back to our cells, or they'll shoot us down. Which would you prefer?"

Thane turned back to his console and followed his orders. If this didn't work, his options were a slow painful death or a quick death. Quick was better.

Cheyenne reported to Jake when she saw the *Independence* begin powering up. Until this point the ships were trying to build speed and traveled in a direct route. The navigation programmed by Arni now introduced evasive maneuvers.

On board the Executor's ship, Luciano's shuttle docked quickly. The Executor raced to the *Chimera's* bridge. He demanded to know the status of the two escaping vessels. The Captain filled him in and resumed his chase. Executor Hale had given no specific orders about the vessels. The Captain knew his duty was to stop them and arrest everyone on board or destroy them if necessary. He attempted to hail the ships and order them to surrender.

Admiral Deacons was sitting in his chair to the left of the Captain on the bridge. He respected the Captain's abilities to run his ship the way he saw fit. He spoke softly to the Captain in deference to his command presence. "Captain, I need those ships disabled so we can board them or force them to land. I really don't want them destroyed if at all possible."

The Captain acknowledged the Admiral's orders. He efficiently began issuing orders. "Helm take us to bearing three four five degrees and twenty degrees' positive pitch. Weapons charge laser cannons to twenty-five percent. Load EMP torpedoes. Be ready to fire on my command. Communications, hail those ships."

The communications officer attempted to contact the two ships without success. The Captain scowled. He didn't really expect this to be quick and easy, but he was an optimist at heart. He could always hope they would respond to his authority. "Alright then, let's give them a bigger reason to listen to us. Fire a laser cannon directly between the two ships. On my mark…

fire!" The cannon belched a fiery red blast and narrowly missed both ships.

Thane yelped. "Chief! That one nearly got us!"

Jake was no less uptight. "Simmer down, Lieutenant. You weren't hit. That was just meant to get our attention."

Thane continued to object. "It worked! It got my attention!"

Jake reassured Thane and the other listening crew members with more confidence than he felt, "This wasn't my plan. It was Arni's. Keep that in mind. Hold her steady."

Thane's brow wrinkled. He looked around at Aulani and Lazaro. "Hold her steady? Marissa has the controls. I'm just babysitting."

The *Valiant's* captain was again hoping the escaping ships would respond favorably to the warning shot. He was slightly disappointed, although not surprised, when the ships kept going. A nearby ensign added to his disappointment, "Sir, they're loading their tachyon nets."

The Captain frowned. "How far away are the other cruisers?"

The ensign glanced at his screen, "They are still outside firing range, but closing fast."

The Captain's frown gave way to a smile. "Let's see if we can get this done before they get here. Lock torpedo tube one on the lead ship and tube two on the second ship. Fire as soon as you have a lock."

Both weapons officers were quiet as they studied their displays. The more experienced of the two piped up quickly, "Captain, I can't get a weapons lock."

The Captain came out of his chair as though it was on fire. "What? Those ships are not equipped with jamming technology. How is that possible?"

The Admiral stepped up beside the Captain, "You could try firing blind. You might get lucky."

The Captain considered his suggestion for a moment. Another idea popped in his head. "Laser cannons one and two, decrease your beam intensity to zero point zero two percent. Adjust to widest possible dispersion. Fire a continuous beam. When you hit those ships, narrow the beam by ninety percent. Hold the lock manually."

One of the laser cannon operators was new to her position. "Sir? The cannons won't even scratch the hull at that intensity."

The Captain gave a curt response, "I'm fully aware of that, Ensign, just follow my orders." The Captain sat back down and continued his orders. "Let me know the instant you have a lock and transmit the trajectory to the torpedo stations."

The scanning station reported, "The other two cruisers are moving into firing range."

Communications followed with, "Admiral Garcia is hailing. He wants to know why we haven't fired on the two ships."

Admiral Deacons moved to the comms station. "Captain, with your permission, I'll update Admiral Garcia. You continue working."

The Captain gave a quick nod and a short "Thank you." He didn't care for Admiral Garcia and was glad to have someone else deal with him. He also needed to be focused on something other than such rhetoric.

Seconds later the lasers reported a lock. The trajectory was adjusted eight degrees to account for the angle difference between the lasers and the torpedo tubes. The Captain began issuing orders. "Fire torpedoes one and two."

Just as the two launched, the ships changed course. The lasers were readjusted more quickly, and new coordinates issued. The tubes fired a second time. This time they got closer. Scanners reported the two ships were reaching net saturation.

Admiral Deacons turned to the Captain. With an upset stomach and a heavy heart, he told the Captain, "Admiral Garcia is ordering you to increase laser power to full intensity the next time you get laser lock. He's attempting the same thing, as is the *Chimera*. He wants those ships destroyed. I can't give the order. I need to recuse myself from this."

The Captain was confused by the Admiral's confession. "Admiral, who's on that ship?"

He looked away. "My nephew and his wife." The Admiral knew his entire family was on board the two ships. He had to feign ignorance of the last part, lest his alliance with Pateras be discovered.

The Admiral's words slowly sank in. The Captain realized why Admiral Deacons had taken a back seat on a mission of this importance. He hastily nodded his understanding and turned back to his duties. "Keep closing on those two ships. Get those lasers readjusted. I want all four forward torpedoes ready to fire, alter trajectory to three degrees off center. Cannon one fire at plus three degrees on the X-axis, cannon two minus three degrees on the X-axis, cannon three minus three on the Y-axis, cannon four plus three degrees same axis. Lasers change your color to the opposite end of the spectrum. Hustle people. Communications, see if you can jam the signals between those ships. The second ship appears to be running in tandem with the first." The Captain thought perhaps the second ship had no qualified pilot. If he could break the comm link, he could stop at least the second ship. He didn't know a very qualified pilot sat at the helm waiting for a chance to exercise his skills.

Jake kept his eyes glued on the scanning display. With the three cruisers getting so close, Jake was getting very nervous. This business of trusting someone other than himself wasn't easy. Something, or someone, told him to forward the next three course adjustments to the secondary ship. "Marissa, send Thane's station the next three course adjustments and send him each succeeding one as we complete one adjustment." He pressed his comm button to address Lazaro. "Lt. Commander, I'm forwarding our current course up to the next three moves on a narrow beam, so it won't be intercepted. Lt. Ryder is not to make the course adjustments on his own unless we lose contact."

"Understood, Chief." Lazaro wondered briefly why he didn't send the entire navigation plan. He realized Jake didn't want the full plan to be out there in case they were caught. Lazaro was exhausted, hungry, and wanted this to be over. His Adrenalin rush did little more than keep him awake.

Jake watched to see if the ships were close to getting another lock on them. He glanced at the scanner, something didn't look right. It took him a minute to realize the lasers were no longer in the same color or temperature range. The *Valiant's* Captain or perhaps Admiral Deacons was very astute. The scanners weren't programmed to detect laser activity at this range. Jake hastily adjusted the scanners. His eyes grew wide as he realized they had their guide and would be firing torpedoes any second. He looked up at Marissa, "Can we activate the tachyon drive?"

"Yes, the net is saturated. Jake, I've lost my control of the second ship." Marissa looked scared.

Jake hoped the others were paying attention. "Adjust course so we are one hundred yards above the *Independence* then prepare to engage the tachyon drive on my mark."

Lazaro watched the scanning displays as intensely as Jake was watching. As soon as he saw Jake move off course, his heart skipped a beat, then made up for the lost beat with interest. "Lt. Ryder! You have the helm control! Prepare to engage tachyon drive."

Thane had been leaning back in his seat with his arms folded across his chest scowling at the controls. As soon as he heard Lazaro, he jumped upright and placed his hands on the controls. "Nets aren't at full capacity yet. Need a few more seconds."

Lazaro looked up and saw the *Evangeline* vanish then reappear as she gave a short burst that put her out of firing range of the three ships. Lazaro glanced at his display. The net was at ninety percent capacity. "Set a course putting us off the *Evangeline*'s port bow and engage the drive now!"

Thane strenuously objected. "The net isn't full!"

"DO IT NOW!" Lazaro shouted as he watched the three ships launching a barrage of torpedoes at them. Lazaro had no way of knowing the projectiles coming from the *Valiant* would only disable them. The ones from the *Chimera* and the *Stalwart* were not simply EMP's, they were armed to destroy.

By pushing Thane to use the net too early, the ship would not reach tachyon induced speeds. By forcing the tachyons through the empty sections of the net they would reach a bradyon induced speed. It was faster than their current speed, but not faster than light speed. The three ships watching, saw the *Independence* light up then flicker and streak across space to take its place beside the *Evangeline*.

Thane blinked as the ship returned to thruster control. "Why did that work? Lt. Commander, what just happened?"

"Later Lieutenant, let's get the net to full capacity then get out of here before those ships catch up. Scanners indicate they're loading their own nets to pursue us. How long to saturation?" Lazaro was relieved his engineering skills weren't compromised by mental fatigue.

"Ten more seconds to saturation. We'll be fully operational before those cruisers are. I'm getting the rest of the navigation information from Marissa again. I guess we moved outside jamming range."

Jake wanted to ask Lazaro about what happened aboard the *Independence*. He decided he could clear the air about it later. The most important thing was they were able to escape the Commonwealth ships. "Lt. Commander, are you still with me?"

"Yes Chief, we're five seconds from saturation. We'll engage on your command." Lazaro had a newfound respect for the Chief. His plan to get the crew out of Commonwealth custody was working.

Five seconds later, the two ships activated their tachyon drives. Their escape route began with several increasingly larger spiral loops around the outside of the star system flooding the area with residual tachyon particles, masking the ship's true trajectory.

• •

The Supreme Executor sat calmly in his chair watching the drama unfold in front of him. The two ships disappeared from the display. The Captain of the *Chimera* was afraid to make eye contact with Executor Hale. The failure to stop the escaping ships gave the man visions of his future as Captain of a freighter in a distant asteroid belt. Surprisingly, the Executor said nothing. The Captain saw him pick up his data pad and press a couple buttons. He set the data pad back down and asked the Comm Officer to send an order to the Admirals to join him aboard the *Chimera*. The Captain was relieved although slightly confused. It seemed the Supreme Executor wasn't surprised the two ships escaped.

• •

The two escaping ships dropped back down to thruster speed at the established coordinates. Jake ordered the initiation of docking maneuvers. The *Evangeline* positioned itself above the *Independence*. The ships were capable of docking two ways. One way was side by side. It was intended for short quick easy accessibility. The ships could not remain docked side by side and resume using the tachyon drive. The bridge between the two ships was too flimsy to handle such stress.

The second docking maneuver, placing one ship sitting directly on top of the other, aligned the frames of the ships in a far more stable position. Docking clamps added to stability, along with symmetrical space bridges or structural tubes connecting the two ships. The tubes, once secured, allowed the passengers to traverse back and forth via an elevator. The tubes and docking clamps were equipped with tachyon webbing making the two ships capable of resuming use of the tachyon drive. Jake got the ships secured and a hard-wire link between the engines. Lazaro tried to join Jake on the bridge to oversee the initiation of the joint activation of the tachyon drives. Jake allowed him to stay long enough to resume trans-light speeds, and get both crew and passengers squared away. Before resuming course, Jake went aboard the *Independence* to talk to David's family. The Captain's family was unsettled and unaware of what had just happened. All they knew is they had been escorted to the ship, told they were in danger and being moved to a safer location. Jake informed them David was safe, getting medical treatment, and would be available to talk to them after getting adequate treatment and rest. The family had a million questions. Jake declined to answer all, save the most basic of questions. He secured the secondary bridge and engineering compartments then headed back to the bridge aboard the *Evangeline*.

Both ships now securely underway, Jake sent Lazaro to the Infirmary along with all the remaining crew members including Marissa. He took the next shift alone.

• •

Several hours later, David yawned and stretched. His eyes opened drowsily. He raised his head and lifted himself up onto his elbows. The dim lighting slowly revealed his own crew quarters aboard the *Evangeline*. Confusion set in. How did he get here? Had the last week been nothing more than a horrific nightmare? David softly called out, "Computer, display the date and time on the display screen, please."

An empty spot on the wall lit up briefly with the requested information. No, over a week had passed since he had been in his own bed. The memory of Jake ordering him to the Infirmary flashed in his mind. Maybe this was real, despite the ludicrousness of the idea that Jake was giving the orders. David rubbed his hand over his face and felt several days of beard growth. Memories of pain with every movement resurfaced. He laid back down and stretched again. The pain was gone, only stiffness remained.

David rolled over. He saw Brynna's soft curls on the pillow beside him. She was sleeping soundly with her back to him. At the sight of her, David's tension and confusion began to melt away. His hand moved to gently stroke her arm. Images of Heather flashed harshly through his mind. His hand stopped just short of touching her. His conscience was sharply pierced by the memory of Heather's voice telling him he owed Brynna an apology. It was quickly followed by the image of Brynna's face when Executor Hale forced her to watch him with Heather. He still had very little memory of his time with her.

David never wanted to hurt Brynna. Would she believe his side of the story? Would she believe his lack of memory? Would she forgive him for his indiscretion even if it was induced against his will? He knew they needed to have a long talk and he owed her a very profound apology. David pulled his hand away. He decided he didn't have the right to touch her until he confessed his actions and asked for forgiveness. He also decided it was time to put his "Captain's hat" back on. They would have to discuss this later. "Captain" Alexander slid quietly out of bed and into the shower.

An invisible figure stood there watching the Captain. When David's hand stopped short of touching his wife, the shrouded figure smiled sadistically. His plan was working. He didn't know the Captain's thoughts, but he recognized doubt, fear, and the sounds of an emotional wall going up. "I may not have destroyed you today, but this isn't over yet." No one heard the voice of the Dark Figure, save one. Pateras heard. He watched and said nothing. Luciano left the ship to prepare for the next phase of his plot.

• •

Brynna woke up and rolled over. She wasn't quite ready to wake up yet. The most appealing thought was to snuggle with David to gently ease herself into waking up. With her eyes still shut, she rolled over and slid her hand over to David's side of the bed. It had been long enough since he had gotten up the sheets were now cool. She opened her eyes to confirm what her hand had already told her. David wasn't there. She frowned, so much for her idea of snuggling. She closed her eyes again for a few more minutes. David's absence started to gnaw at her. Her eyes opened again. Okay, time to get up.

Brynna found David shaving in the bathroom. She slipped in to stand behind him. Despite the trauma they had both experienced over the past six days, she smiled as she gently wrapped her arms around his waist. David smiled in return although his conscience prevented him from enjoying the sight of her warm beautiful smile and her loving touch.

Brynna laid her head on his shoulder as David finished up. "Why didn't you wake me when you got up?"

David picked up his washcloth. The laser razors did an excellent job of eliminating facial hair, but he always felt the need to wash his face one more time after shaving. He wet the cloth. He still had his back to her, so he spoke to her reflection in the mirror. "You were sleeping so soundly, I didn't want to disturb you. I don't have any idea how I got back to my own bed, so I didn't really know how long you'd been asleep either." When he finished speaking, he washed his face, neck, and hands with the warm cloth. His shower just didn't wash away the guilt.

Brynna pulled her arms back and moved over to David's side. She pulled his arm turning him slightly towards her. She somehow felt the wall he had put up between them. "David, this may seem like an incredibly trite question, but… what's wrong?"

David winced as several painful thoughts ran through his mind. He fought the urge to shut her down. He reached up and placed his warm hand against her cheek. Brynna could see a mixture of anger and sorrow in his eyes. He struggled to find the right words to answer her. "Let's just say there are a lot of things wrong. I don't have time to go into detail. I need to find out who's running this ship and where we're headed. I need to know what's happened to my family. I need some answers."

David shoved his washcloth in the laundry chute. He walked back into the bedroom to finish putting his uniform on. Brynna watched his brusque movements as she contemplated how to respond to him. "David, we need to talk."

David heard the pain in her voice. He was finished dressing and headed for the bridge. He stopped by their bedroom door. Cradling her face in his hand, he stroked her cheek with his thumb. A small breach in the wall opened for just a second. "I know. Believe me, I know. We will, I promise. Brynna, you're one of the best things that's ever happened to me. You know that, don't you? I know I have no right to ask, but please, give me a little time."

Brynna needed his reassurance. This wasn't nearly enough of what she needed, but it was a start. She gave him a weak smile. "Take whatever time you need, just don't leave me hanging. I showered before I laid down. I'll get dressed and meet you on the bridge shortly, Captain."

David smiled a more assured smile this time. Brynna was a strong and wise woman. It was those characteristics that attracted him to her. He kissed her quickly and headed to the bridge.

• •

Stepping onto the bridge, the Captain found Jake at the helm. He took a sip of a cold cup of coffee and nearly choked on it. The face he made told the Captain a good portion of what he needed to know. The Chief had been at the helm for far too many hours. "Chief, report."

The Chief filled him in on everything. The list of things reported on included the presence of David's family on the ship docked beneath them, their current location and course, and the crew's condition. Marissa had relieved him for four of the last eighteen hours. The doc and Laura were the last two crew members to get rest and would be the last ones available for duty. David asked several questions to clarify the situation. Once he was sure this wasn't some elaborate trickery, he had one more question to ask. Brynna stepped onto the bridge as he was about to make his inquiry.

"Chief, I need to know, honestly, where your loyalties lie. No more lies." As David awaited his answer, he waved Brynna over to her station. "Chief, transfer control to the Commander's station before answering."

Brynna was slightly unnerved at walking onto the bridge and taking over controls she hadn't been briefed on. As her station lit up she perused the displays thoughtfully. Her eyes grew wide as she realized the two ships were conjoined and traveling at speeds well beyond light speed. This type of maneuver required an engineer in both engine rooms. There wasn't one in either place. She said nothing. She kept her eyes glued to the displays. One fluctuation in either engine could rip both ships apart. She allowed herself one quick glance at the Chief. "Chief, how long have you been up here monitoring these displays? Captain, he has engineering readouts, scanners, comms and the normal ship's operations on here, for BOTH ships. This is a lot to keep an eye on."

Jake rubbed his tired eyes. "I know. I've been at it for fourteen of the last eighteen hours. In answer to your question, Sir, my loyalties lie with Pateras. If you don't trust my word, and I wouldn't blame you if you didn't, put us off the ship somewhere. Confine me to quarters, put me in stasis, whatever you must. I hope spacing me is off the list of possibilities. I know what you and the crew went through was because of me and I'm so… *so* sorry. I hope someday you can all forgive me. Arni says he's forgiven me. I'm having trouble believing that. I haven't even asked Marissa to forgive me. I'm not sure she knows this is *all* my fault."

David studied Jake carefully. Was he telling the truth this time? "Chief, how do I know you're telling the truth?"

Jake thought for a moment. Was there anything at all he could say to convince the Captain of his sincerity? "Captain, I told you the only reason I would lie to you was to protect my wife and son. You can check with your uncle about this. I made a deal with Executor Hale to leave free and clear with my wife and son. Executor Hale reneged on the agreement. He was going to arrange for Marissa to have an unfortunate accident. I went to the only one who could help me. Ask Arni. He knows my thoughts and desires."

David glanced back at Brynna who only offered a quick unreadable expression. Returning his gaze to a very tired Jake, he considered all the security chief had done and put himself through. There was no solid reason to continue doubting him. He had been staring at monitors normally watched by six individuals for nearly two straight shifts, he managed to somehow get them out of a firefight they should have died quickly in, alive and well. That was the one thing he didn't get; how did they escape three heavy cruisers? "Chief, how did we get past those flagships?"

Jake looked down at the floor and rubbed his tired eyes again. "I really don't know, sir." He thought for another minute then offered a possible explanation. "Captain… I don't know if this is why, but… I don't know, maybe…"

"Get to the point, Chief," David said impatiently.

Jake looked up with a troubled look on his face. He glanced over at Brynna. He really didn't want to say this in front of her. "The night I came into your cell… to… uh… make sure you weren't expecting me to rescue you and the crew. You asked Pateras to protect the crew. He did what you asked. Every cell appeared to be empty. The surveillance feeds showed the crew were still in their cells, but they were invisible to the naked eye. Maybe Pateras somehow hid us from the three ships. I suppose it's also possible, they *let* us get away. I don't know, sir. I'm just guessing."

David decided walking unobstructed past numerous guards was no different than flying past three heavy cruisers. David looked at the tired security chief. His frame was that of a man with no fight left in him. "Chief, swear to me." He didn't ask for a particular oath and left it purposefully open to interpretation.

Jake stood up from his chair. Snapping to attention, he raised his right hand. "Captain, I swear on my life and the lives of my wife and son, I am loyal to Pateras. I will follow his orders and yours without question. I no longer serve the Commonwealth."

David studied the man. Without moving his gaze, he asked, "Commander, are you satisfied?"

"I think so, sir," came the reply.

"At ease, Chief," the Captain ordered. Jake relaxed his stance. David continued, "Jake, Arni told me you were the reason we were going to have to go through all of that. He also said you were worth it."

David paused to let his words sink in. "I believe him. We're going to need to have a staff meeting with the entire crew and all of this will have to come out. Until they have forgiven you and come to terms with what you did to them, you might need to watch your back and keep a low profile. I will give you my support. Hopefully, that will be enough to assuage any desires for retribution. This may not go smoothly so be prepared for some hard feelings."

"Yes sir, I understand, sir."

"Let me finish. Be prepared for some hard feelings, even from me. I trust Arni and I will forgive you, I do forgive you. I just can't feel very good about you, yet. We need to put some distance between us and the last week. I can't guarantee the crew will forgive you. We will need to get everything, and I mean everything out in the open. I can't guarantee you can even remain with us. I will do whatever I can to guarantee your safety."

Jake nodded. "Yes sir."

David had a small amount of compassion on the man. "Chief, you did an excellent job getting us out of there. Thank you. Go grab some food, take it back to your quarters to eat. For your own safety, I advise you to confine yourself to your own quarters until further notice. Dismissed."

Jake snapped to attention and saluted. He moved slowly to the door to leave the bridge. Before stepping through the doorway, he stopped and turned around. "Captain… thank you."

Captain Alexander pivoted his chair around to face the Chief. "For what, Chief?"

Jake's eyes filled with a myriad of emotions. "For a lot of things. For going through what you did just to save me, for not spacing me, for forgiving me… for everything. I don't deserve any of it. If you believe what Arni said, then I'll do my best to live up to it."

The Captain nodded. "You're welcome, Chief. Get some rest… Oh, one more question; What's our heading? Where are we going?"

The Chief smiled, "Galat III. The course is plugged in. The Dreans have already been notified to send a pod to meet us there in twelve days. The Commonwealth may track us to Galat, but they won't know where we disappeared to."

"Twelve days? We were only five days from Galat on Romajin. Why twelve days?"

"I didn't want to put in our direct course, so they wouldn't be able to figure out where we're going. They may anticipate Galat, Medoris, Drea or Tudoren as good possibilities but when we don't show up right away, they'll start looking elsewhere."

The door to the bridge opened, and Braxton joined the three. David nodded for Jake to leave. Jake headed to the dining hall then to his quarters as ordered.

Braxton took Jake's seat at the helm and began to discuss their current situation. The three put together a duty roster. This was not going to be an easy twelve days. David wanted an engineer in both engine rooms and a bridge officer or helmsman on each bridge around the clock. It was going to require four officers on duty all the time. There wasn't much of a reason to have a comms officer on duty since there was no one out there to talk to. Being on the Commonwealth's most wanted list was going to make for a very lonely existence. They worked out the schedule and posted it to go into effect in four hours. David, Brynna, and Braxton agreed to fill in until the duty roster kicked in. David took over watching the displays while Brynna and Braxton grabbed a bite to eat.

•••••••••••••••••••••••••••••••••

Later David took his turn to get something to eat. He began encountering more crew members in the dining hall. The crew had lots of questions. It was time to move ahead and get everyone up to speed. Touching his comm unit he spoke to the computer. "Computer link me in to all comm stations aboard the *Evangeline* and the *Independence*." The computer beeped its compliance. David began his address. "Attention all crew and passengers of the *Evangeline* and the *Independence*, there will be a joint meeting of all personnel in the gymnasium of the *Evangeline* in two hours. Those personnel on duty please link in through comms. I intend to answer all questions and bring everyone up-to-date at that meeting. Chief Holden, since you've been on duty for fourteen of the last eighteen hours, your presence is optional."

Jake didn't want to disturb Marissa, so he quickly ate and laid down on the sofa in their quarters. He also wasn't ready to answer questions or beg her forgiveness. He asked the computer to wake him in three hours then grabbed a blanket and curled up on the sofa. It took only a minute to drift off. Marissa came out of the bedroom. Finding Jake on the sofa asleep, she smiled. She was anxious to talk to him, but after what the Admiral had done to her, she was just glad to see him alive. She patted her active belly. "It's okay Jake Junior, your daddy's fine." They hadn't named the baby yet. Jake Junior worked for now.

The Captain's announcement woke Jake from his nap. He tried to roll over and go back to sleep, but worry filled his mind. He wondered what the crew would do when they found out the truth about what he'd done. An hour of tossing and turning later, he got up, showered, and got ready for the staff meeting.

David ate quickly and headed to the bridge again. When he stepped onto the bridge, Brynna stopped him. "Captain Alexander, you've seen to the safety and security of your crew. I strongly suggest you check on your passengers and show them the way to the gym before you come back in here taking charge."

David stopped in his tracks. Brynna's tone was insubordinate yet her message was profoundly correct. He blinked in shock a couple times. He did the only thing possible. He said, "Yes, Ma'am," saluted, did an about face, and left the bridge, grinning as he went.

• •

David stepped foot onto the *Independence*. He quickly found his family in the dining hall. When he stepped into the room, all conversation ceased. David's grandmother stood up quietly. She walked slowly over to him, tears glistening on her cheeks. She pulled him down and hugged him tightly around the neck. "I knew he'd protect you," she whispered.

David smiled and returned her embrace. "Gram, we don't need to whisper anymore. We're free to speak the name of Pateras."

Jessica and Abigail could wait no longer. They joined David and Kay in their embrace. Tears flowed freely. Steven and Caleb were less than enthusiastic. Their concerns were for the safety of their families. David had placed them in grave danger as fugitives. David spent the next hour visiting with his family. Steven and Caleb sat on their questions as long as they could stand it. Steven finally got up and refilled his coffee then interrupted the pleasantries. "Excuse me for interrupting, *Captain*, but I think we need some answers."

David stopped playing with his nephew and passed him back to Abigail. "Steven, I appreciate your patience. I'm sorry. I know you need answers. You may not like them, but you deserve to know what's happened."

"I'm going to go over the details at the meeting on the *Evangeline* in an hour. I think Uncle Rob gave you the basics. I can go over it in more detail if you wish," David offered.

"I'm not interested in why you ruined your career or about your… politics… or whatever. I want to know why you dragged this family into it. Why did you kidnap us?"

David was surprised at Steven's tone and choice of wording. He apparently had no clue what the severity of the situation was. Jessica and Kay were equally shocked. David calmly explained, "I didn't bring you here. Uncle Rob brought you to

Romajin. I was in no shape to get you off Romajin. I can only guess that either Uncle Rob or Pateras did that. How did you get aboard this ship?"

Jessica recovered from the shock of her husband's vicious tone and answered him. "A man came to us and told us we needed to be moved for our own safety."

David looked at her curiously. "Did he tell you his name? Was it Gabe?"

"No – o, it was… um… Adam something." Her face clouded as she tried to remember.

David cocked his head sideways. "Adam Franklin?"

"Yes, that was it! Do you know him? Who was he?"

David smiled. "You may not like the answer. He's a superior being who works for Pateras."

As David predicted, Caleb didn't care for his answer. "Oh, come on! You really don't expect us to believe such ridiculous garbage. There are no such things. That's insane."

David got up and approached Caleb and Steven. He leaned over and placed his hands down on the table they were sitting behind. "Let me put this as plainly as I can. Our *mission*, our Commonwealth assigned mission, was to search out a *superior being* known as Pateras and report his followers back to the Commonwealth. The Supreme Executor sent us to find these beings. I'm not insane. They exist. We found them. I've seen them do things not humanly possible. The reason you are here with me is because the Supreme Executor won't hesitate to start killing my family to stop me from spreading what I know about these beings. You are here for your own protection."

Caleb and Steven's faces went white. Steven swallowed hard. "So why do you want to tell people about these beings? Why not keep it quiet?"

David stood upright. He toyed with the idea of whether to go deep into the explanation or keep it superficial. Kay could see by the look on David's face what he was debating. "Tell them the whole story, Son."

"Gram, you don't even know the half of it." David countered.

She smiled knowingly. "I know whatever it is, it's going to be the truth, and it's going to sound incredible. I trust Pateras. I denied him for years out of fear, but I never rejected him deep down."

Steven looked at his mother-in-law strangely. He looked at Jessica. "Do you know what she's talking about?"

Jessica nodded. Her eyes teared up as she relived that dreadful day when Abigail died. "Tell them everything, Son."

"There are two powers trying to claim control of this galaxy. Pateras is the superior power. His head man rejected his authority and tried to take over. He has done his best to stamp out any knowledge of Pateras. Pateras has had enough of his behavior. He's coming for him. The problem is mankind. Humans are the pawns who are going to be hurt in such a struggle. Pateras doesn't want harm coming to man. He's doing whatever he can to protect us. His nemesis is destroying mankind either from the inside or the outside. He doesn't care which."

Caleb shook his head. "Why have we never heard of any of this? How does the Commonwealth fit into this?"

David knew the next part would be hard to swallow. "The Commonwealth is run by whoever is in the office of Supreme Executor. Every Supreme Executor who's held office is Pateras' nemesis known as the Dark Lord. He changes human forms every thirty or so years."

Caleb, Steven, and even Abigail stared at David as though he had lost his mind. David knew he sounded crazy. His eyes darted back and forth between them. "I know this sounds insane. If you had told me this a year ago, I wouldn't have believed it either. I can provide you with evidence in the ship's logs to support what I'm saying if you want to see it. There's one thing I doubt you can argue with. Consider this: why would the Supreme Executor of the Commonwealth, the most powerful man in the Galaxy, take time out of his busy schedule to personally oversee a lowly Captain who's gone off the deep end?"

The three skeptics looked at each other. David had a point. Surely there was more to it than meets the eye. He was right. The Supreme Executor didn't just drop everything and run across the Galaxy on a whim. Steven was the first one to respond. "I think I need to see this evidence. You're right about the Supreme Executor taking a personal interest in your case. That doesn't make sense. For Jessica and Stevie's sake, I'm willing to listen."

Caleb still had a look of disdain on his face. He took one look at Abby's face and his resolve began to melt away. "Fine, for Abby's sake, I'll look at it. I do have another question. What's going to happen to us? We can't keep these two ships traveling adjoined like this indefinitely. Where can we hide from the Commonwealth?"

"We're going to go over that in the joint meeting with the crew in a few minutes. My crew is wanting to know the same thing. There is a plan in place and we have the protection of Pateras. That doesn't mean nothing will go wrong, it just means I trust him more than Executor Hale. If you'll excuse me, I need to spend a few minutes preparing for our meeting. I'll get to work to give you the evidence you've requested." David excused himself and returned to the bridge. He asked the crew to pull chairs into the gym while he made a few notes on his data pad.

• •

David stepped into the gym to begin his meeting precisely on time. Seeing him enter, Thane called the room to attention. The crew obeyed including the personnel only visible by computer screen. David's family looked around awkwardly. David quickly ended their discomfort by calling out, "As you were." He moved to a position most suited for addressing the room.

David looked around at the group assembled in front of him. The crew were awake and alert, yet a certain weariness was still evident on their faces. His family's faces reflected worry and fear. David paused and silently asked Arni for guidance. He knew this was unfamiliar territory for all of them. He really didn't know how to lead his people any longer. As he paused for that one moment, he heard Arni's voice speak quietly within him. "That's what you need to tell them. It's my job to lead now."

David took a deep breath. "I think the first thing we need is to make sure everyone's on the same page. I know some of this information is going to be hard to accept, but for now you'll just have to accept it. I'm not putting it out there for debate."

David was about to tell his family and the crew his true background when Chief Holden slipped quietly into the back of the room. His feelings of guilt over betraying the crew weighed on him so heavily, he had been unable to sleep more than a brief period of time. He needed to face the crew, now. David made eye contact with him. "Welcome, Chief."

Jake was afraid of how he would be received. He still didn't know if the crew would even consider receiving him. The Captain's welcome wasn't surly, sarcastic, or businesslike. It was genuine. It was only two words, but it spoke volumes. Jake needed one ally and it appeared the Captain was that ally. Jake felt like his debt to the Captain was continuing to grow daily.

Only a few of the crew and some of David's family knew about the abduction of David's grandparents' family by the Commonwealth and the death of his Aunt Abigail. David's sister had known she was named after a deceased aunt, but she didn't know the girl had been murdered. Abby assumed it had been a tragic accident or something. David imparted his history and posted pictures of the family from the archived Commonwealth prison records. When Abigail's picture popped up, Abby gasped as she realized how much she and her Aunt looked alike. She had never seen a picture of her missing Aunt before. Tears formed in Kay and Jessica's eyes as they viewed the image they had not seen in nearly fifty years.

Steven realized whatever was going on was very deep-seated and very real. He attempted to comfort his visibly shaken wife. Jessica began to cry outright from the pain she had hidden for such a long time. She finally managed to speak. "This – This isn't right. Robert should – should be here."

Jake stood quietly and walked up beside the Captain. He whispered something to him and slipped a data crystal into his hand. David stepped over to a computer terminal and inserted the crystal. Abigail's prison record faded away and Robert's face appeared on the screen. Hannah was at his side. Robert smiled, though not as strongly as he hoped. "Mom, Jess, Abby… by now David has brought you up to speed on what's going on. I'm sorry I couldn't go with you, but Arni isn't done with me yet. I am recording this message to say good bye because I don't really know if I will ever see any of you again. Just to be clear, I serve Pateras, not the Commonwealth. I have chosen to remain in my current position to do what I can to protect those who serve Pateras. I'm not sure how much help I will be because I wasn't able to help David or his crew very much. I am not the one who got them out of prison on Romajin, Pateras did that. David will get you to safety. I tried to send Hannah with you, but she refused to go. I guess Pateras knew I needed her here with me." Robert squeezed Hannah's hand then continued. "I love you all. Maybe this will be over soon, and we won't have to hide for very long. If it isn't, make sure my great-nephew learns about his great-uncle and his uncle. Trust David, he has your best interests in mind and trust Pateras. Pateras won't fail you like the Commonwealth has. Good bye."

Tears flowed freely again. Caleb was torn between comforting Abby, entertaining Aiden, and demanding answers. Lexi slipped up quietly and took Aiden from Caleb. She walked around the back of the room to entertain him while his parents dealt with the more urgent matters. His parents' tensions only served to fuel his recent crankiness. Caleb demanded to know where they were headed and why their lives were in so much danger.

David stepped forward again. His face grew even more serious than before. "Caleb, the Commonwealth has declared war on Pateras, and they aren't afraid of civilian casualties. They will kill you just because you're related to me, to my sister, my mother, my grandmother. If Executor Hale thinks you have even been in the same room with me for too long, he'd kill you."

"That's ridiculous." Caleb retorted. "The Commonwealth doesn't execute people anymore. That barbarism was done away with a hundred years ago."

David pushed a button on his tablet. Images of the bodies on Galat III appeared on the screen. Several gasps were heard among his family. The crew averted their eyes. David moved closer to Caleb. "You were in my cell on Romajin. You saw what kind of barbarism the Commonwealth is capable of. You want more proof? Here's some of it. We visited this world on our first mission. We befriended these people and invited them to join the Commonwealth. They politely agreed, welcomed our help, and treated us like honored guests. Then, they introduced us to their most honored citizen, Arni Liontari, son of Pateras El Liontari. We left, per our Commonwealth mandate and reported what we found. A couple months later, we were able to visit again. This is what we found. The energy signatures found in those bodies were from the energy weapons used by the Commonwealth Pacification fleet. These people were peaceful. They never even saw who killed them! They died, scared to death! Men! Women! Children! Infants!" The picture of the twins named after Jason and Cheyenne appeared on the screen.

Mercifully, David closed the file and the images faded away. He continued more calmly and quietly. "We knew those people by name. We served the Commonwealth, and it killed them. They had no weapons. They agreed to join the Commonwealth. They didn't fight it. Do you really think he'll spare your lives? Executor Hale wanted to order the deaths of me and my crew. Pateras prevented him from issuing that order. He threatened to kill even the men who guarded me for fear I might corrupt them. Luciano Hale doesn't want any knowledge of Pateras getting out. Since he couldn't execute me, Executor Hale did everything in his power to get me to commit suicide."

Steven spoke up quietly. "You said if we were even in the same room with you too long, he'd kill us. Did you just seal our fate by telling us this?"

David shook his head. "I'm taking you to a place where you'll be safe. It's possible he would have killed or imprisoned you regardless. I can't say for certain. I do know I intend to fight him and that *would* get you killed."

Jessica dried her tears and calmly asked. "David… where are you taking us? Where in this entire galaxy can we hide?"

David glanced at his grandmother and smiled before answering his mother. "We're going to Galat III and a party will meet us there. They'll take you home… to Drea. The party from Drea can't be traced back there. They have a technology allowing them to use tachyons to transport directly from the surface of one planet to another. No one will know where you went."

Kay leaned forward. Her eyes glistened with excitement. "They perfected it?"

Lazaro's eyes mimicked Kay's. "You know about it?"

Kay smiled. "My husband and I worked on that project together before we were taken."

David jumped in quickly. Knowing what he did about

Lazaro's love for engineering and his grandmother's love for engineering and talking, things could go astray quickly. "There are a number of private conversations that will need to occur shortly. Before we start those, let's get the big stuff out of the way. It's going to take twelve days to reach Galat. We're taking an indirect route. The ships will stay conjoined for those days, so we can visit as much as possible. Unfortunately for the crew, that means no days off. We'll have to keep two people on duty on the *Independence* and two on the *Evangeline* at all times. We can't afford to have anything happen to the drive on either ship. It also means we won't match the tachyon signature they're looking for. They'll be looking for two smaller signatures not one larger one. I've made out a duty roster for the crew and sent it out to each of you already. I'll make it available to my family, so they can know where everyone is at any given time. Lt. Flint, I'm afraid I'm going to need you to pull double duty. There's bound to be people needing to work through some anger issues. I would prefer you handle urgent situations first. You may need to arrange to meet with certain personnel while you are on duty in engineering or use a group therapy session. Don't lose your focus of those monitors though. If it's alright with you, please put yourself at the disposal of my family. They are under a great deal of stress as well."

Lexi nodded while bouncing the fidgety baby on her hip. "Yes sir, I'm glad to help." Her smile was warm and welcoming despite the weariness in her eyes.

Kay raised her hand. David felt odd acknowledging her. "Yes… Gram?"

Seeing the peculiarity of his situation, she got to her point quickly. "I am a qualified tachyon engineer. I can pull some shifts. I would feel better sitting in on a couple shifts with your Chief Engineer first. I want to help. I need to be productive for a *good* purpose."

"I appreciate the offer, but that isn't necessary. My crew can handle it." David was glad she wanted to help, but she hadn't worked in nearly fifteen years. He was concerned she wouldn't be up to it.

"You and your crew are putting your lives on the line for me and my family. You've all been through some truly traumatic events… Captain Alexander. The job is mostly babysitting, is it not? There would be a second engineer on duty at the same time, right? You're asking your Lt. Flint to pull extra duty. I'm offering to relieve her of some of that burden, and I am more than capable of babysitting an engine I *helped design*."

David stared at his grandmother for a moment. She was making sense. He looked up at Lazaro then Lexi. They both gave him a slight questioning shrug. "I tell you what. I'll have Lt. Commander Dominick check you out on the engines. If he's comfortable, then you have a deal. If he isn't comfortable turning you loose, then I'm not either. Are you okay with that?"

Kay smiled. "Yes, Captain." Her eyes twinkled again. Today was the first time David had seen that twinkle since before his grandfather died.

Caleb rolled his eyes then slowly raised his hand. "I can pull a couple relief shifts as a pilot."

Abby looked at Caleb and gave him a thankful smile. She was glad her husband was taking the first steps towards accepting his situation. David glanced at the screen showing Brynna. Brynna gave him a similar shrug. "Alright, your duties will be similar babysitting. Take something to do with you. I'll arrange to have you sit in with Thane and go through some simulations before I clear you to take a duty shift. My crew and I appreciate the offers."

Aulani raised her hand. "Captain, what's going to happen to *our* families? Surely they're going to be in the same danger as your family."

Jake stood up slowly. "Captain, I can address this one."

David motioned him forward. Jake nervously addressed the assembly. "I took the liberty of sending messages to your families to warn them to get out of their homes immediately. I gave them each different locations to go to. Apparently, Moderator Tarmon has been sending out teams to several other worlds capable of space travel. These are worlds with minimal populations, mining colonies and other such places. The Dreans will be looking for them on those worlds and taking them back to Drea. I sent the messages the Captain had you prepare in the event we were captured by the Commonwealth along with my message. I can't account for whether they took my warning seriously or whether they followed my instructions verbatim. If they didn't... well, their best bet is to denounce you publicly."

"Isn't there any way we can contact them, personally?" Aulani asked nervously.

David shook his head. "Not right now. If we try to contact them now, the Commonwealth will find out our location and may start tracking your family members. The best thing we can do is ask Pateras to look out for them and stay as far away from them as we can."

Caleb leaned forward. "What about my family? I just totally disappeared off their radar without so much as a *goodbye*. They're never going to know what happened to me. What happens to me when my marriage contract with Abby expires? Can I return home?"

David struggled with how to answer that one. Caleb could never return home. Kay stood up to offer some insight. "Caleb, on Drea, they don't have marriage contracts. Marriages are for life. There are occasional divorces and annulments. They will accept your marriage. They won't accept your expiration date."

David added the one thing no one wanted to hear him say. "Whoever goes to Drea is stuck there until the war between Pateras and the Commonwealth ends and the danger is over. There is no coming back. I can let you record a message for your family and try to get it to them later, but you absolutely can NOT tell them where you are going. They can't contact you in return. This is a one-way trip. I'm sorry. There's just no other way."

Caleb sat back in shock. He looked at Abby. He wasn't sure about being married to her indefinitely. He cared deeply for her, but this was a strange concept. This was only his second marriage. The average was four. Abby did not care for the look he gave her. Panic started to set in, forcing Caleb to see the pain he was inflicting on her.

Steven was less concerned. Jessica was his third wife and he had already thought about making their contract his last one. They had been together for a sizable number of years and gotten comfortable with each other. David even viewed him as somewhat of a father.

David had reached the end of his planned agenda. The only other point was to answer any questions posed. This was the part he didn't look forward to. He decided to preface it carefully. "For the last point on my agenda, I intend to answer any questions you may have if I can. I do not know the full plan of Pateras, nor do I want to know. Pateras asked me a week ago to put the welfare and safety of this crew in his hands. I did, thankfully. If I hadn't, we'd probably all be dead right now. So, what do you need to know?"

Cheyenne raised her hand. "Captain, what about the crew? Are we going to Drea, or are we staying with the ship? Are you giving us a choice?"

David glanced at Brynna again. They hadn't discussed this. Brynna gave him a look that said she was deferring to him. David looked back at Cheyenne. "We have twelve days to make that decision. The choice is yours, but there are some things you need to know before you make that decision. If we all disappear to Drea, the Supreme Executor could find out and focus his attention on Drea. That would put the entire population at risk including our family members who take refuge there. If we stay with the ship and try to fight him, it keeps him from coming after our families. Staying with the ship puts us facing some insane odds. My personal choice is to stay with the ship. We cannot lose more than four crew members and continue this mission, at least not safely. If half the crew stays behind, the other half may have no choice. Ask Arni what he wants you to do. We'll take a vote by secret ballot, just before we reach Galat."

David paused a moment then asked, "What else do you want to know?"

The room got quiet. Jake had backed away to lean against a nearby wall. Thane looked at Jake then back at the Captain. Lazaro studied the interactions between the Captain and Jake then seeing Thane's doubt, he had to ask. "Captain, we need to know what happened. How did we get caught? Did you turn us in, or did Jake?"

"I'm taking full responsibility for this. I just told you, Arni told me what was going to happen and I… did nothing to stop it. This is my fault."

Cheyenne squinted at him. "Captain, that's only part of the truth. You have to tell us everything. We can't function as a crew if we don't know the full truth."

Jake stepped forward. "Captain, I'll take responsibility for this."

The Captain stepped towards Jake to stop him. He whispered softly to Jake, "I can handle this, Chief. I don't want to give them another reason not to trust you."

Jake smiled and shook his head. "Captain, all you're going to do is give them a reason to distrust you. I need to do this. Please, don't stop me," Jake pleaded. He was accepting the Captain's leadership, but per usual, he argued against the Captain's decision. "I need to ask for their forgiveness. Please, Captain."

David nodded and stepped aside. He offered Jake his hand to shake. Jake shook it then moved in front of the assembly. He cleared his throat. "When we were on Tudoren… I stopped fighting this following of Pateras. I suppose it might have appeared I was on board with the Captain's plan. I wasn't. I kept my head down and played along. Before we headed to Romajin, I sent a message to Admiral Garcia telling him where we were headed and that the Captain was still alive. When we reached Romajin, I put a plan in place with Admiral Deacons to have the crew arrested. I agreed to turn you in so long as I could leave with Marissa and our son. Executor Hale agreed. He said it could be arranged, although Marissa would have to go through the re-education if she didn't recant."

The crew began casting looks of anger and hatred towards Jake. The look on Marissa's face was the coldest. Thane jumped to his feet ready to pummel the security chief. David put himself between the two men. Thane shouted angrily, "Get out of my way, Captain! I'm going to shove him out an airlock!" Thane dodged the Captain and took a swing at Jake. David jumped back between the two again, taking the punch to his face. Startled by his own actions, Thane backed off quickly. "Captain, I'm sorry. I didn't mean to hit you. Forgive me."

David wiped the blood from his lip. In the mouth again, why was it always in the mouth? "You want me to forgive you?"

"Yes sir. I'm sorry, sir."

"Are you willing to forgive Mr. Holden?" David ran his tongue across the inside of his swelling lip tasting blood as he did.

"Forgive him? For what we went through? Never!" Thane bristled.

"Then I can't forgive you, Lt. Ryder." David said calmly.

"What? You can't be serious. This doesn't even compare to

what he did. How can you even suggest it does?" Thane argued.

"I told you. I'm taking full responsibility for what happened. I could have taken steps to stop it. I didn't. Pateras allowed it to happen. He… forgive me for this… he wanted it to happen. I'm just as guilty as Jake for betraying you and I did it… for Jake."

Everyone looked stunned as David continued his explanation. "Arni said this was the only way to get through to him. It was the only way to convince him to follow Pateras. He told me I would go through six days of… torture." David struggled with his own memory of the recent days. "He told me I could escape it, but it would cost me Jake's respect, among other things. I agreed to do as he asked. His plan worked. Jake serves Pateras now. If you have a bone to pick with him, then take it up with me."

"Captain, he betrayed us. You didn't betray us." Lazaro joined Thane's protest. "He was thrown in a cell with us. He sat there and lied to our faces. He told us *you* betrayed us."

The Captain began to get angry. "If ANYONE has a reason to hate this man, it's ME! You were treated poorly. I have no argument with that. I am responsible for what happens to my crew. When he betrayed this crew, I felt it *twelve time*s what you did. I endured more torment and beatings than I care to think about because of this man. I was drugged, tortured, and lied to. I have chunks of my days that are missing entirely. I may have even been forced to do deplorable things. I may never even know what I did. Jake came in and beat me *himself*. I was forced to watch Executor Hale humiliate my wife. Do you think any of you has worse reasons to hate him? DO YOU?"

The crew got quiet. His family gripped the arms of their chairs nervously. Jessica glared at Jake. Jake was truly sorry for what he had done. His demeanor reflected his sorrow. Jessica's glare brought a new level of discomfort to him.

Lexi asked the one question she knew would turn the tide.

"Captain… would you do it again? Would you do it for any one of us? Would you do it again for Jake?"

David looked down and around the room at nothing in particular, the memories of his pain still fresh in his mind. His eyes finally landed on Jake. "Arni said Jake would be worth it, so yes, I would go through every bit of it again. Jake got us into trouble and Pateras used Jake to get us out again. He's worth it, like Arni said. I've forgiven him. I'm asking you to do the same."

Jake stepped forward. "Captain… I never officially apologized. I need to apologize."

David nodded and stepped back. Jake's attitude had made a change for the better.

"I am so… so sorry for everything I put you and the Captain through. I was being a good Commonwealth soldier. I thought I was doing the right thing. I was so wrong. I'm sorry it took me so long to figure it out. I wish I had figured it out sooner. I swear, I will do whatever I can to pay you all back for everything I've cost you. Mrs. Deacons, I put your son, Admiral Deacons, through untold tortures watching this nightmare I created. I'm sorry. Mrs. Lance, I hurt your son and your family very badly. I hope someday you can forgive me."

Jake paused for a moment. Tears formed in his eyes. "Marissa, I was so afraid I was going to lose you. Executor Hale ordered your execution." Jake tried to swallow the lump in his throat. "I knew by keeping the baby, you disobeyed orders. I tried to make a deal to see to it you and the baby were safe. I screwed up… badly. I hope… I hope my actions haven't ultimately cost me the one thing I tried to hang onto the hardest. I hope… it hasn't cost me… you. Please forgive me."

He dropped his eyes to the floor to take the pressure of responding off her. David moved over to Jake and shook his hand. Placing his left hand on Jake's shoulder, David offered his forgiveness and promised him no retribution would happen to him.

David turned and locked his eyes on Thane. Maintaining his gaze, he wiped his swollen lip again. Thane's glare was still cemented on his face. Jake moved away from the front of the room. David watched him go with a heavy heart. He thought perhaps the crew would forgive him as their own emotional wounds began to heal. A question popped into David's head. "Jake, I need to ask you something. Arni said you would be watching me and how I handled myself. He indicated my reactions would affect your choices. There at the end, you brought me a hypo-spray with a deadly sedative dose in it. Were you testing me?"

Jake blinked, startled by the question. "No sir. I had already committed to Pateras. Executor Hale ordered me to take it to you. I didn't want to. I was afraid if I didn't, he would know I changed sides. For a minute, I was afraid you might use it. You were in bad shape when I took it to you. I'm glad you were strong enough to resist."

"I wasn't, Chief. I was going to use it after you left my cell. You pushed me… hard. I needed that push. You saved my life. You reminded me why I was there. I had a job to do and it wasn't just my life at stake. I hope I haven't disappointed you, Chief. I owe you one."

"You haven't disappointed me, sir. I think my debt to you is still far greater."

Hearing the exchange, the crew's anger eased. Seeing David forgive Jake and announce his indebtedness made his family less angry as well. Thane was not one to hold a grudge typically. He was too lighthearted by nature. This was still a rough one to get over. His anger slowly began to subside seeing his Captain genuinely forgive his rival. Thane grudgingly offered Jake his hand. "This is going to take some time and several games of Zone to get past. Don't push me until I get past this."

Jake nodded his understanding. He moved back to his seat to let the Captain continue his meeting. "Just to be perfectly clear, the Chief is under my protection. If he has any unfortunate accidents, I'll do twice as much to whoever caused the so-called accident. Are we clear?"

The crew replied with a firm although less enthusiastic, "Yes sir!"

"Are there any more questions?"

Braxton piped up from one of the screens, "Just one, Captain. What are we doing after we drop your family off on Galat?"

David paused to consider the question. "Assuming we have a sufficient crew remaining aboard the *Evangeline*, we need to get the message of Pateras out. I don't know the specifics yet. We probably should warn the other eleven ships. We can't stay in one place too long. I'll probably take us out of our sector. We'll need to discuss that after everyone has had more time to recover."

David dismissed the meeting. Some slowly made their way to Jake to offer him their forgiveness or at least their appreciation to him for aiding their escape. Jake humbly accepted. Marissa was the last to approach him. She waited until the last people were leaving the room. Her words were simple, but sharp. "I'm not happy. We need to spend time with Lexi, a lot of time."

Jake nodded. "I know. I'm sorry. This will never, ever happen again. I swear it."

"In that case, you can sleep in our bed tonight instead of the guest quarters." Marissa turned and left the room.

Jake was grateful for that. He finally felt like he could sleep.

• •

The next twelve days brought up numerous heated arguments accompanied by heartfelt reconciliations. It was going to take time to work out the tension created by the sleep deprivation, indoctrination, and mind-altering drugs. There were many nightmares causing a resurgence of sleep deprivation. Lexi was glad to have someone take her shifts in engineering. Although a clinical psychologist by trade, she enjoyed exercising the mathematical part of her brain in engineering. Her psychology duties were far too consuming right now.

The crew and passengers were able to get in some recreation over their voyage. David teamed up with his younger half-brother for a game of Zone against Jason and Laura. He thoroughly enjoyed the chance to bond with the brother he barely knew. They got in a second game against Caleb and Abby. His family watched both games with an excitement not seen in many years. After the game, Abby congratulated David and Stevie on their win. "Davie, you're better at Zone than I remembered."

David grinned. The crew played regularly as a stress reliever. It was expected he would get in lots of practice. He couldn't resist teasing her though. "I think having a baby just made you soft," he chided.

Abby promptly slapped him across the face with her sweaty towel.

· ·

Four days before reaching Galat, Lexi scheduled a counseling session with the Captain, Commander, Lt. Holden, and Chief Holden. As the five of them sat down to talk, Lexi informed the group the topic of discussion was not about prior wrongs. They were to limit their discussion to the one matter. Lexi invited Jake to start the conversation.

"Captain, Commander, Marissa and I were discussing whether we should join your family in going to Drea. We seem to be having some difficulty with this decision."

David shifted in his seat. "Jake, this isn't a decision I can make for you. I'm not ordering, requesting, or even suggesting any options in particular. Lt. Flint, I know you indicated the topic wasn't to include previous wrongs, but I need Jake to understand, he doesn't owe me anything. You can freely stay or freely go. It's your decision."

Marissa leaned forward in her chair. "Captain, he wants us to go to Drea. I don't want to go. I want to stay with the ship."

"Captain, tell her the ship is no place for a baby. It's against the regs. We can't go on with a baby on the ship." Jake groused.

David looked at Brynna and Lexi. "Did he really just say that?"

Jake gave everyone a befuddled look. "Say what?"

Marissa grinned knowing his case was now a lost cause.

Brynna leaned forward. "Chief, the regs were set up by the Commonwealth and we are now Commonwealth fugitives. The Captain will need to continue following certain regs to insure the ship and crew function properly. He doesn't have to follow all of them. He doesn't have to follow that particular regulation."

Jake's mouth fell open. He looked from Brynna to the Captain. "You're not serious. Captain, is she serious? Would you really allow that?"

David leaned back in his seat and pulled one leg up to rest his ankle on the opposite knee. He leaned his head over, placing his chin on his hand. His forefinger began to absently tap his lips. "The Commander is right. We're criminals. I can follow or not follow this particular regulation. I gave Marissa my word I would protect her and the baby. I hadn't really considered anything other than her remaining with the crew."

"Well… tell her staying is a bad idea!" Jake didn't like the direction the conversation was taking. He had been certain the Captain would back him up.

David looked at Brynna, "Commander, your thoughts?"

Brynna wasn't amused with being put on the spot, but she didn't let it stop her. "It is against the regs for a reason. It's a distraction for the crew. It could decrease the effectiveness of the crew. It will require additional resources. A baby puts the crew at greater risk for being compromised."

Jake seemed to breathe a little easier as he heard Brynna's introspection.

"That being said, losing two crew members could cause the same problems." Brynna finished.

Jake was no longer breathing easier.

The Captain looked at Lexi. "Before I make a final decision on this matter, Lt. Flint, I need to know what sort of impact this will have on the crew."

Lexi's contemplation didn't take long. "It's hard to say. The baby could well become something akin to a ship's mascot. He could serve as a doorway to reuniting the crew. If Jake and Marissa leave the ship, the crew would come back together, but I believe it would take longer. If they are the only ones choosing to leave, it will put the crew in a manpower crisis as the Commander mentioned, but I don't think it would be insurmountable."

"See, they could get along without us." Jake prodded.

"Oh, no. She said it would create a crisis. It doesn't matter. If the Captain decides I can stay, then I'm staying. Jake, I've seen too many children killed by the Commonwealth. I can't sit back in some quiet little corner of the Commonwealth and ignore it. The Commonwealth has tried twice to kill our son. It's not going to get a third chance." Marissa stubbornly announced.

Jake pleaded. "If we don't disappear, the Commonwealth may *have* a third chance to destroy our child. They may even succeed the next time."

The Captain put his foot back down on the floor and leaned forward. "Okay, that's enough. I think you two have had this conversation several times before. My decision is this. No place in this galaxy is going to be safe as long as the Commonwealth is trying to destroy Pateras' followers. Yes, this ship is a primary target. It also has the protection of Pateras. Marissa, if you want to stay here, I will allow it. I'm not going to stop you. The decision is still yours."

The discussion continued for a few minutes until David strongly advised them to discuss it with Arni before reaching a final decision. The two agreed and took their argument back to their own quarters. Lexi seemed surprisingly pleased at the Captain's decision.

• •

Two days before the ship reached Galat, David was preparing for the crew's vote. He walked into his quarters and found Brynna curled up on the sofa reading something on her data pad. He gave her a cold and distracted nod as he sat down at his desk. Brynna started to go on reading. The tension in the room became more palpable as they tried to ignore each other's presence. Brynna finally put down her data pad. "David… we need to talk."

David looked up feeling slightly annoyed. "I'm really busy right now. Can we not put this off until after Galat?"

"David, you're about to ask the crew to vote on their futures, and you and I haven't discussed it."

"What's to discuss? You need to vote your conscience just like everyone else."

"I'm not inclined to want to vote contrary to you. I know you said you needed some time before we discuss what happened on Romajin. I've got the distinct feeling whatever happened is affecting our future. We need to talk about it."

David shut off his computer and headed for the door. "I can't talk about this right now. We can talk after Galat."

Brynna wasn't going to let it go so easily this time. This door had to be opened before Galat. Brynna stood up abruptly. "DAVID! Answer this one question! Do you still love me?"

Her question stopped him dead in his tracks. David stood there with his back to her for a moment as he postulated the cause of her question. A woman of her caliber deserved a far better husband than he had been. How could any man *not* love her? Why would she ask him that? Had he given her reason to doubt his love and devotion? Obviously, he had.

Brynna watched as David balled his fists up. He raised his right hand and hit the door frame with the soft side of his fist. It was a punch of frustration, not one of anger. He turned around slowly to face her. "Brynna, I am so sorry if I gave you cause to question my love for you. I love you more than I thought possible." He moved towards her slowly as he spoke. "What do I need to do to fix this?"

"First thing you need to do is stop shutting me out. I've been trying to give you the time you need. I thought you only needed a couple days. It's been ten days. The longer you wait, the harder this is going to be." Brynna hesitated. "David, you've hardly looked at me or touched me since leaving Romajin. Do you have feelings for that woman on Romajin?"

David looked as though his very soul had been cut to the quick. He grabbed Brynna's hands and sat down on the sofa pulling her down beside him. He finally realized his guilt had been conveying the wrong message to her. "Brynna, no, I have no feelings for… Heather. I don't really know her. I love you and no one else. I've been so… wracked with guilt… I – I don't know." David struggled with how to talk about his pain. "You deserve so much better than this… so much better than me. I wish he had never shown you that surveillance video."

"What do you mean? He told you I saw the footage of the two of you? Were you planning on keeping it from me?" Brynna was ready to lay into him again.

David's face looked almost green. Brynna was afraid he was about to get sick. He had trouble looking her in the eye. He looked down and away as he tried to compose himself and choose his words carefully. "Brynna… I… No, I wasn't going to hide this from you. Executor Hale made sure I would see your reactions when he showed you the surveillance videos of me… with Heather."

"He showed you that?"

David still couldn't look her in the eye. "He attacked me in any and every way possible. Yes, I saw him show you the feed. I am so sorry you had to see that. Executor Hale brought me into his office. He had me injected with some kind of drug. I don't remember much about that day. I remember… small flashes of faces. The next thing I remember… is waking up in bed and you were snuggled up beside me."

David stared into space as he relived the memory. "I started to caress your hair thinking I'd just had a bad dream. I opened my eyes to kiss you… and… it wasn't you. I thought it was you. I have no memory of whatever happened before waking up in bed with her. I – I asked Heather what happened between us. I even used some intimidation tactics to see if her story remained constant. It did."

Brynna sat there quietly listening to her husband. Sensing how difficult this was for him, she held her questions and comments. When he paused again without saying the one thing they both needed him to say, she prodded, "David, did you sleep with her?"

A look of pain engulfed him. "I don't remember. Heather said we did… I did. Brynna, I am so sorry. I never meant to hurt you or be unfaithful to you. Can you ever forgive me?"

Brynna stared intently at him. "Before I answer that, there's something I need to understand. This sounds like you didn't have a choice. If that's true, why have you been avoiding me, making me feel unwanted?"

David sat there in shock for a moment. Unwanted? Never! He no longer felt worthy of her.

Brynna's face began to redden and tears finally started

flowing down her cheeks. The truth of what he had done to her finally dawned in on him. David lifted his hand and cradled the side of her face. He wiped her tears away with his thumb. "By the stars of Raesii," he swore. "Brynna, I never meant to give you that impression at all. You mean the world to me. I haven't felt worthy of you. I did everything I could to resist his attacks. I failed. I failed Pateras and I failed you. I don't deserve someone as special as you. You deserve better than me."

Anger replaced her tears. "David, you don't get to make that decision for me. I decide what's good enough for me, not you. If I thought you weren't good enough for me, I never would have married you. If you have those kinds of doubts about my judgment, perhaps you shouldn't have married me. The next time you think you've done something to hurt me, perhaps you should start by telling me and apologizing. Do you not realize my perspective on this situation?"

David pulled back slightly feeling her anger. "Perhaps not."

"I had two of my crew members and the Supreme Executor telling me you were a traitor. A third crew member reporting similar information, albeit with a different slant. I saw video surveillance of you enjoying the company of our enemies and a beautiful blond woman. The minute we're reunited, you want nothing to do with me. Exactly what was I *supposed* to think?"

David took her hands in his again. "It appears… I have wronged you twice. I'm sorry again. I guess I haven't got the hang of this marriage thing yet. Can you forgive me… for all my offenses? Can we fix this? Please let me try and fix this."

Brynna set her jaw defiantly for a moment. "Yes, I'll forgive you and let you try to fix it. I'll warn you though, it's going to cost you dearly."

David stared at her in shock. He wasn't sure what she meant.

Brynna didn't wait for him to ask. "I'm going to expect to

be treated like a queen every time you step foot in this cabin, Mr. Alexander. You better make sure I can never doubt your love for me ever again."

The tension between them began to melt. Brynna slowly smiled. David got down on one knee. Taking her right hand in his, he lifted her hand to his lips and kissed it gently. He looked up and smiled warmly. "You have my word of honor. You will never have reason to doubt my love and devotion again… Your Majesty."

David's duties to the ship and crew were put off awhile longer. His devotion and duty to his wife now took precedence. For tonight, the two believed the matter of "Heather" was now behind them.

• •

The next morning the crew met briefly to vote on whether to stay behind with the ship or go to Drea. The vote was unanimous. The crew wanted to stay with the ship despite the risks. Captain Alexander was relieved and invigorated by their choices. He wanted more than anything to stop the death and destruction. He knew it would take the entire crew to fight Executor Hale's campaign against Pateras. It would take a lot more than that. Operating the ship with less than twelve people could be enough of a struggle. Pateras would have to orchestrate the fight against Luciano Hale. Captain Alexander didn't have a clue what their first goal should be other than getting his family to safety and getting out of the Galatan star system undetected.

The two ships made a cautious approach to Galat. Once in orbit, the two ships separated and landed. The temperature for this region of Galat was quite cold as they were well into winter. The crew stripped the *Independence* of anything usable. The sofas in the crew quarters of the *Independence* could convert to a bed unlike those on the *Evangeline*. The sofas were exchanged for their more versatile counterparts. The hydroponics equipment was transferred to the *Evangeline*. One room aboard the *Evangeline* was designed to serve as a place of rest and relaxation. It wasn't a full blown holographic imaging suite, but it was designed to provide scenic views and atmospheric conditions to relieve feelings of confinement. Their CIF orders were never to use that room for anything, but what it was intended. David moved the hydroponics equipment in there. He moved the holographic imagers into the gym. It was the largest room on the ship and the imagers would make it seem even larger. Lt. Commander Dominick moved as much of the fuel as possible to the *Evangeline*. The kitchen equipment was also moved into the current dining hall. It seriously decreased their elbow room, but the crew were anxious to have cooking facilities. A few extra pieces of equipment were placed in the cargo hold for future use.

Once everything was squared away, all that was left was to wait on the Drean pod. David spent every available moment with his family, knowing he might never see them again. Too soon the word came down from the bridge of a build-up of tachyon particles a few hundred yards from the ships. David took his mother and grandmother quickly to the landing just outside the airlock, so they could see the pods materialize. Since David's family had not come prepared for winter weather, the spare blankets from the *Independence* were conscripted as cold weather gear.

Col. Bernt, who had been in charge of their security detail on Drea, emerged from one of the pods and approached the ships. David fastened his overcoat and moved down the steps to greet the Colonel. The two discussed business first. David assured Col. Bernt he had scanners on maximum range and hadn't detected a Commonwealth presence. Col. Bernt signaled the pods then commenced discussing lighter topics. He offered greetings from those now considered friends on Drea. "Captain Parker and his wife send their regards."

David cocked his head slightly. "Wife? Do I know his wife?"

"Oh… I may not have told you. He married your attorney, Rachel Johan."

David smiled. "Really?" He doubted the two would have connected more than professionally if it had not been for the crew's presence in the Drean prison. "Please give them my congratulations."

Col. Bernt smiled again. "I brought some friends with me."

David looked up in time to see Moderator Tarmon with her father, Donald Leal, on her arm. David smiled and walked towards the elderly man. Donald smiled warmly. Despite the definitive nip in the air, the warmth of friendship kept them both comfortable. David greeted Moderator Tarmon and invited the two into the ship. He turned in time to see Col. Bernt nod towards the pod. He looked back to see his grandparents' family members walking towards him. He excused himself to greet the second group of visitors.

David moved the group into the gym again and began making introductions. David's grandmother stepped forward and looked at her brother, Zachary Leeto. She reached up and touched his face. "Zach? Is that really you?" Tears began to well up in her eyes.

Zach's eyes teared up equally as quickly. "Tyra? I didn't think I would ever see you again. Thank Pateras."

The two hugged for a very long time. Kay wiped the tears from her eyes. "It's going to take a little time to get used to that."

Zachary looked puzzled. "The Commonwealth doesn't practice hugging?"

Kay laughed. "No, I haven't been called Tyra in nearly fifty years. The Commonwealth changed my name to Kay Deacons."

Kay looked past Zachary and saw her husband's brother and sister. "Oh Joel, you look so much like Saul… uh… Elliot." Tears began to flow again. "I miss him so much. I wish he could've lived to see this day." The three grabbed onto each other tightly and cried, sharing a grief long overdue.

Jessica stepped forward to greet her Uncle Zachary. David introduced his mother to him. Zach's eyes grew wide, "My little *Nessie*? You grew up into a beautiful woman, Vanessa."

David grinned impishly. "Nessie? Oh, that's cute. I'll have to keep that in mind. Maybe Brynna and I can name our first daughter, Nessie."

Jessica glared at David, "Don't you dare. I always hated being called Nessie."

Jessica had little memory of the man. She did remember her previous name and pet names. When Zachary, Joel, and Amanda saw Abigail, the tears began again. She brought back memories of the beautiful twelve-year-old girl who died on Mara. The group had expected her to be grown and have children of her own.

David spent as much time as he could with his family. He was afraid to spend too much time in their current location. He took the time to talk to Donald Leal and Moderator Tarmon. The man had been a valuable source of wisdom and comfort in the days preceding David's decision to join Pateras. The two now shared an even greater common bond. They had both been tortured because of their decisions to follow Pateras. As David struggled to tell Donald the things he had so recently suffered, Donald's eyes teared up. David's rendition brought back painful memories of his own.

After an hour or so, David saw Col. Bernt pacing nervously on the other side of the room. He decided he could put this off no longer. He stepped to the middle of the room and asked for everyone's attention.

"As much as I would love to spend several more hours visiting with everyone, I'm afraid we have to go our separate ways. It's too dangerous for us to stay here. We need to get my family to Drea. I'm afraid it's time to say our goodbyes."

Their guests said goodbye to David and his crew and headed for the pods. David expressed his profound thanks to Moderator Tarmon for coming to rescue his family. Moderator Tarmon was glad to retrieve a few of her long-lost citizens. She assured the young Captain the crew's family would be sought out and taken to safety as well.

David's family had their bags packed and ready to head out the door. There were long hugs and several goodbye kisses from David's grandmother, mother, and sister. David promised to do what he could to look after his Uncle Rob and Aunt Hannah. He assured his family he would talk to them as often as he could. Abby promised to send him lots of pictures of Aiden. Steven promised to take care of Jessica for David. Caleb assured David he would look after Abby and quietly told him he would stay by her side as her husband… permanently. David smiled. He was glad Caleb was making the adjustment. It couldn't be any easier for him to leave his own family behind than it was for David to send his family away.

David and Brynna walked his family out to the pods then watched as the pods soon vanished. David and Brynna spent a few quiet minutes together before returning to the ship.

David moved the ship off the planet's surface then put it down on the dark side of the moon. He wanted to give the crew a little more time to heal emotionally before facing their enemies head on. The duty shifts were cut down to two people instead of four. The crew spent time discussing their fears, pain, and how to put the past behind them. They took the initial steps towards forgiving Jake, but they still had trouble trusting him. Lexi set to work doing what she could to build up their trust again.

Ensign Ryder sat at the comms station. Her task was to lock the ship up tight so no one could access its computers. An unexpected hail came in. "Captain, the Valiant is hailing us. Should I answer it?"

The Captain moved to his station. Glancing around at the bridge crew, David made sure everyone was paying attention. "The Valiant and Admiral Deacons are our enemies. Be very careful what you say and do concerning them. Don't even allow your facial expressions to be read. My Uncle Rob is not our enemy. Know the difference. Ensign, make sure that carrier wave detection program is active. I need to know if they try to slip a signal through under the radar. Bounce the signal a couple times and put it through."

Admiral Deacons' face appeared on the screen. "Captain Alexander, where is your security officer?"

David glanced at Jake, sitting at his station. "He's here on the bridge where he belongs."

Admiral Deacons glared. "You would do best to watch that man carefully. He's not to be trusted."

David squinted at his uncle. "Why is that any concern of yours?" He challenged.

Admiral Deacons continued to glare at Jake's image on the corner of his screen. It was starting to unnerve Jake. "He's responsible for the deaths of every soldier on the CIF base on Romajin. There were ten thousand men and women on that base. They are ALL DEAD because of his actions."

Jake looked up startled. He looked back at the Captain. "I – I don't understand. I didn't do anything to – to the base."

The Captain gave a reassuring glance to Jake then turned his attention back to the Admiral. "Is this your way of trying to track us down, Admiral? If it is, I can assure you, by the time you get here, we'll be long gone."

"You would be foolish to think I'm not tracking your signal. I *am*. I just thought you should know there is no place in this galaxy for you to hide. You might as well turn yourselves in so you can receive a merciful execution. After Mr. Holden's actions, the entire Commonwealth Interstellar Force is out for blood… his, and yours." The Admiral's face was deadly serious although his eyes showed concern.

David folded his arms across his chest. "Why do you think Chief Holden is responsible for anything happening on the Romajin CIF Base? What happened? This is the first we've heard of anything."

"The self-destruct mechanism was triggered just as your ships left the planetary system. Your security chief had gained enough trust to be given access to the computer. Commodore Vardin, and nearly his entire command, are dead. There were a few who were off base, and those guarding the perimeter who survived. The signal was tracked as coming from *your ship*… CAPTAIN."

Jake stood up slowly. He turned halfway between the Captain and Admiral. Looking back and forth between the two, "I swear… I didn't do this. We walked out of there clean… no casualties. I would never do anything like this. Captain… please believe me."

David nodded for Jake to sit back down. "Admiral, I know the Chief betrayed this crew, but he did it so that no one got hurt. Mr. Holden is incapable of coldblooded murder. I think the Supreme Executor orchestrated this to frame us. I don't really care whether you believe me or not. I will do some investigating on my own to clear my man to *my* satisfaction then, I'll move on. You can let the Supreme Executor know his days of murdering the innocent are coming to an end."

David turned around and sat down in his chair. "On a personal note, neither you, nor he, can use my family against me again. I hope you aren't too disappointed." This was David's way of discreetly telling the Admiral their family was safe.

The Admiral's face remained perfectly neutral. "You seem to have a very negative view of me, the Supreme Executor, and the Commonwealth. I would never put our family in danger and neither would the Supreme Executor. I thought for a brief period, your man had killed our family when he destroyed the base. Lucky for you, scans revealed they were no longer on the base or I would have hunted him down myself. The safest thing for you is to disappear with them. You know I still care about what happens to you, right?"

"Based on the things you let Executor Hale do to me, I'm not sure I believe that. Admiral, I think we're done here. Let the war commence."

Admiral reached for his controls to end the communication, "So be it then." The screen went dark.

● ●

Executor Hale pressed a button. The images of the conversation between Captain Alexander and Admiral Deacons faded away. He smiled. He still had Admiral Deacons' loyalty. He pressed another button.

The face of Defense Minister Hamilton Payne appeared on the screen. "Executor Hale, what can I do for you?"

"Get my new troops ready for battle. The other eleven

ships are going to be recalled. If they don't return, send those troops out to hunt them down and destroy them all. I want all twelve of those ships and all twelve crews executed. These troops will answer only to me. Any questions?"

"No Supreme Executor, they will be ready to ship out on schedule. I look forward to seeing them in action."

"You will and soon." The Supreme Executor closed the communication link and smiled sadistically.

"I may not have won this round, but I will win the next. You can count on it!"

Continued in:

The Defender:

Mission Abandoned

Thank you for reading this story, we hope you enjoyed it. We invite you to explore the rest of the books in The Defender series. Books 1-4 are available on Amazon.com and Kindle!

The Defender: The Mission

Volume one of a Sci-Fi Space Opera, takes Capt. Alexander on a series of dangerous first contact missions with low-tech worlds. Their mission is to create allies and identify the strongholds of a new enemy challenging the Commonwealth's powerbase. The enemy proves to be more powerful than imaginable.

The Defender: Defended

Volume two of a Sci-Fi Space Opera, follows the crew of the *Evangeline* to an advanced tech, non-spacefaring world that has a history with the Commonwealth. Secrets brought to light reveal ancient debts yet unpaid. Someone must pay. Capt. Alexander offers his life to settle the debt. It isn't enough!

The Defender: Treasonous Acts

Volume three of a Sci-Fi Space Opera, the crew of a military vessel is divided in their loyalties. The Captain has declared his own treason after seeing the heinous crimes of the Commonwealth. To avoid detection by his superiors, he continues his mission… superficially.

The Defender: In Evil's Grasp

Volume four of a Sci-Fi Space Opera, you are holding this one in your hands now! Leave a rating for this book on Amazon now.

Coming Soon!!!

The Defender: Mission Abandoned

The Defender: Birth of a Revolution

The Defender: Questions of Trust

Tell us what you think!

Leave a comment on Amazon and/or GoodReads

Search for
"Reggi Broach Defender"

www.ingramcontent.com/pod-product-compliance
Lightning Source LLC
Chambersburg PA
CBHW070759120726
47910CB00001B/226